APPOMATTOX

☆ ☆ ☆

THE CIVIL WAR BATTLE SERIES
by James Reasoner

Manassas

Shiloh

Antietam

Chancellorsville

Vicksburg

Gettysburg

Chickamauga

Shenandoah

Savannah

Appomattox

☆ ☆ ☆

APPOMATTOX

James Reasoner

CUMBERLAND HOUSE
NASHVILLE, TENNESSEE

Published by
CUMBERLAND HOUSE PUBLISHING, INC.
431 Harding Industrial Drive
Nashville, Tennessee 37211
www.cumberlandhouse.com

This novel is a work of fiction. Names, characters, places, and incidents either are the product of the author's imagination or are used fictitiously. Any resemblance to persons, living or dead, events, or locales is entirely coincidental.

Cover design by Bob Bubnis, Nashville, Tennessee.

Library of Congress Cataloging-in-Publication Data

Reasoner, James.
  Appomattox / James Reasoner.
      p.   cm. — (The Civil War battle series)
    ISBN 1-58182-357-6 (hardcover : alk. paper)
    1. Brannon family (Fictitious characters)—Fiction. 2. United States—History—Civil War, 1861–1865—Fiction. 3. Virginia—History—Civil War, 1861–1865—Fiction. 4. Appomattox Campaign, 1865—Fiction. 5. Culpeper (Va.)—Fiction. I. Title. II. Series.
PS3568.E2685A87 2003
813'.54—dc22

                                                                    2003015355

Printed in Canada

1 2 3 4 5 6 7 8 9 10—07 06 05 04 03

This book is for all the readers
who have walked with the Brannons
down the long road from peace to war and back again.
Thank you for going along on the journey.

Chapter One

A T FIRST ROMAN TRIED to blink back the tears, but after a moment he gave up and let them flow freely. He stood there beside the mound of freshly turned earth and wept without shame. Mac Brannon stood with him, and tears rolled down the sun- and windburned face of the Confederate cavalryman as well. Mac had lost a brother today. Roman had lost a friend.

No white man ever *be friends with a slave*. Roman had heard that many times at Tanglewood, the plantation owned by the Lattimer family where he had grown up. He had been owned by the Lattimer family, too, specifically by Yancy Lattimer, the young man who one day would have run the plantation if this awful war had not come along and taken his life.

Roman had never believed that he and Marse Yancy were friends, even though they had spent most of their time together. Marse Yancy thought kindly toward him, Roman had no doubt of that. He had always been well treated. Marse Yancy had even taught him to play chess. But friends . . . ? No.

With Will Brannon, it had been different.

William Shakespeare Brannon, named by a father who admired the immortal bard of Avon above all other men. Sheriff Will Brannon for a time before the war, when he'd been the law in Culpeper County, Virginia. Then Capt. Will Brannon of the Thirty-third Virginia Infantry, part of what had come to be known as the Stonewall Brigade after its brilliant commander, Gen. Thomas J. "Stonewall" Jackson.

The famous Stonewall was long dead now, killed by his own men on a dark night in the stygian woods near Chancellorsville, and the brigade named after him had shrunk to a shadow of its former self. The men still alive fought gallantly, however, as they had today—June 3, 1864—in the trees along the edge of a long field just west of the crossroads village of Cold Harbor, Virginia.

Yancy Lattimer's last will and testament had left ownership of the slave Roman to his friend and fellow captain in the Confederate army, Will Brannon. Roman had found Will and put his destiny in the white man's hands. What else was he to do?

Quickly, Will had made it clear that he did not intend to own a slave. His family had never been slaveholders and had too much pride to believe that any man should be subjugated so. Yet when war came, they fought for their homeland and the preservation of that "peculiar institution." Roman couldn't understood their actions, but in the end, it didn't matter. Will Brannon had given him his freedom. Yankee politicians blustered about it, but Cap'n Will had accomplished it. Roman was a free man now, and he had stayed with Will out of friendship and loyalty, serving as a civilian aide, not because he had to but because he wanted to. It was always "Cap'n Will," not "Marse Will." That had been made plain early on, even before the manumission papers had been filed and Roman was granted his freedom officially.

All those memories raced through Roman's mind as he stood beside Will Brannon's grave. Never fully recovering from the awful wound he had received at Gettysburg, Cap'n Will had rejoined the Confederate army as soon as he was able. He fought again, through the battles of the Wilderness, Spotsylvania, and now Cold Harbor. Finally, Cold Harbor had been the death of him, as it had brought death to so many thousands of men on both sides of the great conflict. In recent days, before the battle, Roman had noticed a gray cast to Will's face, had seen the haunted look in his friend's hollow, deep-set eyes. The end had been nigh already. Yankee bullets had cut down Cap'n Will today, but they had really killed him at Gettysburg. In the months since, he had lived and breathed but been a dead man. Toward the end he had known it, just as Roman did.

A great shudder shook Roman's body. Mac put a hand on his shoulder and squeezed hard. "I can't believe he's gone," he said in a voice thick with grief, and Roman felt a flash of guilt. Mac had lost even more today than he had.

"No sir, Cap'n," Roman said as he dragged the back of his hand across his wet eyes. "No sir. I don't expect anybody who knew Cap'n Will will think he's gone."

Mac patted Roman's shoulder again then put on his hat, tugging down hard on the floppy brim in front. "I believe we've done all we can for him. I want to look around, though, and fix this place in my mind. Someday, when the war is over, I'll come back here."

"Yes sir."

Mac moved back a few steps from the graveside. Roman went with him. "What will you do now?" Mac asked. His voice was slightly stronger but still choked with emotion.

Roman blinked again, in confusion this time. "Sir? Why, I figured I'd go with you, Cap'n Mac."

Mac shook his head. "There's no need for that. You're a free man, remember? You can go wherever you want."

"Don't know as I want to go anywhere else," Roman said honestly. "I never give it much thought."

In the wan light from the moon and stars that washed over the battlefield, Mac smiled. "You'd better start thinking about it. You're going to be free the rest of your life, Roman. That's a long time. What do you want to do with yourself?"

Cap'n Mac might as well have been talking some foreign language, Roman thought, or some forgotten tongue no longer understood. Do with himself? How did he know what he wanted to do with himself?

He'd had his moments of dreaming, of course. He supposed everybody did, even slaves. He was good at carving chess pieces and other things out of wood, and he enjoyed it. But he reckoned a fella couldn't spend his life whittling. There had to be more to it than that. But what?

"Cap'n Mac, I . . . I just don't know."

"Some of the men in Fitz Lee's cavalry have brought their . . . servants . . . with them."

Servants. Not slaves. But that's what they were, of course.

"I've always ridden alone, though," Mac went on. "You're a good man, Roman, and I'd be proud to have you with me, but your place isn't here."

Roman wiped away the last of the tears. "Reckon I could go back to Culpeper County. That's home to me. Always has been."

Mac nodded and said, "I think that's a good idea. Go to my family's farm. I know they'd be happy to take you in, and I'm sure they could use a good hand."

"I don't know, Cap'n," Roman said. "Your ma . . . she ain't partial to slaves."

"You're not a slave anymore," Mac pointed out.

"I expect she's even less fond of colored folks who've been freed. She didn't want Cap'n Will to manumit me."

"All that's in the past. And to tell you the truth, Roman, you'd be doing me a favor by going there. I'm not sure what's happening on the farm with Henry and Titus, but considering the hard feelings between them . . ." Mac shrugged. "Well, like I said before, I'm sure they can use the help."

"If you really think it's best, Cap'n, I reckon I can go there."

"Thanks, Roman." Mac put out his hand. Just like his brother, he had never considered himself too good to shake hands with a black man. Roman returned the firm grip. "You know," Mac went on, "Will never would have made it back from Pennsylvania without your help, Roman."

"He was my friend," Roman said. "The best friend I ever had, I reckon."

DECIDING TO go to Culpeper County and actually getting there were two different things, Roman discovered. It was at least a hundred miles from Cold Harbor, northeast of Richmond, to the town of Culpeper, far to the northwest of the Confederate capital and within sight of the great spine of the Blue Ridge Mountains.

The only way to get there was on foot. Roman had no horse, and the Confederate cavalry couldn't spare one. Even if he had been mounted, he wouldn't have gotten very far. The horse would have been confiscated, and there was a good chance he would have been shot as a horse thief.

So he would have to walk back home. He had no doubt he could do it. After all, he reminded himself, he had walked from Virginia to Pennsylvania to find Cap'n Will after Yancy Lattimer's death. That had been a lot farther. But things had gotten worse in the year since then. Large areas of the South had been stripped bare of food and supplies by the two ravening armies jousting with one another across the battered landscape. Refugees who no longer had homes wandered the roads, and many of them would steal, even kill, to stay alive. Roman couldn't bring himself to blame them too much. When faced with the prospect of starving to death—or worse, watching their children starve to death— most folks would do whatever they had to in order to avoid that horror. That sympathy didn't make him any less wary of the refugees, though. And many of them were no-account to start with, men who always sank to the lowest level no matter what their circumstances or surroundings.

So as he skirted Richmond to the north and struck out toward the distant Blue Ridge, he did a lot of walking by night and hiding out by day, finding a good spot each dawn to curl up out of sight and rest. He drifted in and out of a light sleep during the day, always restless, always on the alert for trouble.

Sometimes exhaustion claimed him, pulling him into a deep, dreamless slumber. Such was the case when, with no warning, the cold hard ring of a pistol barrel prodded his forehead and an even colder voice announced, "Lookee what we got here."

Startled, Roman would have jumped up off the ground, even with the gun at his head, but a heavy foot landed in the middle of his chest and roughly shoved him down.

"Don't do that again!" the man looming above him yelled. "I'll blow your damn brains out, you understand, boy?"

Wide-eyed, breathing hard with fear, Roman stared up at the man. He saw a filthy, bearded face. Above it, a gray cap with a torn and broken bill rested crookedly on a tangle of black hair. The man wore a ragged, patched gray jacket. The left sleeve hung empty, the arm either blown off in battle or sawn off by some butcher of a surgeon in a field hospital. Probably blown off clean, Roman thought. A man actually stood a better chance of surviving a wound like that than he did if he was sent to one of those charnel houses masquerading as hospitals.

Why was he even thinking such things at a moment such as this, he wondered, when he was so close to death himself?

He lay in a narrow gully cut by the thin trickle of a creek. The stream was at his feet, and he had crawled under some bushes that grew at its edge, thinking he wouldn't be seen there. But this man had seen him, and Roman knew that discovery might easily prove to be the end of him.

The one-armed man would have been mustered out of the army and sent home to recover from his wound as best he could. The Confederate army, like all armies, didn't care much about a man once he could no longer fight. Maybe he still had a home, but from the looks of him, it was more likely that the war had forced him out of it, forced him to take to the roads and the open countryside to survive. At least he seemed to be alone. Roman swallowed nervously. If there had been a gang of such scavengers, he would have had no chance at all to get out of this predicament. As it was, the odds were extremely slim that he would live longer than a few more minutes.

The man leaned closer to him and hissed, "You got any food?" The smell of rotting teeth almost made Roman gag.

"I . . . I got nothin' to eat, sir." That was the truth. Roman had long since finished off the little bit of hardtack and jerky Mac Brannon had given him before he left the gravesite at Cold Harbor. Once those provisions were gone, he had lived on wild plums and onions. He was so hungry he had forgotten what it was like to have even a half-full belly.

"You lie!" the man said as he pressed the gun barrel harder against Roman's head. "All darkies lie."

"N-no sir. Not me. It's the truth."

"Well, then, if you ain't got any food, what else you got?"

"Nothin', sir."

"You a runaway? Mebbe I could get some money for turnin' you in."

Roman licked his lips. "No sir. I'm a freedman. I got my papers an' everything."

That was one thing Roman did possess, proof that his former master had freed him. The manumission documents were folded, wrapped in oilcloth, and stowed inside his shirt. He kept them with him always, sometimes taking them out and touching them as if they were holy icons.

The man looked him up and down. "You got shoes," he said.

That was true. Roman had shoes, and the soles had only a few holes in them. The crippled Confederate who knelt on the soft earth of the gully bank beside him had bare feet.

"And them pants look better'n mine. Ain't fittin' for a darky to be wearin' better clothes than a white man. Take 'em off."

"I . . . I don't want to."

"I ain't givin' you no damn choice." The man took the gun barrel away from Roman's head then awkwardly, without a second arm to balance him, pushed himself to his feet. He kept the pistol trained on his prisoner. "Now do what I say, or I'll just shoot you and take 'em off of you."

Roman had no doubt the man meant what he said. He sat up, reached for his right shoe, then paused before taking it off and looked up at the man. "You're goin' to kill me anyway, ain't you?" Suddenly, for some reason, he had to know.

The man's creased, filth-encrusted face split in a grin. "Why the hell would I do that?"

"'Cause I used to be a slave, and I ain't no more."

"You think that matters a good goddamn to me? You think it matters now?" The man laughed, and Roman thought he heard an edge of insanity in the sound. "Hell, boy, I don't care no more if all you apes go free. You can go on up to Washington and dance a jig with Abe Lincoln for all I care. I just want somethin' to eat and some shoes. You got the shoes."

Maybe . . . maybe the man would let him go after all. Roman hated to lose the shoes, but he could walk barefooted. It was summer, after all. A fella didn't really need shoes at this time of year. He hated to give up his trousers, too. A man with no pants was a man with no dignity at all. Maybe the one-armed man would just swap pants with him. Ragged they might be, but they were better than nothing.

"All right, sir," he said as he took off his right shoe. "I won't give you no trouble, and you won't kill me." He wanted to get the man to say it.

"Yeah, yeah. Hurry up."

The sound of horse hooves moving slowly along the nearby road took both men by surprise. The one-armed man looked up and turned the barrel of the gun away from Roman. Roman could have jumped him then. The one-armed man looked sick and weak. If Roman ever got his hands on him, he knew he could wrest the gun away with no trouble. But the man had promised not to kill him, and if Roman started a fight, the one-armed man just might get lucky and pull the trigger in time . . .

"Drop that gun!"

The shout came from behind them, again startling both of them and making them jump. The one-armed man wheeled around, waving the pistol wildly in response to the command instead of following it.

Roman looked down the gully and saw another man standing about forty feet away, where the creek made a bend. The newcomer must have slipped along the gully until he reached a spot where he could get the drop on the one-armed man. The stranger was armed with a rifle, one of the new-fangled repeaters with a cocking lever under the breech. Roman had heard of such rifles but had never seen one before.

That wasn't the most surprising thing about the stranger's appearance, however. The most surprising thing was that he was black, as black as Roman himself.

"I won't tell you again, mister," the newcomer said. "Drop the gun!"

The one-armed man pulled the trigger instead, thrusting the barrel of the revolver at the black stranger as if the gesture would give an added impetus to the bullet. The hammer fell with a futile click as the pistol misfired. The rifleman didn't give the one-armed man the chance to try a second shot. His weapon cracked wickedly as the stranger squeezed off a round.

Roman heard the bullet strike the one-armed man in the head. It sounded a little like the blade of an ax biting deep into the wood of a tree. Blood flew through the air, along with splinters of bone and splatters of brain. The one-armed man swayed for a second then toppled onto the bank beside Roman. A good-sized chunk of his skull was shot away.

Roman had seen death before, seen it close up as men were blown to pieces in combat when they were standing only a few feet from him. Still, a shudder went through him as he looked into the staring, unseeing eyes of the one-armed man. The man was dead already, but his legs kicked feebly and his fingers dug into the dirt for a moment before relaxing. He smelled worse in death than he had in life, difficult as that was to believe.

The stranger lowered his rifle and walked along the gully toward Roman and the corpse.

"You all right, son?" he called when he was closer. Despite the way he spoke to Roman, he was only a few years older, still in his twenties, Roman judged.

Holding his shoe, Roman slid away from the dead body and stood up. "I'm fine," he said. "He didn't hurt me."

"Idiot should have done what I told him," the stranger said as he stopped and looked down at the corpse. "Some fellas just can't get used to the idea of a black man telling them what to do . . . even when the black man's got a rifle."

"I'm not sure that was it," Roman said. "I think he was just ... surprised."

"Surprised right to death." The stranger worked the rifle's lever and deftly snatched the empty cartridge from the air as it sprang out of the breech. The cartridge could be reloaded later. He saw Roman admiring his weapon and chuckled. "This here is a Henry rifle. They've been around for a few years. Fifteen-shot repeater. Folks say you can load one on Sunday and shoot it all week."

"Yes sir. You're mighty good with it."

"I've had a lot of practice." The stranger's voice was dry with meaning that Roman couldn't fathom.

The Henry rifle wasn't the only gun the stranger carried. He had a cartridge belt strapped around his waist with a holstered pistol attached to it. He was dressed like a white man, wearing a flat-crowned brown hat, a brown coat and trousers, boots, and a white shirt. Roman had never seen a black man like him.

"Name's Joe Brackett," the stranger introduced himself. He held the rifle at his side in his left hand. With his right, he gestured toward the pistol the one-armed man had dropped. "Reckon that gun is yours now."

Roman reached down and picked it up. He had held a gun only a few times in his life, and the cold metal gave him a feeling in his stomach that he didn't like. He knew enough about guns, though, to see something that made him shake his head.

"What is it?" Brackett asked.

"This pistol's not loaded. Besides that, the sear's busted. He couldn't have shot anybody with it, not even me."

Brackett frowned. "Well, I didn't know that at the time, and neither did you. Fella shouldn't go around acting like he's trying to shoot somebody if he doesn't have the means to do it."

Roman had never heard a black man talk quite like Joe Brackett did. He sounded like he had never spent a day in Virginia or anywhere else in the South.

"Was he trying to rob you?" Brackett went on.

Roman nodded. "He wanted my shoes and my pants. Wanted food more than anything, but I don't have any."

"Yeah, I can see you've got a sort of lean and hungry look about you. Well, come on. I've got some food in my saddlebags."

Brackett turned and climbed up out of the gully. Roman slipped his shoe on and followed him. The road was about fifty yards away. A black-and-white horse stood there, the colors so evenly mixed Roman couldn't tell if it was a white horse with black spots or a black horse with white spots. He had never seen the likes of a horse like that, either.

"I saw that fella creeping around the edge of the gully and figured he was up to something," Brackett explained. "So I sent my horse walking on down the road and slipped around on foot to see what was going on." He noticed Roman staring at the horse. "What, you've never seen an Appaloosa before? I'm not surprised. The Nez Perce Indians breed them, out in Washington and Oregon."

"I never been out there," Roman said with a slow shake of his head.

"Those are states out west. A long way west. I reckon I know my way around out there better than I do this part of the country. I'm a mite lost. Maybe you can set me straight. Which way is Washington City?"

Roman just stared at him for a moment before saying, "Mister Brackett, you really *are* lost."

☆ ☆ ☆

As it turned out, Joe Brackett had taken a wrong turn back in Ohio and had aimed a little south of where he should have been going. That minor deviation had increased with distance until he found himself in Virginia instead of Maryland. He had been pretty circumspect in his travels and hadn't stopped to ask directions. A well-armed black man riding a fine horse would be suspect even in the North.

"Wouldn't be in such a fix if Matthew Hanley hadn't up and died on me," Brackett said that night as he and Roman sat next to the ashes of a tiny fire in a small clearing deep in some woods. Brackett had doused the fire before it grew full dark, just to be sure no one would spot the camp.

"Who's Matthew Hanley?" Roman asked sleepily. He had eaten some salt pork and biscuits from Brackett's saddlebags, and he felt better than he had in quite some time. Even a partially full stomach made him drowsy, though.

"Preacher man from Washington. The city, not the state." Brackett took a thin cigar from his coat pocket, put it in his mouth, and chewed it without lighting it. "He got the idea that he ought to gather up a bunch of freed slaves and take them out west so they could start a community of their own. He needed somebody who knew the frontier to take charge of the whole thing, though, so he went to St. Louis to look for a fella like that. That's where he ran into me."

"You know about the West?"

Brackett snorted around the cigar. "Been over most of it, at one time or another. I worked as a guide on the Oregon Trail, leading whole wagon trains full of pilgrims to what they thought would be the Promised Land. Maybe to them, it is. I was always too restless to light and set in one place for very long, though. Until I got to Last Chance Canyon, that is."

"Last Chance Canyon? Where's that?"

"California. Gold-rush country. Me and a friend of mine, a fella named Fury, helped out some folks who had a gold claim there. Fury, he moved on, but I stayed. You ever seen a rich black man, son?"

Roman had to shake his head. "No sir, I don't reckon I have."

The cigar in Brackett's mouth tilted up at a jaunty angle as he grinned. "Well, you're looking at one now. I was in St. Louis on business, met Reverend Hanley, and decided to throw in with him. We were on our way back to Washington when he took a fever and died. I decided to come ahead on my own." He took the cigar from his mouth and turned it slowly in his fingers. "You know, when Hanley first told me his idea, I thought it was the craziest thing I'd ever heard. But the more I thought about it, the more I figured it might be worth a try." The cigar jabbed toward Roman as Brackett grew more animated. "I'll tell you one thing. All those slaves who're going to wind up free when this war is over think that everything's going to be milk and honey when that time comes. Well, that's not the way it's going to be. Life will still be damned hard for them down here in the South, maybe almost as hard as when they were slaves. And it's not going to be much better up north. Those Yankees talk about equality, but I promise you, most of them sure as hell won't practice what they preach. Out west, though, it's different."

"Folks out there don't care if a fella's black?"

"Oh, they care." Brackett laughed humorlessly. "I've been called enough names in my time to know that. But if you work hard and if you're good at what you do . . . if you're the sort of man who'll do to ride the river with, as they say . . . after a while they don't think near as much about the color of your skin. That's why I think maybe Reverend Hanley had himself a good idea."

"It sounds like a good place," Roman said. He wasn't as sleepy now. Brackett's words had engaged his interest.

Brackett replaced the cigar and said, "Come with me."

Roman sat up straighter. "To Washington, you mean?"

"Yeah. I need somebody who knows this country to help me get there. But after that, you can come west with us, be a part of the group."

The possibility was intriguing, but frightening at the same time. "I don't know . . ."

"You told me you're a free man. You can go where you please, do what you want. Once we get away from all these Rebels, the Yankees won't interfere."

"You're sure?"

"Nothing in life is guaranteed, son," Brackett said. "Best you get used to that if you're going to live free."

Live free . . . It had a mighty nice sound, Roman thought. But he had promised Cap'n Mac that he would go back to the Brannon farm in Culpeper County.

"If I go," he said, "I got to send a letter to some people and explain things to them."

"Folks where you come from, you mean?"

"That's right. Some friends of mine. White folks."

Brackett arched an eyebrow. "Best friend I ever had was a white man, but I didn't expect to run into that back here."

"Man's got to take his friends where he finds them, and you'd never find a better one than Cap'n Will."

Brackett put out a hand. "So we've got a deal?"

Roman hesitated only a second before clasping Brackett's hand. "Deal," he affirmed. He hoped Mac would understand.

As for Cap'n Will . . . Roman was convinced Cap'n Will wouldn't have minded at all.

Chapter Two

S WEET MUSIC DRIFTED THROUGH the night. A man could close his eyes and almost imagine he was back home, Mac Brannon thought. Almost.

But then, inevitably, the realization crowded in that the music he heard came from the camp of the enemy. Also, the melodies were counterpointed by the rattle of drums as the Yankees used the pounding beats to signal troop movements. The Federal infantry was on the move tonight as Gen. Philip H. Sheridan maneuvered his army into position for an attack on the Confederate line.

It was the evening of September 18, 1864. For months, battles had raged up and down the length of the Shenandoah Valley, west of the rounded peaks of the Blue Ridge. The Shenandoah was perhaps the only part of the Confederacy where farms still functioned at a level anywhere close to how things had been before the war. The farmers in the valley had gotten their crops planted the previous spring, and milk cows still grazed, pigs still rooted and wallowed, and chickens still scratched in farmyards. What came out of this valley fed practically the whole Confederate army. Not only that, but as long as the Shenandoah was in Confederate hands, it could serve as a back door into Washington, D.C., should the rebellious Southerners somehow manage to launch another assault like the one back in July that had penetrated beyond the Monocacy River to the outskirts of the capital city itself before being turned back. Such a thrust was unlikely now, but it was a worrisome enough possibility, combined with the valley's importance to the Confederacy as a source of food and supplies, to prompt Ulysses S. Grant, the commander of all Union forces, to send "Little Phil" to the Shenandoah with orders to drive out the Rebels, no matter what it took. Sheridan had worked hard at his task, but so far, Gen. Jubal Early's army had held off the Federal invasion despite being outnumbered more than two to one.

Now two divisions of Early's army were centered on a shallow plateau east of the town of Winchester, facing Sheridan's forces. Winchester had been the scene of two earlier battles, and the town had changed hands numerous times during the three and a half years of the conflict. Tonight the Yankees were camped down the road, along the turnpike that led to Berryville. From the plateau the fires of the enemy were visible, looking for all the world like winking eyes in the darkness. And the music they played could be heard by the tired, hungry, battle-weary men of Early's command.

Mac tried not to think about home as he ran a comb over the sleek hide of the big, silver gray stallion that had carried him safely through so many battles. He was all too aware that Culpeper County was only a few score miles away, on the other side of the Blue Ridge. His mother Abigail, his brother Henry, and his sister Cordelia were back there, trying to keep the Brannon family farm intact despite desperate conditions. From everything Mac had heard, Culpeper and the surrounding countryside were well behind Yankee lines and occupied by Federal forces. He hoped that conditions weren't too bad on the farm. He hoped as well that Henry was controlling his temper anytime he had to deal with the Yankees. Henry could be hotheaded at times.

Not as hotheaded as brother Titus, of course. But Titus was gone. Mac had gotten a short note from Cordelia, smuggled through the lines somehow and sent to him while he was at Petersburg a month earlier. Titus had left the farm, and no one knew where he had gone. It was suspected that he had something to do with the fiery destruction of the main house at Mountain Laurel, the plantation owned by Duncan Ebersole. Ebersole, whose daughter Polly had been married to both Titus and Henry Brannon before she was murdered, was dead as well, his life claimed by the flames that had consumed Mountain Laurel.

Death and tragedy were everywhere, Mac thought. The war was burning up the South, just as the fire had burned Ebersole's house to the ground.

Wherever Titus had gone after leaving home, it was likely he was fighting the Yankees. No one hated Northerners more than Titus. Mac supposed he had good reason to hate them, having survived long, hellish months in the Union prison compound at Camp Douglas, just outside Chicago. That experience would have killed a lot of men; indeed, the cemetery at the camp was packed full, according to Titus. But he had lived through it, had escaped and made his way home, but when he got there he was colder, more ruthless and brutal than ever. Mac hardly knew Titus anymore.

A footstep made Mac pause in his grooming of the stallion. He looked around, saw a familiar figure approaching, a pipe clenched in his teeth. The glow from the burning tobacco in the bowl revealed the man's bearded face. Once that face had been handsome and boyish, quick to laugh. Why shouldn't Fitzhugh Lee laugh? He was a member of the most illustrious military family in the entire South, the nephew of Gen. Robert E. Lee himself, as well as being the close friend and protégé of the Confederacy's most dashing cavalry commander, Gen. James Ewell Brown "Jeb" Stuart.

But now Fitz Lee's face revealed lines of strain. Stuart was dead, fallen at the battle of Yellow Tavern, the victim of a bullet fired by a fleeing Yankee. And though Robert E. Lee was alive and still firmly in command of the Army of Northern Virginia, that army was bogged down and besieged at Petersburg, south of Richmond. After being defeated at Cold Harbor, Grant had sent his army wheeling around, intending to strike at Richmond from the south. Robert E. Lee had blocked his path at Petersburg, but a stalemate had developed. Neither army seemed willing or even able to move.

Action continued along the other fronts, however, and that explained why Mac and Fitz Lee were here, along with the rest of the cavalry division commanded by Lee. They had arrived in the Shenandoah Valley only a couple of weeks earlier, having been sent to reinforce Jubal Early.

Fitz Lee sucked on his pipe for a moment, making the glow even brighter, then he took it from his mouth and used the stem to point down the Berryville turnpike.

"The enemy seems quite gay tonight. It sounds like we're confronted with an army of meadowlarks."

"I doubt if they'll fly up like meadowlarks when we make a loud noise at them, General," Mac said.

Lee chuckled. "No, probably not. But I wish they would." Then he grew more serious. "I can tell by that drumming, though, that Sheridan's up to something. I expect he will come calling in the morning. Probably marching right down the turnpike from Berryville."

"Probably," Mac agreed. Scouts estimated that Sheridan had more than thirty-seven thousand men at his disposal. Early's force numbered just over eighteen thousand. The odds, though still in favor of the Federals, hadn't been quite as bad until Early had sent an infantry division and a battalion of artillery south to join the embattled army at Petersburg a few days earlier. Care had been taken to disguise the departure of those troops, but Mac had a feeling that Sheridan had gotten wind of it anyway. That was why Sheridan had moved up so quickly to Berryville as Early was settling into a defensive line east of Winchester. Sheridan liked to strike while the iron was hot.

Adding to the problem was that Early had gone off to Martinsburg, twenty miles northeast, with Robert Rodes's and John B. Gordon's divisions, to threaten the yards of the B&O Railroad there. Stephen Ramseur's infantry division had been left at Winchester, along with cavalry divisions under Fitz Lee and Gen. Lunsford Lomax. Another infantry division, commanded by Gen. Gabriel Wharton and even more undermanned than Ramseur's, was positioned at Stephenson's Depot, a stop on the railroad four miles north of Winchester.

"I've just come from a meeting with General Ramseur and General Lomax," Fitz Lee went on. Mac had served as Lee's aide for the past couple of years, but the two men were friends as well, and Lee liked to mull over strategy and tactics with Mac. "General Ramseur's division has taken up a post at the mouth of Berryville Canyon to meet any Federal advance."

Mac nodded as he resumed combing the stallion. He was familiar with the terrain, having ridden over it during scouting missions in recent days. "That's good thinking. The canyon isn't much wider than the road itself. Sheridan may find himself in a bit of a bottleneck if he comes through there."

"Yes. There was some talk of pulling back and concentrating the army so that we could meet the enemy at Front Royal or Mount Jackson. But General Early seems to think this is the place to stop Sheridan, and that we have sufficient forces to do so. So that's what we're going to do."

"Yes sir," Mac said. Orders were orders. He knew that, even though his mind was not of a military bent and never would be.

His brother Will, on the other hand, had taken to soldiering right away. A natural leader, Will had served as an infantry captain from First Manassas until his death at Cold Harbor. Though more than three months had passed since Will had fallen, his loss was still a sharp pain to Mac. Will had been the oldest of the five Brannon brothers, followed by Mac, Titus, Cory, and Henry. Cordelia, the only girl, was the baby of the family. Now Mac was the oldest, and he worried about his brothers and sister. He always had, even when Will was alive. He had been closer to Will than any of the others. They had been good friends as well as brothers. The loss of Will, Mac sensed, was something from which he would never fully recover, no matter how long he lived.

Which, of course, might not be very long, not with all those thousands of Yankees just down the road.

"We'd better get some sleep," Fitz Lee advised. "No telling when the enemy will be up and around, but I'd wager it'll be before dawn."

"Yes sir. I'll turn in soon." Mac patted the stallion's shoulder, feeling the powerful muscles under the smooth, silver gray hide. "I haven't heard much music in a while. Thought I'd listen a while longer."

Lee sighed. "Yes, it was different when Beauty was still alive, wasn't it?" he said, using the nickname by which he had known General Stuart since they were both cadets at West Point. Stuart's camps had always been full of music and laughter, and even on the eve of a battle, ladies came to visit. There was nothing improper about it—Stuart had been, above all else, a gentleman—but he was the sort of man who was always surrounded by women, reveling in the pleasures of adoring female company. A woman's laugh, a sigh, a fluttering of lashes, the touch of a lady's fingertips on his arm . . . those things were the stuff of life itself to General Stuart.

His death had taken away more than his leadership and tactical brilliance. When his spirit departed, it took with it the joyous air that had surrounded him. Now the cavalry camps were solemn places where men went about a grim, deadly business.

Perhaps that was the way it should have been all along, Mac thought. War *was* a grim, deadly business. And no amount of lace and perfume and banjo music could make it otherwise.

A TWISTING, tree-lined stream called Opequon Creek meandered between the Confederate and Union lines and crossed the Berryville turnpike at a place known as Spout Spring. Just west of the creek, the road entered a narrow canyon. Starting at 2 A.M. on the morning of September 19, 1864, Sheridan's men began moving west along the turnpike and toward the creek. Gen. James H. Wilson's cavalry division led the way. Three corps of infantry followed.

By dawn the leading elements of the Federal advance had reached Spout Spring and crossed the bridge over Opequon

Creek. Wilson's men cantered carelessly through Berryville Canyon unopposed until they reached the western end of the defile. Awaiting them there was Confederate Gen. Stephen Ramseur's infantry division, which was supported by a single battery of artillery.

In the graying light, guns roared and hoof beats thundered as the Yankees launched a cavalry charge. At the top of a gentle slope, Ramseur's men took cover behind some old earthworks from a previous battle. It wasn't a bad spot to make a stand, but the Federal cavalry attack was unexpectedly strong, and Ramseur had not positioned enough men here to hold back the Northern horsemen.

Soon the Confederates were forced to fall back to a barn on a farm belonging to a family named Dinkle. The thousands of Federal infantrymen who had followed Wilson through the canyon emerged from it, and their line surged forward, ready to drive the Confederates back even farther toward Winchester.

Sheridan knew that Early's forces were stretched out, some of them as far away as Martinsburg. A quick, smashing blow could destroy this part of Early's army, Sheridan reasoned, and then the other parts would fall one by one, like dominoes.

Berryville Canyon wasn't the only place the Yankees struck in the early morning of September 19. To the north, more Federal cavalry, two divisions commanded by Gens. Wesley Merritt and William W. Averell, headed for a pair of fords across Opequon Creek. If they were successful in crossing the creek, they could then turn south and launch a devastating attack on the Confederate left flank.

STREAMERS OF mist hung in the air as the small group of cavalry led by Fitzhugh Lee galloped toward Opequon Creek. That mist would burn away later in the day as the sun rose higher, but it would be replaced, perhaps, by clouds of powder smoke, Mac thought. He already heard the sounds of battle to the south, around the turnpike.

Scouts had brought word of the Federal cavalry movements to the north that threatened Stephenson's Depot. Now Lee was going to see for himself what the Yankees were up to. Gen. John McCausland's cavalry brigade was already up there, ready to meet the enemy, but they probably wouldn't be strong enough to hold back the Yankees by themselves. Lee was charged with maintaining a screen of cavalry from the turnpike north to the railroad. That line was going to be stretched mighty thin, Mac knew. But McCausland's cavalry and Gabriel Wharton's infantry would have to stop the Union flanking movement if the defense of Winchester was going to have any chance of being successful.

Mac spotted the rail line in the distance when he caught sight of its embankments through the trees. A few minutes later Lee's cavalry rode up to the depot to find a meeting of generals. In addition to Wharton and McCausland, Mac recognized Gens. John C. Breckinridge and, surprisingly, Robert E. Rodes. He hadn't known until this moment that Rodes had returned from Martinsburg.

The generals welcomed Lee to their conversation. As Lee's aide, Mac stood nearby. He heard Rodes explain that a dispatch found in the Martinsburg railroad station the day before mentioned Grant's presence in Sheridan's camp. Early immediately had grasped that Grant was there for one reason and one reason only: to order Sheridan into battle. Accordingly, Early had sent Rodes's and Gordon's divisions back to Winchester as quickly as possible. The overnight march had brought Rodes's men to Wharton's aid; Gordon's force was still on the way, though not far behind.

"Now we have a chance to surprise Sheridan with a bigger force than he's expecting," Wharton said. The general, with his long black beard, was from Culpeper County, though Mac did not know of him before the war. Still, it was nice to see someone from home would be in command of part of the upcoming battle. Better Wharton than him, he thought wryly.

For a few moments, Lee only listened to the discussion, somewhat impatiently slapping the gloves he held in one hand against his thigh. Finally he said, "Most of my men are in position to cover General Ramseur's left. I'll personally take a smaller force to watch the Valley turnpike, in case the enemy tries to cut it north of Winchester."

The suggestion met with agreement from the other generals, and Mac thought it was a sound idea, too. If the Federals gained control of the Valley turnpike north of Winchester, the Confederates in the town and those at Stephenson's Depot would be effectively cut off from each other. The first step in destroying an army was separating it.

Lee pulled on his gauntlets and swung up into the saddle. Mac and the other members of Lee's staff mounted as well, and a courier galloped off to fetch the other two brigades. Those brigades would be posted on either side of the Valley turnpike between Winchester and Stephenson's Depot, Lee explained to Mac as they hurried southwest along the road.

The noises of battle several miles to the south continued, though more sporadically now. Mac had heard the crackle of rifle fire and the dull boom of artillery almost since the sun came up. He wasn't sure what was going on, but he felt relatively certain the Yankees were testing the strength of the line that Ramseur had established on both sides of the Berryville pike. Knowing that the Yankees were already assaulting the Confederate center and that they were also preparing to try a flanking attack to the north, Mac wondered what was going on south of the turnpike. It seemed likely to him that Sheridan would make a move in that direction as well. A classic enveloping maneuver was in the making. If they weren't careful, Mac realized, he and his comrades could find themselves in the jaws of a trap themselves.

☆ ☆ ☆

THAT WAS exactly what Sheridan had in mind, but as usual in war, not everything went according to plan where huge numbers of men were concerned. Miscommunication among the Federals caused one of the infantry corps to bring their supply wagons and ambulances with them when they started through Berryville Canyon. The narrow confines of the canyon worked against them so that it wasn't long before a natural bottleneck occurred and brought the Yankee advance to a standstill. Thousands of infantrymen were stuck behind the wagons, unable to get through and deploy for battle. Many of these men were part of the division that was supposed to swing south around the Confederate right, so the scheduled flanking maneuver in that area failed to get under way.

This delay gave Rodes's and Gordon's divisions time to arrive on the scene from Martinsburg. These footsore, weary, battle-hardened troops lined up on Ramseur's left, forming a solid line from the turnpike to a small creek called Redbud Run. When the Federals started through this area, they would find much stiffer resistance waiting for them than they had been led to believe was there.

The firing in the Confederate center slackened as the Union troops struggled to move into position to launch their main attack. Both sides seemed to pause and draw a deep breath. Hell might be coming . . . but it wasn't here yet.

NORTH OF Winchester, along the railroad and the Valley turnpike, fighting had flared up already as Merritt's and Averell's cavalry made contact with Breckinridge's infantry.

Mac heard the fierce outbreak of gunfire as the Yankee cavalry pushed toward Stephenson's Depot. He sat mounted beside Fitz Lee, and he and the general looked at each other in awareness. They both knew it wouldn't be long before they were in the thick of the fight.

Sure enough, only a short time later Mac saw men in ragged gray and butternut uniforms moving back through the trees on both sides of the turnpike. Those were infantrymen from Wharton's division, and though they paused along the way to fire their rifles at as-yet-unseen foes behind them, they were in retreat.

McCausland galloped up to Lee. A lean-faced Irishman with a slightly drooping black mustache, McCausland had led a cavalry raid earlier that summer into Chambersburg, Pennsylvania. In retribution for the burning of homes and farms in the Shenandoah Valley by a Yankee army commanded by Gen. David Hunter, Sheridan's predecessor, McCausland ordered that Chambersburg's business district be put to the torch. Afterward. it was safe to say that in Pennsylvania there was no more hated Confederate than McCausland. Today, however, they were a long way from Chambersburg, and McCausland's cavalry fought not for revenge but for survival.

"We were holding them for a spell," he told Lee, "but that was just Merritt's bunch. When Averell's division took a hand too, they started pushing us back." McCausland wiped a hand over his face. "They fight like madmen, those Yankee troopers. Especially Custer's men."

Custer. Mac knew the name. It was said that Custer was young, one of the youngest generals in the Union army, and he was impossible to miss on the battlefield, what with that long yellow hair of his. Mac had seen him on several occasions in the past, at various cavalry clashes, including the one at Gettysburg on the third day of that epic battle.

"What about Wharton's men?" Lee asked.

"They're trying to stiffen, but I don't know how successful they're going to be, General."

"Hold out as best you can," Lee muttered. "Make the enemy pay a price to get this far, and when he does, we'll hit him with fresh troops."

McCausland nodded. "I understand, sir." He turned and trotted his horse back toward the retreating line of gray.

A short time later, Jubal Early himself rode up, accompanied by General Breckinridge. Lee saluted as he greeted them.

"What in hell's goin' on here?" Early demanded. With his grizzled beard and blunt, often profane speech, he seemed more like a mountaineer than a general. "You boys got to protect this flank so's we can hit them Yankees right in their guts."

"We'll hold this side of the line, General, have no fear about that," Lee replied. "Our men are fighting splendidly."

Only someone who knew Lee as well as Mac did could detect the faint hollowness in his tone. Mac had no doubt that Lee meant what he said. But Lee was enough of a realist to know that he and the other commanders in this area were outnumbered.

Still, they didn't have to actually defeat the Yankees who were trying to push past Stephenson's Depot and down the Valley turnpike toward Winchester. All they had to do was put up enough of a fight to delay the Federals. If the tide of battle down the Berryville turnpike, west of Opequon Creek, were to swing in favor of the Confederates, chances were that Sheridan would recall this flanking maneuver and use his cavalry to bolster the center of his line. They needed time for that situation to develop, Mac thought, and it was the job of Lee, McCausland, Wharton, and the rest of the men up here to buy that time.

"All right," Early said grudgingly. "But if you get a chance, you hit them sons o' bitches with everything you got, you hear me, General?"

Lee nodded. "I hear you, sir," he said. "I surely do."

ALTHOUGH JUBAL EARLY considered Sheridan to be overly cautious, Sheridan showed none of that on this day. Impatient with the delay at Berryville Canyon, Sheridan ordered a major assault around midday, even though some of his men were still bogged down in the canyon. A signal gun barked its message, sending thousands of blue-clad soldiers surging forward.

They found themselves pushing through a thick stand of trees then emerging into a broad field that offered little if any cover. Beyond the field lay a shallow but steep ridge, and Ramseur's, Rodes's, and Gordon's men were dug in atop that height. Cannon began to belch fire and lead as the Yankees started forward across the field. Minié bullets from Confederate muskets whistled around the heads of the lucky ones. The unlucky ones fell as lead thudded into them. Dust puffed from blue woolen tunics at the impact of the bullets. Blood welled from the wounds, hiding the ragged, black-edged holes torn in the fabric. The storm of death grew more and more fierce as the Union men advanced.

Still, there were too many of them. For each Yankee who fell, ten more charged onward, shouting and firing up at the defenders. The wave of blue climbed steadily up the hill, and suddenly, the Yankees were among Gordon's men, fighting hand to hand and driving the Confederates back into some thicker woods.

The Federals gave chase until they ran into artillery fire from batteries in the woods as well as flanking fire from a section of horse artillery dispatched to this part of the battle by Fitzhugh Lee in response to a message from Gordon. The Confederate retreat, which had threatened for a moment to become a rout, became instead a counterattack.

Uncertainty among the Federal commanders led to the left side of their attack veering too far in that direction. Suddenly their front was stretched out too far, and it split in the middle, leaving a gap. Watching through field glasses as clouds of smoke swirled and roiled across the battlefield, Rodes and Gordon both spotted the Union error and acted quickly to exploit it. They conferred briefly and decided to strike straight ahead, driving a wedge into the gap and widening it. Outnumbered as they were, victory might be out of their grasp no matter what they did, but it seemed to both officers that they would at least have a better chance if the enemy were divided and confused.

Both men issued orders to launch the assault on the Federal center, but as they did so, a shell burst nearby. Rodes staggered and fell forward, blood welling from a horrible wound behind his ear where a piece of shrapnel had struck him. An able commander from the battle of First Manassas onward, he lay dead on the field. Quickly his staff loaded his body into an ambulance and rushed away with it, fearing that if the news of Rodes's death became widely known, it would dishearten his men.

Although distraught at the death of his friend and comrade, Gordon had no choice but to carry on. Assuming command of Rodes's division as well as his own, he ordered the attack. With Rebel yells ringing from lips blackened by gunpowder, Confederate troops surged into the hole in the center of the Union line. The Yankees were taken by surprise, and in fierce hand-to-hand combat, they were driven back toward Sheridan's command post in the rear. For a moment, the pendulum swung. After almost being routed, now the Southerners found themselves on the verge of making the Yankees turn and run.

If the odds had not been so great in the Federals' favor, that might have happened. As it was, Sheridan quickly called up reserves and threw them into the battle. The Confederate thrust was stalled then turned back.

After a couple of hours of nonstop fighting, a lull settled over the battlefield in the early afternoon of September 19. Listening to the quiet, Jubal Early—Old Jube, to some of his men—was convinced that he had won. Stymied by the Confederate resistance, Sheridan should withdraw.

But Little Phil was just getting started.

MAC LEANED forward anxiously in the saddle. He could see the Yankees now, moving through the woods a couple of hundred yards to the north. Some of the Union cavalrymen were on horseback, but others were fighting dismounted, their Spencer repeaters barking rapidly as they drove the Confederate infantry before them, advancing relentlessly along the turnpike.

Mac looked back at the line of gray-clad cavalrymen awaiting the order to attack. To the left, Col. George S. Patton's infantry brigade had moved up and waited for orders as well.

Beside Mac, Lee smiled and leaned forward to pat the neck of his horse. "Well, Nellie," he said to the animal, "it's come to us again. Time to do our job." The general straightened and looked over at Mac with a curt nod. He drew his saber from its scabbard and held it over his head. Sunlight reflected off the blade.

"Gentlemen . . . ," Lee began, his voice rising as he drew out the word then finished with a shouted command. *"Charge!"*

The cavalry thundered forward. Across the road, the infantrymen received their orders at the same moment. They surged toward the Yankees, shouting their defiance.

Mac carried two pistols and had two more close at hand in saddle holsters. He guided the stallion easily with his knees as the cavalry swept toward the Federal horsemen. As he began to fire, alternating with the pistols, Mac wondered where Custer was. Would this be the day he had a shot at the flamboyant Yankee general? Mac felt no hatred for Custer, but he knew the man's death would be a blow to the Union cause.

The lines of blue and gray came together with an explosion of gunfire and the ringing of steel against steel as men fought with sabers. Mac emptied his pistols, jammed them back in their holsters, and drew the other two revolvers. He blinked as the acrid powder smoke stung his eyes and tried to make him cough. In the madness of blood and killing that ebbed and flowed around him, he looked for a new target wearing Yankee blue.

Instead he saw the bearded, gray-clad form of his friend and commander, Fitzhugh Lee, as the general waved his saber to urge his men forward. Then, to Mac's horror, a shell burst beside Lee, throwing up a dense cloud of dirt and black smoke.

"General!" Mac shouted as he sent the stallion lunging toward the spot. Cold fear clutched at his heart. "General Lee!"

Chapter Three

MAC FLUNG HIMSELF OUT of the saddle and stumbled forward. He heard a shrill screaming and thought at first the horrible sound came from Fitzhugh Lee. Then he realized it was a horse in agony. He batted at the smoke that drifted in front of his face and blocked his vision.

Spotting a huddled shape on the ground in front of him, he dropped to his knees beside it. Blood soaked into the legs of his trousers from the puddle in which he knelt. He reached out and grasped the shoulder of the man who lay face down before him. As gently as possible, he turned the man over and saw Lee's face. His features were drawn tight in pain and as pale as milk. But to Mac's immense relief, the general's eyes fluttered open, and he looked up with something approaching awareness. Lee was alive. "M-Mac . . . ?" he muttered.

"Right here, General," Mac assured him. "Just hang on. You'll be fine."

The screams of pain from the nearby horse fell silent. Mac glanced around, spotted Nellie, Lee's usual mount, lying on her side. The horse's legs thrashed a final time then grew still in death. The bursting shell had torn a hideous wound in her belly and side.

Mac loved animals, always had, and his heart went out to the poor beast that had just expired. But he had much more pressing worries at the moment, such as the condition of Lee. A quick examination told him that the general had been wounded in the right thigh. Mac tore away more of the burned and shredded cloth to lay bare the injury.

Shrapnel from the shell had ripped a huge gash in Lee's leg. The wound bled freely, the blood puddling around and underneath his sprawled body. Mac tore off the general's belt and wrapped it around his leg above the gash, pulling it as tight as he could. Then he used his saber to cut a large piece off the general's coat. Wadding up the fabric, he pressed it hard to the wound and held it there, trying to stanch the flow of blood.

He wasn't aware that help had arrived until several men of Lee's staff knelt around him and reached forward to help care for the general. Lee was still conscious, although just barely. He summoned the strength to grasp at Mac's sleeve.

"W-Wickham!" he gasped. "Tell . . . Wickham . . . to carry on . . . Mac . . ."

Mac nodded. Gen. Williams Wickham, a brigade commander and second in command to Lee, would take charge of the division. "Of course, sir," he acknowledged.

"H-Help him . . . all you can."

Again, Mac nodded, knowing that his service as one of Lee's aides was over. Even if the general survived this wound, he would be out of action for a long time. The war might even be over before he could return to command.

First Stuart, and now Fitz Lee, Mac thought bitterly, blinking back tears. War took the best of men and struck them down without mercy.

Medical orderlies rushed up and took charge of Lee, placing him on a stretcher and carrying him toward the rear. Mac stumbled to his feet, dragged the back of his hand across his eyes, and looked around for his horse. He had to find General Wickham and report that Lee had been wounded. There was still a battle to fight, he thought. The Yankees, damn them, kept right on coming.

THE TIDE of blue creeping down the Valley turnpike was simply too much to be stemmed. During the fighting, Patton had been fatally wounded about the same time as the bursting shell had unhorsed Fitz Lee and put him out of action. The line of infantry collapsed without Patton's leadership, and the cavalry under

Wickham and McCausland could not stand up to the Federal attack, either. In midafternoon, couriers arrived bearing orders from Breckinridge for all the troops on the left flank to fall back and form a defensive line stretching east from the turnpike.

Meanwhile Sheridan's reserves, led by Gen. George C. Crook, were moving north across Redbud Run. The original battle plan had called for Crook's men to flank the Confederates to the south, but now he was headed the other direction. After crossing the creek, Crook wheeled his forces left, which put them in direct opposition to the line Breckinridge was forming from what was left of the defenders from Stephenson's Depot.

The other flank wasn't completely neglected. Since leading the initial attack through Berryville Canyon, Gen. James H. Wilson's cavalry had spent the day at the far left end of the Union line. Now these horsemen moved forward to the Valley turnpike south of Winchester. By taking control of the roadway, they could cut off the best route for the Confederate army to take if they were forced to retreat . . . a possibility that had begun to look more and more likely with each passing hour.

WILLIAMS WICKHAM was a distinguished-looking man in his midforties with a neatly trimmed salt-and-pepper beard. He listened as Mac informed him of Fitz Lee's wounding and turning over command to him. With a nod, Wickham thanked him and added, "I know General Lee has relied on you in the past, and you have served him well."

"But you have your own aides, sir, and the other members of your staff," Mac said. "You don't need my help."

"Actually, I do. I just received word that the commander of the Ninth Virginia was killed. I want you to take command of that regiment . . . Major."

Mac swallowed hard. He knew the promotion was a brevet commission, brought on by battlefield necessity. Still, the rank was a higher one than he had ever thought to attain when he enlisted in the cavalry as a private. A part of him worried about being given a command under fire, about having the responsibility for the lives and safety of other men in his hands, but he suppressed those feelings. This was no time for self-doubt.

He could only accept the challenge and ask what Wickham's orders were.

"General Early has ordered that General Lee send some men down the Valley pike to turn back the Federal cavalry approaching it south of town. Since I've assumed command from General Lee, I'll follow that order by dispatching your regiment and a couple of others. Gather your men, Major, and fall back to Town Run until you're joined by the rest of the force. Then deal with the Yankees as best you can, but don't let them have that road."

Mac acknowledged then wheeled around and led the stallion several yards away before mounting and riding along the line of cavalrymen on the northern outskirts of Winchester.

"Ninth Virginia!" he shouted. "Form up on me!"

Several lieutenants and sergeants gathered around him in response to his call. He introduced himself and explained that he had just been placed in command of the regiment. He didn't mention that he didn't have any command experience. He could only rely on what he had learned from riding with Fitz Lee for the past couple of years. Other cavalrymen might have garnered more fame to themselves, but as far as Mac was concerned, there was no more capable officer in the Confederate cavalry than Fitzhugh Lee.

Mac knew from maps of the area that Town Run was a creek that meandered through the southern part of Winchester before flowing south and east to merge with Opequon Creek. The Valley turnpike entered the town just below the creek. As soon as the junior officers had rounded up the regiment, Mac set off for the area at a canter, the other troopers following closely behind him.

Meanwhile, the battle continued to the east. Federals hammered at the three divisions of Ramseur, Gordon, and the late
Rodes. The Southerners clung stubbornly to their positions
along the Berryville turnpike, but they were being forced farther and farther back. A line of Confederate artillery posted at
the very center of the maelstrom somehow kept up a thunderous fire. That barrage was about the only thing holding the Yankees at bay.

At times such as this, Mac thought as he listened to the roar
of artillery and the crackle of musketry, it seemed that the whole
world was caught up in battle and always had been. It seemed
almost inconceivable that silence and peace had once reigned
over the land. Such things were dim, far-off concepts. The only
realities were fire and blood and sudden death.

Yet Mac and his men enjoyed a brief respite as they moved
into position to blunt the Federal cavalry movements. At the
moment, no one was shooting at them, despite the chaos nearby.
A few stray shells landed not far off, and as they arrived at Town
Run, a cannonball smashed down one of the trees on the bank.
But that was as close as the battle came to them for a short time.

Two more cavalry regiments galloped up a few minutes later.
Their commanders rode over to talk to Mac. Both men were
colonels, but there was no condescension in their manner. They
were all in this fight together.

"We'll move south along the turnpike," one of the colonels
announced. "If the Yankees are down here, I reckon we'll run
into them soon enough."

Mac nodded his understanding of the task. The situation
was simple: Find the Yankees, fight them, and drive them from
the roadway.

The three regiments moved out briskly, one staying on the
turnpike and the other two flanking the road. Mac's unit was to
the right. The turnpike curved to the southeast, following the
course of the creek for a mile or so. The sounds of battle faded a
little as the cavalrymen put more distance between themselves

and the fighting. Even so, Mac could tell that the combat was still fierce.

Scouts galloped ahead, but it wasn't long before they came galloping back. "Yankees just around the bend!" one shouted as he waved his cap over his head. "Just around the bend!"

Mac looked to the other two commanders and saw them draw their sabers. He knew what was coming next. Pulling his own saber from its scabbard, he lifted the blade above his head then slashed down with it, bellowing, "Charge! Charge!"

All three cavalry regiments leaped ahead, racing along the turnpike toward the enemy.

The blue-clad Federals came into view. Their scouts must have seen the Confederates coming, because they were charging, too. It required only a matter of moments for the two forces to come together, slamming into each other with a clash of sabers and the loud popping of pistols.

To his surprise, Mac found himself strangely calm as the chaos surged around him. He had ridden into battle enough times at the side of Fitz Lee so that leading a charge was familiar to him. This was nothing he hadn't done before, only Lee wasn't with him this time. Yet in a way the general *was* here, seeming to hover at Mac's side, watching over him like a guardian angel. Mac hoped the feeling didn't mean that Lee had died of his wounds. He couldn't spend much time worrying about that, however, because he was too busy fighting.

The two forces were fairly evenly matched. Mac thought the Federals might have them outnumbered slightly. But as he fought with saber in one hand and pistol in the other, he saw that his men were more than holding their own. Some of the Yankees were down, and others were beginning to pull back.

The stallion suddenly danced aside without any prompting from Mac. He heard a saber whistle past his ear and knew that if his horse hadn't acted, he would have been struck down from behind. This wasn't the first time the stallion had demonstrated an almost supernatural awareness of danger. Mac had come to rely on the horse's keen senses and uncanny instinct. He twisted in the saddle and spotted the cavalryman who had almost killed him. The man was off-balance from the missed blow, and Mac didn't give him a chance to recover. He thrust the pistol at the Yankee and pulled the trigger.

The hammer clicked on an empty chamber.

The Yankee's eyes lit with ferocity. He brought the saber around in a backhanded swing aimed at Mac's neck. Mac barely had time to parry the blow with the empty pistol. The stallion spun halfway around, putting Mac in position to chop at the Yankee's forearm with his saber. The man screamed as the blade bit deep into his arm and grated on bone. The razor-sharp steel sheared on through the arm, severing it halfway between wrist and elbow. The cavalryman sagged forward as blood spurted from the stump. Losing consciousness, he toppled from the saddle.

The Yankee would probably bleed to death before help got to him, Mac thought, but that was all the thought he spared for his fallen enemy. The clash continued fiercely all around him, and he had to keep fighting. He holstered the empty revolver and drew one of his other guns. It bucked in his hand as he fired slowly, deliberately, picking his targets in blue as the battle swirled around him . . .

He hadn't realized it was late afternoon, approaching nightfall, until shadows began to creep across the land. The Yankees had retreated but still threatened the turnpike. The Ninth Virginia and the other two cavalry regiments held them back, fighting skirmish after skirmish as the number of Confederate infantrymen moving south along the road increased. Finally, Mac realized that a full-scale retreat was under way. General Early had abandoned Winchester to the Yankees.

A furious cavalry charge on the northern flank of the battle had turned the tide at last, Mac discovered later. Averell's and Merritt's horsemen had slammed into the Confederate left with such force that it was overwhelmed and pushed back into the center where the three divisions of Ramseur, Gordon, and Rodes were still fighting. Crook added his infantry to Merritt's cavalry, and Averell circled still wider and struck the Confederate rear. Chaos and confusion spread rapidly, and the defenders broke and ran through the streets of the town, pouring out its southern end.

Ramseur rallied his men enough to get them to fight a rear guard action against the pursuing Northerners. With that valiant effort, and with the cavalry screening them to the east, Jubal Early's army was able to withdraw from Winchester without being destroyed. That evening, Sheridan rode into the town and wired the news of his victory to Washington. Once again, control of this Shenandoah Valley community had changed hands.

Newly promoted Maj. Mac Brannon didn't care about Little Phil's triumph. He had a command of his own to worry about. He might be new at this, but he was determined not to let his men down.

He wasn't going to let Fitz Lee down, either. When the fleeing army finally came to a halt, long into the night and far down the valley from Winchester, Mac forced himself to ignore his exhaustion and asked around until he found out that Lee had been taken to the town of Mount Jackson to be cared for. Mac would have gone to see him, but he couldn't leave his men.

This, then, was what it was like to be a commander. He leaned against the stallion and closed his eyes for a moment, fighting the weariness that threatened to overwhelm him. Always thinking, always worrying, always carrying the burden of responsibility . . . it took a special sort of individual to live up to that, and Mac wasn't sure if he would ever be that kind of man.

Over the coming days and weeks he would find out. The Yankees would test him, immerse him in a crucible of fire. He had no doubt of that.

☆ ☆ ☆

EARLY HAD chosen to make his stand at Fisher's Hill, a steep ridge that was broken only by a small gap through which ran the Valley turnpike. From the turnpike, the ridge stretched east to the even more rugged heights of Massanutten Mountain. The western slope of Fisher's Hill was not quite as steep, which made it easily defensible.

Massanutten Mountain, another long, high ridge, paralleled the Valley turnpike and separated the main portion of the Shenandoah Valley from the smaller, narrower Luray Valley. It was to Luray Valley that Mac and the Ninth Virginia, along with the rest of Wickham's cavalry, found themselves bound the next morning after the retreat from Winchester. Early feared that Sheridan would send some men around Massanutten Mountain and through the Luray Valley so they could cross back into the Shenandoah through New Market Gap and menace the Confederate rear. If Sheridan attempted this maneuver, it would be the cavalry's job to prevent it from being successful.

As Mac and the other horsemen trotted along the road toward Millford Pass, he thought about what he had heard that morning during a hasty breakfast. Many of the wounded had had to be left behind during the retreat the day before, and those who had been brought along were going to be moved even farther up the valley, away from the Yankees. That news had come as a relief to Mac, because it meant that Fitz Lee would continue to be out of harm's way while he recuperated from his wound.

He felt a bit guilty for thinking such a thing, however. He ought to be telling himself that Sheridan's army would be stopped cold at Fisher's Hill. After all, the steep, heavily wooded ridge was some of the best ground for fighting a defensive battle he had ever seen.

But making a stand required plenty of men as well as officers to lead them. Early was in shorter supply of both those commodities today than he had been twenty-four hours earlier. Outnumbered to start with, Early could ill afford any casualties, let alone the high number the army had suffered at Winchester. Of

course, it was rumored that the enemy had lost even more men
. . . but they had more to lose.

Mac sighed. Brooding over battle tactics involving the entire
army wouldn't do him any good. He had one regiment to think
about, the Ninth Virginia. His regiment, now. That was still an
odd thought.

The cavalry crossed the ridge at Millford Pass and rode into
the Luray Valley. This was really just a section of the Shenandoah Valley, and it shared the Shenandoah's lush fields and
gently rolling hills and winding streams. Grain mills dotted the
landscape. A good road ran from Front Royal, at the head of the
valley, down to New Market Gap. If the Yankees showed up as
Early feared, it was likely they would come down this road, so
Wickham's cavalry was positioned along and on either side of
the pike to wait.

Even with Massanutten Mountain in between, it was possible that the cavalrymen in the Luray Valley would be able to
hear the sounds of battle if Sheridan attacked Early's stronghold
at Fisher's Hill. All day long on September 20, however, silence
reigned. A few times Mac thought he heard the distant popping
of rifle fire, but he could have imagined that. It seemed likely
that, for whatever reason, Sheridan had not moved against the
Confederates on this day.

Nor did any Federal forces show up in the Luray Valley.
Scouts rode out and came back to report to General Wickham
that the Yankees were nowhere in sight. Mac wondered that
night if General Early had sent them on a wild goose chase. If
there was no real threat on this side of Massanutten Mountain,
they might as well be on the other side with the rest of the army,
ready to help out as best they could when Sheridan finally
launched another attack, as he was bound to do.

On September 21 the situation changed. Scouts galloped into
camp with the news that a large number of Yankee cavalrymen
had been spotted on the road from Front Royal. Wickham immediately sent out two regiments for a reconnaissance in force.

The Ninth Virginia was one of the two. Mac trotted the stallion along at the head of the column. Lt. Angus McCreary, who had been aide to the regiment's previous commander, continued in that position for Mac and rode alongside. His thick, reddish side-whiskers and bushy mustache were fairly bristling with anticipation of meeting the enemy.

"Want me to ride ahead and see what I can see, Major?" McCreary asked.

"The scouts are already out, Lieutenant," Mac replied. "They'll let us know soon enough if we're about to run into any Yankees."

He understood how McCreary felt. He had ridden on many scouting missions for Fitz Lee. A man usually felt a little better about his chances if he were well informed and knew the enemy's whereabouts and strength. It was the uncertainty that wore on a man's nerves, grinding him down.

"Yes sir, but any time you want me to go have a look, you just let me know."

"I'll do that, Lieutenant," Mac promised, managing to keep the dry humor that he felt out of his voice. McCreary seemed like a good man. Mac didn't want to offend him.

After a few moments, McCreary said, "Do they call you Mac, sir? Since your name's MacBeth, I mean?"

The question took him by surprise and seemed a bit familiar for a junior officer to be asking of his regimental commander. On the other hand, Mac had never been a stickler for such things. He said easily, "That's right, they do. I'll wager you get called Mac, too."

"Yes sir." McCreary grinned. "A couple o' Macs, that's us."

"I suppose so, Lieutenant," Mac said, and this time he couldn't stop himself from chuckling.

A moment later, all thoughts of humor fled abruptly as he spotted a couple of scouts coming toward them at a gallop. Heeling the stallion into a run, he rode out to meet the men; McCreary trailed behind him.

The scouts brought their lathered mounts to a halt as Mac reached them. "Yanks up ahead, Major," one of them reported without preamble. "No more'n a half-mile down the road."

"How many?" Mac asked.

"Ten or twelve, maybe. Looked like a patrol out in front of the main bunch."

"Did they see you?"

"No sir, I expect not. We hightailed it back here mighty quick. I'm pretty sure they didn't see us."

Mac nodded. He knew a dozen Yankee cavalrymen wouldn't be wandering around the Luray Valley alone. Their presence had to mean that Sheridan had sent a force around the northern end of Massanutten Mountain, just as Early had expected.

He turned his head and barked an order at McCreary. "Get everyone off the road, Lieutenant. Have the men pull back into the trees so they can't be seen."

"Going to ambush that Yankee patrol, Major?" McCreary asked with a grin.

"I don't want them riding back to the rest of their outfit with the news that we're up here. Step lively, Lieutenant."

"Yes sir!" McCreary wheeled his horse around and hurried to pass on Mac's orders to the regiment.

Within moments the Ninth Virginia had vanished into the woods on either side of the road. They were lucky there was some good cover along this stretch, Mac thought as he backed the stallion out of sight into the trees. He drew a deep breath, leaned forward in the saddle, and waited. The second regiment was at least a mile off to the west, near the base of the ridge, and it was unlikely the Yankee patrol would run into it.

A few minutes passed, the time stretching out unnaturally, as it always did when a battle was brewing. A twelve-man patrol would have no chance against a regiment. Mac hoped the Yankees would do the logical thing and surrender. If Yankees were sensible, though, he told himself, they wouldn't be fighting this war in the first place. Compromises would have been possible that could have averted the Northern invasion. As early as 1838, at a conference in Philadelphia, moderate politicians from the South had floated a plan whereby slavery would be phased out over a period of ten or fifteen years. That plan had been summarily rejected by the Yankee leaders in attendance.

Mac put those thoughts out of his head. Politics was beyond him. It would be fine with him if the war ended today and all the Yankees went home so he could go home, too. But as long as they were here where they didn't belong, trying to impose their will on people as if nobody below the Mason-Dixon Line had any rights at all, he supposed he would fight.

The sound of hoof beats in the roadway made his features draw tighter. He didn't need the field glasses stowed in his saddlebags to see the blue-clad riders who came cantering down the road. Mac let the Yankees ride past him. Then he glanced toward McCreary, raised his hand, and waved it forward to signal the men forward.

With Mac leading the way, the regiment rushed out of the woods on both sides of the road, converging on the startled Yankees trapped between them. Several of the blueclad cavalrymen tried to draw pistols or raise carbines, but the Southerners were on them too fast. Mac was practically on top of the Yankees when he pulled the stallion to a halt and leveled his pistol at the captain who seemed to be in charge of the patrol. "Don't move!" Mac called. "I strongly urge you to surrender!"

Outnumbered more than ten to one, the Federals looked around helplessly. Mac saw the fight go out of them. The Yankee captain sighed and lifted his hands. "Looks like you've caught us fair and square, Major," he said to Mac. "I value the lives of my men too highly to squander them to no purpose."

"I'm glad to hear it, Captain," Mac said sincerely. "Please order your men to drop their weapons."

The Yankee withdrew his saber and extended it to Mac.

With a shake of his head, Mac said, "Keep your saber, Captain. I want only your guns."

"Gracious of you," the Yankee muttered. "But then, you Rebs are known for such things, aren't you?"

Mac suppressed a flash of irritation at the bitter edge in the man's voice. Still, he supposed he couldn't blame the man for being bitter. After all, he had just ridden right into a trap.

When the Union cavalrymen had been disarmed, Mac said to the captain, "Would you be willing to tell me the strength and position of your forces in the Luray Valley?"

The officer's back stiffened. "No sir, I would not."

Mac wasn't. "Very well. Lieutenant McCreary, detail a group of guards to escort these prisoners to the rear."

McCreary nodded. "Yes sir. And the rest of us?"

"We'll continue with our mission, of course."

"Yes sir!"

The Yankee captain looked like he wanted to say something else, but he maintained his silence as he rode off with the rest of the captured cavalrymen. Mac was pleased with the outcome of this encounter. He had taken a few prisoners without firing a shot, and more important, he had prevented any of the Yankees from turning around and racing back to the main body of cavalry. It was a good day's work, he thought.

But the day was far from over.

Chapter Four

OLD JUBE WAS NO fool. He knew how Sherman liked to launch a frontal attack while simultaneously sending some of his men around to strike the enemy's flanks and rear. Where the Confederate army was situated on Fisher's Hill, a Federal flanking maneuver to the Confederate right was impossible. The ridge butted up against Massanutten Mountain in that direction. This is what led Early to suspect Sheridan would attempt to utilize the Luray Valley and get behind the Confederates that way.

Sure enough, Little Phil had sent two cavalry divisions commanded by Gen. Alfred Torbert into the Luray Valley. Meanwhile, Gen. George Crook's men moved west, toward North Mountain at the other end of Fisher's Hill, their objective being to position themselves for an attack on the Confederate left. Sheridan took pains to conceal this movement, wanting Early to be surprised when Crook struck.

Despite the apparent strength of Early's position atop Fisher's Hill, Sheridan considered that he had the Rebels right where he wanted them. Crippled by a flank attack, a frontal assault would drive the Southerners backward into the waiting gun sights of Torbert's cavalry, who would have cut off their route of retreat. Early's army would be trapped and destroyed.

That was Sheridan's plan, anyway . . .

☆ ☆ ☆

A SHORT time after Mac's regiment had captured the Yankee patrol, the other regiment came riding in from the west, joining forces with the Ninth Virginia. The other commander hadn't seen any Federal cavalry at all.

"They're up ahead somewhere," Mac informed him. "That patrol wasn't here by itself."

The colonel nodded. "I agree, Major. We'll continue toward Front Royal."

The two regiments rode on together. As the afternoon passed and the sun dipped lower toward the heights of Massanutten Mountain, Mac began to wonder if he had been wrong. Maybe the patrol had been wandering around on its own.

He reined in suddenly and reached for his field glasses. Some movement up ahead caught his eye. It was on the other side of a long, shallow depression with a creek wandering down the center of it. Mac caught his breath as he glimpsed a large group of Union cavalrymen.

The Yankees had come to a stop, too, and one of their officers held his field glasses up to his eyes. Mac realized the man was looking straight at him, just as he was looking at the Yankee. The realization gave him a start, and he lowered the glasses.

"Well, they know we're here," he said to McCreary.

"Yes sir, I reckon they do. What do we do now?"

Mac raised the glasses to his eyes again and swept his gaze across the countryside on the other side of the low ground. Almost everywhere he looked he saw blue-clad riders. There was a whole blasted division over there, he thought. Maybe more. He and the others were outnumbered, and there was no good place for the men to form a line on foot.

Mac took a deep breath. If they couldn't fight a defensive action, then they would have to fight an offensive one. He tucked the glasses away. As the idea took shape in his mind, he turned to McCreary and said, "Lieutenant, prepare to charge."

The order, given in a calm, quiet tone, caused McCreary to lift his eyebrows for a second, then a broad grin broke out on his ruddy face. "Yes sir!" he said.

Mac knew he should have conferred with the colonel, but there was no time for that. Every instinct in Mac's body told him this moment had to be seized. Fast, unexpected action was their only chance. He drew his saber and raised it over his head. Behind him, McCreary and the other officers called out commands, ordering the men to prepare to attack. Mac looked over his shoulder. When McCreary gave him a curt nod, Mac swept the saber down. "Charge!"

With Rebel yells pealing the air, the Virginians thundered down the gentle slope. Mac followed the road, staying right in the middle of it. There was no bridge over the creek, but there was a shallow ford where the road crossed the stream. Mac went straight across, the stallion's pounding hooves throwing up a great spray of water. Late afternoon sunlight sparkled and danced among the droplets as they hung in the air to be joined by thousands of others as the rest of the regiment splashed across behind Mac. It made for a beautiful sight, but he never looked back to see it.

His attention was focused ahead of him, where the Yankees were galloping to meet the charge.

But not all of them, Mac noted. The Federals had split up, with part of them staying in reserve while the rest charged. Mac wasn't sure what to make of that. The Union commander was either overly cautious or overly confident. Either way, Mac intended to demonstrate to the man that he had made a mistake.

With sabers swinging and guns blazing, the two groups of cavalry came together. Like all such engagements, any orderly plan of attack was soon discarded. The fight was a bloody melee. Clouds of dust from the road and spurts of powder smoke from gun muzzles clogged the air, making it difficult to see or breathe. Horses whirled and reared. To a detached observer, the battle appeared to be nothing but confusion and chaos. Yet, within the clash, there were small pockets of intense fighting where a man could concentrate on one or two of the enemy at a time.

Mac found himself between two Yankees. Both of them hacked at him with sabers. He parried one thrust with his own blade and leaned far over in the saddle to avoid the other, clamping his legs tightly around the stallion's flanks as he did so. He couldn't lean far enough, though, and the second Yankee's blade slashed across his right arm, leaving a shallow but painful cut. The stallion whirled, driving a shoulder against one of the other horses and knocking it back, giving Mac some breathing room. His wounded arm refused to work when he tried to raise his pistol. Grimacing in pain, he forced the arm up anyway and fired. The bullet smashed into the shoulder of the cavalryman who had wounded him. The man managed to stay in the saddle, but he dropped his saber and clutched at the injury. He was out of the fight, at least for the time being.

The other attacker was still in it, though, and from the corner of his eye Mac saw the Yankee swinging another saber blow at him. He ducked just in time. The point of the blade caught his hat and sent it spinning off his head. Slight pressure from his knees made the stallion lunge toward the other horse. Mac straightened his saber arm and thrust the blade straight out. It went in under the Yankee's right arm. The man gasped in pain and swung a backhanded blow that made Mac rip his own blade free and dart back. Blood bubbled from the Yankee's lips as he swayed, fighting to stay in the saddle. He failed, falling from his horse as he lost consciousness.

Mac wheeled the stallion, ignoring the pain in his arm as he looked for another foe. Most of the men around him wore Confederate gray, he saw. As the dust cleared slightly, he spotted a good number of Federal horsemen galloping back the way they had come from.

The Yankees were retreating, Mac thought as a savage grin pulled his lips back. They had been outfought, and now they were running for their lives.

Mac wanted them to keep running. He waved his saber over his head and bellowed, "Ninth Virginia, follow me!"

With that, he gave chase to the fleeing Yankees.

It was a crazy thing to do. Later, when he thought about it, he knew that. Outnumbered as they were, he and his men had emerged victorious from the brief fight because they had surprised the Federals with their aggressiveness. But now, riding straight toward a much larger force was sheer madness.

If any men of the Ninth Virginia realized the folly of the chase, they didn't show it. Nor did they hesitate to follow Mac. Shouting and grinning, they charged right at his heels.

The fleeing Yankees reached the rest of their comrades . . . and kept going. Not only that, but many who hadn't taken part in the fight wheeled their horses and retreated as well.

Mac howled when he saw that. The Yankees were running! Running, by God! And within seconds it wasn't an orderly retreat but a rout. The Federal horsemen tucked their tails between their legs and headed back to Front Royal as fast as they could go.

Reason slowly crept into Mac's brain. He hauled back on the reins, bringing the stallion to a trot. The others followed suit. Cheers and laughter filled the ranks as the Confederates realized they had routed a much larger force. Finally, Mac came to a stop and looked back.

To his surprise, he saw that the rest of Wickham's division had come into view, riding hard to catch up with the two regiments out in front. Either scouts had brought news of the battle, or Wickham had heard the shooting and sent his men hurrying forward. What the Yankees didn't know was that, even with these reinforcements, the Confederates were still considerably outnumbered. If they had only stood their ground and fought, they probably would have emerged triumphant, Mac thought with a laugh. But for a moment, it must have looked as if every cavalryman in the Confederacy was charging toward them, and the Yankees' nerve had broken.

They might try to come back again, but night was not far off, and Mac was confident that it would take time for the Federals to regroup and figure out their next step. For now, at least, they would not use the Luray Valley to menace the rear of Jubal Early's army. Williams Wickham's cavalry—Fitz Lee's cavalry, in actuality, Mac thought—had done the job required of them.

He had never been more proud to be a member of this fighting force.

☆ ☆ ☆

DESPITE THE fine work of the Confederate horsemen in the Luray Valley, Sheridan proceeded with his planned attack on Fisher's Hill at dusk the next day, September 22. Crook struck hard on the Confederate left, taking the Southerners by surprise because they had failed to notice the Federal troops shifting toward North Mountain. Dismounted cavalry from Lunsford Lomax's division defended this end of the Confederate line, and there were too few of them to hold back the attack.

Unknown to Sheridan, Early had already decided to withdraw from Fisher's Hill, and he planned to do so as soon as it was good and dark. The Confederate commander had concluded that despite the natural advantages of the terrain, he lacked the manpower to hold the ridge against a determined assault.

By striking with Crook's forces before Early had a chance to retreat, Sheridan inflicted more casualties on the Confederates, losses they could ill afford. Not only that, but as the Rebels fled down the Valley turnpike that night, Sheridan was convinced that they would run right into Torbert's cavalry and have their escape blocked.

It was not until the next morning that Sheridan received the unpleasant news that Torbert had never reached New Market Gap. The Federal cavalry had been forced to turn back, Torbert reported to Sheridan, and had regrouped at Front Royal. The message implied that Torbert had encountered a large force of Confederate cavalry in the Luray Valley, but Sheridan knew better. He knew from battlefield reports which units Early still had with the main body of the army.

Torbert had turned tail and run from no more than a division of cavalry—no doubt an undermanned division, at that. He probably had outnumbered the Confederates more than two to one.

Furious that his man had failed to block the turnpike, Sheridan ordered the pursuit to continue. Gen. William W. Averell's cavalry was supposed to lead the chase, but astonishingly, Averell lagged far behind the rest of the army. Sheridan had been let down again by his cavalry, and his fury at this led him to relieve Averell of command, even though Torbert's mistake had been as crucial, if not more so.

The Confederate retreat continued to Harrisonburg, Port Republic, and up into the Blue Ridge Mountains themselves. Sheridan stopped at Harrisonburg, unwilling to chase the enemy into the mountains, where the Federals might find themselves at a disadvantage due to the terrain and their lack of familiarity with the countryside. But it was a victory of sorts anyway, and Sheridan did not hesitate to proclaim it as such. Early's army had been driven out of the Shenandoah Valley. The Union controlled the Valley from one end to the other.

But the enemy was still in the mountains, and the day might come when the fight would resume. Meanwhile, Sheridan still had work to do.

☆ ☆ ☆

MAC HAD never seen so much smoke in his life. Everywhere he looked across the Shenandoah Valley, from the Blue Ridge in the east to North Mountain in the west, columns of black smoke rose into the crisp blue autumn sky.

Phil Sheridan was burning the Valley, waging war now not on enemy soldiers but on civilians as well. Mac could barely contain his fury at the thought of what was happening.

A little more than two weeks had passed since the Confederates' defeat at Fisher's Hill. During that time Early had worked to regroup his army. In fact, he had received reinforcements from Robert E. Lee in the form of the same infantry division Early had sent to help Lee at Petersburg before the battle at Winchester.

Additional cavalrymen had come trotting in as well. Among them was the six-hundred-man Laurel Brigade commanded by Thomas L. Rosser, who earlier had been a cavalry commander under Jeb Stuart. He merged his brigade with what was left of Fitz Lee's, taking command from Wickham, who resigned to take a seat in the Confederate House of Representatives to which he had been elected the previous autumn. No one faulted Wickham's actions while he had been in command, but Rosser and the Laurel Brigade had a sterling reputation. The only possible drawback was that Col. Thomas Munford had taken over Wickham's old brigade, and there was a longstanding feud between Rosser and Munford over Munford's failure to be promoted, which he blamed on Rosser.

Mac didn't particularly care who was in charge. He wanted only to fight Yankees and avenge the Valley for the destruction wreaked by Sheridan. There were times he told himself he was almost as full of hate for the Yankees as was his brother Titus.

But what they were doing in the Valley, oh, Lord, what they were doing . . . !

Sheridan was determined that the Shenandoah would no longer be the breadbasket of the Confederacy. He was angry, as well, at the losses his army had suffered at the hands of irregulars and guerrillas, partisan rangers led by men such as John S. Mosby. Guerrillas operated on their own, with little supervision or even contact with the Confederate command. They attacked communications and supply lines and carried out daring raids on Federal camps and patrols. Mosby's Rangers were inflicting about as much damage on the Yankees as the regular army was. More, in recent days.

So, in retaliation, the Yankees burned fields and haystacks, barns and houses of the farms in the Valley. For the past four days, though, since October 5, the wanton destruction had become even worse. A pall of smoke hung over the Valley as far as the eye could see, blotting out the sun and casting a seemingly perpetual twilight over the land.

Early and the rest of his army were on the move, hoping to catch up to Sheridan as the Yankees moved down the Valley, devastating it. Rosser's cavalry was out in front, leading the pursuit. The day before, October 8, they had skirmished with Yankee cavalry in the rear of the Federal column, and Mac had seen Custer again, riding out boldly in front of his men. In fact, just before the battle, Custer had galloped close to the Confederate line and doffed his hat in a mock salute, exposing his long blond hair. Mac had heard later that Custer had performed the gesture as a greeting to Rosser, an old friend of his from their days together at West Point. There might be some truth to that, but Mac figured that Custer had been showing off a little, too.

Angus McCreary coughed as he trotted his horse alongside Mac's stallion. "All this blasted smoke in the air!" he complained. "'Tis like ridin' through the brimstone-laden confines of Hades itself!"

"It's hell, all right," Mac said, thinking of the destroyed homes and crops they had seen along the road. When winter came this year, some people in the Shenandoah would starve to death, he thought bitterly. He had spent most of his life as a farmer. He knew how much hard work, sweat, and blood, had gone into the soil to produce the lush green fields. Now those fields were nothing but a vast expanse of ashes. No place to live, nothing to eat . . . how had it ever come to this? How?

There were no answers.

"Major!" McCreary's voice intruded sharply into Mac's brooding reverie. "Major, there's a whole bunch o' bluebellies up yonder!"

They were a short distance south of Fisher's Hill, approaching a small stream known as Toms Brook. On the other side of the creek, Federal cavalry moved up and dismounted, forming a line that bristled with repeating rifles and carbines. Beyond them were more horsemen, so many horsemen, in fact, that Mac tried and failed to see either end of the line of mounted men. Everywhere he looked, there were Yankees.

Without realizing what he was doing, Mac reined in and stared at the spectacle. McCreary and the rest of the regiment did likewise. The line of Confederate cavalry was quite long, extending perhaps five miles across the Valley. But the Union line was as long and much deeper.

"My God, Major," McCreary said in a hushed voice. "What are we going to do?"

"Fight. That's all we can do. That's why we've been chasing them for days now." Mac looked slowly across the Valley, noting every column of smoke that marked the destruction by the Yankees. "We'll fight," he said again, his voice shaking a little with anger.

McCreary took off his cap, turned it over a couple of times in his hands, then jammed it back on his head. "Yes sir!" he said with an angry nod of his own. He turned and shouted back at the regiment, "Prepare to charge!" All along the line, mile after mile, similar orders were called out.

But the Yankees struck first, shots ringing out from their horse artillery before the Confederate big guns could be brought into action. Shells arced over the open ground that bordered Toms Brook and slammed into the earth among the Confederate cavalry. Rosser ordered his gunners to open up as quickly as they could, and within minutes the Rebel cannon, mounted on light-weight limbers, was wrestled into position and roared out an answer to the Federal barrage.

Meanwhile, the dismounted Union cavalrymen surprised the Southerners by charging on foot, firing as they came and forming a skirmish line that advanced steadily toward the Confederate front.

Finally, orders to charge rang out along the long line of Southern horsemen. Mac sent the stallion lunging straight ahead. He saw the dismounted Yankees peeling away, opening a path for the mounted attack that followed right behind them. Yet Mac had expected as much. Men on foot couldn't stand up to a cavalry charge, but the rest of the Yankee cavalry could.

With shells from both sides bursting among them, the two lines of riders smashed together. Mac left his saber in its scabbard and fought with his pistols, firing with both hands and guiding the stallion with his knees. He alternated his shots from right to left as he charged into the blue horde. Lead sizzled and hummed around his ears. The arm that had been wounded in the Luray Valley was still stiff and sore, but he ignored the discomfort. He knew that his life might end at any second, so a piddling little scratch had no importance.

When the hammers of both guns clicked on empty chambers, he thrust the weapons back in their holsters and grabbed the reins. The breakneck pace of the charge had taken him almost all the way through the Union lines. Wheeling the stallion, he saw only bluecoats around him, closing in. With a strident yell he sent the stallion smashing through the ring of horsemen as they tried to surround him. When he was through the Yankees, he reined to a halt and turned the stallion again. Half a dozen Union cavalrymen were coming after him.

With the stallion standing firm in the midst of chaos, Mac drew his second set of pistols. A defiant shout rang from his lips as he began firing both guns as quickly as he could cock the hammers and pull the triggers. The shots rolled out like thunder as lead scythed through the startled Federals.

Mac emptied the pistols, blowing four of his pursuers out of the saddle. But two men made it through the fusillade, and both of them slashed at him with sabers. Mac blocked one of the blows with the barrel of his left-hand revolver. The other strike got past his attempt to parry it, but luckily it was the flat of the blade and not the edge that smacked against his temple. The impact was enough to blind him for a second and make him sway in the saddle.

He held on for dear life as the stallion suddenly reared up on its hind legs and lashed out with its forelegs, the steel-shod hooves slashing at the Yankees. The men had no choice but to haul back on their reins and give ground. When the stallion's legs came back down, he gave a mighty bound that carried him past the enemy. Mac clung to the saddle and shook his head, trying to clear the cobwebs from his brain.

The stallion twisted and galloped to the south. When Mac could think clearly again, he realized that the big silver gray horse had carried him safely out of danger yet again. As he looked around, he saw that the Confederate line was re-forming for another charge.

With his head still ringing a little from the blow, Mac reloaded his pistols and got ready to ride into battle again. He had lost track of his regiment, but that didn't really matter now. Once in the midst of battle, it was pretty much every man for himself.

For the next two hours, charges and countercharges played themselves out across the fields bordering Toms Brook. Vastly outnumbered, the Confederates fought valiantly as ever, but the odds against them were too great. If they had had any support . . . But the rest of the army was too far behind to be of any help. When at last one cavalry unit was forced to turn and flee, it was the beginning of the end. Within a short time, all of the Confederate cavalry—Rosser's Laurel Brigade, the survivors from Fitz Lee's division, the men of Gens. John Imboden and Lunsford Lomax—all these gallant men had no choice but to race back up the Valley while the Yankees nipped at their heels like the hounds of hell.

Mac was sick at his stomach as he rode. Sick from the blow on the head, from breathing too much powder smoke, and from the bitter knowledge that the once seemingly invulnerable Confederate cavalry had been whipped today, whipped worse than ever before. Individually, the men had acquitted themselves as well as could be expected—better, really, considering the odds against them. But it hadn't been enough. Not nearly enough.

Mile after mile passed under the hooves of the galloping horses. The chase didn't come to an end until the Confederate horsemen reached the rest of Early's army near New Market. There the infantry waited, and the Yankee cavalry gave up the pursuit rather than face the masses of riflemen who were dug in on Rude's Hill. Mac reined to a halt once he was within the Confederate lines and turned to look at the Yankees. Exhaustion and despair etched weary lines on his gaunt, powder-grimed face as he watched the Federals withdraw down the Valley. Even from this distance he sensed the smug satisfaction they had to be feeling right now. He wanted to hate them for it.

But he couldn't. To his surprise, he found that he was too tired even to hate . . .

☆ ☆ ☆

OVER THE next few days Mac did the best he could to round up his regiment so he could determine how bad his losses were. He never found some of the men, including Angus McCreary. The lieutenant had been either killed or captured by the Yankees, Mac deduced. He felt McCreary's loss keenly. He had grown accustomed to the affable Scotsman. Needing an aide, he promoted one of the sergeants, a man named Blaisdell, to lieutenant and gave him the job. But it wasn't the same.

Bitterly disappointed by the rout of his cavalry, Early still was not ready to give up the fight. He continued to pursue Sheridan's army down the Valley, skirmishing successfully with Crook on October 13. Although the brief battle resulted in the Federals retreating, it was a decidedly mixed victory. Up until this point, Sheridan had not known for certain that Old Jube still had some fight left in him. Now that the Union commander was aware of Early's determination to continue the conflict in the Valley, he took steps to counter the Confederate's aggressiveness, recalling a corps he had previously sent out of the Valley.

The Union army camped along the banks of Cedar Creek, a short distance north of Strasburg. For several days Mac's regiment and other cavalry units carried out scouting and reconnaissance operations, locating the Yankees and estimating their strength. What they couldn't know was that Sheridan himself was no longer with the army. Continuing disagreements among the highest levels of the Federal command—U. S. Grant, chief of staff Henry Halleck, Secretary of War Edwin M. Stanton, even President Lincoln himself—had caused Sheridan to start back to Washington for a council of war. He made it as far as Front Royal before he was given a telegram, a Confederate message that had been intercepted, indicating that fresh troops led by James Longstreet were on their way to join Early and give him the strength he needed to crush Sheridan's army.

As it turned out, the message was a forgery, sent by Early to be intercepted by the Yankees. Longstreet wasn't on the march at all. Early hoped that the dispatch might scare off Sheridan. It had exactly the opposite effect, sending Little Phil hurrying back toward Cedar Creek, along with the troops he had taken with him when he left.

By the predawn hours of October 19, Early was ready to launch an assault on the Federals camped along Cedar Creek. The Valley turnpike crossed the creek, and Early intended to take two divisions down the road and into the center of the Union camp. At the same time, John B. Gordon would lead three more divisions to strike the Federal left. Also the plan called for the two cavalry divisions to split and hit the enemy's flanks, Rosser going left and Lomax going right. Chances were the attack would not come as a complete surprise to the Yankees, but Early hoped to hit them fast enough and hard enough to win a victory before they knew what was going on.

A thick fog hung over the rolling landscape, making the hours before dawn even darker than usual. Mac felt it on his face like clammy fingers as he rode slowly toward Cedar Creek at the head of his regiment. Blaisdell was close beside him.

All night long the Confederates had been maneuvering into position. Gordon's divisions would have the honor of launching the attack and striking the first blow against the Yankees. That burst of firing would be the signal for the other parts of Early's army to strike.

When he judged that they were where they needed to be, Mac lifted a hand to call a silent halt. In the darkness, however, complete silence was not possible. He heard the faint jingle of harness chains, the murmur of whispered commands, but the damp, heavy air had a tendency to muffle such sounds. Mac hoped that would be enough to keep the enemy from hearing their approach.

Now that they were in position, there was nothing to do but wait. He shifted in the saddle, arching his back and stretching weary muscles. Over the past two months he and his men had been in the saddle almost every waking hour and had taken part in fight after bitter fight. They had suffered losses in men and horses, but it was perhaps the horseflesh they could least afford to lose. Not only that, but their supplies of ammunition and powder were running low, and many of the men had no sabers and were using weapons captured from the enemy. Still, victory was possible in the Shenandoah Valley. Mac had begun to doubt that the Confederacy would ever be able to achieve an overall victory in the war; the North simply had the upper hand in manpower, firepower, and supplies. But a negotiated settlement, peace with honor, was still the goal. Anything but allowing Grant his nickname—"Unconditional Surrender."

The sudden rattle of gunfire in the distance to the east shook Mac from his thoughts. He inferred the sound of fighting to mean that Gordon's men were advancing across Cedar Creek and into the very midst of the Yankee camp.

"Forward," Mac said quietly but clearly, and he put the stallion into a walk. The pace increased until the big horse was trotting. The fog along the ground was still thick, but overhead the sky had begun to turn gray with the approach of dawn as the riders splashed across the creek.

They expected to take the Federals by surprise, but to his shock, Mac heard bugles nearby and saw blue-clad horsemen galloping out of the mist. The Yankees had either known they were coming or were simply in a state of alert. Instead of dashing into the camp and inflicting damage on their unsuspecting enemies, the Confederates found themselves meeting stiff opposition.

Mac shouted for the charge, and for what seemed like at least the thousandth time, the two mounted masses clashed, fighting savagely with saber and pistol and carbine. The fact that the Yankees were already in the saddle complicated things tremendously. If the attack had gone according to plan, anybody on the ground would have been an enemy. But with the Yankees mounted, in the dim light it was almost impossible to tell friend from foe until two men were practically on top of each other. Mac nearly shot a couple of his own troopers before he realized who they were. He had no idea how close he came to being shot by his own men, but he was sure such things were happening.

The confused battle lasted only a few minutes before the outnumbered Confederates were forced to retreat. Mac hated to shout that order, but everywhere he looked his men were dying.

"Fall back!" he bellowed. "Fall back and regroup!" The fight wasn't over, he vowed. The regiment just needed a moment to catch its breath.

The Yankees weren't going to give them that moment, however. Even as Rosser's division retreated, the Federal horsemen continued to press forward. Back across Cedar Creek went the Confederates, fighting every step of the way, and all they could hope was that the rest of the battle was going better for their side.

UNFORTUNATELY FOR the Southern cause, that was not the case, although for the most part the battle went well in the beginning. The assaults led by Early and Gordon pushed back the Union line but soon began to lose strength. Although there were moments during the long, bloody morning of October 19 when the Yankees' defensive line appeared to be on the verge of collapse, somehow it stayed together and kept the Confederates from overrunning it. Not only that, but the Confederate cavalry had been unable to occupy its Federal counterpart and keep the Yankee horsemen out of the main battle. The ranks of Union infantry were bolstered by blue-clad cavalrymen.

At midday Early paused in the attack, despite objections from Gordon. Early thought his men were worn out and needed the respite before launching another attack later in the afternoon. That decision allowed the Yankees to rest and shore up their lines as well.

The delay was an important factor in another way. It gave Philip H. Sheridan time to reach the battlefield.

Sheridan found his men battered and bloody but still full of fight. Their enthusiasm grew even more as Sheridan rode up and down his line in plain sight, rallying the troops. For most of the day, the Yankees had been fighting a defensive battle. Now, with Sheridan prodding them, they would go on the attack.

Late in the afternoon, as artillery roared on both sides, the Yankees charged with rank after rank of infantry. Then, with a rolling thunder of hoof beats, the Federal cavalry attacked. For a short time, the Confederates stood up to these smashing blows, but then their lines began to crumble. Cannons fell silent, battle flags were lost, and men turned and ran for their lives.

Although the retreat would go on for hours, until the tattered remnants of Early's once-proud army fled all the way to New Market, the battle of Cedar Creek was over.

And so was the struggle for the Shenandoah Valley. Now a devastated shambles of the beautiful land it had once been, it truly belonged to the Yankees.

Chapter Five

T HE LATE FALL AND winter of 1864 were not kind to the Confederacy. In Virginia the bloody siege of Petersburg continued, already the longest, costliest siege of the war in terms of human lives lost . . . and with no end in sight, it could only get worse. In Georgia, the vital city of Atlanta had fallen to Gen. William Tecumseh Sherman in September, and after resting his troops he marched across the state to the sea during November and December, devastating everything in his path before reaching the coastal city of Savannah. Just before Christmas 1864, the Confederates still in Savannah withdrew into South Carolina, abandoning the city and its vital port to Sherman. Elsewhere, in Tennessee, Confederate Gen. John Bell Hood, having failed to save Atlanta from Sherman after taking over command from Gen. Joseph E. Johnston, turned his attention to an ill-advised attempt to capture Nashville. This plan came to ruin when a momentous clash with the Yankees at Franklin practically wrecked Hood's army. The Confederates suffered even more losses during a climactic battle with Federals just outside Nashville on December 16, and Hood was forced to retreat back toward Alabama. The Confederacy was shrinking, and everywhere the beleaguered Rebels turned, the Yankees seemed to be waiting for them.

But the fight was still a long way from over.

THIS WAS the most miserable Christmas Day he had ever spent, Henry Brannon told himself. He swayed in the saddle from exhaustion as his horse plodded along a frozen, deeply rutted road. The air was cold enough to chill him to the very bone. But at least it wasn't sleeting or snowing right now. Give it time, though, he thought.

And after due consideration, he amended his judgment: The previous Christmas Day, in 1863, hadn't been very good, either.

That was the day his brother Titus had come home.

Titus, who everyone in the family had believed dead ever since the battle of Fredericksburg. Titus, who, when he left Culpeper County to join the army, had been married to Polly Ebersole. Over time Henry had fallen in love with his older brother's widow, had gotten her with child, and had married her. But Polly wasn't really a widow at all, because Titus wasn't dead. Instead, he spent long, hellish months in a Yankee prison camp. When he escaped and made his way back to Virginia with the help of a woman named Louisa Abernathy, he showed up at the door of the Brannon family farmhouse on Christmas, only to find that his wife was now married to his little brother and carrying Henry's baby.

No wonder things hadn't gone well after that, Henry thought as he rode along with the Nathan Bedford Forrest's cavalry.

Forrest was guarding the rear of the shattered Confederate army that had tried and failed to take Nashville back from the Yankees. For more than a week now, Forrest and his cavalrymen had been up to the task, fighting skirmishes with the Yankee horsemen who harried the Rebel column and burning bridges so that the Northern invaders couldn't use them. This morning the Southerners had pulled out of the town of Pulaski, leaving a small force behind to torch the bridge over Richland Creek. The Federal pursuit had gotten there too quickly, however. The Yankees had put out the fire and saved the bridge, and now they were close on the heels of the Confederate rear guard.

Henry's friend Ernie Murrell rode alongside him. "Reckon we're gonna have to stop before much longer and fort up to make a stand," he said. "Otherwise them Yanks'll be ridin' right up our backs. Hell of a way to spend a holiday, ain't it?"

Henry dragged the back of his hand across his mouth, feeling the rasp of beard against skin that was cracked and bloody from the cold. "Yeah," he answered. "Not much of a celebration."

There hadn't been much of a celebration at the Brannon house the previous Christmas, either. Provisions had been scarce, and presents were out of the question. Then had come the knock on the door as a cold wind raged outside . . .

The rage had come into the house with Titus. The return of a brother from the dead should have been a joyous occasion, but Titus had brought nothing but hate and grief with him. Hatred for Polly and for Henry, because of what Titus considered their betrayal of him . . . and ultimately grief over the deaths of Polly and the child she was carrying, deaths that Henry would always link in his mind with Titus, even though he hadn't caused them directly.

Henry didn't know if the pain of his loss had faded with time or if he was too numb and beaten down to feel much of anything anymore. He had left the farm, the last of the Brannon brothers to go off to war, but not to escape the sorrow of losing his wife and unborn baby. He had left because he had killed one of the Yankees who now occupied Culpeper County, a brutal sergeant who had attacked his sister, Cordelia, and Louisa Abernathy, who was staying with the family. To spare his loved ones—and he had to admit, to spare himself the fate of a firing squad or a hangman's noose—he had taken off for the tall and uncut and wound up riding with Forrest's cavalry as part of Hood's army in its disastrous excursion into Tennessee. Henry's brother Cory had ridden with Forrest in the past, had in fact served as scout and aide to the general. Henry wasn't that close to Forrest and likely never would be, but he admired the man's daring.

The road ran between some hills, and orders came back along the column for the men to fan out and position themselves on those wooded slopes in preparation for an ambush. Murrell's prediction was about to come true. Forrest, as usual, was going to get in the first blow rather than wait for the enemy to seize that advantage.

Henry and Murrell left the road and headed up the hill to the right, riding into the trees and then turning their horses so they faced toward the oncoming Yankees. Most of Hood's depleted army pressed on south, of course, but soon a good number of cavalry and infantry were deployed on these hills, along with several batteries of artillery situated in strategic positions. All they were waiting for were the Yankees . . . and the order to attack.

Both those things came along in short order.

Henry was armed with a Spencer carbine he had taken from a dead Federal cavalryman. He checked the rifle's loads and then tugged down on the brim of his hat. He didn't like fighting. It filled him with anxiety. When he was younger, he had longed to follow his brothers off to war, thinking that it must be the most glorious enterprise in the world. In the past year he had learned the truth of the matter. Combat was confusing, maddening, utterly terrifying. Yet once the battles started, he was able to shove those feelings far back in his mind and ignore them. He had decided that living through a battle was largely a matter of luck, but staying calm at least improved the odds.

He didn't have to wait long this time, and he was glad of that. A tall, bearded man on a white horse rode by, his long coat flapping behind him. He brandished a pistol and shouted, "Charge, boys, charge!"

Henry hadn't spotted the Yankees yet, but obviously Forrest had, because the general was leading the attack himself . . . also as usual.

The cavalrymen followed Forrest out of the trees, and as Henry and Murrell emerged onto the open slope, Henry saw the blue-uniformed riders below on the road. The Yankees milled around as if unsure of what to do. The long-barreled pistol in Forrest's hand exploded, and in response to that signal, guns roared all over the hillsides, pouring bullets into the Federal cavalry.

Forrest's horse artillery began to speak. Shells burst among the Union troopers, knocking down men and horses and leaving craters in the frozen mud of the road. Hundreds of men, ragged as scarecrows and many of them without shoes despite the cold, came yelling from the trees and rushed down the hills in the wake of the cavalry.

Henry held his fire until he was almost at the bottom of the slope, not trusting his marksmanship from horseback. When he started shooting, he was close enough so that it was difficult to miss the Yankees. He emptied all seven rounds in the Spencer's magazine into the milling mass of the enemy.

From the corner of his eye, he saw Forrest, as magnificently deadly as ever, riding tall in the saddle into the midst of the Northerners. The general had drawn his second revolver and blasted both of them at the foe, emptying a saddle with almost every shot. Henry had heard it said that Forrest was the single most dangerous man on either side of the great conflict, and at moments such as these, when the general struck down his enemies like some sort of avenging angel, Henry well believed it.

He couldn't afford to sit there gawking in admiration, however, not with the fight still going on. Shifting the now empty Spencer to his left hand, he used his right to draw his pistol and opened fire with it.

The day was overcast and gloomy to start with, and as clouds of powder smoke began to clog the air, it became even more difficult to see. Henry and Murrell guided their mounts along the edge of the road, toward the rear of the pursuing party. Suddenly Henry saw a Federal battery up ahead. The Yankee drovers were trying to get the teams of mules pulling the cannons turned around. They didn't want the artillery to fall into Confederate hands.

Murrell let out a whoop of excitement and sent his horse lunging straight at the nearest group of teamsters. Henry followed. A couple of the soldiers turned to fight. Murrell shot one of them with his pistol. Henry rode over the other man. The Yankee let out a scream as the horse trampled him into the mud. The other teamsters broke and ran, abandoning a cannon on its gun carriage.

Murrell grabbed the team's harness and tugged hard on it, starting the mules moving up the road again. He looked over at Henry and proudly grinned. "We got us a Yankee cannon!" he shouted in triumph. Henry just nodded and smiled tiredly, falling in beside Murrell.

The battle was strung out for a good distance along the road. Most of the Yankees had turned and were retreating as fast as they could in the face of Forrest's furious attack. Panic was contagious. Federal cavalrymen fled from the tattered Confederate infantrymen. Within minutes, it was a total rout.

Of course, the victory would be short-lived, Henry thought. The Yankee cavalry wasn't that far in front of the rest of the army being led by Gen. George H. Thomas, the so-called Rock of Chickamauga and Hammer of Nashville. Vastly outnumbered by that army, Forrest's rear guard couldn't hope to stop them. But this skirmish had at least slowed down the pursuit for a while. Every minute they could buy for the rest of Hood's men was precious. If the army could reach the Tennessee River and cross over it, perhaps the Yankees would give up the chase.

Forrest rode by and saw the captured cannon. "Got you a Yankee long gun, did you?" he asked Murrell.

"Yes sir, General!"

"What you goin' to do with it?"

Murrell frowned for a moment. "Well, sir, I don't rightly know. Give it to our artillery boys, I reckon. I'm a cavalryman, not a gunner."

Forrest nodded. "That's a good idea. Maybe it'll make up for the fifty or sixty cannon we lost back up the road in Franklin and Nashville." He spurred away.

The general's scathing sarcasm wasn't lost on Henry. He had heard around the campfires that Forrest had no patience for the ineptitude of his fellow officers, even so-called superior officers. He had given Gen. Braxton Bragg a tongue-lashing when Bragg failed to take advantage of his victory at Chickamauga and had ridden away on his own, taking his cavalry with him, without waiting for an official transfer or new orders. Forrest fought his own way, on his own terms.

If the Confederacy had had more officers like him, Henry thought, they might have stood a better chance in this war.

JUST AS Henry expected, the rest of Thomas's men moved up quickly and made the rearmost members of Forrest's cavalry ride for their lives. The fall of night slowed everyone's pace, and the crucial gap remained between hunters and hunted. The next day, the day after Christmas, the main body of Hood's army reached the Tennessee River at the village of Bainbridge. Disorganized the army might have been, but the engineering companies still functioned well enough to throw a pontoon bridge across the river. The troops began to march across the swollen stream, hoping to find a safe haven on the other side.

Several miles back up the road, where a small stream called Sugar Creek crossed it, Forrest and the cavalry halted to wait once again for the Yankees. The road just south of the creek was crowded with wagons from the ordnance train. The mule teams that ordinarily pulled the wagons had been unhitched and taken to Bainbridge to assist in the construction of the pontoon bridge. The mules were supposed to be returned to Sugar Creek later in the day, once the bridge was up, but until they got back, those wagons and their contents were sitting ducks for the Yankees, if the pursuit should arrive in time.

Henry waited tensely with the other cavalrymen, expecting to see the Federals come marching into sight at any time. As the day passed, however, the Yankees didn't show up.

"What do you reckon is keeping them?" Henry asked Murrell as the two men stood beside their horses, ready to mount at a moment's notice.

"This weather's just as bad for them as it is for us," Murrell replied, waving a hand around him to indicate the icy mist and fog that filled the air and chilled man and beast to the bone, making them miserable. "And they got an even bigger bunch than we do to keep movin'. But they'll be here sooner or later, never you worry about that. That ol' Rock o' Chickamauga wants Hood, wants him bad."

Henry nodded. He didn't think Thomas would give up the pursuit, either, at least not this side of the Tennessee.

More hours dragged past, still with no sign of the Union army. The mules were brought back during the afternoon, as promised, and soon the balky creatures were hitched up again to the ordnance wagons. The wagon train moved out, heading slowly down the road toward Bainbridge.

The fog had grown even thicker, so that by late afternoon it was difficult to see more than a few feet in any direction, especially around the creek. Not long before dark, Forrest rode along the stream, pointing to some of the men who waited there. "You and you and you," he said, indicating Henry, Murrell, and a few other men. "Stay here in plain sight on the bank. The rest of us are pulling back a ways."

"Sounds to me like you plan on usin' us as bait, General," Murrell drawled.

"You got any objection to that, son?" Forrest's tone was sharp.

"No sir," Murrell replied quickly, not wanting to risk the general's wrath. "In fact, it sounds like a mighty good idea to me."

A grin flashed across Forrest's face. "We won't be far off. As soon as the Yankees show up, you boys mosey on down the road. They'll follow you."

"Yes sir," Henry said, thinking that he understood what Forrest had in mind. He would have to wait and see how things played out to be sure, though.

He and Murrell and the other men swung up into their saddles and waited at the edge of the road by the creek as the rest of the cavalry moved farther south, vanishing into the fog. The fog did more than obscure one's vision; it muffled sounds as well. Once the others had pulled back, they might as well have disappeared from the face of the earth. Henry could neither see nor hear any sign of them.

And he couldn't hear the approach of the Yankees, either, until the enemy was almost at the creek. Then, suddenly, the soft thudding of hooves and the occasional jingle of a harness chain were audible. Henry swallowed hard as he heard the sounds coming nearer.

"Get ready, fellers," Murrell hissed. He dismounted, and Henry wanted to ask him what he thought he was doing, only Murrell held up a hand to forestall any questions. Murrell picked up one of his horse's hind legs and began to examine the hoof as if something was wrong with the shoe. Henry had to admit that Murrell's actions provided an explanation of why he and the others might be lagging behind the rest of the rear guard. They wanted the Yankees to think that Forrest's cavalry was nowhere around Sugar Creek.

Like ghosts, the riders in the forefront of the Federal pursuit loomed out of the fog on the other side of the creek. Murrell ignored them for a moment, giving them a chance to get a good look at him, and then he let out a yelped "Son of a bitch!" as if he had been taken by surprise. He leaped into the saddle.

Henry and the other men wheeled their mounts and kicked them into a gallop, following Murrell's lead. Shouts came from across the creek as the Yankees spurred ahead faster now. Henry, Murrell, and the others thundered down the road while the pursuers splashed across the stream and gave chase. A glance over his shoulder told Henry that there were more than a few of the Yankees. In fact, they kept coming out of the fog, dozens—no, scores—of them. There was a whole damned regiment back there, Henry thought wildly, closing in not more than fifty yards behind him.

Suddenly, from lines stretched out on both sides of the road, yellow and orange flame tore holes in the overcast. The fog wasn't thick enough to muffle the roar of gunfire as Henry and the others reached the site of the ambush. They reined in, slowing their mounts as volley after volley crashed out from the rifles of Forrest's men. Then, with high-pitched Rebel yells, the Confederate horsemen charged the startled Federals.

The Yankees never had a chance to ready themselves to meet that charge. Forrest and his men were already on top of them, cutting them down with rifle and pistol fire at close range. The Yankees turned to run but found themselves slowed by the creek at their backs. The Confederate riders fell on them and fell hard, blasting men from their saddles. Forrest led the advance on across the creek, continuing the slaughter. The Yankees began to surrender, seeing that their only other choice was to die.

Their supposed flight had carried Henry, Murrell, and the handful of other riders past the main group of Confederate cavalry, so by the time they got turned around and joined the fight, most of the combat had spilled back across the creek. Henry and Murrell came upon some Yankee stragglers who threw down their guns and lifted their hands. Murrell grinned and called to them, "Howdy, boys! Nice of you to come visitin'. Light down from them horses and sit a spell."

The prisoners dismounted. Henry covered them with his Spencer while Murrell gathered up the reins of their mounts. Forrest's men would make good use of these Yankee horses. After all, the failed invasion into Tennessee had taken a high toll on horseflesh.

A short time later Forrest came trotting back along the road, trailed by his men and the prisoners they had taken. Most of the Yankees had gotten away, but it would take them a considerable amount of time to regroup because they had gotten so scattered in the thick fog. Before the pursuit could be reorganized, there was a good chance the ordnance train would reach the river at Bainbridge and cross over. Once again Forrest's rear guard had done its job.

When they camped that night, Forrest sought out Henry, Murrell, and the other picked men. He shook their hands and congratulated them. "Good work, Brannon," he said to Henry. "Reckon I wouldn't have expected any less, though. That brother o' yours was always a fightin' fool. Wish he hadn't stayed behind with Bragg. That sumbitch got a lot o' good men killed there on Lookout Mountain and Missionary Ridge. Hope Cory wasn't one of them."

"Yes sir," Henry agreed. "I hope so, too."

"You'll see him again one o' these days. All you Brannons will meet up, either here or in the Promised Land."

Henry had to swallow the lump that came into his throat. "Yes sir," he managed to say.

He hoped fervently that he would see all his family again this side of heaven. But under the circumstances, he supposed that when it came to reunions, he would just have to take what he could get.

SOMEWHAT TO Henry's surprise, the Yankees didn't show up on their tail the next day. Without any Federals harassing them, the Confederate rear guard was able to ride on south to Bainbridge at an almost leisurely pace. Arriving at the Tennessee River, they found that elements of Hood's army were still engaged in crossing on the pontoon bridge. Forrest and his men stood guard while the retreat continued and didn't cross over until evening had fallen.

The next morning, December 28, the last of the infantry crossed, taking up the pontoons as they went. Henry and the other cavalrymen sat in their saddles watching as the last troops reached the south bank of the river. The bridge was gone now, and the fast-flowing stream would be impossible to cross without something spanning it. The question was whether or not Thomas would want to go to that much trouble, especially considering the fact that, in the interim, the Confederates would be lengthening their lead on any further pursuit.

"Lookee there!" Murrell said excitedly as the last of the infantry marched away. He pointed across the river.

A tired grin stretched across Henry's face as he saw the blue-uniformed riders galloping toward the river. The Yankees had arrived, but not in time.

Murrell put his fingers in his mouth and whistled in glee as the Federal troopers came to a halt on the north bank of the Tennessee. He edged his horse closer to the water, took off his hat, and waved it in circles over his head. "You boys come too late to the dance!" he shouted.

Henry doubted if the Yankees had heard the whistle or the taunt. But they could no doubt see Murrell out there capering around in plain sight.

"Come on, Ernie," Henry called to his friend. "Let's get out of here."

"In a minute," Murrell replied. He gave a Rebel yell and waved the hat over his head again.

Henry saw the spurt of smoke from a rifle in the hands of one of the Yankees on the far shore. "Ernie!" he yelled, knowing he was already too late with the warning.

Murrell let out a startled exclamation as something plucked the hat right out of his hand. He turned his head and watched for a second as it sailed away behind him. Then he yanked hard on his horse's reins and brought the animal around in a tight turn. "Let's get the hell out of here!" As his mount broke into a gallop, Murrell leaned down with the grace of a born horseman and snatched up the hat that had been shot out of his hand by the Yankee sharpshooter a moment earlier.

Henry had already turned his own horse and heeled it into a run. Murrell caught up with him and showed him the hat, poking a finger through the hole in the crown. "Damn Yankee ruined a perfectly good hat!" he said indignantly.

Murrell's hat had been soaked and torn and covered in mud so many times that it barely resembled headgear. Henry grinned and said, "Better to get your hat ventilated than your head!"

"Well, yeah, I reckon I can't argue with that."

Without looking back, they rode away from the Tennessee River and the Federal cavalry milling around in frustration on the other side. Murrell had been damned lucky, Henry thought.

But after everything that had happened, it was about time the Southerners had a little bit of luck.

Chapter Six

A DEEP GLOOM HUNG over the ranger camp that had nothing to do with the weather on this Christmas Day 1864. A few days earlier, while having a meal at Lakeland, the home of a friend, Lt. Col. John Singleton Mosby had been shot by a Yankee raider firing through a dining-room window. The wound was severe, and when the Federal cavalrymen burst into the house a few minutes later, the officer in charge examined the injury and decided that the wounded man had no chance of survival. But when he asked Mosby who he was, the partisan leader had the presence of mind to identify himself as a lieutenant in the Sixth Virginia Cavalry. One of the ladies of the house also thought quickly enough to hide Mosby's hat and uniform coat under the bed. The Federals would have liked nothing better than to get their hands on him, wounded or not.

Instead, the Yankees had left him at Lakeland, accepting the lie about his identity and assuming he would die from his wound. Four days later, however, Mosby still clung to life. He had been taken to another farmhouse and then to a hiding place in the woods to keep the Union men from finding him if they figured out who he really was and came looking for him. Nearly all the rangers who had ridden with him in the Shenandoah and Loudoun Valleys, the area east of the Blue Ridge that some called "Mosby's Confederacy," vowed vengeance on the Yankees for striking down their beloved commander.

Titus Brannon didn't have to take any extra vows. He had already devoted his life—what was left of it—to killing Yankees.

He sat beside a small fire, staring into the flames. He knew better; looking into a fire for very long ruined a man's night vision, and he might need it in a hurry if trouble broke out. But Titus was lost in memory, as he so often was these days, and didn't think about what he was doing.

There was little coherent about his thoughts. Instead, a kaleidoscope of images revolved crazily through his head, pictures burned into his brain by anger and sorrow and hate.

Polly, beautiful blonde Polly, his wife, the only woman he had ever loved . . . Tree-shaded Dobie's Run, the creek that ran through the Brannon farm in Culpeper County, where as a boy Titus had fished and hunted and swam . . . The battlefield at Fredericksburg, where Union soldiers had died by the thousands on the open ground between the town and Marye's Heights—and where Titus himself had been taken prisoner . . . Old Judge Darden, red-faced and wheezing, declaring that Titus and Polly were still married, no matter what anyone said, no matter how fat her belly got with his brother Henry's bastard . . . O'Neil, the brutal Yankee sergeant at Camp Douglas who had tried so hard to break Titus's body and spirit and had failed at both, dying at Titus's hand instead . . . Duncan Ebersole, Polly's father, possibly the most evil man on the face of the earth, who had paid the ultimate price for the ultimate crime . . . Nathan Hatcher, dead now, too, as far as Titus knew, lost during the long trek from Illinois to Virginia . . . Danetta Wiley, not quite as blonde as Polly, not quite so lovely, but still capable of starting to melt the frost that surrounded Titus's heart—until the Yankees came on their burning raid that had ended it all between them . . . Bob McCulloch, a friend when Titus had thought he would never again have one, also dead, a victim of Sheridan's vengeance on the Shenandoah Valley . . .

Titus gave a little shake of his head and looked away from the flames. No, he didn't need any more reasons to hate the Yankees and want them all dead. He had plenty already.

The scrape of a footstep on the frozen ground behind him made Titus tighten his grip on his rifle and glance around. Even in the middle of the rangers' camp he was alert for trouble and poised for violence.

Adolphus "Dolly" Richards, the commander of the battalion to which Titus belonged, sat down on the log beside him.

"Evenin'," Richards said with a nod. "How are you, Titus?"

"Fine." That hadn't been true for a long time, but Titus kept what he felt to himself. As far as he was concerned, it was no one's damned business how he was.

"Bill Chapman's riding down to see General Lee at Petersburg," Richards went on, referring to another of Mosby's lieutenants. "Our rations are getting mighty short up here."

Titus grunted. "He thinks Lee's goin' to give him a wagon train o' supplies, does he?" It was common knowledge even in the Loudoun Valley that the troops in the trenches at Petersburg were slowly starving to death, as were the people of Richmond whom they protected. Grant might not have to defeat the Confederate army by force. Hunger might do it for him if he waited long enough.

"No, he wants permission to move some of the men somewhere else for the winter. It was the colonel's idea."

That caught Titus's interest despite his calculated indifference. "How is the colonel?"

"Hanging on as best he can. As soon as he's a little stronger, we're going to start moving him around so the Yankees can't get a bead on him. By now they've probably figured out who they let slip through their fingers, and they're not going to be happy about it."

Titus didn't care if the Yankees were never happy again. It would be all right with him if every single one of them stayed miserable from now on.

"What do you want from me?" he asked.

"The colonel's going to need some fellas to look after him—" Richards began.

"I ain't no doctor."

"I don't mean look after him like that. He's already got our best surgeons tending to him. He needs people to guard him and move him from place to place. You know, make sure he stays safe. You're one of the best scouts and fighting men we've got,

Titus. I want you to take over the detail that'll protect the colonel."

Titus frowned. Guarding Mosby while the colonel was recuperating didn't sound very exciting, and it didn't sound as if there would be many opportunities to kill Yankees. Still, a fella never knew what might come up. Trouble was certainly possible, because it was likely the Federals would be searching for Mosby. And besides, it was the dead of winter—one of the worst Virginia winters in anyone's memory—and there wasn't much going on anyway.

"All right," Titus said with an abrupt nod. "I'll do it."

Dolly Richards clapped a hand on his shoulder. "Thanks, Titus. I knew I could count on you."

"Colonel Mosby better get well in a hurry, though," Titus said as Richards got to his feet. "I don't want to wait too long before I get back to killin' Yankees again."

WOULD THERE ever be another Christmas when the sun shone and peace reigned over Virginia? Cordelia Brannon asked herself as she rubbed her hands together and drew her blanket closer around her shoulders. Her breath fogged in front of her face. The fire in the fireplace was out, the last of the wood in the wood box having been burned earlier in the evening. Tomorrow she would have to take an ax and go out to chop more. They could have busted up another chair and burned it, she thought, but the furniture left in the house was already scanty. Too much of it had gone to warm the remaining members of the family against the chill of this dreadful winter.

Not that there was much left of the Brannon family, at least here at home in Culpeper County. Just Cordelia and her mother, Abigail. Then there was Louisa Abernathy, who, while not a blood relative, was almost like a member of the family now. She had been here a year and had no place else to go.

A year, Cordelia thought. A year exactly since Louisa had hammered her fist against the door and begged to be let in out of the storm. Titus had been with her, half-dead from a fever. Louisa was a Quaker and had served as an inspector of prisons in the North, a position that had taken her to Camp Douglas on the outskirts of Chicago. There she had met Titus, and her sympathy for his plight had led her to help him escape, along with fellow prisoner Nathan Hatcher. Nathan was from Culpeper County, too, and for a short time, Cordelia had considered him her beau. Potential beau, anyway. Nathan's feelings about the war had doomed that romance.

How odd, she told herself as a shiver went through her. She had driven Nathan away because he had said that he could not support the Confederacy. And now she was very much afraid that she had fallen in love with a Yankee.

"My, spring is going to be mighty welcome this year," Abigail Brannon announced. She sat on the divan next to Cordelia, also wrapped in a blanket. Louisa sat in the rocking chair near the unlit fire. A single candle burned on the mantel. Soon they would blow it out, and all three of them would crawl into the same bed, fully dressed and with a pile of blankets on top of them. But Abigail never turned in until she sat for a while with the Bible open in her lap, even though the light was too dim for her to read the words in the Good Book. Just holding the thick old volume with its cracked black leather binding was a comfort to her, she claimed. Cordelia wasn't going to take that away from her.

"I never saw a prettier place than Virginia in the springtime," Louisa said. "Even my home up in Pennsylvania wasn't as nice as this."

"You shouldn't say that, my dear. A person's home is always the nicest place there is, no matter what it's like." Abigail couldn't resist adding, "Even if it's full of Yankees."

Louisa didn't seem to take offense. She didn't support either side in the war. Her faith didn't allow her to believe in war or in

violence of any kind. She claimed that the actions she had taken
to help Titus had separated her from her religion and damned
her, but Cordelia knew that wasn't true. No matter what she had
done, in her heart Louisa was still a Quaker and still a good
person, and Cordelia was sure the Lord would forgive her.

Cordelia was about to say something about Culpeper County
being full of Yankees these days, when a knock sounded at the
door. The heads of all three women jerked up. No doubt they
were all thinking the same thing, about how a knock on that
same door the previous Christmas had heralded changes that
shook the Brannon family to its very core.

"Don't answer it," Louisa whispered.

Abigail looked like she wanted to agree, but her natural hospitality got the better of her. "See who it is, Cordelia," she said
crisply. "I won't let anybody stand outside my door on a night
like this."

Slowly Cordelia stood up. As she started toward the door, the
knock came again. Then, over the sound of the wind, a voice
called, "Miss Brannon?"

Cordelia relaxed. It was just Joseph.

Just Lt. Joseph Keller of the Union army, one of the enemies
of the Confederacy.

"Mrs. Brannon?" Joseph shouted. "Miss Abernathy?"

Cordelia shot a glance over her shoulder at her mother as she
paused at the door. Abigail didn't like Joseph, didn't like the
way he had been coming around for months, ostensibly to see if
Henry had returned but really to see Cordelia. At least that was
what Abigail suspected, and of course, it was true.

Cordelia opened the door, and Keller stepped inside quickly,
so that what little heat there was in the room wouldn't escape.
As she closed the door, he tugged off his black kepi. His sandy
hair was cropped short, and he had a neatly trimmed beard. Tall
and broad-shouldered, his brawny frame housed a truly gentle
man. That was one reason Cordelia loved him—even though it
was treason for her to do so.

Joseph nodded first to Abigail. "Good evening, Mrs. Brannon. And Merry Christmas."

Abigail sniffed, "Nothing much merry about it for folks living under the iron heel of a conquering army."

Cordelia saw the way Joseph's face fell. He had probably hoped that Abigail would make allowances since it was a holiday and all. But he didn't know Abigail Brannon nearly as well as Cordelia did. Making allowances for anything was not part of her nature.

"Good evening, Lieutenant," Louisa said. "What's that you have there?" She gestured toward the wicker basket in his hand.

Cordelia had seen the basket, too, but she didn't allow herself to hope that it might contain food. Keller had been bringing them food for months, but usually he had to steal it from the army's supplies, and Cordelia was afraid he would get into trouble because he was trying to help them.

Only in recent weeks had he begun to get some of his normal coloring and strength back. He had been badly wounded by a deserting sergeant who had come to the Brannon farm to kidnap Cordelia. The man's name was McCafferty, and he had stabbed Joseph in the belly when the lieutenant encountered him and realized the sergeant was deserting. For a time Cordelia feared Keller would not recover from the wound. But he'd been stubborn, and slowly but surely he was getting to be himself again. Louisa had also been hurt during McCafferty's attack, but she had recuperated quickly.

Joseph extended the basket toward Abigail. "It's not much, ma'am," he said. "A few biscuits and some fried chicken. But I thought it might brighten your holiday."

Abigail lifted a hand but hesitated. It had taken her awhile to accept the idea of letting a Yankee help the family. Pride had waged a stubborn war with necessity. But in the end, Abigail had been able to tell herself that the Yankees had taken this food from Confederates in the first place, so it was all right if they gave back a little of it.

Cordelia felt her stomach clench at the mention of biscuits and fried chicken. All they'd had to eat recently was some watery potato soup. If her mother didn't accept Joseph's gift, then she would, she told herself.

"Thank you, Lieutenant," Abigail said grudgingly as she reached up to take the basket. "Cordelia, Louisa, come over here and share in this food. We'll eat here, where it's a bit warmer."

Warmth was largely an illusion, because the fire in the fireplace had been out for quite some time. But Cordelia and Louisa crowded onto the divan with Abigail, and the three women began to eat.

Joseph walked over to the fireplace and stood there, his hands clasped behind his back. After a few minutes, he said, addressing the question to Cordelia, "I don't suppose you've heard anything from your brother Henry?"

She shook her head. "Nothing. Not a word since he left."

"I'm very sorry," Joseph said with a sigh. "I still feel like it's my fault for not catching on sooner to what McCafferty had planned. If you do hear from Henry, please tell him that he's free to return to Culpeper County anytime he wants to."

"As long as he signs a formal Yankee loyalty oath?" Abigail asked sharply.

Joseph looked pained. "I can't do anything about decisions made by my superior officers, ma'am. But I suspect that the war will be over soon, and none of us will have to worry about loyalty oaths anymore."

Cordelia winced, sure that Joseph had said the wrong thing and that Abigail would explode in anger at the very idea of the Confederacy's being defeated. But her mother surprised her by saying nothing. Abigail was as staunch a Confederate as ever, but she was no longer the firebrand she had been four years earlier, before the war. She had lost too much since then, had seen too much hardship.

The food in the basket was delicious to Cordelia. She had to force herself not to wolf it down. When she and Abigail and

Louisa were finished, Joseph said, "Please, keep the basket. I don't need it." Nor did he want to be seen riding back into Culpeper with it, Cordelia thought. That could give rise to awkward questions from his superiors.

"Thank you," Abigail said stiffly. No matter what the circumstances, she was polite, even to Yankees.

"I guess I'd better be going." Joseph put on his cap. "I tied my horse in the barn, out of the wind, but I'm sure the poor animal is pretty cold anyway."

Cordelia got to her feet. "I'll see you to the door."

Louisa stood up quickly. "Goodness, that was a fine meal, Lieutenant Keller. But I'm so full now it's making me sleepy. I believe I'll turn in."

Joseph tugged on the brim of his cap. "I'll say good night, then, Miss Abernathy."

Louisa looked down at the woman still seated on the divan. "Abigail, are you coming up with me?"

"I suppose." Abigail frowned at Cordelia as if to say that she knew perfectly well what was going on and didn't approve of it one bit, but she stood up and went to the stairs with Louisa. "Hurry upstairs, Cordelia," she said over her shoulder as she and Louisa started up the steps.

"Yes ma'am. I'll be right there as soon as I show Lieutenant Keller out."

Joseph was already at the door. Cordelia dawdled a bit getting across the room, giving her mother and Louisa time to reach the top of the stairs and disappear down the hall. She was grateful to Louisa for orchestrating this moment alone with Joseph. And she supposed she was grateful to Abigail as well for going along with it, no matter how reluctantly.

She looked up at Joseph, and he took her in his arms and kissed her. She felt safer in his embrace than anywhere else these days, and when he broke the kiss, she pressed her face against the front of his black woolen greatcoat, trying not to think about the blue uniform that was under it. When she looked up at him a few moments later, she said, "Do you think it's true? I mean, that the war will be over soon?"

"I hope so. I don't see how the Confederates can hold on for more than a few months. I hope it's true, for the sake of you and your family, Cordelia."

She frowned slightly. "What about for your sake, and the sake of all the soldiers, Joseph?"

"For the others . . . of course. As for me . . ." A pained look crossed his face. "Cordelia, I've not yet done anything in this war to help end it. I've never even heard a shot fired except in practice and drill."

"But . . . but that's all right, isn't it? There's no need for you to fight—"

"I joined the army to do my part," he said. "So far, I don't think I've done that." He took a deep breath then went on, "That's why I've requested a transfer."

"A . . . a transfer?" Cordelia repeated, her eyes widening in surprise. "You mean you're leaving Culpeper County?" The very notion of that filled her with fear. She wasn't sure she and her mother and Louisa would have been able to remain on the farm for this long if Joseph hadn't helped them. Without him around, they might have been forced to abandon the farm and take to the roads like so many thousands of homeless refugees throughout the South had done.

And it was more than just fear for herself and her family that caused her reaction to the idea. Joseph wanted to transfer to another part of the army so that he could fight. And if he fought, he might be hurt . . . or killed.

"I don't know," he said in reply to her question. "Requesting a transfer and being granted one are two different matters. It's entirely possible that my request will be denied. Even if it isn't, these things take time." A wry smile tinged with bitterness came over his face. "The war may be over before anyone gets around to acting on my request."

"I hope so," she said fervently.

He frowned. "Cordelia? What's wrong? I realize this would mean that we'd be separated for a while, but I could come back—"

"Unless you were dead." She put her hands against his chest and held him off as he tried to draw her closer. "And even if you don't get hurt, you want to go off and kill my friends and neighbors. Maybe even my brothers!"

"My God," he muttered as his frown deepened. "I hadn't thought about that. I just . . . I just wanted to do my part . . ."

"Your part to crush my people and destroy my country."

"It's not a country. The Confederacy doesn't really—" He stopped short. "We've avoided having this argument until now. I would prefer to continue avoiding it."

"You're the one who wants to change everything."

"No, I just want—" Again, he stopped short. This time, he shook his head wearily. "I'm sorry, Cordelia. I shouldn't have told you until I knew for sure one way or the other. All this may come to nothing."

"For your sake, Joseph, I hope so. But until you know, perhaps it would be better if you didn't come out here anymore."

"You don't mean that!"

"Yes, I do," Cordelia said, forcing herself to be resolute.

"All right," he said grudgingly. "If that's what you want. But I don't like it."

"Ever since the war started, there have been a lot of things that none of us have liked. But it's bigger than all of us, Joseph. It can't be stopped. It just has to . . . end."

"I pray that comes soon," he murmured.

So did Cordelia. But she feared the end could not come soon enough.

THIS WAS the end, Cory Brannon thought as he looked out at the gray waters of Port Royal Sound, South Carolina. The South was dead. But like a chicken with its head wrung off, the carcass kept bleeding and flapping around.

He felt disloyal for thinking such thoughts. Not so much disloyal to the Confederacy, but to the men he had served with, men such as Forrest and Gen. William J. Hardee, his current commander, and Abner Strayhorn, who had fought beside him all the way from Tennessee, through the slow retreat from Chattanooga to Atlanta, through the doomed defense of that city, and then across Georgia to the beautiful, stately seacoast city of Savannah, the city that had been abandoned to Sherman's Yankees four days earlier.

It was not only thoughts of the living that preyed on Cory's mind. The dead haunted him, too. Capt. Ezekiel Farrell, who had taken a starving, half-frozen wharf rat under his wing and started the process of turning Coriolanus Troilus Brannon into a man. Ike Judson, who had piloted Cap'n Zeke's riverboat, the *Missouri Zephyr,* up and down the Mississippi and been a friend to Cory, although he might have denied that. Col. Charles Thompson, Cap'n Zeke's brother-in-law and beloved uncle of Cory's wife, Lucille, was simply one of the finest men Cory had ever known. Lt. Hamilton Ryder, Cory's partner in a perilous mission behind enemy lines, a mission that had cost Ham his life. All dead now, taken by this endless war.

And then there were those whose fate was unknown, most notably Lucille, who had started for Texas with Colonel Thompson's wife, Mildred. Had they arrived there safely? Cory had no way of knowing, stuck in South Carolina more than a thousand miles away. His friend Pie Jones was supposed to be somewhere in Texas, too, with his wife, Rachel. Again Cory had no idea if they were even still alive. The uncertainty nagged at him day and night. Since falling in love with Lucille, he had been separated from her on several occasions. They had spent too much time apart. He missed her terribly.

Maybe the thing to do was just give up. Surrender now. End the suffering.

But that would mean admitting that the Yankees had won. His friends, both dead and alive, were not the sort to capitulate so easily.

And Cory could not bring himself to let them down, no matter how much the old rootless wanderer buried deep inside him wanted to take the easy way out.

After blowing up the navy yard at Savannah and tramping across the hurriedly constructed bridges that spanned the Savannah River, the army under Hardee had marched up the coast to Port Royal Sound and camped there. The general intended to move on to Charleston and begin working on the defenses of that city, but his small, eight-thousand-man army needed a chance to regroup and catch its breath. And it was Christmas, too. Some of the men might want to celebrate.

Not surprisingly, Abner was one of the celebrants. He came up behind Cory in the twilight. "Here you go, Cap'n."

Cory had been standing near his tent, looking over the sound. He turned to see Abner holding out a cup toward him. Tendrils of steam rose from it.

"It ain't real coffee, but it'll warm your old bones," Abner went on with a grin. He had a second cup in his other hand.

"I'm not that old, Sergeant," Cory grumbled. "Younger than you, in fact."

"Yeah, maybe when we was both privates. But you're an officer now. You got the weight o' the world weighin' you down."

Cory took the cup, which was filled with a bitter brew made from roasted grain. It was what passed for coffee these days. He took a sip and looked up in surprise. "There's whiskey in this!" he hissed.

"'Bout half and half," Abner said, pride in his voice.

"Where in the world did you find—no, never mind, I probably don't want to know."

"No sir, I reckon not. I will say, though, there's a lieutenant colonel who's gonna be mighty surprised when he fetches out his flask and goes to take a nip before bedtime tonight."

Cory held up a hand to stop Abner from saying anything else. He took another swallow of the spiked brew and felt its warmth spread through him.

There had been a time, back in New Madrid, when he had stayed drunk most days. Every coin he earned on the docks got spent at Red Mike's or in the other dram shops. He had been about as disreputable a character as anybody would ever want to run into. His mother would have been mortally ashamed of him.

But he had left those days behind him. They had been swept into the past, first by love and then by war, the two most calamitous uproars known to mankind, he thought wryly. Now he could take a drink without plunging into an abyss of drunkenness.

"I hear tell we'll be movin' out again sometime soon," Abner said, interrupting his thoughts. He took a drink from his cup.

"That's the general's plan, but he hasn't made any firm decisions yet." Cory was an aide to Hardee, so he was privy to most of what the general had in mind. Abner, in turn, was assigned to him, an aide to an aide, so to speak.

"You reckon old Sherman's a-gonna come after us?"

"He chased us all the way across Georgia to Savannah," Cory said. "I don't think he's likely to stop now." He finished the last of the liquid and felt a pleasant lassitude stealing over him. He was still cold but not quite as chilled as he had been by the raw wind coming off the sea. "I expect it may take him awhile to get started, though. Now that he's got a good seaport at his disposal, he'll probably want to bring in plenty of supplies."

"Wish we could get some of those."

Cory shook his head. "Not likely." The Union blockade and the blight on the land caused by war had combined to strip the South of nearly all provisions.

"Well, a fella can always dream, I reckon."

That sounded good, he thought. But too often dreams became nightmares. And even when they didn't, his dreams were always the same, and they made the pain inside him even sharper.

Dreams of Lucille . . .

Chapter Seven

WAS IT REALLY CHRISTMAS? Lucille Farrell Brannon thought so, but she couldn't be sure. After a while all the days started to run together, so it was difficult to keep track of things like dates or even days of the week. It seemed as if they had been traveling across this rolling Texas landscape for months rather than weeks.

Lucille perched on the wagon seat, taking her turn at the reins. Her aunt, Mildred Thompson, was in the back of the wagon. Allen Carter, who handled most of the driving, sat up front beside Lucille, his hat tipped back on his curly, graying hair. The other two members of the party—Carter's son, Fred, and the Englishman, Phineas Carnevan—rode horseback on either side of the wagon.

Phin Carnevan edged his mount closer and called out, "I'll ride on ahead a bit and see if I can find a good place to camp."

"All right, but be careful," Lucille warned him. "You know what they said back at Veal Station about the Indians."

Several days earlier they had passed through the tiny community of Veal Station northwest of Fort Worth. There was nothing to it except a church, a few houses, and a log building that served as a ranger outpost. All the rangers had been on patrol at the time, searching for hostiles. The preacher at the church had spoken to the travelers, warning them that bands of Comanche and Kiowa roamed the territory to the west, emboldened by the fact that the war had drawn away many of the male settlers. The U.S. Army, which had set up a string of frontier forts in North and Central Texas, was gone now, too, of course, and the Confederate government didn't give a hoot what happened so far from Richmond. The only force for law and order in this part of the world was the loose-knit Texas Rangers organization, and the rangers were stretched mighty thin.

Lucille worried about the Comanche and Kiowa war parties, but they weren't going to stop her from reaching the Brazos River. Cory had been talking for years about settling on the Brazos one day, and she knew that when the war was finally over, that was where he would look for her. After fleeing Vicksburg, she and Mildred and the Carters had stayed for a time in East Texas, and that was where they had met Carnevan. A British sea captain who had been smuggling goods through the Yankee blockade to Texas, he had been double-crossed by his partners, who tried to murder him. Lucille, Mildred, and the Carters had helped Phin to get away from the men who wanted to kill him and had nursed him back to health. He was relatively young and strong . . . and handsome. Lucille had to admit that, although only to herself. She was a married woman, after all, and loved her husband very much.

Carnevan heeled his horse into a fast trot that carried him ahead of the wagon. Fred Carter looked over at his father and asked, "Can I go with Phin, Pa?" Fred, in his early twenties, had the mind of a child, but he was courageous and fiercely loyal to his father and their friends.

Allen Carter waved a hand toward his son. "Sure, go ahead. But keep an eye out for trouble. And watch Phin. Do what he does if there's a problem."

"Sure, Pa." Fred galloped after the Englishman.

Carter shifted on the wagon seat, his wooden pegleg scraping on the floorboards. As a sergeant in the Confederate army, he had lost his right leg at the battle of First Manassas, the first real battle of the war. "I reckon that boy really looks up to Carnevan," he said. "Told me the other day he wants to be a sea captain when he grows up."

"That's nice," Lucille said. She and Carter both knew that Fred would never grow up any more than he was now, but it was good that the young man could still dream.

"Yeah, I suppose so. Lord knows he wouldn't want to grow up to be like his old man."

Lucille glanced over at Carter. "Allen, that's not like you. I've never known you to feel sorry for yourself."

"Every cripple does, sooner or later." Carter thumped his peg against the wagon box. "Me and Fred are two of a kind, me crippled in my leg and him crippled in his head. Best he learns to accept that."

"I think he accepts it. He seems to understand his limitations. But you can't blame him for wanting to be more than he is. Everyone does, regardless of their situation."

Carter shook his head. "Oh, I don't blame him. I'm just not sure I like him bein' around Carnevan so much. It puts ideas in his head." Carter looked over at Lucille with narrowed eyes. "I'd say that Carnevan's got ideas in his head, too, especially where you're concerned."

Lucille felt warmth spreading across her face as she blushed. She hoped that in the fading light of day the reaction wasn't too obvious. "You're wrong, Allen. Phin is a gentleman. He wouldn't do anything improper."

Carter turned his head and spat off to the side of the wagon. "Ain't no man ever drawn breath who's so much of a gentleman that he don't think things he shouldn't."

"Well, I don't know that I can argue that point one way or the other." Truth to tell, until she'd met, fallen in love with, and married Cory, she had been pretty innocent in the ways of the world, despite growing up on a riverboat. "But I still don't think you have to worry about Fred's being around Mr. Carnevan."

"Thought you usually called him Phin."

"We're all traveling together. We might as well be friends."

"I don't think that's what he wants."

Lucille searched her mind for some way to distract Carter from this subject, but she didn't have to go to that much trouble. A second later, Carter straightened on the wagon seat and muttered, "They're comin' back in a hurry."

Lucille saw the same thing. Phin and Fred rode hard toward the wagon, dust swirling up from the hooves of their horses.

They wouldn't push the animals like that unless there was some sort of trouble. Hauling back on the reins to bring the team of mules to a halt, Lucille called her Aunt Mildred to the front of the wagon.

A moment later, Mildred Thompson stuck her head through the opening between the canvas flaps that closed off the back of the wagon. "What is it?" she asked worriedly. Clearly she had grasped the urgency in Lucille's tone.

"Phin and Fred were looking for a place to camp. Now they're coming back in a hurry."

Carter turned half-around on the seat. "Better hand me that scattergun, Mrs. Thompson," he said to Mildred.

Quickly Mildred passed the loaded shotgun to Carter, who gripped it tightly as he and the two women waited for Carnevan and Fred to reach the wagon. Lucille's eyes scanned the landscape to the west, beyond the two riders. She saw nothing but more of the same sort of country they had been passing through for several days: wooded, rolling hills with occasional rocky ridges and brushy, meandering creeks.

Suddenly, on one of the highest bluffs, she spotted movement. The bluff was at least half a mile away, so she couldn't see that well, but she thought there were riders up there. In this part of the country, chances were that meant a war party.

Lucille's breath seemed to freeze in her throat. If she could see them, then surely the keen-eyed savages could see the wagon. Lucille had never been around Indians before. What would they do? She had heard stories about murder and torture and mutilation . . .

With a thunder of hooves, Carnevan and Fred galloped up to the wagon and brought their mounts to skidding halts.

"Did you see them?" Fred asked excitedly. "Did you see the Indians?"

"I saw riders up on that bluff yonder," Carter said, confirming that he had noticed the same horsemen as Lucille. "Are you sure they're Indians?"

"Who else could they be?" Fred said.

"Rangers, perhaps?" Mildred suggested.

Carnevan shook his head. "Not unless the rangers have taken to wearing buckskins and feathers in their hair and riding ponies without saddles. I wish I had my old spyglass, but my eyesight is still quite good without it. They're Indians. I'm certain of that."

"Damn," Carter muttered more than under his breath. It was an indication of how worried he was that he didn't apologize to the women for his language.

Lucille tried to keep her voice calm and steady. "What should we do?" she asked.

Carnevan turned in the saddle and pointed to the northwest. "There's a small hill over there with a thick stand of trees on top. I think we should camp there tonight. I believe we can defend the place, if it should come to that."

Lucille had known when they started for the Brazos that they might have to fight hostiles somewhere along the way. Still, knowing that and being faced with the immediate prospect of doing so were two different things. She couldn't keep a small shudder from running through her. But she forced her fear down and commanded, "All right, let's go."

With that, she called out to the mules, flapped the reins, and got the team moving again.

As she drove toward the hill, she considered their armament. They had a shotgun, a single-shot rifle, and several pistols. That wasn't much in the way of firepower if they had to fight off Indians. However, if it was only a small band of warriors menacing them, the Indians might think twice about pushing an attack once they'd been met with hot lead. Lucille didn't know. She had no idea how Indians fought—or how they thought, for that matter. They were as mysterious to her as Yankees.

Lucille glanced toward the distant bluff. She couldn't see the riders up there anymore, but that didn't mean they weren't there, watching and waiting for the best time to attack.

When the wagon reached the bottom of the hill, Lucille brought the vehicle to a stop. She studied the approach for several minutes and didn't see any way to get the wagon to the top of the slope. The trees were too close together, and the wagon wouldn't fit through the gaps between the trunks.

Allen Carter reached the same conclusion. "We'll have to unhitch the team and leave the wagon here," he prompted. "We can lead the mules up the hill and tie them to the trees on top."

"What if the Indians sneak up and steal things out of the wagon?" Mildred asked.

"We'll take everything we have to have to the top of the hill with us," Lucille said. "If we lose the rest of it, then so be it."

"You're right, Mrs. Brannon," Carnevan said. "And in my opinion, our scalps are the most important things of all."

"You think the Indians are gonna try to scalp us?" Fred's excited tone disappeared, replaced by worry.

Carter said firmly, "Nobody's goin' to get scalped, son." He started to climb down from the seat, moving somewhat awkwardly because of his wooden leg. "Fred, I want you to help me unhitch these mules. Be careful, though. You know how contrary they are. They'll up and bite you if you don't keep an eye on 'em and watch what you're doin'."

Lucille knew that giving Fred a chore was the best means of getting his mind off their danger. She jumped from the wagon box to the ground, knowing that if she hesitated, Phin Carnevan was liable to try to help her. She didn't need that distraction right now.

She went to the back of the wagon, pushed the canvas aside, and reached in to grab a sack of flour in one hand and a bag of beans in the other. From the front of the wagon, Mildred suggested, "Better take a pistol with you, dear."

Lucille nodded in agreement and put the beans down. She leaned farther into the wagon and plucked a Colt navy revolver off a built-in shelf instead. It was fully loaded. They had taken to leaving all the weapons like that ever since the wagon rolled

out of Fort Worth, which was pretty much the last bastion of civ-
ilization in this part of the state.

Carnevan appeared beside her and picked up the beans,
along with several sides of bacon wrapped in oilcloth and burlap.
He wore his pistol in a holster strapped around his waist, so he
had both hands free. She would have to get a holster like that
one of these days, Lucille told herself. It was certainly a more
convenient way to carry a gun.

It struck her then just how far she had come from the opu-
lent salon of her father's riverboat. In those days, despite her
occasional tomboyish tendencies, she never would have considered carrying a gun.

But those were the days before violent times had forced her
to kill several men . . .

As the sun touched the horizon to the west and began to sink
below it, Lucille and her companions spent the next half-hour
unloading what they could from the wagon and carrying it to the
top of the hill. Carter and Fred brought the mules up, along with
the saddle horses, and tethered all the animals to the trees.
There was no water up here, but they had canteens and could
make do until morning. Nobody was particularly thirsty or
hungry anyway, but Lucille knew how quickly that would
change if they were besieged. After the time she had spent in
Vicksburg, she knew all about sieges.

Every chance she had, she looked all around, searching for
any sign of the Indians. She didn't see anything moving except,
from time to time, a squirrel. At this time of year, there weren't
even many birds around.

The trees were evergreens—cedars, she thought, or perhaps
junipers. She wasn't an expert on such things. They grew in
ragged formations that covered most of the hill. At the top, the
hill flattened into an area of perhaps twenty feet by forty feet.
Several of the trees up here were dead and had fallen over. Allen
Carter studied them for a moment then said, "Looks like light-
ning got them."

"Perhaps we can use the trunks for cover if need be," Carnevan suggested.

Carter rubbed his jaw in thought and nodded. "If the Indians come, best we stop 'em before they ever get up here." His broad face was red from exertion. Climbing up and down the hill had not been easy for him with the peg leg.

The sun was down by this time, and shadows began to close in under the trees. A cold wind whipped the top of the hill. Mildred asked, "Can we make a fire?"

"I don't see why not," Carter replied. He left unspoken what the rest of them, with the exception of Fred, were thinking. The war party already knew they were there. A fire wouldn't give them away.

The dead trees all around them provided plenty of dry wood. Within minutes Carter had a blaze going in the shallow depression in the ground that had been left where one of the trees had been uprooted. The five of them gathered around it for warmth as well as for the sense of comfort provided by the merry, dancing flames.

"Now what do we do?" Carnevan asked.

"Have something to eat then wait for morning to get here, I guess." Again Carter left something unspoken, but Lucille knew what else they would be doing.

Praying that the Indians did not attack . . .

MILDRED FRIED bacon and made biscuits. Carnevan and Carter stood guard while Lucille talked to Fred and kept his mind off the danger. She even tried to make a game out of looking for things moving around in the dark, figuring that having two more pairs of eyes watching for trouble couldn't hurt anything.

When the food was ready, they took turns eating, although no one except Fred had much of an appetite. Mildred put more wood on the fire, keeping it built up. Everyone was tired and on edge, but despite their efforts to stay alert, it was Fred who noted the first sign of something about to happen.

"Pa," he said, "I think I hear somebody comin'."

Lucille had sat down earlier on one of the fallen logs. Now she stood up, her senses straining to see if she could hear something, too. After a few seconds, she heard the faint thud of a horse's hooves.

No, she quickly realized. The sound came from more than a single horse. There were several down there, perhaps as many as a dozen. Lucille's heart thudded heavily in her chest. If there was a fight, their small party would be outnumbered by far more than two to one.

She struggled to bring her fear under control. She had faced peril before, sometimes with Cory at her side, but sometimes not. The first time she had ever killed a man, she had been alone, with only herself to depend upon. At least tonight she had friends with her, good friends.

Phin Carnevan moved closer to her. "They're down there, all right," he said quietly. "Mrs. Brannon . . . Lucille . . . whatever happens tonight, I want you to know—"

Whatever he wanted her to know would have to remain unsaid, because at that moment, a voice shouted from the bottom of the hill, "Hello, the camp! All right for a bunch of Texans to come up and sit a spell with you?"

Lucille's knees suddenly went weak with relief. She made an effort to stiffen them and keep herself from collapsing. Around the fire, there were similar reactions. Mildred pressed a hand to her breast and uttered, "Oh, my." The simple words sounded like a prayer of thanksgiving. Carter blinked, swallowed, and dragged the back of his hand across his mouth. Carnevan's face remained impassive.

Fred said, "They're not Indians after all." He managed to sound vaguely disappointed.

Carter cupped a hand to his mouth and shouted back, "Come on up, but come slow and easy!" He looked over at the others and added quietly, "They may not be Indians, but we still can't be sure they're peaceable."

As if the spokesman for the newcomers had heard Carter, the man called, "Sure thing, mister, but you don't have to worry. We aren't looking for trouble."

The five people on the hilltop stood there waiting, guns in hands, as the strangers climbed the slope, leading their horses. The first man to reach the top and walk into the circle of firelight was tall, broad-shouldered, barrel-chested. He wore denim trousers, a thick flannel shirt, a cowhide vest, and a high-crowned black hat. His face was weathered but friendly. He nodded and smiled. "Evenin', folks. Saw your wagon down below and figured you might've come up here to fort up. Have you seen any Indians?"

"We sure did," Carter replied, acting as spokesman for the group. "They were on top of a bluff over yonder, not long before dusk." He waved toward the west, indicating the direction where they had seen the Indians.

The newcomer nodded. "Yep, that's one of their usual look-out spots." Behind him, several roughly dressed men appeared with their horses. All the strangers were well armed. Each man had at least one pistol, and some of them carried rifles as well. The leader went on, "Name's Griffin, Jim Griffin. I'm a captain in the Texas Rangers, and these boys are part of my troop."

Lucille's relief grew even stronger. She counted ten men, including Captain Griffin. The Texas Rangers were known for being fierce fighters, and surely any war party would think twice about attacking such a large group of them. Perhaps if the rangers were heading toward the Brazos River, she and her companions could accompany them the rest of the way.

"I'm Allen Carter. That's my boy Fred over there, and the other fella's Phin Carnevan. These ladies are Mrs. Thompson and Mrs. Brannon."

"Ladies," Griffin murmured as he politely touched the brim of his hat. "If I may be so bold, where are your husbands?"

"Fighting for the South," Mildred replied, her chin lifting with pride.

"That's right," Lucille added.

Griffin nodded. "Well, I'll pray that the good Lord watches over 'em until the war is over. In the meantime . . ." He turned his head and spoke to one of the other rangers. "Curt, see to posting some sentries. Those Indians these folks saw were probably scouts from Black Sky's bunch."

"Sure thing, Cap'n," the ranger responded.

"Black Sky?" Carter said.

Griffin nodded. "Comanche war chief. He's been raiding in these parts the past couple of weeks. Got a good-sized bunch of warriors with him."

"They won't bother us now that you're here, will they?" Lucille asked hopefully.

"Wish I could guarantee that, ma'am. But from the reports we've heard, Black Sky has forty or fifty warriors with him. I don't reckon Comanche'll be too scared of a single patrol of rangers."

The fear came back inside Lucille at Griffin's words. It looked like they were still in danger and couldn't relax after all. Still, having Griffin and the rangers with them at least increased the odds of survival.

Or maybe it was just a matter of being able to put up a slightly better fight before the Comanches overran them and murdered them all.

THE RANGERS had some coffee with them, real coffee, not the roasted-grain substitute. Lucille had no idea where they had gotten such a precious commodity, but she didn't ask questions. She just felt grateful that the Texans were willing to share. The coffee smelled heavenly as it brewed in a battered tin pot over the fire. It tasted even better when she sipped it from a steaming cup a short while later.

122 • *James Reasoner*

Griffin sat down at a respectable distance on the log beside her. Lucille asked, "Do you have a regular ranger post in this area, Captain?"

"No ma'am, we sort of use my ranch as our headquarters. It's called the JG Connected, and it's over yonder a ways to the west, on the Brazos."

"The Brazos River?" she asked, feeling excitement quicken inside her.

"Yes ma'am. El Brazos de Dios . . . 'The Arms of God,'" as the Spanish folks who came through here a long time ago first called it. The longest, prettiest river in Texas, with some of the best farming and ranching land along it you'll ever find. If things around here ever get tamed down a mite, you'll see this country grow up in a hurry."

She nodded. "I've heard a lot about the Brazos River. My husband used to talk about it all the time. He knew someone in the army who came from here, and that man told Cory all about what a great country it was."

Griffin looked sharply at her. "Cory Brannon? That'd be your husband, ma'am?"

"That's right." Lucille gave a little laugh. "He goes by Cory, but his real name is—"

"Coriolanus Troilus Brannon," Griffin finished for her before she could go on.

Lucille almost dropped her cup, which would have wasted the rest of the coffee and been a real shame. She stared at the burly ranger captain for a moment, so surprised that she was unable to speak. Finally, when she could, she asked, "How in heaven's name did you know that?"

"Pie told me," Griffin replied.

Lucille stared even harder. "Pie?" she repeated. "Pie Jones?"

Griffin nodded. "One and the same. The big fella is also part of this troop. He's not with us on this patrol because he and his wife are looking after a ranch down south of my place. Spread belonged to a family named Harrigan, only the Comanches got

all of them except a youngster called Tad. Pie and Miss Rachel
have taken over running the place and looking after the boy. I
reckon the ranch is as much theirs now as it is Tad's. Pie rides
with us when he can, but he's a mite shorthanded with just his
wife and the boy to help him run the spread."

Lucille was amazed at the coincidence that had brought her
and her companions in contact with these men who were friends
with Cory's old friend Pie. And yet it wasn't that much of a coincidence, she realized as she thought about it. When Pie and
Rachel left Louisiana heading for Texas, Pie had heard a lot
about the Brazos River country from Cory. With the war and all,
there weren't that many settlers out here. It made sense that
people who were acquainted would stand a good chance of running into each other.

"Pie talks a lot about his old pard' Cory," Griffin went on.
"He's mighty proud of the way the two of them helped set up
that supply line from East Texas over to Vicksburg."

"My Uncle Charles was in charge of that," Lucille said.
"Aunt Mildred is his wife."

Griffin nodded. "Yes ma'am, I remember Pie talking about
Colonel Thompson, too. Well, I'm more pleased than ever that
we happened along. We can ride with you on over to the river
and see that you get to the Harrigan place safely."

"Assuming that this Black Sky and his war party don't wipe
us out."

"Well, there's that." Griffin looked a bit surprised by the
bluntness of her comment. "But I reckon you always have to
hope for the best."

"I used to . . . until I spent some time in Vicksburg."

"Pretty bad, was it?"

"Bad enough," Lucille said. She was certain she would never
forget the hunger and disease that had gripped the city as it lan-
guished under the siege laid by U. S. Grant's army. Nor would
she forget the incessant pounding of the Yankee artillery and the
way the inhabitants of the doomed city had been forced to cower

in caves under the houses as that devastation rained down on them from the heavens . . .

But she didn't have to dwell on those evil memories, she told herself with a little shake of her head. Instead, she asked, "How are Pie and Rachel?"

"Why, they're doing just fine. Pie's turned out to be a good ranger, and I'll reckon he'll be a fine rancher, too. And Miss Rachel looks after Tad and works right at Pie's side . . . well, as much as she can, anyway, since she came down with her, ah, delicate condition."

Despite the threat of impending attack, Lucille couldn't help but smile as she exclaimed, "Rachel's expecting?"

"Yes ma'am. I reckon her being in the family way is one more reason she'll be happy to see you and Mrs. Thompson. I don't have a whole heap of experience in that area, you understand, but I figure a lady likes to have other ladies around her at a time like that."

"Yes, indeed," Lucille agreed. She hoped Rachel was pleased about the situation. Rachel deserved to be happy. She had had to endure so much unhappiness in her life . . .

Born on a plantation near Baton Rouge, the daughter of the plantation's owner and an octoroon slave, Rachel's red hair and fair skin made her appear just as white as anyone else. But in the eyes of the law—as well as in the eyes of most people in the South—she was still a slave. After the death of the man who had sired her, the plantation owner's widow had sold her, not wanting to keep such a blatant reminder of her husband's infidelity around the place. Rachel had wound up belonging to a tavern owner named Grat in northwestern Louisiana.

Lucille didn't know all the details of the degradation through which Grat had put Rachel. She didn't want to know. All that mattered was that Rachel was a fine person and Pie loved her, so he and Cory had helped her get away from Grat. When the tavern keeper showed up later looking for Rachel and had threatened to take her back with him, all of them, Lucille included, had helped Pie and Rachel escape. The two of them had ridden away, bound for Texas, and that was the last Lucille had seen or heard of them. It was wonderful news to find out that they were alive and doing well.

It would be even more wonderful if she could see them soon . . . but that was pretty much up to Black Sky and his war party.

Curt came over to the log where Lucille and Griffin sat and reported, "Ever'thing's quiet, Cap'n. No sign o' hostiles."

Griffin grunted. "That's about what I expected. Black Sky probably has a pretty good idea that these folks saw him earlier. He knows they will have told us, and he knows we'll be watching for him. That's why he'll wait until later, when he thinks we won't be as alert."

"I've heard it said that Indians won't attack at night," Lucille commented.

"They'll attack whenever it suits them best, day or night," Griffin said. "But it's true that some of them prefer not to fight in the dark. They think if they're killed, their spirits will have a harder time finding where they're going."

"That's why some fellas like to shoot a Comanche's eyes out once he's dead," Curt put in. "Blinds him in the spirit world."

Lucille looked up at the lanky, lantern-jawed ranger, somewhat horrified not only by what Curt had just said but also the nonchalant way in which he had said it. But she realized that these men lived in a violent world and had no doubt grown accustomed to death and horror.

Sort of like the rest of the South over the past four years.

Griffin noted her reaction. He said, "That'll be enough, Curt. I want four men on guard all night."

"Yes sir. Carter and that Englisher have offered to pitch in and stand their turn, so we got enough men for that."

"I can stand guard if I need to," Lucille offered.

Griffin shook his head. "No ma'am, that won't be necessary. In fact, if you and Mrs. Thompson want to go ahead and bed down now, that'd be just fine. It's a shame there's no way to get that wagon of yours up here so the two of you could be just a mite warmer."

"We'll roll up in blankets. I'm sure we'll be fine."

Griffin stood up and touched the brim of his hat again. "Yes ma'am. Sleep well."

"Thank you, Captain," she said, but she thought the same thing she had earlier.

How well she slept on this night was pretty much up to a Comanche war chief called Black Sky . . .

Chapter Eight

T HE TEMPERATURE CONTINUED TO drop, the wind whistling down from the north across the Texas plains. Lucille wrapped herself in several blankets, but the chill still seeped through and settled deep in her bones. The rangers let the fire go out—it would be easier to keep watch without it burning, Captain Griffin explained—but under the circumstances, Lucille didn't think it would have helped much, anyway.

Except for some high, patchy clouds, the sky was clear overhead. The stars shone with a brilliant luster, and there seemed to be millions of them scattered across the heavens. They gave off plenty of light, and when the moon rose as well, it was almost as bright as day. The moon was nearly full. Lucille found herself staring up at it, and that was what she was doing when she dozed off . . .

She didn't know how long she had slept when she opened her eyes next. The great glowing orb in the sky had shifted quite a bit, though, so she figured it was well after midnight. She wasn't sure what, if anything, had awakened her. Maybe just the cold. A shiver ran through her.

"Lucille?"

The whispered voice came from somewhere close by. She barely heard it over the snores that she knew came from Allen Carter. She turned her head and saw someone spreading a blanket on the ground next to her.

"I'm sorry if I woke you," the man said softly, and now she recognized his voice as belonging to Carnevan. "I just came off watch and thought I'd get some sleep."

"It's all right," Lucille told him, pitching her voice so quietly that it wouldn't disturb any of the others. Mildred lay curled up about ten feet away, and Fred Carter was on the other side of her. Fred's father lay just beyond him. The rangers were scattered around the clearing on top of the hill, except for the ones who were standing guard.

Carnevan stretched out on top of the blanket rather than rolling up in it. He wore a thick sheepskin coat, so he probably wasn't too cold. He pointed up into the sky. "See that?"

"What? The moon?"

"One of the rangers told me it's called a Comanche moon, because they like to raid by its light."

"That's comforting," Lucille said dryly.

Carnevan seemed not to notice the tone. "I'm told it's unusual for a war party like the one led by Black Sky to go on a raid in the middle of winter like this. Usually, the Indians stay close to their home villages during the winter and raid at the other times of the year. The fact that they're out now is a sign that their autumn buffalo hunt didn't go well."

"You've learned a lot."

"I wanted to keep my mind off of . . . things."

She didn't ask what things he meant. He was probably talking about the danger in which they found themselves, she told herself. If he was referring to something else . . . well, she didn't want to know about it.

Carnevan turned on his side so that he faced her. "Lucille . . . ," he began.

"It's very late," she said before he could go on. "And it's too cold to talk."

"Perhaps—"

"I think I'll go back to sleep now," she said. Whatever he was trying to say, she didn't want to hear it.

"All right," he said after a moment of awkward silence. "It'll be dawn in a couple of hours. You should rest while you can."

She rolled over, putting her back to him. Over the next few minutes she forced her breathing to become deep and regular, as if she had dozed off again. But in reality her eyes were wide open and her head was dizzy from the thoughts racing through it. For a second she had thought about how nice it would be to curl up under a thick layer of blankets with Phin Carnevan holding her. It would be warm, or at least not so cold, and it had been so long since she had experienced the pleasure of having a man's arms around her.

But she didn't need just any man's arms around her, she reminded herself. She needed Cory to hold her. And until he returned to her, she had to deny herself the pleasure of being embraced. Resolution grew stronger within her. Perhaps it was wrong to ignore the situation that had developed, she decided. It might be better to have a long talk with Phin and bring everything out into the open. The more she thought about it, the more she felt that that was the correct course of action. They both needed to air out their feelings, so that they could put all that behind them and be good friends. She would definitely have a talk with him, she vowed.

Assuming, of course, that they lived through the night.

THE COMANCHES didn't wait until dawn. They came a half-hour before that.

The moon hung low on the horizon, and the stars seemed to have lost their luster. The sky's earlier widespread brightness had now faded. Although the four rangers standing guard were awake, their eyelids were heavy. Even though they knew this was the most dangerous part of the night, the human body had its limits. Staying awake and alert was almost impossible.

The Comanches knew that, too.

Lucille gasped and sat up, fighting against the blankets that enveloped her. The flat crack of the rifle shot that had awakened her still echoed across the landscape. Somewhere close by, a pistol roared and a man cursed. More rifles blasted, and a high-pitched shout seemed to freeze the blood in Lucille's veins.

Finally, she succeeded in throwing the blankets aside. A pistol lay on the ground close beside her. She had placed it there before she went to sleep. Now she felt around frantically, trying to locate the weapon.

As her fingers closed around the smooth walnut grips of the gun, a hand came down hard on her shoulder. She screamed and twisted around, bringing up the gun, but she couldn't seem to find the trigger.

That was a good thing, she realized a second later as Phin said from above her, "Stay down, Lucille!" He knelt at her side. His other hand gripped a pistol.

All around the top of the hill, the rangers were firing on the Comanches. "Make your shots count, boys!" Griffin bellowed. A moment later, Lucille heard the familiar roar of a shotgun and knew that Allen Carter had joined the fight.

A couple of shapes scuttled across the clearing toward them. One reached out to grasp Lucille's free hand. "Are you all right?" Mildred asked as she squeezed Lucille's fingers.

"Yes," Lucille said. "Is Fred with you?"

"Yes, he's scared."

Fred clapped his hands over his ears and wailed, "It's loud, it's loud! Why do they keep shooting?"

Mildred put her other arm around the young man's shoulders and drew him closer. "There, there," she said. "It'll be all right. You'll see, Fred. Everything will be fine."

The two women and Fred huddled together next to one of the fallen trees. Carnevan got to his feet and stood over them in a protective stance. He held the pistol ready to fire if any of the attackers made it through the circle of defenders at the top of the hill.

The firing continued, hot and heavy. Lucille wished she could get a better look at what was going on, but at the same time, she knew she would be in even more danger if she was where she could see. For the moment all she and Mildred could do was wait and comfort Fred.

Suddenly, one of the rangers cried out and fell backward. He sprawled on the ground and lay still. Even in the poor light,

Lucille could see the dark pool that spread around his head. She bit her lip to fight off the horror. She couldn't let herself succumb to her feelings. In the midst of danger like this, emotion was an enemy, too. She had to think clearly and calmly, so she would know what to do if she had to take action.

From the sounds of the firing, the attack came from all sides of the hill at once. The Comanches had surrounded the height before they attacked. At least one of the rangers had been killed, so that left a maximum of ten men to defend the hilltop. And that was too big an area, Lucille thought. There had to be gaps through which a warrior might come.

A rush of footsteps sounded on the other side of the log. Phin turned toward the noise. Lucille came up on her knees, pulling away from Mildred. She leaned forward, resting both arms on the top of the log as she gripped her right wrist with her left hand to steady the pistol. As she drew back the hammer she saw shadowy figures charging toward them. For an instant she hesitated, not wanting to accidentally shoot one of the Texans, but then she noticed the feathers worn as decoration on the heads of the men. Holding her breath, she squeezed the trigger.

Carnevan fired an instant before Lucille, but the shots were so close together they sounded like one. At the same time, one of the Indians fired, orange flame gushing from the muzzle of a rifle. Lucille didn't know where the Comanche's bullet went, but she wasn't hit and since Phin didn't cry out, she assumed he wasn't either.

The attackers stumbled, though. One warrior went to his knees; the other pitched forward on his face. The one who was still upright tried to bring his rifle to bear on the people behind the log. Lucille expected Phin to shoot at him, but when she glanced to her right she saw that the Englishman was down, too. She hadn't even heard him fall.

She didn't know how badly Carnevan was hurt and didn't have time to check him. Instead, moving as quickly and smoothly as she could, she cocked the pistol again, lined the barrel on the wounded Comanche, and pressed the trigger. The gun bucked against her palm as it blasted out the shot. The Indian jerked backward and collapsed before he could fire a second time.

If Phin was dead, at least his murder had been avenged, Lucille thought, but that was scant comfort at a time like this. Breathing hard, her pulse hammering inside her head, she drew the revolver's hammer back again and kept the weapon trained on the edge of the hill, just in case any more Comanches scrambled to the top of the slope.

"Aunt Mildred," she said tensely without looking around, "Phin's hit! Can you see to him?"

"He's alive, Lucille," Mildred replied. "Seems to be breathing all right."

Lucille drew a shuddery breath. That was something anyway. She still had no way of knowing how badly Carnevan was wounded.

The shooting began to die away. After a few more minutes of sporadic fighting, Griffin called, "Hold your fire, rangers!" No more gunfire rang out.

"Reckon they're gone, Cap'n?" Curt asked from the other side of the hilltop.

"I don't know. You can never assume anything where those devils are concerned. Stay alert, boys. Who's hit?"

Several men replied but downplayed their injuries, insisting the wounds were nothing more than scratches. Curt grimly reported, "Hudson's dead, Cap'n. So's Jellicoe. They got him first. One o' the sons o' bitches slipped up and cut his throat."

"So we lost two good men," Griffin said.

"And Black Sky lost a dozen or more, I'll bet a hat on that. That's why he turned tail and run."

"We'll see," Griffin said. "It'll be light soon. Let's just hang on until then."

With the rangers ready to fight and keeping watch as the sky turned gray with the approach of dawn, Lucille thought it was safe to turn her attention to Carnevan. She put the gun down and knelt beside him, opposite from Mildred. Fred Carter sat nearby, rocking back and forth a little as he talked to himself in a soft voice. Lucille couldn't make out the words. At least he was calm.

She ran her hands over Phin's body, searching for wounds. Under other circumstances, it would have been uncomfortable and awkward for her to touch him like that, not to mention highly improper. Propriety took a back seat to necessity, though. She didn't find any blood on his clothes, which was a bit puzzling. What had happened to him?

"I think it's his head," Mildred said, as if she had heard the question in Lucille's mind.

Catching her breath in fear that Carnevan was badly injured, Lucille's fingertips explored his head. She found a sticky wetness that had to be blood in his hair, above and a little ahead of his right ear. Her fingers searched more and discovered a welt from which the blood had oozed. She realized that the Comanche's bullet had creased the Englishman's skull. She probed around the injury and thought that the slug hadn't done any more damage, but she couldn't be sure. She was no doctor. She hoped, though, that getting barked by the bullet like that hadn't done anything more than knock him out.

Griffin came over and hunkered on his heels. "How bad is Carnevan hit?" he asked.

"Not too bad," Lucille replied. "At least, I hope not. It looks like the bullet just creased his head and knocked him out."

"Better keep an eye on him," Griffin advised. "Getting hit on the head is a tricky injury. Sometimes it doesn't seem too bad, but it's worse than it looks."

"We'll hope for the best."

Griffin nodded. "Nothing wrong with that."

Allen Carter came over holding the shotgun. He put his hand on Fred's shoulder. "Are you all right, son?"

Fred looked up at him. "I . . . I'm all right now, Pa. But I sure was scared when those Indians came. It wasn't fun. It wasn't fun at all."

"No, it wasn't fun at all," Carter said as he squeezed the young man's shoulder. "And I was scared, too."

Fred stared at his father. "You were scared, Pa? You? I didn't think anything ever scared you."

"I sure was. I couldn't let it stop me from doing what I had to do, though."

Curt was standing close enough to overhear the conversation. "That's right, Fred," he added in his twanging voice. "I reckon the bravest feller is the one who's scared the most but goes on anyway."

Fred nodded and used the back of his hand to wipe away some tears on his cheeks. "I'll remember that," he said.

A few feet away, Phin Carnevan suddenly stirred, letting out a groan as he did so. Lucille leaned forward and rested a hand on his shoulder to keep him still. "Don't move, Phin," she told him. "You've been wounded."

His eyes blinked open, and as she saw him staring up at her in confusion, Lucille realized that the sky had lightened enough now for her to see more clearly. "Wha . . . what h-happened?" Carnevan asked.

"You were hit by a bullet," she said. "It grazed your head. But I think you're all right. You were just knocked out."

Carnevan closed his eyes again. "It hurts like blazes," he said in a stronger voice.

Griffin patted his other shoulder and advised, "You just take it easy for a spell, Carnevan. You've got a couple of good nurses looking after you."

"The . . . the Indians . . . ?"

"Gone, at least for now. And I'm hoping we did enough damage to them that Black Sky won't come back and risk any more men."

That was a hope Lucille fervently shared.

Dawn arrived quickly, the sun poking its head above the eastern horizon. When the rangers scanned the countryside around the hill, they didn't see any Indians anywhere. Several men went down to check on the wagon, and they reported that the vehicle was unharmed. "Reckon they figured on waitin' until after they'd done massa-creed us to loot it," Curt said.

"You folks were lucky all the way around," Griffin said. "And I reckon we were, too. You were a big help in fighting them off."

Lucille knew that she and Carnevan accounted for two of the Comanches. When she looked around, though, no bodies were in evidence except those of the two unfortunate rangers.

"The Comanch' take their dead and wounded with them when they break off an attack," Griffin explained when she asked him about it. "When they get the chance, they usually mutilate the bodies of the whites they kill, and I guess they're afraid we'll do the same to them."

"Like shooting out their eyes to blind them in the spirit world," she suggested.

Griffin shrugged. "Yes, that happens. So I guess they have a good reason for taking their dead with them, at least to their way of thinking."

By this time Carnevan had recovered enough to sit with his back propped against the log and sip a cup of coffee. When he was finished, Lucille knelt next to him and cleaned the shallow graze on his head. Carnevan winced as she did so, but he made no complaint. When she was done she tore a strip off her petticoat and bound it around his head as a bandage.

"I must look like a bloody pirate," he said with a chuckle.

"Naw, you ain't near as bloody as you was," Curt said. "Miz Brannon done cleaned off most of the blood."

Carnevan laughed again and didn't bother to explain the British vernacular. He put a hand on the log and pushed himself to his feet. "I think I can ride now," he declared. The rangers had saddled their horses in preparation for leaving. However, Phin swayed suddenly on his feet and nearly fell, catching himself with a hand on the fallen tree.

Griffin noticed and suggested, "You'd better ride in the wagon, Carnevan. Be better that way, and we can move faster."

The Englishman nodded in agreement, but Lucille could tell by his expression that he didn't like it.

A few minutes later, accompanied by several rangers, Carter and Fred took the mules down the hill and hitched them to the wagon again. Everyone had made a quick, cold breakfast, and the party was ready to move out as soon as one more chore was taken care of.

Some of the rangers had dug a pair of graves near the edge of the hilltop where there was a good view in several directions. Everyone gathered around and removed their hats. The two dead men, Hudson and Jellicoe, were wrapped in blankets and lowered gently and carefully into the graves.

Griffin stood beside the graves and offered a brief eulogy: "Lord, You've seen fit in Your great wisdom to call home a pair of the finest men to ever set foot in Texas. Al Hudson and Tom Jellicoe were good rangers and good friends, and everyone who ever knew them would say that they'd do to ride the river with. So, Lord, we all know that now they're riding the river with You. Watch over them, keep them safe, and anytime You get in a tussle with the devil, You just call on them, because they'll sure back Your play. Nothing left to say, Lord, except . . . amen."

"Amen," echoed the men gathered around the graves. Lucille, Mildred, and Fred wiped away tears, and Allen Carter and Phin Carnevan looked misty-eyed as well.

Most of the rangers stayed on the hill to fill in the graves and pile some rocks on top of them. Griffin went down the slope with Lucille and the others, explaining that they would carve headstones for the two men and return later to place them on the graves.

With the extra saddle horses tied behind the wagon, Carter took the reins and got the mule team moving. Lucille sat beside him while Carnevan and Mildred rode in the back. Several of the Texans stayed with the wagon; the others, true to their name, ranged out ahead and to the sides. Lucille still felt a little nervous, so she watched the landscape carefully, alert for any sign of return by Black Sky's war party. But except for the rangers, they might as well have been alone on the face of the earth.

Griffin kept everyone moving at a steady pace all day, pausing only when it was necessary to rest the animals. He explained to Lucille that he wanted to reach the Brazos by nightfall. He had the party swing to the southwest. "We'll head for the Harrigan place," he explained. "Since Pie and Rachel are friends of y'all's, I figured that was where you'd want to go."

"That sounds wonderful," Lucille agreed. "I'm looking forward to seeing them again."

Now that it was daylight, she could see the horses better, and she was especially impressed with the one that Griffin rode. Its hide was a beautiful copper color except for its face and legs, which were white, and some small white marks on each side of its belly. On the left side of the horse's neck was a white distinguishing mark shaped like an arrowhead. Its muscles moved with power and economy under the sleek sorrel hide.

When Lucille commented on the mount, Griffin looked pleased. He patted the animal's neck. "Yes ma'am, this old paint of mine is quite a horse. Name's Sizzle. We've been together for quite some time. One of these days we'll show you a few tricks I've taught him."

"I'd like to see that," Lucille said with a smile. She thought that if all Texans were like Griffin and Curt and the other rangers, she would be mighty glad her aunt and her friends had decided to head for the Brazos River.

Late in the afternoon Griffin pointed to a line of trees in the distance. "That marks the river," he said. "We'll be there before dark, just like I hoped."

Carter commented, "I never thought we'd get here without running into those Indians again."

"I reckon they've headed farther west, back to Comancheria. That's what they call the part of West Texas where their villages are. They'll hunker down and lick their wounds for a while." Griffin's normally jovial face grew solemn. "But I expect we'll see ol' Black Sky again sooner or later. As Curt says, you can bet a hat on that."

If Lucille never saw another hostile Comanche, that would be all right with her, she thought. But she supposed such threats were part of living out here. You had to take the bad with the good. It was that way no matter where a person lived. In the rest of the Confederacy, there had certainly been more bad than good over the past few years.

The sun had set, but the western sky was still filled with red light when the wagon came within sight of a sturdy-looking cabin about fifty yards from the river. It had two squarish rooms separated by an open area in between, with a single roof over the entire structure. A rock chimney rose at each end. Griffin pointed to the open area. "That's called a dogtrot. Most folks around here build their cabins like that."

Lucille nodded. She saw that a couple of the rangers had ridden on ahead. Their horses were tied to an upright post in front of the cabin. Several figures emerged from the cabin and gazed toward the approaching wagon and riders. Lucille felt a tingle of recognition go through her. Pie Jones was a massive individual, tall enough to tower over most men, and at first glance he seemed almost as broad as he was tall. Next to him, with his arm around her shoulders, stood a redheaded woman who could only be Rachel. Both of them waved an excited greeting toward the newcomers.

Lucille wanted to tell Carter to hurry, but she restrained the impulse. They would get there in due time.

When the wagon finally rolled to a stop in front of the cabin, Lucille fairly leaped down from the seat. Rachel rushed forward to embrace her, and Pie put his brawny arms around both young women. "Lucille, is it really you?" Rachel asked.

"It's me," she replied with a laugh as she returned the hug. She drew back a little and looked down at Rachel's gently rounded belly. "I heard the good news. Congratulations."

Rachel blushed in the fading light. "Thank you."

Pie looked down at both of them from his great height and grinned. "Dang, but it's good to see you, Lucille! Where's Cory?"

He knew immediately from her expression that he had said the wrong thing and started stuttering apologies. She stopped him. "No, it's all right, Pie. You couldn't have known."

Pie swallowed hard. "He ain't . . . he ain't dead, is he?"

Lucille shook her head. "No, I'm certain he's not. I'd know it if he was gone. I can feel that in my bones. But I don't know where he is or how he's doing."

"He's bound to be all right," Rachel said. "I didn't know Cory for that long, but I could tell that he knows how to take care of himself."

Remembering the wretched, pitiful wreck of a young man Cory had been the first time she'd seen him, Lucille knew that hadn't always been true. But Rachel was right: Over the past few years Cory had become a survivor.

"As soon as he can, he'll come out here and find us," Lucille said with a smile. "You remember, Pie, how he always talked about settling here on the Brazos."

"Yeah, I sure do. Reckon I beat him to it, but he'll still come." He turned and held out a hamlike hand toward a youngster with blond hair who stood shyly in the dogtrot behind them. "Come on up here, boy." As the teenager came forward, he introduced Tad Harrigan. "He lost his folks awhile back, so him and Rachel and me all sort of been lookin' out for each other."

Lucille smiled at the young man. "Hello, Tad."

"Ma'am." He ducked his head bashfully.

Pie clapped an affectionate hand on Tad's shoulder. "See that young feller there?" he asked, nodding toward Fred Carter. "His name's Fred, and he's an old pard' of mine. Why don't you help him get those horses unsaddled and in the corral?"

"Sure, Pie," Tad agreed, obviously happy to have some chore to do. He approached Fred and introduced himself. Within minutes the two young men were grinning and talking together as they led the horses away.

Meanwhile, Pie grabbed Allen Carter's hand, pumped it, then pulled the older man into a backslapping hug. "How you doin', Sarge?" Pie asked.

"I haven't been a sergeant in almost four years, and you know it," Carter said, but his smile took any sting out of the gruff-sounding words. "It's good to see you, Pie."

Pie moved on to Mildred, and he got as shy and bashful as Tad had been. "Howdy, Miz Thompson."

"Oh, come here and give me a hug, you big old bear," Mildred told him. With a grin, Pie did as she told him, his massive form dwarfing her petite one as he embraced her.

"I reckon the colonel's off with Cory?"

"I wouldn't be a bit surprised," Mildred said. "Those two have become inseparable."

"I never was much of a military man, but the colonel, he's about the finest officer I ever did see."

Mildred squeezed his arm. "Thank you, Pie."

Carnevan had climbed out of the wagon as well. Pie turned to him and stuck out a hand. "Don't reckon I know you, mister, but if you're travelin' with these fine folks, I'm mighty glad to meet you."

"Phineas Carnevan," the Englishman introduced himself as he shook hands. "But you can call me Phin."

"I'm Pie Jones, and this here's my wife, Rachel."

Carnevan bowed politely to Rachel. "The honor is entirely mine, madam."

Rachel laughed, a little flustered but pleased by Carnevan's fancy manners. She said, "All of you come on in the house. I'll have supper on the table in just a little while." Looking over at Griffin, she added, "That goes for you and the rest of the boys, too, Cap'n Jim."

"Much obliged, ma'am," Griffin said. "I think we'll be a mite crowded if all of us try to squeeze into that cabin, though."

"Don't worry about that. We'll manage." Rachel looked at Lucille and the others. "You brought us our friends. That's the best Christmas present anyone could ask for, even on the day after Christmas."

It was almost full dark now, but candlelight shone warmly through the gaps around the shutters on the cabin's windows. The night would be cold again, but Lucille knew they would all be warm and safe inside. Rachel was right, she thought.

Good friends were just about the best present anybody could want.

Chapter Nine

T HE TEMPERATURE IN THE Dakota Territory was well below freezing on Christmas Day 1864, but the weak, watery sunlight that washed over the parade ground at Fort Rice provided an illusion of warmth. Pvt. Nathan Hatcher, late of the U.S. Army, now a member of the First U.S. Volunteer Infantry Regiment, huddled in his greatcoat and watched the Stars and Stripes ascend the flagpole at the west end of the parade ground, directly in front of the office of Col. Charles A. R. Dimon, the commander of the regiment.

A week or so earlier Dimon had ordered the erection of the flagpole on the parade ground, but today was the first time the American flag had been raised over Fort Rice. To make it a special occasion, the colonel had invited Two Bears, the chief of the local Yanktonai Sioux, and all his people. They were considered friendly Indians, and while they were at the fort, they were given rations to help see them through the bitterly cold winter.

Just as the flag reached the top of the pole, a gust of wind swept across the parade ground. It caught the flag and unfurled it. Cheers rang out from the assembled soldiers as Old Glory flapped in the wind, its colors brilliant against the washed-out blue sky. Evidently caught up in the spirit of the moment, the Indians on their ponies yipped and shouted and pumped their feather-decorated lances in the air above their heads.

Nathan had to swallow hard as he looked up at the flag. He loved his country, and to see its glorious symbol flying, even here in this godforsaken wasteland called Dakota, moved something deep inside him. His love for the United States made it bitterly galling that some people still regarded him as an enemy of his country, a traitor who had turned against his own land.

Unable to support the Confederacy or to believe in slavery, Nathan had left Culpeper County, Virginia, to enlist in the Union army. He had abandoned his job as a law clerk and a potential career as an attorney. He had left behind as well the young woman he had believed he might come to love, Cordelia Brannon. His convictions had made him a pariah, but they were his and he could not deny them, even though, as a Southerner, he hadn't exactly been welcomed with open arms by the Yankees.

Through as strange a twist of fate as any he had ever heard of, he wound up in Confederate gray at the battle of Fredericksburg. The Union soldiers who had taken him prisoner had been unwilling to listen to him. To them he was a dirty Johnny Reb, and that was that. So they shipped him off to Camp Douglas, a prisoner-of-war camp near Chicago.

And that had almost been the death of him.

If Titus Brannon, one of Cordelia's brothers, hadn't wound up in the same prison, Nathan probably would have died at Douglas. It was Titus who taught him how to survive. After their escape together, Nathan had made it part of the way back to Virginia before he and Titus were separated, and he was recaptured. This time the Yankees had sent him to Rock Island, another notorious prison camp, and Nathan had been certain he would not live through another bout of captivity.

Rescue had come in an unexpected form. All he had to do was swear allegiance to the Union and join the army. The Yankees recruited hundreds of Confederate prisoners, swore them in, and sent them west to protect the frontier . . . since of course they didn't trust former Confederates to fight their own countrymen. These prisoners were called "Galvanized Yankees," and now Nathan Hatcher was one of them.

Colonel Dimon—small, handsome, and a bit of a martinet when he wanted to be—stood in front of the men and raised his voice to make a speech. "Let Fort Rice stand as a monument of what soldiers once Rebel, now Union, can do for the cause they have espoused," he said and continued for several more minutes of flowery rhetoric. Nathan paid little attention to what he was saying. He looked around the fort instead, taking note of the improvements that had been made during the past month. New officers quarters and new barracks for the enlisted men had been completed, along with a bathhouse. Dimon was a stickler for cleanliness and insisted that all the soldiers bathe once a week, even during colder weather, when ice had to be melted in huge pots over roaring fires to provide enough water for the men to wash.

Completing the improvements to the fort was only one of the tasks assigned to the First U.S. Volunteers. Using horses obtained from the Indians, they patrolled the area for hostiles. They also drilled frequently, and Dimon and his junior officers conducted a variety of classes on subjects ranging from tactics to discipline. The colonel believed in keeping his men busy. When they weren't in class or drilling or patrolling, they cleaned the fort from top to bottom. Although Dimon was not widely loved, no one in his command could deny that he ran things in a taut, efficient manner.

Once the flag-raising ceremony was over and Dimon finished his speech, the Indians were allowed to help themselves to the rations set out for them. Immediately, a small-scale frenzy broke out as the Yanktonai began to feast. Nathan had never seen anyone consume so much food and feared that the stomachs of some of them might actually burst.

He was sitting on a wagon tongue, balancing a plate on his knee, when Patrick and Elizabeth Cardwell came over to him. Elizabeth was the only woman at Fort Rice; one of the few women within a hundred miles, in fact. Somehow, at every step of the journey, she had convinced the colonel and the other officers to allow her to accompany her husband. Now she gave Nathan a friendly hug and a "Merry Christmas."

"Merry Christmas to the two of you as well," he replied, summoning up a smile. With a nod toward the feasting Indians, he added, "Quite a celebration, isn't it?"

Patrick chuckled. "Those lads are going to be sick at their bellies tomorrow, I'll wager. They're going at it like they want to pack away enough food to last them the entire winter, like a hibernating bear."

"I just hope they don't eat us out of house and home," Elizabeth said.

"There should be a supply train from Fort Sully sometime in the next couple of weeks," Nathan said. "I think we can last until then."

Elizabeth frowned worriedly. "But what if something happens to the wagons so they're delayed . . . or worse, don't get here at all?"

"Then I suppose we'll try to make it through the winter living on buffalo steaks, like the Indians," her husband said. "We might get a bit hungry, but I don't think we're likely to starve to death."

Perhaps not, Nathan thought, but more of them might die of dysentery. That ailment had proven already to be the most dangerous killer on these lonesome plains.

Elizabeth crossed her arms and hugged herself. "Well, spring can't get here soon enough to suit me. I'm tired of the cold weather. Besides, I'm hoping that more ladies will move into the area over the spring and summer. Being the only female amongst hundreds of males gets a bit tiresome. Perhaps even Mrs. Kelly will be released by her captors."

Nathan wasn't convinced that Fanny Kelly was still alive. The woman had been a member of a small wagon train of immigrants that had been attacked by Indians the previous summer. Kelly had been carried off along with several other captives. Recently Colonel Dimon had heard rumors from some of Two Bears' people that the band that held Kelly prisoner was in the area. Immediately, Dimon had led a patrol to search for her, but they'd had no luck in finding the woman. Nathan believed it was just as likely that the rumor was false and that Fanny Kelly, if she was still alive, was nowhere near Fort Rice.

He didn't say that to Elizabeth Cardwell, though. There was nothing wrong with having hope, whether it was justified or not.

Sometimes—especially during a long, cold Dakota winter—hope was one of the main things that kept a person going.

A COLD wind blew in Washington, D.C. Folks tended to forget that, at heart, Washington was a Southern city, Roman thought as he walked down the street with Joe Brackett. Right across the Potomac was Virginia, and Washington was only about 150 miles north of Richmond itself, the capital of the Confederacy. Southern or not, though, it could get mighty cold during the winter.

Only a week remained in the Year of Our Lord 1864. But despite the fact that it was Christmas Day, the business of governing the country and fighting a war went on. Plenty of folks were on the streets today . . . civilians in town clothes and bowler hats, soldiers in blue with yellow braid decorating their uniforms, ladies in long woolen dresses with gloves on their hands and fur mufflers wrapped around their throats. And many of those people, Roman noted, cast suspicious glances at the two well-dressed black men who walked among them.

"These folks all look like they want to ask us what the hell we're doing here," he muttered to Brackett.

Brackett grinned and rolled his cigar from one corner of his mouth to the other. "Noticed that, did you? Some of these Yankees may be full of high-flown talk about everybody being equal, but when they look at us, their faces still pinch up like some Georgia cracker's."

They turned into a side street near the Capitol and entered a building. After going through a foyer and climbing a narrow set of stairs, they came into a cramped office with a single grimy window. A coal-oil lamp hissed on the desk that took up most of the room.

An attractive black woman sat behind the desk with several ledgers spread open in front of her. She glanced up at Roman and Brackett, but only for a second. Then her eyes—an unusual but appealing shade of hazel—returned to scanning the columns of figures and the lists of names entered into the ledgers.

"Hello, Mary," Brackett said in greeting as he took off his hat and hung it on a nail by the door. "Hard at work, I see, even on Christmas Day."

"Somebody's got to do it," the woman said. "You may know just about everything there is to know about the West, Joe Brackett, but you don't know anything about arranging for wagons or buying supplies or putting together a list of travelers."

"Say, I've led more than one wagon train in my time!" Brackett looked a little offended, but Roman thought he was just putting on an act. Brackett liked to tease Mary Campbell.

That was her legal name, since she had been called Mary by her mother and had belonged to a man named Campbell, but those days were in the distant past. She was a free woman now, and she sometimes called herself Mary Lucky because, as she put it, she was a lucky woman to have been granted her freedom. Of course, it was only right that she was free, she usually went on to explain, because everybody deserved to be free, no matter what color his or her skin was. For several years she had worked for the Reverend Matthew Hanley, a renowned abolitionist preacher, first as his housekeeper and then, after he'd discovered that she could read and write and cipher, as his secretary and bookkeeper.

She had taken it hard when Roman and Brackett arrived in Washington and broke the news that Hanley was dead. For a time, she had been so grief-stricken that Roman had wondered if there had been something more than a business relationship between the two. As he got to know Mary better, he realized that wasn't true. She simply had a great deal of admiration for the man, and she shared his dream of taking a wagon train of freed black immigrants West to form their own community and seek their own destiny. Mary had feared that Brackett would abandon the plan, but he had assured her that he intended to follow through on Hanley's idea.

In the weeks since then, the three of them had worked together to organize the pilgrimage. Brackett had brought a death certificate signed by the St. Louis coroner so that the reverend's estate could be probated. Hanley's only living relative was an unmarried sister. She shared his abolitionist beliefs and had placed the inheritance in a trust to be used to finance the expedition. She had to sign all the documents involved with the preparations, but so far she had been completely cooperative.

Despite the fact that Brackett was a free man, most white businessmen were leery of entering into contracts with him. Roman knew that grated on Brackett, but the Westerner managed to keep his temper. This project in which they were all involved was too important to allow anyone's wounded pride to jeopardize it.

Roman had helped as much as he could. He knew how to read and write, although numbers were still somewhat mysterious to him. He helped Mary Lucky by carrying out whatever tasks she assigned to him.

Now, with a tired sigh, she closed the ledgers. "If nothing unexpected happens," she said, "I don't see why we can't leave as soon as the weather starts to improve. We have enough members signed up to take fifteen wagons west. The wagons will be delivered sometime in February to Independence, Missouri, and our supplies will be ready in March. You said April would be a good time to depart, Mr. Brackett?"

"That's right." Brackett propped a hip on a corner of Mary's desk. "Not too early in April, though. Sometimes you can get a spring storm on the Great Plains that'll drop a foot of snow on the ground. If we don't run into anything like that, we ought to reach Oregon sometime in late summer or early fall."

"What about Indians?" Roman asked.

Brackett looked at him and frowned. "What do you know about Indians?"

Roman reached under his coat and pulled out a rolled-up pamphlet of some sort. "I was reading this *Almanack*—"

154 • *James Reasoner*

"Let me see that." Brackett held out his hand.

Roman hesitated but gave the pamphlet to Brackett, who unrolled it and grinned at the garish illustration on the cover that showed a man in buckskins and a coonskin cap struggling with several painted, feather-bedecked savages. "This is one of those *Crockett's Almanacks*," Brackett said. "Don't you know all these stories are just made up, Roman?"

"They are?"

Brackett laughed and tossed the pamphlet back to him. "Pure fancy, dreamed up by fellas who don't have anything better to do and don't want to work at a real job. There are Indians out west, sure. I've seen plenty of them in my time. And some of them don't like white men."

Mary said, "Then they shouldn't bother us."

Brackett shook his head. "The Indians don't see it that way. To them, we may not be white but we might as well be, because we're not them. A lot of tribes have a name for themselves that translates to "the People." What that means is, they consider themselves the only real people. Nobody else counts."

"Like plantation owners," she said crisply.

"I never knew any plantation owners. What I'm getting at is that some of the Indians are hostile, some are friendly, and some don't really care one way or the other as long as they're left alone. The trick to crossing the plains is to know which ones are where and to avoid the ones who'd like to lift our hair." Brackett's smile widened. "I know the trick. I'll get us where we're going; don't worry about that." He leaned over and stacked up the ledgers. "Now Roman and I came down here to get you and take you back to the boarding house, Mary. It's Christmas. Ought to be some celebrating done."

The three of them had rooms in a boarding house that catered to freed blacks. Quite a few of the immigrants who would join the wagon train in Missouri lived there as well. When the time came, Roman thought, they would make quite a crowd on the train heading west to Independence. That town on the

Mississippi River was the jumping-off place for most of the wagon trains heading west across the plains.

The Mississippi River, the Great Plains, the Rocky Mountains . . . those were just words to Roman, not real places. Not yet. But soon, he thought as he left the office with Brackett and Mary, soon he would see them for himself, and they would become real. They were going to Oregon, and beyond Oregon was the Pacific Ocean itself. Imagine that. A black man who had been born and raised in Virginia, clear across the continent; a man who had, until the war came, figured that he would never set foot outside of Virginia; a man who still hadn't been anywhere else except across Maryland and a little ways into Pennsylvania and now in Washington City . . . that man might just wind up standing on a hill in Oregon and looking out at the Pacific Ocean.

Wouldn't that be something, now?

No one felt much like celebrating Christmas in the Shenandoah Valley . . . at least no one on the Confederate side, anyway. No doubt, Philip H. Sheridan probably thought it was a fine holiday, Mac Brannon told himself as he walked down the hill toward the large pasture where the regiment's horses were picketed. He had just emerged from the crude cabin he shared with Blaisdell, part of the winter quarters for Rosser's cavalry. A cold gray dusk settled on the land. Mac wanted to check on the stallion before full night fell.

Cabins, tents, and lean-tos were scattered across the hillside near the town of Staunton. Following the defeat at Cedar Creek, the remnants of Jubal Early's army had scattered, making it more difficult for the Yankees to pursue them. There had been some fighting at Waynesborough, but for the most part, what was left of the Confederate army in the Shenandoah Valley had successfully avoided engagements with the enemy.

And to tell the truth, the army now had other enemies in addition to the Yankees. They also had to fight disease, hunger, and desertion.

These once-rich lands had been scoured almost clean by Sheridan's fiery raids back in the fall. Yankee foragers—and, to be honest, Confederate scavengers too—had grabbed all the livestock and supplies they could. Some of the civilians in the valley remained on their farms, eking out a miserable existence, but many of them had abandoned their land and taken to the roads, seeking anyplace better than here. Unfortunately, in the South these days, there was no good place to go. The Yankees squeezed them on all sides, and everywhere the Yankees went, devastation followed. Some of the soldiers still talked about winning the war, but most of them didn't say much about that these days. Instead, they did a lot of sitting, huddling around campfires, staring at nothing. When they talked, it was of home and family and the things they had left behind, all the things that had been carried away and lost forever in the storm of war.

Some of them got to missing it so bad they went home, slipping away on dark nights without so much as a by-your-leave. Losing them was bad enough, but usually they took horses with them, too, and the cavalry really couldn't afford that. Not many of the men had tireless mounts like Mac's big, silver gray stallion, horses that could be ridden day after day with little rest and scant forage and still remain fresh and strong. Even the stallion was starting to look a bit gaunt these days, Mac thought, and his heart went out to the gallant animal every time he noticed that.

Maybe it was time they went home, too.

No sooner had the thought passed through Mac's mind than he quashed it. Brannons had plenty of faults: They were stubborn, opinionated, hot-tempered, restless. But they weren't quitters. Never had been. Once they started something, they saw it through to the end.

In this case, Mac didn't think the end was going to be long in coming. With this cold, wet, miserable winter holding Virginia in its grip, there hadn't been much fighting lately. Down south of Richmond, the siege of Petersburg continued, with occasional attacks and counterattacks but nothing really settled. When spring came, though, Grant wouldn't be satisfied with just sitting in the trenches in front of Petersburg. He would find some way to force the issue. Every spring for the past three years, Grant had launched a campaign. Mac didn't expect the spring of 1865 to be any different.

He nodded to one of the guards posted near the horses. "Evenin', Major," the man said then broke into a fit of coughing. The wracking spasms shook him for more than a minute. He wiped a hand across his mouth. "Sorry, sir."

Mac saw dark streaks on the man's hand and knew they were blood coughed up by the soldier. "You're sick, son," he said. "You shouldn't be on duty."

"Tell that to the sergeant of the guard . . . sir."

Mac didn't blame the man for sounding a little insubordinate. Under the circumstances, he was willing to overlook the infraction. Yet he viewed his willingness to do so as just one more indication that he wasn't a soldier at heart. A real officer would have cracked down on a trooper who spoke to him like that, no matter what the circumstances.

"Carry on," Mac said curtly. He strode across the pasture toward his horse.

The stallion whickered a soft greeting as Mac came up. He patted the big horse on the shoulder and said quietly, "How are you doing, fella?" The stallion turned his head and bumped his nose affectionately against Mac's arm.

For long minutes, Mac stood there talking to the stallion . . . talking about the war, about his home and family, about the way the stallion had shown up so mysteriously on the Brannon farm and had seemed to taunt Mac for months before Mac finally caught him. That was only a little over three years in the past, but it seemed much longer to Mac. It seemed as if the war had been going on forever and that it would never end, which was odd, he realized, because only a short time earlier he had been thinking about how the conflict couldn't possibly continue for much longer. The war loomed so hugely over men's lives that it affected everything, even their perception of time. In fact, Mac had no idea how long he had been standing in the cold field, talking to his horse.

Some people would think he was crazy. Titus, for one. Even when they were boys, Titus had thought that his older brother Mac was a little unbalanced because of the way Mac roamed the woods and spoke to all the animals just like they could understand what he was saying. Titus spent time in the woods, too, but he always took a rifle with him and went there to hunt and to kill. Craziness went both ways, Mac thought. He had never been able to understand what satisfaction Titus got out of hunting, other than meat for the table. Mac had no objection to that. But he just couldn't comprehend the pleasure Titus seemed to take from the crack of a rifle, the kick of the recoil against his shoulder, the stinging smell of the powder smoke. And the sight of an animal bleeding and kicking out its life on the ground . . . When he was a boy, the mere thought of hunting had made Mac feel a little sick.

Well, he had seen plenty of death since then, he told himself as he closed his eyes and leaned his head against the stallion's shoulder for a moment. He had seen countless men and horses die. He had killed men himself, so many that he no longer knew how many human lives he had ended, how many beloved sons and brothers, husbands and fathers he had turned into nothing more than meat rotting in the ground. He shuddered as he tried to push the awful thoughts out of his head.

The hissed curse behind him broke him out of his reverie.

He turned sharply and saw three men standing in the darkness. Night had fallen, and he had only now noticed. Another Christmas Day was gone, fled almost without notice.

"Sorry, sir," one of the men said. "We didn't see you over here. Didn't mean to disturb you."

Mac drew a ragged breath. "That's all right." He hadn't recognized the man's voice. "What outfit are you with?"

"Don't tell him," one of the other men cautioned the first. "He's an officer."

Mac stiffened. Why would these men want to conceal their identities, unless . . . ?

"Damn it!" the first man swore in reply. "Now you've gone and done it."

Mac saw the second man move and heard the sound of a pistol being cocked. "It don't matter. Soon as he saw us, we had to kill him."

"You're deserting," Mac accused.

"You're damned right! We ain't a-gonna stay here and starve to death. Old Jubilee won't never whip the Yankees. There ain't no point in it no more."

"So what are you going to do? Go home?"

The third man laughed. "My home's in Winchester. I never even got to see my wife and my little boy when the Yankees chased us through there. I can't go home."

"So you'll be a deserter and a bummer and scavenge off your own people?" Mac didn't bother trying to keep the righteous anger out of his voice.

"A man's got to live," the second man answered, still pointing the pistol at Mac. "Got to do whatever he has to, to get by."

Mac squared his shoulders. He was angry with these men, but he was angry with himself, too, because only a few minutes earlier he had almost been willing to give up, just like them. "You're not going anywhere," he said. "One pistol shot and you'll have everyone in the camp up and about. The guards will come to see what's wrong."

"We paid off the closest sentry to let us through. We'll get away. But there won't be no shootin'."

Mac started toward the hillside camp. "You can't stop me without shooting me."

"The hell we can't. Doolittle, use your knife!"

One of the figures suddenly lunged. Mac knew how much danger he was in. If the men could kill him quietly, without raising an uproar, they stood a good chance of slipping away from the camp and taking some good horses with them when they deserted. Mac couldn't allow that to happen. He twisted desperately aside as the man thrust the knife at him.

The blade went harmlessly between Mac's left side and left arm. He clamped his arm down, trapping the attacker's forearm. He twisted farther and threw his hip into the man's midsection, just like he was back home wrestling with one of his brothers on the grassy bank of Dobie's Run. With a startled yelp, the man came up off his feet as Mac continued to pivot. The deserter flew through the air and landed hard on his back.

A rush of feet behind him warned Mac. He tried to turn but managed only to get his head out of the way of the clubbed revolver that swept down in a blow that would have crushed his skull had it connected. As it was, the butt of the gun smashed into the top of his shoulder. Ice and fire burst simultaneously through Mac's left arm, and then the arm went completely numb. He could no more feel it than if it had fallen off his body.

The deserters didn't want to risk a shot, and that was still to Mac's advantage. He lowered his head and bulled forward, butting the man with the revolver in the chest. The collision knocked the man backward. He struggled to keep his feet but failed. His balance gone, he fell to the ground hard enough to knock the air out of his lungs and leave him lying there gasping for breath.

Mac's right arm still worked just fine. That hand went to the flap of his holster and jerked it open. He drew the revolver and swung it up to point it at the third man, who shifted nervously back and forth, trying to make up his mind whether or not to run. As the barrel of the gun came in line, he decided. He thrust his arms into the air. "For God's sake, don't shoot, sir!"

Just then the first man, the one with the knife, tried to get to his feet. He barely made it to his knees before the stallion's low-

ered head slammed into the small of his back and knocked him
forward. This time his face landed on the ground first, stunning
him. He lay there groaning softly.

Mac took several quick steps back and swung the revolver
from side to side, covering the other two men. The one who'd hit
Mac with the gun had dropped the weapon when he fell. He
reached for the gun, and Mac warned him, "Touch it, and I'll kill
you." The gentle young man who talked to animals was gone,
replaced now by the hard-bitten cavalry officer Mac had become.

"Wh-what are you gonna do?" asked the man who had surrendered without a fight.

"Turn you over to General Rosser," Mac snapped. "He can
decide whether or not to execute you."

"We . . . we didn't actually desert—"

"No, you just attacked and tried to murder me." Mac shook
his head. "I don't think that'll get you much sympathy."

"It's not fair!" whined the man still on the ground. "We can't
win the damned war, not any more! Why do we have to keep
fightin'?"

"Because this is Virginia," Mac said. "Because this is our
home, and the Yankees don't belong here."

Because there was nothing else they could do except surrender, and the politicians and the generals weren't ready to do that
yet, Mac thought. Their pride—and perhaps some misplaced
hope for a miracle—still made them shy away from taking that
final, ultimate, irrevocable step.

But even as the words came from his mouth, Mac heard the
hollow sound of them and knew he couldn't make good on his
threat. It was very likely if he turned these men over to Rosser,
the general would have them hanged or shot by a firing squad.
Three more deaths. Mac wouldn't be to blame for them; the
men had made their own decisions and could be held account-
able for them. And yet, if he turned them in, his hand would
be on them and he would have hurried them on their way to
their fate.

Without thinking about it anymore, he said in a choked voice, "Get out of here."

"Wh-what?" Hope sprang into the voice of the man who stood with his hands up. "You're lettin' us go?"

"I'm not letting you desert," Mac said. "Pick up your friend and get back to your company. As far as I'm concerned, the three of you just came out here to check on your horses before going to bed."

"What's the trick?" the other man asked suspiciously.

"No trick." Mac gave an empty laugh. "Consider it a Christmas present."

And as he watched the two men help their groggy friend to his feet and the three of them hurry away into the darkness, he thought there was a good chance none of them would be alive when Christmas rolled around again. The three men had gotten one last present—their lives—and Mac had gotten to give one final gift.

Chapter Ten

SNOW SWIRLED THICKLY IN front of Mac's face as he made his way through the camp. Two weeks had passed since his encounter with the would-be deserters on Christmas night. The change of years from 1864 to 1865 had brought no relief, either in the weather or in the shortage of supplies. In fact, both were worse. A series of storms had dumped several feet of wet snow on the ground. To keep men from starving, whole regiments that had been raised from the surrounding area at the beginning of the war were now sent home. They might not find provisions any more plentiful there, but at least the army wouldn't be responsible for feeding them.

Mac couldn't go home. Culpeper County was well behind enemy lines, a fact that worried him a great deal. He had heard about the horrors wreaked down in Georgia by Sherman's army as it marched to the sea, and he knew firsthand what the Yankees were capable of from witnessing the fiery devastation of the Shenandoah Valley. But he hadn't heard reports of atrocities from the Culpeper area, so he hoped for the best where his family and the farm were concerned.

Today Thomas L. Rosser had summoned his commanders to a meeting, and that was Mac's destination. He didn't know what it was about. Probably nothing good, he thought with the pessimism that unfortunately had become second nature for him.

Rosser's headquarters were in a small log cabin. When the sentry at the door admitted Mac, he stepped into welcome warmth. A fire crackled merrily in the hearth. Rosser sat at a rough table with a map spread out before him. Several other officers stood around. The general returned Mac's salute and said, "We'll get started momentarily, Major."

Over the next few minutes, several more men came in. Each time the door opened, snow and cold air blew in with the

165

newcomers. Mac rubbed his hands together. It really wasn't that cold inside the cabin. He thought that the chill must have seeped into his bones until it was there permanently. The heat of summer might be required to get rid of it.

Finally Rosser said, "All right, gentlemen, gather around and we'll get down to business." He jabbed a finger at a spot on the map. "Some of our men have returned from a scouting mission into West Virginia, and they tell me that the supply depot at Beverly is fairly bulging at the seams with arms and provisions, especially food." Rosser looked around at the faces of the officers. They had grown excited as he spoke. "Boys, I'll tell it to you true . . . we need those supplies."

Everyone nodded. A look at the map told him that Beverly was at least seventy-five miles from their current camp near Staunton. Seventy-five miles over frozen roads, in weather like this with a couple of feet of snow on the ground, would be an arduous journey. And yet, if there was as much food at that Federal depot as the general said, it might mean the difference between life and death for this army.

"I propose we capture those supplies," Rosser said, putting into words what his officers had already figured out. "I'm asking for volunteers."

"I'll go, sir," Mac said instantly, and that declaration was echoed immediately by all the other officers.

"I expected as much," the general said with a nod and a little smile. "But the call for volunteers extends into the ranks as well. I won't order any man out into weather like this unless he's willing to go." Rosser came to his feet. "Go back to your regiments and let everyone know that we'll be leaving for Beverly tomorrow morning. Anyone who wants to go with us should be ready to ride then."

Mac suspected there would be no shortage of volunteers.

☆　☆　☆

HE WAS right. At least three hundred men assembled at the edge of camp. Some were mounted, but with the cavalry short of horses, most of them would have to march to Beverly.

Rosser split the volunteers into two columns, one commanded by Col. Alphonso Cook and the other by Col. William Morgan. Mac, as part of the mounted detachment, advanced ahead of the marchers. To initiate the action Rosser rode to the head of the columns and took off his hat, sweeping it through the air above his head as he shouted the order to advance. The thick snow muffled the tramping of feet as the men shouldered their rifles and began to march.

Mac wasn't sure who was colder, the men on horseback or the men on foot. At least the men on foot got to get their blood pumping by marching. He felt his blood growing more and more sluggish in the frigid temperature. On the other hand, the men on foot had to force their way through the deep snowdrifts, whereas the riders broke a path through the drifts as best they could. Before this trip was over, frostbite would probably claim some toes, he thought.

The snowfall had tapered off to an occasional fat, wet flake. During the day, it stopped completely, although the sky remained overcast with thick gray clouds. It could start snowing again at any time, Mac told himself . . . and probably would.

Hours passed as the columns advanced through the snow, and men who had been excited and enthusiastic about the raid on the Yankee supply depot had to be asking themselves what they had been thinking when they volunteered. Capturing food and arms from the Federals was all well and good, but not if a fella froze to death before he ever got around to it. Still they trudged on, snow crunching and sliding under their boots and shoes, many of which had holes in them. Socks got wet and froze, and the chill sank deeper, ever deeper.

Mac rode with his shoulders hunched forward. When he grew drowsy, he forced himself to stay awake. He didn't believe that he would freeze to death on top of the stallion, but he didn't want to risk it. He knew that men who allowed themselves to doze off when they were out in the elements like this sometimes never woke up.

With such a thick overcast, night fell early, and everyone was glad of it. They found a place to camp in some woods and built tiny fires that helped to warm them a little. Rosser wouldn't allow any big blazes, saying that they would be too easy to spot if any Union scouts were out and about.

"Why would the Yankees be out in such damned awful weather as this?" Blaisdell asked when he heard the order against large fires.

"We're out here, aren't we?" Mac said.

Blaisdell didn't have any reply for that.

By THE night of January 10, 1865, Rosser and his men were camped on top of a hill overlooking a road marked on the map as the Philippi turnpike. No fires were built at all on this night. Lights were visible a short distance to the south, marking Beverly and the Yankee supply depot. Mac stared at the yellow glows, knowing that each represented a window into a place that was warm and cozy. If for no other reason, he hated the Yankees for that.

The snow had stopped, and late that afternoon the clouds had begun to break at last. Now, as the exhausted men sat on rocks and fallen logs and watched clouds of fog form from their breath, stars appeared in the night sky above them. The heavenly lights were brilliant pinpricks against the deep black. Mac tilted his head and looked up at them and somehow felt better. Probably since the beginning of time, he thought, men had been looking up at the stars and drawing strength and renewal from them. The stars were visible proof that the universe was a big place, and in the long run, man's petty squabbles didn't really amount to all that much. Not a hill of beans, really, Mac told himself. No matter what happened here tonight, no matter how this long, seemingly endless war turned out, those stars would continue to burn, changeless, eternal. Life would go on.

He caught his breath as a light suddenly streaked across the sky and disappeared with a flare of fire. One of the stars he had been watching had just fallen . . .

And he felt colder inside than he ever had before, even when Will died.

"Major? What's wrong?"

Mac gave a little shake of his head and looked over at Blaisdell. "What?"

"You shuddered real strong just then, Major. You feeling feverish?"

"No. No, I'm fine." Mac forced himself to draw a deep breath. He patted Blaisdell's shoulder. "Just thinking about all those good Yankee rations we'll be eating soon."

"You think they'll have any coffee? I'd sure admire to drink a cup of nice hot coffee, Major."

"That sounds good," Mac agreed. "Let's hope they have coffee."

He supposed that his lifelong closeness to nature had made him something of a believer in signs and omens and portents. He was just a naturally superstitious sort. At times he had even wondered if the silver gray stallion he rode was real, or if it was some kind of spirit horse made flesh. Now he had to ask himself if that falling star meant something. Was it a sign that his own life was about to end?

He couldn't allow that to affect his behavior tonight. He had ridden into danger many times since joining the cavalry, knowing full well that he might not survive the action to come. He could do no less tonight just because a star had fallen from the heavens.

Rosser didn't order an attack right away. He wanted the men and horses to rest, although he issued a warning for the men not to fall asleep, lest they freeze to death. The officers would stay busy making sure everyone was awake. Also he wanted to wait until later so that everyone in Beverly would be asleep. Even the few Union soldiers left on guard at the supply depot would be groggy.

The stars wheeled through the sky overhead as the hours passed slowly. The men grew impatient. No one had had a good meal for days, and they all knew there was plenty of food less than a mile away. All they had to do was go and get it.

Finally, Rosser passed the word. Mounted men swung up into their saddles. Foot soldiers readied their rifles. The cavalry would lead the attack into town; the infantry would sweep in close behind them.

The stallion shifted restlessly underneath Mac. The horse was ready for action. Mac remembered the falling star then pushed the thought out of his mind. He was ready, too, and when the command came to move forward, he put the stallion into a walk.

The Confederates moved slowly and quietly into position, poised on the edge of the settlement. Beverly wasn't a very big place, just a main street with a few businesses, a scattering of residences, and a line of warehouses that had been constructed by the Yankees. All the buildings were dark now. The hour was long after midnight. Scores of tents had been set up for the soldiers, and fires burned low in front of some. No one was moving around, though. None of the Yankees seemed to suspect that a sizable Confederate force lurked on their doorstep.

They found out in a hurry, though, when Rosser gave the order to attack.

The horses lunged forward in a gallop. Mac unsnapped his holsters and drew his pistols; he guided the stallion with his knees. The thundering hoof beats of the horses created a commotion that spilled startled Yankees in long underwear out of their tents. Gunfire began to crackle as the few Federals who were armed put up a feeble defense.

Mac rode close to the tents, making a couple of Yankees leap desperately out of the way of the charging stallion. He fired a shot into the shoulder of another man who was trying to bring a rifle to bear. Then the cavalry was past the tents and bearing down on the warehouses as the Confederate infantry overran the Union camp and began mopping up the opposition.

Bullets suddenly whipped around Mac's head. He saw muzzle flashes from behind a short stack of crates in front of one of the warehouses. Several of the guards had sought cover there to make a stand.

Crazy thoughts tumbled through Mac's brain. If the falling star really was an omen . . . if this was the night he was fated to die, no matter what he did . . . then there was no point in being careful, was there?

He leaned over slightly in the saddle, veering the stallion and sending the horse straight toward the pile of crates.

The Yankees must have thought him mad, galloping right at them with pistols blazing and a Rebel yell torn from his throat. But they kept shooting anyway, sending a hail of bullets around Mac . . . a storm that never touched him.

Then, as the stallion loomed up in front of the startled guards, the big silver gray horse left his feet in a soaring leap that carried him and his rider up and over the crates. Both pistols bucked and roared in Mac's hands as he fired right and left at the same time. The Yankees scattered frantically to avoid being crushed as the stallion came down among them. Some of the blue-clad soldiers fell, wounded by Mac's bullets; the others threw down their rifles and stuck their hands in the air, surrendering before the lunatic on the big stallion could do anything else crazy.

Mac pulled the horse in a tight circle, covering his prisoners with empty guns, although the Yankees had no idea about that, of course. Within moments, more of Rosser's men rushed up to take over. Mac holstered his guns. Then and only then did his hands tremble a little.

He was still alive, and as he listened to the scattered firing die away completely, he realized the battle was over. Again he had survived it after all, this time despite the heavenly omen, if an omen it had been.

The thought made him jerk his head around and peer over his shoulder. All it would take was one Yankee who hadn't been captured, one man with a rifle who stood up from concealment, unnoticed, to draw a bead on the tall man on the silver gray horse . . .

Then Mac began to laugh. He leaned forward in the saddle, resting his hands on the stallion's neck. The stallion turned his head to look back at the man as Mac kept laughing.

"Major?" Blaisdell asked as he rode up. "Major, you all right?"

"You keep asking me that, Lieutenant," Mac replied as he lifted a hand to wipe tears away from his eyes, tears that rolled down his cheeks because he was laughing so hard.

"Well, begging the major's pardon—"

"I'm acting like a madman, I know." Mac laughed again and then brought himself under control. "I'm fine, Lieutenant, not hurt at all. Casualties?"

"A few wounded but none killed, at least not in our outfit," Blaisdell reported. "And Major . . ." The young officer's voice was eager. "I snuck a peek in one of these warehouses. They're stuffed to the rafters, just like we thought. There's enough food here to feed everybody in the command, not to mention a lot of rifles and ammunition!"

"It sounds like we did a good job," Mac said. Now that the fighting was over, a great weariness threatened to steal over him. He hoped he could get some sleep before they had to start back to Staunton.

"Yes sir. We were lucky."

Lucky? It was about time the Southerners had some good luck, even on such a small scale. Fortune had not smiled much on them for a long time. But luck could change without warning, Mac thought. Sometimes good luck was nothing more than bad luck delayed.

And sometimes stars fell from the sky.

☆ ☆ ☆

"WHAT'S THIS say?" Ernie Murrell asked as he held out a piece of paper toward Henry Brannon. One of Murrell's cracked and broken fingernails tapped a sentence on the paper.

Henry leaned closer and read the words by the light of the campfire. "'Kindness to bad men is cruelty to the good.'"

"That's why we're goin' after them deserters? Because they're bad men?"

Henry nodded in agreement. "And if we let them get away with what they're doing, we'll also be harming the good people of the Confederacy."

"Well, I reckon that makes sense. I got to tell you, I'm a mite worried about goin' out to fight our own boys when there's Yankees not that far off."

"We can fight the Yankees better if we get everybody back where they belong," Henry pointed out.

"Reckon that's true." Murrell went back to laboriously studying the documents in his hand by the light of the fire. It was a declaration from Bedford Forrest that had circulated among the cavalrymen following the general's recent promotion. He had been placed in charge of all cavalry in this part of the Confederacy as well as overall command of the Department of Mississippi, East Louisiana, and West Tennessee. From what Henry had seen of Forrest, it was a move that was long overdue.

Much had changed in the month since the retreat from Nashville. Although John Bell Hood still found it difficult to accept the blame for the debacle, he had asked to be relieved of command. Gen. P. G. T. Beauregard in Richmond had complied, placing Gen. Richard Taylor in charge of what was left of the army, for the time being, anyway. Rumor had it that Gen. Joseph E. Johnston would soon return to assume command. Meanwhile, seeing what bad shape his cavalry was in after fighting the rear guard action all the way back from Tennessee, Forrest had taken the bold step of giving furloughs to many of the men who lived in Tennessee, Alabama, and Mississippi. Those men could reach their homes without much trouble, and while they were visiting with their families, perhaps they could also gather up supplies, fresh horses, and new recruits for the cavalry. Of course, some of the men would never come back, and Forrest knew that. But his expectation was that enough of them would return, rested and better supplied and better mounted, to make the gamble worthwhile.

That was exactly how things had worked out. The cavalry was now in much better shape than it had been immediately following the retreat. But as the only effective fighting force in the area, Forrest's cavalry now had more responsibilities as well. One of them was to round up the gangs of deserters that roamed the countryside looting and wreaking as much havoc on the civilian population as the Yankee army ever had.

That was the errand in which Henry, Murrell, and the rest of their patrol were engaged. They had been chasing a good-sized band of deserters across northeastern Mississippi for two days now. When they caught up with the deserters, the men would have the choice of returning to their regular companies or being thrown in prison. Either way, their depredations would cease.

The weather was still cold, wet, and miserable. The warmth from the campfire was most welcome as Henry, Murrell, and the other men huddled around it. They had already eaten their scanty supper and soon would turn in, rolling up in their threadbare blankets for another night of shivering, restless sleep.

As Henry felt himself growing drowsy, his thoughts returned to the farm the patrol had ridden up to that afternoon. The barn was just a heap of smoking ashes, and everything of value had been stolen from the house. An elderly couple lived there, the old man sporting a long white beard that was streaked with blood. One of the deserters who had raided the place had smashed the old man in the mouth with a rifle butt. The injury made his voice thick, his words difficult to decipher. The old woman never spoke at all, just stood there sobbing with her apron over her face.

The story told by the old man was a familiar one. The foragers had descended on the farm, a few on horseback but most on foot, and had demanded that all the couple's valuables be turned over to them. Of course, the old people had little or nothing of value . . . a few clothes, a couple of pots and pans, some pewter handed down through the old woman's family from colonial days. As for livestock, they had a single cow and four chickens. All of it was gone now, taken away by the raiders, who had brutalized the old man and torched the barn for good measure before they left.

A fresh surge of anger welled up inside Henry. Wasn't it bad enough that the Yankees had invaded the Southern homeland? How could anybody do such things to their own people?

But then he remembered some of the things that had happened in his own life and knew that some people were capable of almost anything, no matter how low. His own brother Titus was proof of that.

The captain in charge of the patrol ordered guards posted and told the rest of the men to get some sleep. Henry was about to spread his blankets on the ground when he heard a sudden, unexpected gunshot. He jerked his head up and saw the captain stagger. The man pressed a hand to his chest and looked down in surprise at the blood that covered it. Then he pitched forward on his face, either unconscious or dead.

"It's an ambush!" Murrell shouted as more shots rang out all around the camp.

Henry threw himself to the ground, snatched up his Spencer, and rolled over, trying to put as much distance as he could between himself and the fire. He didn't want to give the enemy a better target than he had to.

He had no idea who the enemy was. The ambushers might be Yankees. They might be the gang of deserters, although such aggressive action against a group that could fight back was out of character for them. Henry didn't know, didn't care. He scrambled into the brush and lay belly-down on the ground as bullets whined through the air and smashed into tree trunks and broke off branches that were bare with winter.

Henry used the barrel of the rifle to part the brush a little so he could peer into the clearing where the campfire had been built. Several members of the patrol lay on the ground. Some writhed in pain; others were motionless and probably dead. Henry didn't spot Murrell anywhere among the downed men and was grateful for that. His friend must have dived for cover as soon as the shooting started, too.

Shouts of alarm came from the area where the patrol's horses had been picketed. Henry began to wriggle backward on the ground toward it. Fear made his heart thump heavily in his chest. If they lost their horses, they would have little chance of getting back to Forrest's headquarters in Corinth, Mississippi. Instead, they would be sitting ducks for any Yankee cavalry that happened to come across them. The horses had to be protected or all was lost.

When Henry was several yards away from the clearing, he came up in a crouch and started to force his way through the brush. Someone screamed in mortal pain. More shots blasted. He ducked around a tree and almost ran into a man. It was too dark to see much, but a stray beam of starlight reflected off the blade of a saber as the man hacked at Henry's head.

Desperately, Henry ducked under the swiping blow and rammed the barrel of his carbine into the man's belly. He could have pulled the trigger and blown the man's spine apart, but he didn't. He didn't want to kill anybody without knowing who it was. For all he knew, he was fighting a friend of his. As the shadowy figure grunted in pain and doubled over, Henry jabbed him again in the belly then slammed his fist against the side of the man's head. The man went down to his knees and toppled over, all the fight gone out of him.

Henry leaped over his fallen foe and hurried on toward the horses. He broke into a second clearing and saw several men struggling near the spooked mounts. The light was a little better here, and he could tell that the ambushers wore ragged remnants of uniforms and battered slouch hats. They were deserters, then, and not Federal troopers. That knowledge didn't make Henry feel any more kindly toward them. If anything, he despised them even more than if they had been Yankees.

He ran up behind one of the deserters who struggled with a cavalryman from the patrol. With a swift stroke of the Spencer's butt to the back of the head, he laid out the deserter. The other man, who'd had his hands full, gasped, "Thanks, Brannon."

One of the frightened horses let out a shrill whinny. Henry spun around and saw another deserter trying to untie the animal's picket rope. Leveling the carbine, Henry called, "Get away from that horse!"

With a snarl, the deserter did as Henry told him. The man wasn't giving up, though. He jerked a pistol from behind his belt and thrust it toward Henry.

Without waiting for the deserter to fire first, Henry pressed the Spencer's trigger. The carbine kicked against his shoulder as it fired, flame belching from the barrel. The slug caught the deserter in the right shoulder, driving him backward and making him drop the pistol. The man fell to the ground, where he writhed and clutched at his injury. Henry hadn't wanted to kill him and was glad to see that he hadn't. Of course, the deserter still might bleed to death or die of blood poisoning from the wound, but such dangers were of his own making.

A shout of warning jerked Henry around. He saw the man he had helped earlier collapse as yet another raider ripped a heavy, long-bladed knife from his belly. The deserter whipped the knife toward Henry in a backhanded slash. Henry barely had time to bring up the Spencer and parry the blade with the carbine's barrel. There wasn't time to work the carbine's lever. Henry rushed forward instead, bulling into the man and smashing the

Spencer across his face. The man stumbled backward but didn't lose his grip on the knife. Henry's hand dropped to the holstered pistol at his waist. He drew the revolver, cocking it as he did so, and fired in one smooth motion. The deserter rocked back, hit in the body. He spun slowly off his feet and landed face down.

Henry felt a flash of regret, knowing that he had probably killed this man, but there hadn't been much else he could do. He had acted quickly and instinctively, without any real thought other than wanting to save his own life.

"Henry!"

It was Ernie Murrell's voice. Henry turned and saw his friend rush up to him. Murrell seemed to be unhurt. As the shooting and yelling came to a ragged halt, Murrell asked, "You all right, Henry?"

"I'm fine," Henry assured him. "Just a little winded."

Murrell chuckled. "Yeah, it was a mite fast and furious there for a minute. But I reckon we done for about half the bunch and the others run off."

"They were the deserters we've been after," Henry said.

"Yep, figured that much when I seen they wasn't wearin' Yankee blue. I reckon they got tired o' bein' chased and decided to come after us instead. That was a mistake."

"What will we do with the prisoners we took?"

Murrell shook his head. "Take 'em back and let the general decide, I reckon. I ain't got much use for anybody who'd bush-whack fellas who're supposed to be on the same side as them."

Henry felt the same way. It would be all right with him if the deserters who had been captured were locked up until the war was over. However, as shorthanded as most of the army units were these days, he knew it was likely they would be pressed back into service. Putting up the best possible fight against the Yankees had to come before all other considerations.

The war wasn't over, and until it was, they had no choice but to battle on.

Chapter Eleven

T ITUS STRETCHED HIS LONG legs toward the fireplace, enjoying the warmth that soaked into his booted feet. He lifted a cup of tea and sipped from it. A sigh escaped from him.

After everything that had happened to him over the past few years, he knew better than to think that his luck had changed. More tragedy and evil likely were right around the corner, as they always had been in his experience. But a man would be a fool not to enjoy such pleasurable moments when they came to him, he told himself.

"You remind me of a cat," Mosby said from the other armchair, where he sat with a blanket wrapped around his legs. The two men were in the bedroom on the second floor of the farmhouse in Amherst County that belonged to the colonel's parents. The house reminded Titus a great deal of his family's farmhouse, although it was better furnished. Alfred Mosby, the colonel's father, had been a more successful farmer than John Brannon.

"A cat?" Titus repeated. "How's that, Colonel?"

Mosby sipped his own cup of tea then said, "You sit there in utter repose, looking half-asleep. And yet, if danger were to threaten, you would move instantly, and your response would be deadly. Your claws are sheathed, but they can come out in a hurry."

Titus chuckled. He wore two pistols and had a heavy Bowie knife sheathed at his waist as well. He supposed the weapons were what Mosby meant by his "claws."

"I don't reckon I'll need to be scratchin' anybody around here, Colonel."

"You never know. It seems safe, but . . . you never know."

The two of them, along with several other rangers assigned to guard the colonel, had been at the Mosby farm for almost a week. After moving from isolated farmhouse to isolated farmhouse—

some called them "safe houses"—in an effort to avoid the colonel's capture by the Yankees, Mosby had decided to go to his parents' place to finish his recuperation.

Already Mosby looked better, although he was still pale. Always slender, now his face was almost gaunt because of the weight he had lost while he was laid up. He had started growing a beard to distract from that thinness.

A cold January wind rattled a window pane, making Titus even happier that he was inside where it was warm and dry. The hour was growing late. Mosby would want to turn in soon, Titus supposed. When that time came, Titus would go to the room next door, where one of the rangers always slept, handy in case of trouble.

A quiet knock sounded on the bedroom door. "Come in," Mosby called in response.

The door opened, and one of the family's slaves looked into the room. "Colonel," the man said, "they's a gentleman downstairs lookin' for you. Says it's mighty important that he talk to you, but he wouldn't give me no name."

Titus saw a change come over Mosby. The colonel straightened in the armchair and seemed filled with purpose and resolve as he set down the teacup. "What does this man look like?"

"He's a big fella, Colonel, 'bout as tall as Mister Brannon here, but I reckon he's packin' more meat on his bones."

"I'm not that skinny," Titus protested.

"Lean . . . like a cat," Mosby said with a chuckle. Then he grew more serious and instructed the slave, "Send the man up here, please."

"Yes sir."

After the slave had withdrawn, Titus said, "Beggin' your pardon, Colonel, but are you sure this is such a good idea? Lettin' a stranger up here to see you, I mean."

"I don't think a Yankee would waltz into my parents' house and ask to see me," Mosby said. "At any rate, I think I know this man, and he's not a stranger to me or to you. You'll see."

The colonel unwrapped the blanket from his legs and stood up. He was fairly steady on his feet, although he moved a bit stiffly due to the bandages still wrapped tightly underneath his clothes. Titus got up too and moved behind the chair where he had been sitting. He rested his left hand on the back of the chair and his right on the butt of the Colt at his hip. He was ready for trouble if it came to that.

A light tap sounded on the door. Mosby invited the man in.

As the colonel had predicted, Titus recognized the man immediately. The newcomer was tall, broad-shouldered, and powerful looking, as the servant had indicated. He was handsome as well, with a quick smile and curly brown hair.

"Hello, Lewis," Mosby greeted him.

"Colonel," the man said in a soft Southern drawl. He looked at Titus and nodded. "Hello, Brannon."

Titus grunted. "Lewis Powell. What're you doin' here?"

Powell grinned and gestured toward Mosby. "I came to see the colonel, of course." He stepped closer and extended his hand. "How are you, sir?"

Mosby clasped his hand warmly. "Getting better every day," he said. "Please, have a seat." The colonel glanced at his bodyguard. "Titus, you can retire for the evening if you wish."

"You sure about that, Colonel?"

"Of course," Mosby answered without hesitation. "I trust Lewis with my life. He's one of us, after all."

That was true enough. Lewis Powell was one of Mosby's Rangers. Titus had known him for months, ever since he had fallen in with the partisans in the first place. Powell was a member of Dolly Richards's company and had been part of most of the raids that had taken place. Titus recalled fighting alongside him when the rangers captured a huge Union supply train on the Berryville turnpike.

"All right, Colonel," Titus said, relaxing. Chances were, Powell was going to be added to the guard detail. That was all right with Titus. More men meant less work for him.

He paused and shook hands with Powell on his way out of the room. "Good to see you again," he said.

"Titus . . . ," Mosby said, causing Titus to pause in the doorway and look back.

"Yes sir?"

Mosby was frowning a little now. "Perhaps it would be better if you didn't say anything to anyone about Lewis's visit."

So Powell was just here on a visit. That was a mite odd, Titus thought. And so was the fact that Mosby wanted the visit kept quiet. But Mosby could give any orders he wanted, and it would be Titus's job to follow those orders . . . no matter how strange.

"Sure, Colonel. As far as I'm concerned, Powell ain't even here right now."

Mosby nodded. "Good. I thought you'd understand."

Titus didn't understand, not a bit. But he would go along with whatever Mosby said. He went out of the room and eased the door closed behind him. On the other side of it, Mosby and Powell began talking. Titus heard them, but he couldn't make out the words, only the voices.

The same thing was true when he entered the small bedroom next to Mosby's bedchamber. The wall was thin enough so that Titus could hear them talking, but he couldn't understand a word they were saying. He thought the voices had an urgent tone to them, though.

He took off his guns and the knife and placed them on the small table beside the narrow bed. Still fully dressed otherwise, he stretched out on the bed and blew out the candle on the table. Darkness closed down over the room. In that darkness, Titus lay there and stared up at the ceiling. He remembered the sudden animation on Mosby's part when the slave announced the visitor. Mosby had suspected then that it was Powell; he had practically said as much to Titus before Powell came upstairs.

As far as Titus knew, Powell was just another ranger. He had no special connection to Mosby. Something was going on, though, that he didn't know about. Titus was sure of that.

Whatever it was, it didn't have anything to do with him. Titus grunted again, rolled onto his side, closed his eyes, and went to sleep.

Like a great cat, though, he slept lightly, ready to awaken instantly and unsheath his claws.

THE NEXT morning Mosby didn't say anything about Powell's visit, and Titus followed the colonel's lead by keeping quiet about it, too. It had been late when Powell arrived. Most of the household had been in bed already. It was likely that only a handful of people knew Powell had been there. These were people who would lay down their lives for the colonel without hesitation, so they were more than happy to do him the simple favor of keeping his secret.

A couple of days passed without incident. Then a letter arrived from Richmond, and as the colonel sat reading it in the farmhouse parlor, a taut look of anger came over his face.

Titus lounged near the parlor fireplace. "Something wrong, Colonel?" he asked.

Mosby slapped the letter down on a side table. "It's that blasted General Lee, causing trouble for me again!"

Titus was surprised by the colonel's outburst as well as the disrespect expressed toward the army commander. "You don't mean Robert E. Lee, sir?" he asked.

"No, no," Mosby said with a wave of his hand. "His nephew, Fitzhugh Lee. The two of us have never gotten along. Back when I was scouting for General Stuart, I think Lee believed I was trying to replace him as Stuart's favorite."

Titus had heard quite a bit about those days, fairly early in the war, from his brother. Mac, of course, had ridden with Fitz Lee's cavalry since that first ride around McClellan back in the summer of 1862, and he seemed to think the general hung the moon. On other occasions since joining the rangers, Titus had heard Mosby talk about the friction between Lee and him. He figured it would be wise not to mention Mac's connection, both professional and personal.

"Lee is laid up in Richmond, recuperating from a wound like me," Mosby went on. "I suppose he's got nothing better to do than think of ways to stir up trouble." The colonel tapped the letter on the table. "This is a request for complete muster rolls for our companies. General Lee has been assigned to the Office of Conscription while he recuperates, and he seems to think we're stealing conscripts from the regular army. Hmmph! As if I've ever made any man ride with me who didn't want to."

"Yes sir," Titus agreed. "As far as I can see, all the boys are right where they want to be."

Mosby looked up at him. "I'm going to have to see about this. It may even require a trip to Richmond to get everything straightened out. But in the meantime, I want you to carry a letter to Major Richards for me."

Titus's eyebrows lifted in surprise. "Me, sir? But it was Dolly—I mean Major Richards—who assigned me to look out for you in the first place."

"I'm aware of that," Mosby said testily. "Now I'm countermanding that order. There are plenty of the boys around here to see that the Yankees don't bother me, and I need a man I trust, a man who can take care of himself on a fast, hard ride, to deliver that letter."

Titus shrugged then nodded. "Yes sir, whatever you say. Want me to fetch you a pen and some paper?"

"Please. I'm going to instruct Major Richards to redouble his efforts in assistance to the local conscription officers. I won't have Fitzhugh Lee besmirching my good name and the reputations of my men." Mosby pointed a finger at Titus. "You stay up there and help Major Richards all you can, Titus."

"Yes sir."

As far as he was concerned, though, Titus thought, he didn't see why the Confederacy even needed conscription officers.

Why would anybody need to be conscripted to go off and kill Yankees? It was the most natural thing in the world.

A COUPLE of hundred miles separated Amherst County, where Mosby was recuperating, from the settlement of Bloomfield, where the company of rangers under Dolly Richards had their winter camp. The rest of the rangers, commanded by Maj. William H. Chapman, had moved to the Northern Neck, the area of Virginia between the Potomac and Rappahannock Rivers, for the winter.

Titus made the ride alone on the rangy lineback dun that had become his personal mount. He followed back roads to avoid any roaming Federal patrols, although it seemed unlikely to him that the Yankees would be out and about much in the cold, icy January weather. Except for the siege at Petersburg, down south of Richmond, there wasn't much action going on. Everybody was waiting for the weather to improve.

Titus knew the location of all the safe houses and stayed at one of them whenever he could. When he couldn't, he found himself an isolated spot to camp for the night. The miles fell behind him, and a little more than a week after leaving Amherst County, he rode up to the rangers' winter headquarters.

A sentry showed him to the cabin where Dolly Richards had his quarters. Richards looked up in surprise from the table where he sat as Titus came in. "Titus!" he exclaimed. "You're supposed to be with the colonel. Has something happened?"

"No sir," Titus tersely answered, reaching into his coat and withdrawing the sealed envelope. "Colonel Mosby gave me new orders, Major, and he sent you this message."

Richards read the contents quickly and gave a curt nod. "I understand. We're to aid the local conscription officers in their efforts." He looked up at Titus again. "And you're to stay here and assist me in doing that."

Titus nodded glumly. "Yes sir."

"That work doesn't sound appealing to you at all, does it?" Richards asked with a grin.

"Well, sir, now that you mention it . . . At least while I was helpin' to guard the colonel, there was a chance some troublesome Yankees might come along lookin' for him."

"And then you'd have a chance to shoot more of them." Richards finished the thought that Titus hadn't put into words.

"Well . . ."

Richards's grin widened. "Don't worry, Titus. I've been making some plans I think you'll like. They'll have to wait, though, until this conscription mess is taken care of."

"Yes sir. The colonel, he said he was going to write to some other officers he knows and call in some favors, ask them to help him get Fitz Lee off his back."

"Let's hope it doesn't take long." Richards's expression became more serious. "We've got more important things to do."

For the next few days, like it or not, the rangers rode with the local conscription officer for Loudoun County, traveling from town to village to hamlet, and stopping as well at farms along the way. The officer had census lists from before the war and used them to figure out which men of military age had not yet served in the army. The Confederacy had need, in these dark days, of every able-bodied man who could come to the nation's defense . . . especially those who had not yet done their part. As Titus rode along with the group accompanying the conscription officer, he found himself thinking about his brother Henry. He wondered if Henry had ever left the farm and joined up before the Yankees moved in and occupied Culpeper County. If Henry hadn't gotten out before, he wouldn't be able to now.

Surprisingly, Titus found himself thinking about his little brother without feeling the usual hatred for Henry. He knew better than to believe that time had begun to heal the hurt of the way Henry and Polly had betrayed him. But though the pain was still there, maybe some of the edge had gone off it. Maybe someday he would be able to see Henry again without wanting to smash a fist into his face.

But probably not. Titus wasn't even sure he wanted to give up the hate and resentment he felt. A man needed something to keep him going, and that was as good a goad as any.

As the end of January approached, word came from Mosby that Fitzhugh Lee had dropped his request for muster rolls. Titus figured that one of Mosby's friends had intervened and gotten Lee to ease off. He didn't really know or care what had happened. The only thing that mattered was that now the rangers were free to carry out their natural activities once more.

Dolly Richards gathered a group of thirty handpicked men, including Titus, and laid out a new plan. On the other side of the Blue Ridge, in the lower end of the Shenandoah Valley, the Baltimore and Ohio Railroad ran from Harpers Ferry to Martinsburg. Just as in the glory days of Mosby's Rangers, Richards wanted to execute a swift, hard-striking raid against the railroad, tearing up the tracks and perhaps capturing some supplies if they came across some at any of the depots.

The plan sounded fine to Titus. Sheridan was still somewhere in the Shenandoah. There was no guarantee the raiders would run into Little Phil—in fact, Richards probably wanted to avoid Sheridan if at all possible—but Titus would welcome the chance to settle the score with the Yankee general, if it came to that. Sheridan owed him a lot for Bob McCulloch's death and the way Danetta Wiley had turned her back on him.

As the rangers got ready to ride, Titus gave in to an impulse and asked Richards, "Where's old Lewis Powell? Seems to me like this would be just the sort of raid he'd want to be part of." Titus hadn't seen Powell since returning to Bloomfield, and he was curious what had happened to the man after Powell left the Mosby farm in Amherst County.

Richards's face hardened. "You haven't heard about Powell?"

Titus shook his head, thinking that perhaps Powell had been killed on his way back up here.

"He left us," Richards went on. "Slipped off, nobody's sure where or when."

"You mean he deserted?" Titus had a hard time believing that. Powell had always seemed like a good ranger, the sort who disliked Yankees almost as much as Titus himself did.

"I reckon so. Anyway, he's gone, and good riddance."

Titus frowned but didn't mention Powell again. It still struck him as mighty odd that Powell would ride all the way to Amherst County to see the colonel and desert so soon after his visit. If Powell meant to take off, why had he bothered to see Mosby? And why had Mosby been expecting him?

Unable to answer those questions, Titus put them out of his mind. He had to concentrate on the job at hand, which was raiding the B&O and making life miserable for some Yankees.

The rangers left their winter quarters on January 30 and headed northwest toward Snickers Gap. They crossed the Blue Ridge into the Shenandoah Valley the next day and continued down the valley toward Harpers Ferry. The Union army believed it was in control of the Valley, but the rangers moved through it with ease, taking little-used roads and trails and riding over open country when need be. That night, in winter darkness, the riders approached the rail line between Harpers Ferry and Martinsburg.

Following Richards's orders, Titus and two men rode ahead to scout the terrain and the enemy's strength. They proceeded slowly so their horses wouldn't make much noise. When Titus, in charge of the scouting detail, called a halt and listened intently, he heard other horses moving somewhere nearby. Twisting in the saddle, he hissed at the other men, "Get back!"

The three of them quickly drifted into the shadows cast by bare-limbed trees that grew alongside the railroad. A few minutes later, with a jingle of harness, a large Union cavalry patrol came trotting along the roadbed. Titus and his companions waited until the Yankees were gone, then they moved quietly along the tracks in the direction the blue-clad cavalrymen had come from.

Within minutes Titus smelled smoke. A moment later he spotted campfires, dozens of them, glowing up ahead. The other rangers saw the same thing. One of them came up alongside Titus and whispered, "Looks like a damned big camp."

Titus nodded. The campfires spread out along the tracks for half a mile or more. Not only that, but the Yankees weren't all asleep, either. A lot of them were up and about despite the late hour and the cold weather. With a heavy tramping of feet, a large infantry detail marched by on the other side of the tracks, separated from the three Confederate scouts by no more than fifty yards. Titus and his companions were cloaked in deep shadows, however, and the Federals never noticed them.

"I ain't sure this raid is a good idea, Titus," the third man said. "Major Richards didn't say nothin' about there bein' this many Yanks over here."

"I don't reckon he knew," Titus growled. "From what we've heard, Sheridan's supposed to be somewhere close to Winchester. Shouldn't be so many of the bastards around the railroad."

But the Yankees were there, no doubt about that, and Dolly Richards would have to decide what to do. With less than three dozen men, it would be crazy to attack a Yankee camp of such large size. It would be worse than crazy, Titus thought. It would be suicide.

But it was Richards's decision to make, and there were worse ways to die. Titus said softly, "Let's go find the major."

The three men turned their horses and headed south, away from the railroad. They hadn't gone very far, however, when a voice in the darkness suddenly challenged them. "Who's that? Stand fast, you men!"

The flat Midwestern accent marked the man as a Yankee. Titus was ready to kick his horse into a gallop and try to get away when his keen eyes spotted only two figures on foot blocking the way. He didn't want any shooting to alert the rest of the Union soldiers nearby. With a sudden lunge, he left his saddle in a dive toward one of the men.

Titus's fingers closed around the barrel of the rifle in the man's hands and wrenched it upward. An instant later he crashed into the man and bore him backward. At the same time, his two companions sent their horses right at the second Yankee. With a yell of fright, he threw himself out of the way. Luck was with the partisans. Neither of the Federal pickets pulled the trigger on their rifles.

Titus landed with his knees in the belly of the man he had tackled. He wrenched the rifle out of the man's grip and hit him across the face with the stock. The Yankee sagged limply on the ground, stunned by the savage blow.

The two other rangers flung themselves from their saddles and swarmed the second picket, knocking the rifle from his hands and hauling him to his feet. The man was clearly terrified. He stuttered and begged for mercy.

Titus stepped up to him, drawing the knife from his belt as he did so. Laying the razor-sharp blade against the Yankee's throat, he ordered, "You make any more noise, and I'll quiet you down permanent-like."

The man shuddered but fell silent.

"Come on," Titus said to his companions. "We'll take these damn Yanks back to the major and see what he wants us to do with them."

If it had been up to Titus, some slashes with his knife would take care of the situation. Two dead Yankees didn't amount to much, but it was a start on a good night's work. However, he knew that Richards might want to question them. It was obvious from what he and the other scouts had seen that the B&O Railroad wasn't as lightly defended as Richards had believed it to be.

With their two prisoners, the rangers moved quickly and quietly through the night. A short time later, they were challenged again, but this time by guards that Dolly Richards had posted.

Titus kept his knife at the back of one of the prisoners as they were brought to Richards. "What's this? You got you some Yankees, Titus?"

"Yes sir, and these two are just the start," Titus said. "There's a whole bunch more of them all along the railroad."

"What? I didn't think there would be many Federals around here except for maybe a small cavalry patrol."

"We saw cavalrymen," Titus confirmed, "but it wasn't a small patrol. More like a whole damned regiment. There's a big infantry camp over there, too, and they're marchin' around like they're guardin' the tracks, even in the middle of the night."

Richards muttered a curse. "Aren't there any smaller camps around here?"

"I don't rightly know, sir," Titus said. "But I reckon we got somebody here who can tell us." His hand closed hard on the shoulder of the prisoner in front of him. "How about it, Yank?"

The Union soldier had recovered some of his courage. He said, "I'm not telling you anything. You can go to hell, Reb."

Titus stepped forward, his left arm going around the neck of the prisoner. It clamped down on the man's throat like a bar of iron. Titus forced the prisoner's head up and back, stretching the skin tight over his throat. The blade of Titus's knife pressed to that skin, hard enough to draw a trickle of blood.

"I may go to hell," Titus said with a grim chuckle, "but you'll be there before me, you son of a bitch."

"Titus . . . ," Richards said warningly.

Titus flashed the officer a grin. "Don't worry, Major. We don't need this one. I'm bettin' the other fella can tell us everything we need to know."

"W-wait!" gasped the man in Titus's grasp. "I . . . I'll tell you what I know!"

"Sort of thought you would," Titus drawled.

He released the man and stepped back. The prisoner swayed and almost fell to his knees before catching himself. He lifted a hand to the shallow cut on his neck and muttered as he brought away bloodstained fingertips.

The other prisoner had been impressed by the near-death of his comrade, too. Both Yankees cooperated, answering all the questions Dolly Richards asked them. It seemed that Sheridan had expected a raid on the railroad, so he had stationed the large force along the tracks just in case.

There was another camp in the area, though, a much smaller cavalry camp about a mile away. When Titus fingered the blade of his knife, the prisoners were only too happy to reveal the countersign that would get the raiders past the sentries on duty at the camp.

"Well, it's not like wrecking the railroad, but I suppose we've got to take what we can get," Richards said when the prisoners were taken away. "We'll only need a small group for this." He picked out Titus and eight other men. "The rest of you start back home."

"What about these two?" One of the rangers jerked a thumb at the prisoners.

"Take them with you for a ways then let them go," Richards ordered, disappointing Titus a little. "Make sure they've got a nice long walk back here."

As the raiders were getting ready to ride, one of the men said to Titus, "What would you have done if those Yankees hadn't talked?"

"Killed them, of course," he replied without hesitation. "Cuttin' throats is sort of messy, but it's nice and permanent."

A short time later, the small band rode out. They had good directions to the Federal camp and had no trouble finding it. A row of hastily erected cabins with canvas roofs housed the troopers; across from the cabins were the stables where the horses were kept. It looked to Titus like the stables were sturdier than the cabins. Enough lantern light came from the windows of the cabins to illuminate the open area between the rows of buildings.

"We want the horses," Richards whispered to his men. "There'll be sentries in the stables, I reckon. Take 'em as quiet as you can."

The rangers dismounted and stole forward, moving quickly but silently. Titus drew his knife as he approached one of the stables. Nothing was better than cold steel for killing without any big ruckus.

The stables were constructed like sheds, with roofs that slanted down from front to back. Each was big enough to house two or three horses. Titus spotted a guard lounging on a stool in front of the nearest one. He circled to the rear of the building, put the blade of the knife between his teeth, and reached up to grab the beams of the low roof. A second later, he was on top of the stable, having pulled himself lithely to the roof.

He crawled to the front of the building and looked down on the guard. The Yankee soldier had no idea he was up here, Titus thought. He took the knife from his mouth and poised himself to spring.

His boots made small thuds as he dropped to the ground beside the startled sentry. The trooper started to his feet, but he had barely moved before Titus's arm looped around his neck. The blade bit deep into the man's back as Titus jerked him around. He felt the knife grate against a rib, then slip past the bone to pierce the guard's heart. The Yankee spasmed and then went limp in Titus's grip.

He lowered the corpse to the ground and looked up the rough street between the stables and the cabins. He saw somewhat the same scene repeated as the rangers dealt with the other Union sentries. However, there was a major difference, he noted with a quirk of his mouth. It looked like the others were capturing and disarming the Yankees rather than killing them. To each his own, Titus thought. But it seemed to him like a waste of a perfectly good chance to kill the enemy.

For a few moments, everything went smoothly as the rangers took care of the guards and began untying the horses in the stables. A horse-stealing raid was better than nothing. Mosby's men could always use extra mounts.

Then, as a Union trooper who was unaware of what was going on walked up to relieve one of the captured sentries, a ranger stepped out of the shadows and ordered him to drop his gun. The Yankee reacted quicker than his fellows had. He sprang backward and lifted his rifle. His finger clenched on the trigger before anyone could stop him, and although the bullet flew harmlessly into the air, the roar of the shot echoed through the camp.

"Get to your horses! Get to your horses!" Richards shouted. He knew, as did all the other rangers, that the camp would be in an uproar within seconds.

Titus had just led two horses from the stable when the shot sounded and all hell broke loose. Dragging them by their harnesses, he headed for the edge of camp where the rangers had left their mounts. When he got there, the other men were already scrambling into their saddles. Titus followed suit and drew his pistols as he settled onto the back of the dun. He let out a whoop as he kicked the horse into a run.

The entire party of rangers galloped down the street, driving the stolen horses in front of them, yelling and shooting as Yankee troopers hurried out of the cabins. Most of the Yankees hurriedly ducked for cover as Confederate lead raked the buildings. Only a few of them managed to get off some return fire, and it was ineffective. Within moments the fight, such as it was, was over. The rangers rode off into the night, taking the stolen horses with them.

Titus smiled grimly as he holstered his pistols and leaned forward over the dun's neck. As battles went, this one hadn't amounted to much at all. And a few horses weren't much to show for a raid deep into Yankee-held territory.

But these days, they took what they could get, whatever the Yankees were stupid enough to give them. For now, it would have to do.

Chapter Twelve

SOUTH CAROLINA HAD BEEN the first Southern state to secede from the Union back in December 1860, a time that must have seemed like the dim past to those who had been engaged in the great conflict for nearly four years. It was also the site of the first shots fired in the war, when Confederate batteries shelled Fort Sumter in Charleston Harbor. Of all the rebellious states, none was more despised by the Yankees than South Carolina, and once Savannah was abandoned by William J. Hardee's army just before Christmas 1864, everyone on both sides figured it was only a matter of time before William Tecumseh Sherman turned north and led his rampaging hordes through South Carolina. Looking at the utter devastation left behind by Sherman's army on its march from Atlanta to the sea, frightened South Carolinians asked themselves what Sherman would do to them and their state.

They had to wait awhile to find out.

With Savannah now under his control, Sherman was content to let his men rest for a few weeks while supplies were brought in by ship. He planned to cross the Savannah River into South Carolina around the middle of January. This delay, while no doubt welcomed by the weary Union soldiers, also gave the embattled Confederates a chance to make some moves of their own. Hardee relocated the eight thousand men of his army from Port Royal Sound northward along the coast to Charleston, where he joined forces with a division of state militia. That brought Hardee's command to approximately eleven thousand men.

Even farther up the coast, Confederate Gen. Braxton Bragg headed a force of six thousand at Wilmington. They would back up Hardee's army. The only real hope of stopping Sherman, though, lay hundreds of miles to the west, with the remnants of the Army of Tennessee, now bivouacked at Tupelo, Mississippi.

Although grievously weakened by Hood's disastrous invasion of Tennessee, the Army of Tennessee still had considerable numbers. P. G. T. Beauregard, trying desperately to put together a force large enough to blunt or even halt Sherman's inevitable advance, ordered thousands of men from the Army of Tennessee to head east. These soldiers, tired and hungry and cold, but still willing to fight, piled onto rattletrap train cars that rolled east toward Augusta, South Carolina, 150 miles inland on the Savannah River. Their goal was to link up with the forces arrayed along the coast and form a barrier to Sherman's plans.

The question was whether or not old Uncle Billy would make his move before the Confederates were ready.

In mid-January the skies opened up and poured buckets of rain on Savannah and the South Carolina coast. Sherman was stubborn, however, and wanted to initiate his planned march anyway, but the roads were impassable and the river was rising, forcing his men to relocate their camps. Not even the fiery-tempered Sherman could command the forces of nature.

Sherman planned to advance through South Carolina in the same manner in which he had marched to Savannah, splitting his army into two columns. The right-hand column, commanded by Gen. Oliver O. Howard, would head up the coast toward Charleston; the left-hand column under Gen. Henry W. Slocum would move toward Augusta, the same destination Beauregard had in mind for the Army of Tennessee.

Slocum's men were bogged down at Savannah, unable to get across the river. All the bridges and causeways were either underwater or had been washed out completely by the flooding. Howard, on the other hand, was able to get a portion of his men out of Savannah by boat before the deluge began. This half of the army sailed up the coast to Beaufort, where it waited for the rest of the column. Finally, toward the end of January, the rains slackened, and the remaining Federals in Savannah moved out.

Directly across the river from the city, where Hardee's troops had gone when they were evacuated, stood a small village that had been dubbed Hardeeville, after the Confederate commander. The Yankees burned it, totally destroying the tiny settlement. A few days later, the same thing happened to the town of Robertsville. Sherman was picking up where he had left off. The pattern of wanton destruction that had left a wide stretch of Georgia in ruins was being repeated in South Carolina.

The march did not come easy, however. The rains had left much of the terrain in a state that could only be described—and generously at that—as swamplike. As a result, Sherman's men didn't really march, they waded. And their heavy supply wagons were constantly stuck in the mud. Progress was slow and painful.

Despite the obstacles, the Union army moved steadily northward. The Yankees were coming, and there seemed to be little anyone could do to stop them.

"YOU WANT I should take a shot at 'em?" Abner Strayhorn asked as he crouched behind a fallen tree. His boots squished in the mud when he shifted a little and rested the barrel of his rifle on the log.

"No, hold your fire," Cory told him. "No point in standing up and yelling at the Yankees that we're here."

Abner snorted. "You don't reckon they could ever catch us, do you? In this muck?"

"I don't want to take a chance." Cory leaned against the log. Through field glasses he studied the Union troops slogging through the shallow water a couple of hundred yards away. "We have to let the general know what's going on, and we can't do that if we're dead or captured."

Rifle fire crackled in the distance. "Reckon that's some o' our boys snipin' at them damnyanks," Abner complained. "I don't see why I can't take a potshot or two at 'em . . . sir."

"Don't start that," Cory snapped. "Every time I won't let you do something, you blame it on my being an officer."

"Was a time you'd have tried to knock down one or two o' them Yankees yourself," Abner grumbled.

Cory lowered the glasses. "Yes. I used to be impulsive and reckless, too."

Abner glared at him for a second then chuckled. "Ol' General, he done the right thing makin' you an officer, Cory. You taken right to it."

God forbid, Cory thought. He had never intended to be a regular soldier, let alone an officer.

But those were the twists that fate had taken.

More shots sounded, closer this time. Cory quickly lifted the glasses again as he heard a distant cry. One of the Yankees hauling on a mule harness, trying to get that brute and the others in the team to pull the wagon to which they were hitched out of the mud, collapsed against the balky animal. The man slid down into the mud.

Angry shouts floated through the gray, misty air. Orange flame lanced from the muzzles of the Yankees' guns as they fired on the Confederate snipers. A haze of powder smoke drifted around their heads.

Cory heard a low hum and recognized it as the sound of a minié ball tumbling through the air somewhere close to his ear. The Yankees were firing blindly because there was little chance they could actually see the sharpshooters targeting them, but a lucky shot could be just as deadly as an aimed one. Cory put down his field glasses and plucked at Abner's sleeve. "We've seen enough. Let's get out of here."

He moved back deeper into the trees, the mud sucking heavily at his boots with every step. Abner followed, still muttering about taking a shot or two at the Yankees. The two men reached their horses, still tied up in the brush.

All morning Cory had watched the Federal column, studying the regimental flags, trying to estimate the enemy's strength. General Hardee in Charleston had sent Abner and him to determine just how much of a threat Sherman's army posed.

As far as Cory could tell, it was a formidable threat. He figured at least half of the men who had marched to Savannah with Sherman were now on the way toward Charleston. He didn't know where the other half of the Yankee army was, but wherever they were, they were up to no good for the Carolinas.

Hardee's army was outnumbered four to one, Cory estimated. They could put up a good fight, but they couldn't win. Not without help. He knew that troops were on the way from Mississippi.

Reinforcements would have to reach South Carolina soon . . . or else it would be too late.

If it wasn't already too late—for South Carolina and for the rest of the beleaguered Confederacy.

DESPITE APPEARANCES, Sherman's first goal was not Charleston but Columbia, the state capital. His easternmost column, Howard's, gradually swung inland and headed almost due north rather than follow the coastline northeastward toward Charleston. Travel conditions improved somewhat as the Federals moved away from the coast.

By this time Cory and Abner were back in Charleston, having ridden as fast as their horses could gallop over the muddy roads. Cory cleaned off his boots before entering Hardee's headquarters in a commandeered residence, but he was afraid he would track mud into the general's office anyway. These days, that was hard to avoid.

The dapper general with a gray spadelike beard looked up from the desk where he had been studying a map of the coast. "Well, what news have you to report, Captain?" he asked.

"Nothing good, sir," Cory replied. "At least half of Sherman's army is on its way north from Savannah. Scouts report that several towns have been burned to the ground already. Our skirmishers have been unable to slow the advance." He paused then added, "The weather seems to be our most effective ally.

The flooding has kept the Yankees from moving as fast as they might otherwise."

Hardee nodded slowly. He didn't seem surprised by the bad news. "General Beauregard and I have consulted on the matter, and it has been decided that the best course of action under the circumstances will be to evacuate Charleston."

"Evacuate the civilians, you mean, sir?"

"No," Hardee said. "Our army will withdraw from the city and move farther up the coast."

In other words, Cory thought, they were running again. Just like they had run at Chattanooga, Atlanta, and Savannah. They had put up a fight now and then, here and there, along the way, but for all intents and purposes, for more than a year now the Confederate army had been running away like whipped dogs with their tails between their legs. It didn't seem to matter who the commander was—Johnston, Hood, or Hardee—or what the circumstances, the end result was the same. The Southerners retreated, and the Yankees kept coming.

"Begging the general's pardon, sir," Cory grated. "Don't you think it's time we made a stand?"

Hardee's eyes narrowed. Placing his palms on the desk, he answered, "You've just returned from a hazardous, difficult mission, Captain. No doubt you're exhausted. You should return to your quarters and get some rest . . . now."

"But, sir—"

"Cap'n, we better do like the general says," Abner interrupted. He had a worried look on his face.

Cory rubbed his fingertips against his temples for a moment. His question had bordered on insubordination and was yet another sign that he really wasn't cut out to be a soldier. He was too quick to speak his mind, too quick to allow impatience and frustration to get the better of him.

"My apologies, General," he said.

"You are dismissed, Captain." Hardee's tone softened a bit as he looked away. "There are eight thousand of us."

He said nothing else. He was too proud to explain himself, but the simple statement was explanation enough. If the odds had been anywhere near even . . . if the Yankees had not had an overpowering advantage in men, munitions, and supplies . . . then this campaign, indeed the entire war, likely would have been a much different story.

But as it was, this story was nearing its ending, Cory sensed. All that was left was the turning of a few more pages.

BY MID-FEBRUARY Howard's column was approaching Columbia. The capital city's population had swelled over the past couple of months as South Carolinians from across the state fled their homes and sought refuge there, deluding themselves into thinking that it was beyond the realm of possibility for the Yankees to ever penetrate that far inland. These newcomers were about to find out how wrong they were.

On February 16 Confederate Gen. Joseph Wheeler's cavalry rode into Columbia. Wheeler's men had been ranging through the middle of the state, trying without success to put up some opposition to the advance of Slocum's column to the west. Now they had come to protect Columbia from the Yankees, Wheeler explained to the city authorities. That may well have been what the general had in mind, but it soon became apparent that the men nominally under his command had a different idea. The gray-clad horsemen began to loot the city instead, breaking into shops and homes and helping themselves to whatever they wanted. Citizens watched aghast as the men who were supposed to protect them now robbed them instead.

Word arrived shortly that the Federals were approaching the city. Some of the cavalrymen broke off their wanton rampage and returned to the duty that had brought them here. They rode out of Columbia, halfheartedly skirmished with the Yankee cavalry in front of the main column, and then beat a hasty retreat. The few horse soldiers left in the city pulled out as well, leaving the capital undefended.

Slocum's men marched into the city early the next morning. Sherman himself accompanied the column, and he met with the mayor of the city to assure him that Columbia would not be destroyed. That soon proved to be a promise that not even a general could keep.

Seeking to keep the conquering troops in a good mood, the residents passed out whiskey by the bucketful to the Yankees. This gesture soon backfired as the drunken soldiers began to loot whatever Wheeler's rogues had left behind. Bales of cotton were set afire in the streets, and the flames soon spread to nearby structures. Reveling soldiers cheered as the blaze raced through building after building. The people of Columbia fled their burning homes and businesses and watched in horror as their city was destroyed around them.

Before leaving Savannah, Sherman had said that the time had come to teach the people of South Carolina a lesson and to punish them for their traitorous behavior. With the burning of Columbia, he made a good start toward that goal.

GENERAL HARDEE was not a well man. Cory knew that just by looking at him. Eventually, the general was confined to his bed for several days, but by February 17 he insisted that he had recovered sufficiently to be up and around and in charge of the evacuation of Charleston. At the same time, he blamed himself that the task was not yet done. His army probably would have been far from the city had it not been for his illness.

Now, though, the troops were lined up and awaiting the word to march out. Hardee issued orders for the cotton stored in warehouses to be burned rather than let it fall into Yankee hands. Engineers placed explosives on ships in the harbor and blew them to dust. Smoke and flames rose into the night sky. It was Savannah all over again, Cory thought bitterly as he watched the destruction unfolding at the hands of his own comrades.

"Mighty hard to swallow such a pill, ain't it?" Abner asked as he stood next to Cory on the porch of Hardee's headquarters. He rested the butt of his rifle on the planks and leaned on the barrel.

Cory silently nodded. He had seen victory in several clashes when he was riding with Forrest's cavalry and with the army at Chickamauga, and he had seen defeats at Chattanooga and Peachtree Creek. The defeats had not been as galling, though, as running away without a fight. That seemed like it was getting to be a habit.

Yet he couldn't fault Hardee and Beauregard for the decision to abandon Charleston. Hardee's small army couldn't hope to stand up to the sledgehammer strength of Sherman's army. Any attempt would result in the futile deaths of thousands of men, not to mention the wave of destruction a battle might unleash on the city and its inhabitants. A significant part of military strategy was knowing when to retreat and when to make a stand. Cory didn't pretend to understand such things. What he knew of soldiering he had learned from Bedford Forrest, and even Forrest had been known to retreat when he had no other choice, such as at Fort Donelson, where he had slipped away before his cavalry could be destroyed by the Yankees. By doing so, he and his men had lived to fight on many other days, in many other places.

The swift rataplan of hoof beats drew Cory's attention from his dark thoughts about the evacuation. A young trooper drew his mount to a halt in front of the headquarters. The horse heaved, and its head drooped, showing how hard the animal had been ridden. The young rider looked frazzled as he swung down from the saddle and hurried to the porch.

Snapping a quick salute, the youngster asked, "Is General Hardee inside, sir?"

"He is," Cory replied, spotting the leather dispatch pouch looped around the young man's neck. "Do you have a message for him?"

"Yes sir, I do. From General Wheeler."

Cory frowned. He didn't know Wheeler, but he knew Forrest had little respect for the man. He held out his hand. "I'm one of the general's aides. I'll take the dispatch to him."

"No offense, sir, but I'm supposed to deliver it personally."

The last Cory had heard of Wheeler, the general's cavalry had been somewhere in the center of the state. If there were important developments elsewhere in South Carolina, Hardee needed to know about them as soon as possible. "Come with me," he said.

Hardee was getting ready to depart as Cory ushered the messenger into his presence. The general had been one of the last to leave Savannah, and Cory figured the same would be true here. Hardee paused in drawing on his gauntlets and raised his eyebrows quizzically. "What have we here, Captain?" he asked.

"A dispatch from General Wheeler, sir."

The young cavalryman stepped forward, saluted, and withdrew a folded paper from the pouch. He handed it to Hardee then moved back discreetly.

Hardee broke the seal and quickly read it. He already looked pale and drawn from his illness. As the message soaked in on him, he became even more wan. Without looking up he said in a strained voice, "Columbia has fallen to the Yankees. By nightfall, the city appeared to be in flames."

Cory knew that it would have taken a large force to capture the capital city. He leaped to the obvious conclusion: "That Yankee column was headed for Columbia, not here, sir. We don't have to evacuate Charleston after all."

Hardee shook his head. "The decision has already been made. This changes nothing."

"But sir—"

"It changes nothing, Captain," Hardee repeated in a heavy voice. "Think about it. With Columbia in Federal hands, the Yankees now hold the interior of the state. If we stay here, the Army of Tennessee has no chance of reaching us." The general crumpled the paper in his hand. "We're cut off as long as we remain in Charleston, Captain Brannon. We must leave so that we have at least a chance of linking up with the rest of our people."

When Hardee put it like that, Cory understood. Sherman had been devilishly clever, disguising his real objective of splitting South Carolina in half. Now he had accomplished that, and it stood to reason that his next move would be to turn toward Charleston to the east and Augusta to the west. Sherman was about to perform the same daring maneuver that Forrest had once pulled off: He was going to charge in two directions at once.

Of course, Sherman might have something entirely different in mind, but that was what he would have done, Cory thought. He grimaced to himself at the idea he might be thinking like a Yankee now.

Hardee turned to the messenger and rested a hand on his shoulder for a moment. "I'd offer you a fresh horse, son, but we don't have any. You'll have to get back to General Wheeler's command as best you can."

The young cavalryman nodded. "Yes sir. I understand."

"But we can offer you a little food and some grain for your mount. Captain, see to that, will you?"

"Of course, sir," Cory said.

"Let me take care of it," Abner offered. He took the young man's arm. "Come along with me, fella."

They left, and as they went, Cory watched Hardee finish putting on his gauntlets. "Are you sure you're all right, General?" he asked.

"I fear none of us are all right," Hardee said with a sigh. "Not anymore."

Cory knew exactly what he meant.

☆ ☆ ☆

THE EVACUATION proceeded without incident. Instead of following the coastline, the Confederates marched inland this time, heading almost due north from the city along the road that led to Florence in the northeastern corner of the state. General Beauregard had decided that Florence, along with the settlement of Cheraw farther north, would serve as the rendezvous for the Confederates scattered throughout South Carolina.

When and if those forces succeeded in coming together, they would have a new commander. Gen. Joseph E. Johnston, who had been replaced by John Bell Hood while the army was in Atlanta the previous summer, had been reinstated by Robert E. Lee. On February 23 Johnston accepted the assignment with misgivings. Desertion had shrunk the numbers of reinforcements making their way to South Carolina. Even at full strength, the army that was being assembled to face Sherman would be outnumbered by a considerable margin.

But unless Sherman was stopped somehow, eventually he would link up with Grant's army in Virginia, and that would be the end.

Chapter Thirteen

W HOO-EEE!" ERNIE MURRELL YELLED as he waved his hat over his head. "Look at 'em go!"

Beside Murrell, Henry Brannon leaned on a split-rail fence and watched the horses thunder past on the crude racecourse that had been staked out that morning. Half a dozen animals were entered in this race. Their riders leaned low over the horses' necks. Some of them used switches to whip their mounts; others used their hats. The course was a short one, only a quarter of a mile, and it wouldn't take long for the horses to run it. While those seconds sped by, however, the several hundred spectators gathered around the course shouted and whistled and cheered on their favorites. Their enthusiasm was contagious, even to those like Henry who didn't really care which horse won. He found himself leaning forward and intently following the race as it unfolded.

Over the past couple of weeks, Forrest's cavalry had shifted southward, following the railroad and the Tombigbee River from Corinth, Mississippi, to the settlement of Verona. Henry had heard rumors that soon they would move even farther south, to a place called West Point. He didn't know why the cavalry's camps had been relocated, but he was sure Forrest had a good reason. To get farther away from Yankee Gen. James H. Wilson's cavalry, maybe.

Henry and Murrell had been among the scouts who had crossed the Tennessee River in far northwestern Alabama to spy on what the Yankees were up to. They discovered a large cavalry force, probably the largest mounted command anybody had ever seen in this area. Wilson had more than twenty thousand blue-clad troopers camped along the river. Henry had studied them from a rise several hundred yards away and had given up counting them. There were just too many, like fleas on

213

a hound dog in midsummer. When he turned his spyglass on the stacks of arms around the camps, he saw that most were Spencer repeaters, like the one he had captured from a Yankee. Forrest's men were not only outnumbered, they were outgunned as well.

Yet when the time came, they would not be outfought. That was the hope, anyway.

Morale was still high even though news of the massive Federal cavalry had gotten around. The horserace was one sign of the high spirits. Friendly banter about whose horse was the fastest had been going around for quite some time, and today the proud horsemen involved had decided to settle the matter.

When the race was over, men gathered around the winning rider, shouting and pounding him on the back in congratulations. Money was in pretty short supply these days, but coins changed hands anyway as bets were paid off. Some of the wagers had been made in other currency, such as tobacco or squares of hardtack. The losing horsemen quickly worked the crowd, promoting a rematch.

Murrell nudged Henry. "Look yonder," he prompted, indicating with a jerk of his chin the cabin where Bedford Forrest made his headquarters.

Henry saw the general lounging in the open doorway with a shoulder propped against the jamb. Forrest was grinning in clear appreciation of the race. That was a bit of a surprise, because the general had let it be known that while he enjoyed a good horserace, the cavalry could ill afford to wear out animals like that. The race had been a small show of defiance on the part of the men, just as they sometimes shot off their guns for no good reason, wasting powder and lead.

Spotting Forrest, the winning horseman led his animal to the general's cabin. "Did you see that, General? We won!"

"You sure did," Forrest agreed. "And on account of that, I reckon I'll give you a prize."

The horseman stared. "A prize? Really?"

Forrest nodded gravely. "Sure enough."

The winning rider turned to the others and shouted, "You hear that, boys? General Forrest is givin' me a prize! Let's hear it for him!"

Shouts of appreciation rose from the assembled cavalrymen. Henry and Murrell joined in, Murrell somewhat more enthusiastically than Henry, who thought he saw something in Forrest's dark-eyed gaze that didn't bode well for the celebrants.

The winner asked, "What kind of prize are you a-gonna give me, General?"

Forrest looked at him and announced, "Well, son, you only have to split and carry rails for three hours, instead of four like all these other boys." He waved his hand to indicate the other riders and the rest of the crowd.

Silence. The winner goggled at Forrest for a moment then said, "But . . . but . . ." He stopped with a shake of his head and a shrug of his shoulders as he accepted the inevitable. "Oh, well. I reckon any prize is better than none. Thanks, General."

That prompted laughter from the crowd, and Forrest himself chuckled at the hangdog expression on the man's face. The fellow was right.

These days, any prize was better than none.

SELMA WAS one of the Confederacy's last bastions of manufacturing. Situated well inland in Alabama, the war had not yet reached it. Nevertheless, Forrest and Gen. Richard Taylor, commander of the troops left behind when the rest of the Army of Tennessee started eastward to aid in blocking Sherman's coastal advance, were convinced that Selma was the ultimate goal of Wilson's massive cavalry buildup. So Forrest began to shift his men southward during February 1865. If Wilson captured Selma, yet another wedge would have been driven deep into the Southern heartland.

Establishing a temporary headquarters at West Point, Forrest shepherded the Confederate army southward toward Selma. Although nominally under Taylor's command, Forrest was in charge of this campaign, if campaign it could be called. In an unusual move for the daring Forrest, he was preparing to fight a defensive battle.

In the camp at West Point, whenever his company wasn't on patrol, Henry spent hours playing checkers with Murrell and the other men. Growing up in Virginia, he had played checkers with his older brothers, most of whom had beaten him unmercifully whenever they had the chance. Only Mac had ever taken pity on him and let him win a game once in a while. When Henry figured that out, he stopped playing with Mac. He wanted to win or lose fair and square, with no punches pulled on either side.

Accordingly, he had become quite a player. Murrell beat him only once or twice out of every ten games. It got to the point in the camp that men actually gathered around to watch whenever Henry played checkers. Some of them even bet on the outcome.

The board was set up on a stump near one of the campfires. Although still cold and dreary most of the time, the weather had improved a little.

Henry drew his coat tighter around him as he studied the checkerboard then glanced up at his opponent. Today he was playing a man from another company, a tall, burly, craggy-faced man whose last name was Conrad. Henry didn't know him very well, but as they had played over the past hour, he had gotten to know the man better. He knew that Conrad took the game seriously and didn't like the fact that he was losing.

Henry moved one of his checkers. The hasty way that Conrad reached forward to counter the move told Henry that his opponent had fallen for the bait. Not hurrying, Henry reached out and jumped three of Conrad's checkers, collecting them and placing them to the side. Conrad stared at the board for a while then frowned in anger.

"You tricked me," he accused.

"Part of the game," Henry said. His tone was level, not friendly but not hostile, either.

"Still, it don't seem right." Conrad was in bad shape now, with only a few checkers left and a limited number of moves he could make—and most of them were bad. He could postpone the inevitable defeat with a proper move, but any hope of winning was gone.

Henry waited patiently. The spectators standing around the stump were quiet. This little area had a hushed atmosphere to it, almost like a church, even though the rest of the camp was filled with the usual noises made by men and horses.

Conrad made his move. As Henry expected, it was the wrong one. He jumped two more checkers and said, "King me."

The burly man uttered an expletive, then his hand shot out and upset the board, flipping it back into Henry's lap. Checkers went flying.

"I'll crown you, you son of a—" Conrad began as he lunged up from his stool and swung a heavy fist toward Henry's head.

Henry let himself go over backward on his stool, putting him out of reach of Conrad's sweeping blow. He rolled over and came up with an agile bound. Conrad leaped over the stump and rushed him, still swinging wildly. The crowd yelled in glee. Nothing broke up the monotony of camp life like a fight.

A part of Henry's brain was amused by the sheer absurdity of brawling over a lost game of checkers. But at the same time, he knew this was a serious situation. Conrad's pride was wounded, and that made him even more dangerous. He would like nothing better than to give Henry a sound thrashing, even though it wouldn't change anything. Conrad had still lost.

Henry ducked a punch, twisted, reached up, grabbed his opponent's arm, and threw a hip into him. Back on the farm, Henry had wrestled a lot with his brothers, too, and they hadn't taken it easy on him in that pastime, either. With a startled yell, Conrad's own weight and momentum jerked him off his feet as Henry pivoted.

The big man sailed through the air and crashed heavily to the ground. Henry hoped that would take the fight out of the man, but Conrad rolled over, pushed himself to his hands and knees, and shook his head like an old bull. He glowered up at Henry and growled a curse.

"Let it go," Henry advised him. "It's not worth it."

"I'll show you what it's worth," Conrad threatened as he came to his feet.

Once again he rushed forward, but this time he approached Henry in a more cautious manner. That wasn't good, Henry thought. Conrad was taller, heavier, and had a longer reach. His scarred, broken-nosed countenance was mute testimony to his experience as a brawler, too. He started a fast left toward Henry's belly, and when Henry's arms dropped, Conrad's right came up and over and tagged him hard on the jaw.

The punch exploded like a bomb and sent Henry staggering back. He thought he was going to fall, but he caught his balance and stayed on his feet. Before he could set himself, though, Conrad was on him, stinging his midsection with quick blows. Henry threw a fist into Conrad's face and connected solidly, but the bigger man shrugged it off. He rocked Henry back another step with a hard left to the chest, then sank a right to the solar plexus that left Henry gasping for air. Desperate, Henry ducked under a roundhouse left and threw himself forward, tackling Conrad around the waist.

He drove hard with his legs, and the impact was enough to topple Conrad like a tree. Conrad landed on his back with Henry on top of him. Henry aimed a knee at Conrad's groin, no longer caring about whether or not he was fighting fair. He was fighting for survival. Fair had nothing to do with it. But Conrad twisted and took the knee on his thigh. It had to hurt, but it didn't incapacitate him. He reached up, got a hand on Henry's throat, and flung him aside.

Henry went rolling. Some of the excited spectators had to skip backward to give him room. Conrad came after him. A vicious kick glanced off Henry's hip. Conrad aimed another kick at him, clearly trying to stave in his ribs. Henry got his hands up in time, caught Conrad's foot, and heaved. With a yell, Conrad went over backward.

That gave Henry enough of a respite to get to his feet. He hurt all over, and he still hadn't gotten all of his wind back. But Conrad was getting up again, fire still in his eyes.

"Wait . . . wait a minute," Henry gasped. "This is stupid! A game of checkers isn't worth . . . isn't worth . . ."

"You cheated," Conrad snapped. "You couldn't have beat me if you hadn't cheated!"

Henry knew that wasn't the case, but Conrad was too full of rage and injured pride to listen to reason. All he wanted to do was keep slugging away at his enemy, even though it wouldn't accomplish anything except more unnecessary punishment for both of them.

He rumbled forward, not as wildly as in his first charge but not with the second attack's caution, either. Henry had gotten in enough licks so that Conrad was feeling some pain, too. He wanted to end this battle while he still could.

So did Henry. He summoned up some unexpected strength from somewhere deep inside him and parried Conrad's first two blows. That brought him close enough to snap a fast right to Conrad's chin. This time the bigger man wasn't able to ignore the punch. He hesitated, and in that split second Henry jabbed a left that opened up a cut over Conrad's right eye. Blood welled from the injury and dripped into the man's eye, partially blinding him. He howled in pain and rage and tried to grab Henry in a bear hug.

Henry slipped away to the side and slapped a right against Conrad's left ear. Then a left shot home to the body. Conrad threw an uppercut. Henry stepped back so that Conrad's fist barely grazed him. He smashed the side of his right fist against the big man's right ear in a backhanded blow. Conrad staggered, and Henry could have tripped him then. He didn't, though. He wanted to end this with his fists. He peppered the burly man with a couple of fast lefts then swung a right that flattened Conrad's nose and made blood spurt. The bigger man went down, his face covered with crimson. He looked a little like a piece of meat on the chopping block when the butcher is through with it.

Butchery was what it had been, all right. Henry felt sick.

He became aware that the shouting had stopped. In fact, an eerie silence hung over the area around the stump where the fight had taken place. The only sounds Henry heard were the rasp of his own breathing and the bubbling rush of air through Conrad's shattered nose.

He looked around and saw the general standing in his customary long coat and wide-brimmed hat. Forrest's hands rested on the butts of the pistols that he carried reversed on each hip.

"You plan on puttin' that much into it the next time you fight the Yankees, Brannon?"

Henry dragged the back of his hand across his mouth then nodded. "Yes sir," he said. "I sure do."

"There's a rule against brawlin', you know."

"Yes sir." Henry didn't mention the fact that Conrad had started the fight by attacking him. He had defended himself, that was all. His own pride wouldn't allow him to say that, though.

"There'll be extra duties for the both of you. I'll speak to your company commanders. In the meantime, carry on." Forrest started to turn away but then stopped to look back at Henry. "All you Brannons are fightin' fools, aren't you?"

"Yes sir, I reckon."

Or maybe just fools, Henry thought, to be fighting an unwinnable war in the first place.

MAC CAME to attention and saluted the man behind the desk, who stood up and returned the salute solemnly.

A smile broke out on Fitzhugh Lee's face, and he came around the desk to embrace Mac and clap him on the back.

"What are you doing here in Richmond, Mac?" Lee asked. He waved a hand toward the chair in front of the desk. "Sit down, sit down. We don't stand on formality, two old comrades in arms such as ourselves."

"Well, sir," Mac said as he settled himself on the chair and held his hat on his knee, "General Rosser's cavalry has been detached from duty in the Shenandoah and summoned here to join the army at Petersburg. I'm not sure what we're going to do there . . ."

"No, there's not much room for cavalry during a siege," Fitz said with a shake of his head. "About all you can do is scout the flanks and watch for enemy maneuvers in that direction."

"Yes sir, I expect that's right. I've been told the Yankees have designs on the Southside Railroad and some other routes leading into Richmond and Petersburg from the west. If those were to be cut, the siege couldn't continue for very long."

A strained look appeared on Lee's bearded face. "I'm not certain how much longer the siege can continue even under the best of circumstances. The army is low, Mac, mighty low."

That opinion came as no surprise to Mac. For months now the bloody standoff had gone back and forth along the trenches and fortifications just south of Petersburg. Several large battles since the previous summer had killed thousands of men but had done nothing to change the basic situation. And the flow of supplies into Richmond was being squeezed off gradually. If the capital were to be isolated, the supplies coming to the troops in the trenches would stop completely. That was why it was vitally important for the railroads and turnpikes leading into the city from the west to remain open.

"What about you, sir?" Mac asked. "How are you doing?"

The wound Fitz Lee had suffered at Winchester had taken a toll on the general. Mac could readily see that. Lee's long, thick beard was touched with gray, and his youthful face had lines and wrinkles that hadn't been there before the injury. But his vitality was still there, although somewhat diminished.

"I'm fine, fine," Lee insisted with a wave of his hand. "I'd be better, though, if I could get out from behind this desk. General Rosser is a good man, of course, but . . ."

"But a good many of the cavalry he commands are still your men, General," Mac finished for him when Lee couldn't go on.

Lee looked away for a moment, moved but clearly not wanting to show the depth of his emotion. He was in control of himself when he looked back and said briskly, "I've seen the reports. You've done a fine job with the Ninth, Mac. I would have expected no less from you. I would have long ago given you a command myself, had you not been so valuable to me. My staff's gain was the cavalry's loss."

"It's kind of you to say so, sir. But when you return to command, I'll be more than happy to relinquish my regiment to another officer for a place on your staff again."

Lee sighed. "I don't know if it will ever come to that, Mac. I really don't. My recovery is almost complete, but I'm not sure there's time—"

Silence shrouded the office as Lee abruptly fell silent. Both men knew what the general meant. February would soon be drawing to a close. March would mean the coming of spring, and spring would mean . . . what?

No one knew the answer to that question. No one, perhaps, save for a hard-drinking, cigar-chewing, tightlipped Yankee general named Grant.

THE SNOW was still a foot deep on the ground in Mosby's Confederacy. Titus had remained there instead of returning to Amherst County. Dolly Richards had received word that Mosby had recovered enough to travel to Richmond for meetings with the president and Robert E. Lee. Nothing more had been heard from Fitzhugh Lee. It appeared that the younger Lee's efforts to interfere with the rangers were over.

To boost their morale, some of the rangers had organized a fox hunt in early February. More than a hundred men had taken part, and somehow they had managed to gather a large number of hounds. Titus had looked on with a mixture of boredom and amusement as the mass of riders dashed around the countryside, despite the snow, and the floppy-eared hounds lumbered through the woods trying to catch a scent of their quarry. Whenever they did, their mournful baying shattered the cold air and prompted enthusiastic shouts from the hunters, who again dashed back and forth some more. All that effort, Titus thought, just to scare up a handful of mangy foxes who were already half-starved from the hard winter.

The rangers spent some of their time patrolling the roads, but these days few Yankees were to be found in Loudoun and Fauquier Counties. Sometimes Titus looked longingly toward the Blue Ridge Mountains. They were over there, he thought, right there in the Shenandoah Valley. It would be easy for the rangers to cross over and find a fight, as they had done back at the end of January when they raided the Federal camp near Harpers Ferry. But Mosby had given orders that they were to stay put.

On the night of February 18 Titus was at one of the safe houses not far from the settlement of Markham. The family that owned the house had made the rangers welcome, of course, feeding them a decent meal and offering them a good place to sleep. After supper, the rangers got up several domino games in the parlor. Warmth and laughter filled the air.

Titus lounged near the fireplace and watched the games for a while before he grew bored. He shrugged into his coat, put on his hat, and picked up his rifle as he started outside. He intended to walk out to the barn and check on the horses. The farmer and his young sons had promised to care for the animals, but Titus liked to see to such things himself. Sometimes the rangers' lives depended on their mounts. The animals had to be well cared for.

It was a cold night with a crystal-clear sky. Stars glittered in the heavens overhead. Titus went into the darkened barn, felt around until he found a lantern, and was about to strike a match and light it when he heard the muffled thunder of thudding hoof beats nearby.

That could be some more rangers coming in, he thought. On the other hand, that was unlikely. Most of the patrols were already at one of the safe houses by this time of night. Titus set the lantern down and gripped his rifle tighter as he went to the door of the barn and peered out through the narrow opening.

His eyes narrowed with hatred as he saw the blue-uniformed troopers sweep into the yard before the house. Yankees! Almost every fiber of Titus's being urged him to fire into the crowd of Federal cavalry. But the part of his brain not blinded by hate warned him that if he did so, he would be signing his own death warrant. He estimated there were more than a hundred men in the Union party.

Less than a score of rangers were in the house. They had no chance. Brandishing carbines, the Yankees dismounted and stormed the place. Titus listened but didn't hear any shots. Mosby's men had been taken by surprise and captured without putting up a fight. Doubtless they had not wanted to endanger the lives of their hosts.

Titus didn't know if he could have let himself be captured like that. He had sworn a vow that he would never again be made a prisoner of the Yankees. He would have forced the raiders to kill him, and he would have taken as many of them to hell with him as he could before he went down.

With triumphant shouts, the Union cavalrymen dragged and prodded their prisoners out of the house. The rangers came along grimly. One of the Yankee officers waved a hand and called out, "Get their horses. And some of you men better search that barn while you're at it!"

Titus drew back from the door as several troopers started toward the barn. He looked around desperately, knowing that if he didn't get out of there in a hurry, he would be trapped. But there was no rear door, no place to run.

Maybe he could hide. He hurried over to the ladder that led up to the hayloft. Slinging his rifle over his shoulder by its strap, he started to climb.

He scurried up the ladder like a squirrel up a tree and dove into the thick pile of hay in the loft, pulling it over him so that he couldn't be seen. With his heart pounding, he lay motionless and hoped that if the Yankees looked up here, they wouldn't notice that the hay had been disturbed recently.

He heard the heavy tread of their feet as they came into the barn. The troopers talked among themselves, pointing out the places they should look. The sound of their Northern accents made Titus's jaw clench. He forced himself to be calm, to breathe slowly and evenly.

Some of the Yankees saddled and led out the rangers' horses. They didn't seem to notice that they had one more horse than they did prisoners. Just as Titus thought they were about to leave without searching the loft, he heard one of them start up the ladder. A moment later, something poked into the pile of hay not far from Titus. The Yankee was using his bayonet like a pitchfork, jabbing around the pile to make sure no one was hidden in it!

Titus waited it out and hoped for the best. There was nothing else he could do. The bayonet came prodding through the hay only inches from his face. He held his breath as it was withdrawn then thrust down again. This time it passed between his arm and his side. The next time he felt it close by his knee. Three times the Yankee had barely missed him.

But three times was the charm.

The trooper turned away and called down to his comrades, "Nobody up here!"

"Let's go, then. We've got all the Rebel bastards."

Not all, Titus thought as he closed his eyes in relief and listened to the Yankee climbing down the ladder from the loft. Here was one of the Rebel bastards who intended to do everything in his power to make the raiders pay for what they had done tonight.

Chapter Fourteen

T HE LAST TITUS HAD heard, Dolly Richards had been heading for Green Garden, his family home near Upperville
and one of the rangers' safe houses. Richards had to be told that
there were Yankees abroad tonight, if he didn't know already.

As soon as the Union cavalrymen were gone, Titus climbed
down from the loft and hurried into the house. The family inside
looked distraught over the raid, but they were more surprised to
see that one of the rangers had avoided being caught up in the
Yankee net.

"Did the bastards say where they were going?" Titus asked,
not bothering to watch his language around the womenfolk.

"From what one of the officers said, I think they came over
Ashby's Gap earlier tonight," the homeowner told him. "They'll
probably go back that way."

"Have you got a horse I can ride?" Titus asked.

The man shook his head. "No, I've got a couple of mules,
though. My boys ride 'em sometimes."

With a sigh of resignation, Titus nodded. A mule would have
to do.

A short time later, he headed north, riding bareback on the
rangy, hardheaded mule. The creature's spine was so bony it was
almost like riding a picket fence, Titus thought. He could put
up with the discomfort, though, if it meant that he could organize a rescue party for his captured comrades.

He bounced along a back road that led toward Upperville,
swaying with the mule's ungainly gait. His keen ears listened
intently for the sound of anyone else on this cold, dark night.

He had nearly reached the intersection with the road that ran
between Upperville and the settlement of Paris, at the foot of
the Blue Ridge, when several riders burst out of the trees and
surrounded him. Titus's hands closed around the butts of his

229

pistols as he determined to sell his life dearly. But before he could draw and fire, a familiar voice called, "Titus! Is that you?"

"It's me, Major," he responded to Dolly Richards's question. "I reckon those stinkin' Yanks didn't get you after all."

"Not for lack of trying," Richards said as he pulled his horse's head around and motioned for the other men to sit easy in their saddles. "They came busting into my folks' house all ready to grab me. They had one of our boys with them who had turned traitor and led them there. But they didn't get me. We heard them coming in time for me to get behind a fake panel in the wall."

Titus nodded. He knew that such hiding places had been set up in most of the safe houses, and tonight that precaution had paid off, saving Dolly Richards from capture by the Yankees. As one of Mosby's most trusted right-hand men, Richards would have been quite a plum for the Yankees if they could have gotten their hands on him.

There were other men in the grip of the enemy, though, and they were important, too. "Another bunch of 'em grabbed up everybody in my patrol except me," Titus said.

"When did this happen?" Richards asked grimly.

"About an hour ago. I don't reckon they've had time to get back through the gap yet."

"Do you know that's where they were going?"

"That's where they came from," Titus said, going on to explain what the homeowner had overheard. "It makes sense they'd go back the same way."

Richards nodded in agreement. "Then that's where we'll hit them," he said.

That sounded good to Titus. Ashby's Gap was fairly wide and had a good road running through it, but the confines were close enough so that a quick, hard strike could be successful, even against a larger force. Titus didn't know how many men Richards had with him, but it was a safe bet the Yankees would outnumber them.

By this time it was after midnight. Richards called the rest of his party out of hiding. Titus estimated there were about thirty men in all. The Yankees outnumbered them more than three to one. The rangers would have to hope that they could hit the enemy hard enough and fast enough to cut those odds down in a hurry. The fact that most of the partisans carried at least a pair of revolvers would help. From what Titus had seen, most of the Yankees had been armed with carbines. At close range, Mosby's men would have more firepower.

They rode east toward Paris and Ashby's Gap beyond. Before they reached the settlement, more riders appeared in the road ahead, coming toward them. The rangers drew their guns in anticipation of a fight, but a moment later a Southern voice hailed them.

The newcomers rode up. There were ten of them, all rangers from the Paris area. "Howdy, Major," one of them greeted Richards. "I reckon you heard about what happened?"

Richards nodded. "We're on the trail of the Yankees right now. Did they do any damage in Paris?"

The spokesman shook his head. "They were just huntin' rangers. They left the civilians and the buildings alone, thank God. Wouldn't have put it past 'em to burn down the town." The man leaned over and spat. "They had quite a few prisoners with them, includin' Jeremiah Wilson."

Richards started in surprise. "Wilson's supposed to get married tomorrow!"

"Yep. The gal he's supposed to get hitched to saw him being taken away by the Yankees and ran out to ask the officer in charge if they'd let him go on account of that. But that Yankee major just sneered at her and said he had no plans to release any prisoners for any reason."

"We'll just see about that," Richards said, his voice low and hard with anger.

"We were on our way to see if we could round up some help to go after 'em. I reckon that's what you got in mind, Major?"

Richards said, "That's right. We'll try to catch up to them before they can get through Ashby's Gap."

The leader of the Paris group turned his horse around. "We better be ridin', then."

Now forty strong, the rescue party galloped west along the snowy road toward the Blue Ridge. If the Yankees weren't stopped before they reached their strongholds in the Shenandoah, it was likely the prisoners would spend the rest of the war as captives.

The sky behind them grayed then turned red with the dawn. The sun rose, heralding a clear, cold day. The riders thundered through Paris and started up the winding road toward the gap. The fact that they hadn't caught up with the Yankees before sunrise meant that they wouldn't take the enemy by surprise. That couldn't be helped now.

They rode up the slope into the long gap itself. Up ahead at the side of the road stood the whitewashed sanctuary known as Mount Carmel Church. As Titus leaned forward in the saddle, his keen eyes spotted blue-clad riders trotting along past the church. The other rangers saw their quarry, too, and urged their mounts to greater speed. Titus bit back a curse as the horses pulled away from the slower mule. He damned his luck at being stuck on such a beast instead of having his speedy dun under him.

Keeping up as best he could, he drew his pistols. The Federal rear guard heard the sound of approaching hoof beats in the early morning air and turned to fight. Gunfire roared, the sharp cracks of carbines blending with the vicious snap and growl of pistol shots.

Although outnumbered, the daring aggressiveness of the rangers carried them charging forward into the midst of the Yankee rear guard. Men twisted in their saddles, guiding their horses with their knees, blazing away with revolvers in both hands. The Yankees had been ready for a fight, but they were not prepared for the ferocity with which the rangers struck.

Titus saw a riderless horse dashing along the road toward him. It was a Union mount. He didn't know what had happened to the horse's rider and didn't care, either. Instinctively, he reached out and grabbed the dangling reins to haul the runaway animal to a halt. After several yards, the horse finally came to a stop. Immediately, Titus threw himself from the back of the mule into the saddle without touching the ground in between. He jerked the animal's head around and jabbed his booted heels into its flanks. The horse lunged back into the melee that still filled the roadway.

With his guns bucking in his hands, Titus sprayed lead into the Yankees. He saw that the rear guard was breaking apart, unable to stand up to the fierce attack. Dolly Richards shouted for his men to follow him and burst out of the confusion to gallop toward the main body of the enemy troops.

A few of the rangers stayed behind to mop up the shattered rear guard and take charge of the surrendering Yankees. The rest charged ahead past the church.

The Federal troopers tried to turn and fight, but as they did so, the men they had taken prisoner revolted. The rangers' hands were tied, so all they could do was send their horses lunging into the Yankee mounts. But that was enough to cause considerable distraction. Titus, Richards, and the other partisans drove hard among them, picking their shots carefully now so as to avoid hitting their captive comrades. Some of the Yankees fell bleeding from their saddles while others managed to hang on and continue the fight despite being wounded. Within minutes the tide of battle turned, and the Confederates were no longer outnumbered. Strident yells went up from the prisoners as they realized they were about to be freed.

Titus emptied his guns, but there was no time to reload. He reversed his grip on them instead and struck out with the butts, slashing blows that thudded home on the heads of the Yankees he rode past. More than once he felt the satisfying crunch of a shattered skull.

Seeing that they were beaten, some of the Union cavalry-men fled toward Berryville. By far the majority of their number were killed, wounded, or captured, though. Meanwhile, the former ranger prisoners whooped as their friends cut them free from their bonds.

Dolly Richards grinned at one of the men. "Looks like you'll be able to make that wedding of yours after all, Jeremiah."

The man pumped a fist in the air. "And I want all you boys to stand up with me when I do!" he declared. That was greeted with enthusiastic shouts.

A few rangers chased after the fleeing Yankees to make sure they didn't turn back and reenter the fight. Doubling back and launching a counterattack seemed to be the farthest thing from the minds of the Union troopers, though. They had been whipped, and all they wanted to do was put some distance between them and their pursuers.

With the freed prisoners riding proudly alongside them, the rangers headed back down out of the gap toward Paris, prodding their Yankee captives in front of them. One ranger had been killed in the brief battle and another had been wounded, but that was the extent of their casualties. Titus knew they had done good work this morning.

The people of Paris were waiting anxiously for them when they reached the settlement. They jeered the captive Yankees then cheered wildly for the victorious rangers. Jeremiah Wilson's fiancée spotted him and ran forward to greet him eagerly. Wilson swung down from his horse and grabbed her up in his arms, twirling her around as they embraced to the shouted congratula-tions of the crowd.

"Mighty touching, isn't it?" Dolly Richards said quietly to Titus.

"Yeah. Touchin'." Titus was glad they had freed the prison-ers and killed some Yankees. But he knew in the long run it wasn't going to make much of a difference. It sure as hell wasn't going to save the Confederacy, he thought.

But let them bask in it as long as they could, he told himself. He was afraid that before much longer, there wouldn't be anything to cheer about south of the Mason-Dixon Line.

☆ ☆ ☆

A FEW days later a relatively healthy John S. Mosby returned to Fauquier County to resume command of his rangers. While in Richmond, he had had his photograph made. Posed in a stiff, straight stance in full uniform, with his beard bristling, he looked every inch the warrior. And the men of Dolly Richards's three companies greeted him as they might a conquering hero.

But there was nothing to conquer. Mosby nodded with pleasure when told about the fight at Ashby's Gap, but unless the Yankees tried something like that again—unlikely given the spectacular failure of their last raid—there was no one to fight on this side of the Blue Ridge.

Therefore, the attention of the rangers turned to a more mundane task: foraging for food and other supplies.

The people of Mosby's Confederacy had always welcomed the rangers with open arms and all the generosity they could muster. They had opened their homes and their larders to the partisans. But now, as February turned to March and the snow began to melt with a constant drip-drip, the hospitality of the citizens in Loudoun and Fauquier Counties was strained. The winter had been hard. Food was scarce. Some families barely had enough to feed themselves, let alone to support the rangers. And some even had to leave their homes, unable to make it any longer and eager to find some place that might be better.

Those people would be searching for a long time before they found such a place in the South . . .

The cheers vanished and were replaced by a sullen, suspicious silence when the rangers rode up to the places where they had been welcomed only weeks earlier. Mosby's men were not only foragers, but at the colonel's orders, they continued their efforts at conscription, despite the fact that the pressure from Fitzhugh Lee had ceased. No one wanted to enlist in the army anymore, though. The men were still loyal to the Confederacy; there was no mistake about that. But no one wanted to volunteer to fight for a losing cause, and they tried to avoid being forced into service as well. People had started to talk about peace. Another summer of war, another summer when the fields were empty and barren instead of being filled with crops, might mean the end forevermore of the South. Confederacy . . . Union . . . it really didn't matter what a piece of ground was called when it was uninhabitable.

After a particularly frustrating day during which they had been turned away empty-handed from farm after farm, Titus sat brooding beside a campfire with several other rangers. Mosby was among them, sipping silently from a cup of what passed for coffee. They were taking a chance by having a fire. In the past week or so, reports circulated that Yankee patrols were venturing over the Blue Ridge again. This was a small group of rangers. If a band of Federal cavalry fell on them, they might not be able to fight their way free.

At the moment, however, the mood in the camp was so bad that the men might have welcomed such a fight.

After a few minutes, Mosby dashed the bitter dregs of the brew into the flames and stood up. "I believe I'll have a look at the horses," he announced. "Titus, come with me."

Titus got to his feet. He had no interest in checking the horses, but Mosby's behavior had him a bit curious. For one thing, it wasn't the colonel's habit to do such a thing, and for another, if the colonel wanted to look at the horses, he could have done it just as well alone.

As they strolled away from the camp, Mosby said in a quiet voice, "You know, with things the way they are, this war can't go on much longer."

"You're not tellin' me anything I don't already know, Colonel," Titus said.

"Perhaps not, but the reason I asked you to come with me was so I could tell you some things you don't know."

Titus had figured as much, but he said simply, "All right."

The two men paused near the picketed horses. Darkness concealed Mosby's face, but Titus could hear the strain in his voice. "Something has to be done. We can't win this war by normal means."

"If I can speak plain, sir, I ain't all that sure we can win it by any means."

"Maybe not. But we'll stand a better chance if some plans from Richmond succeed. Do you want to hear about them, or would you rather not? I warn you, Titus, once you've become a part of this, there'll be no backing out."

Titus frowned in surprise. Mosby had something in mind, something big. Something that might change the course of the war. "Before you say anything more, Colonel," he answered, "how 'bout answerin' a question?"

"What is it?"

"Why me? Whatever you want to tell me, whatever it is you want me to do, wouldn't it better if you got somebody like Major Richards or Major Chapman?"

Mosby chuckled, but there was no humor in the sound. "Major Chapman is already part of the effort. And while Dolly is a fine soldier and one of the best men I've ever known, I'm not sure he's the right sort to be mixed up in this." Mosby paused. "I need someone who's not afraid of anything as long as he has a chance to hurt the Yankees."

"Then I'm your man," Titus declared without hesitation. "Deal me in, Colonel."

"All right. You know I've had several meetings with President Davis and General Lee in recent months."

"I've heard as much," Titus confirmed.

"Those meeting were to discuss various plans involving the kidnapping of President Lincoln and Secretary of War Stanton as well as the destruction of the White House by explosives."

Titus's breath froze in his throat as the enormity of these goals hit him. Kidnapping Lincoln and Stanton . . . blowing up the White House . . . Yes, those things might have an affect on the war, and that was putting it mildly.

"Colonel," Titus said slowly, "you're gonna have to tell me more about this."

"Of course. You recall Lewis Powell?"

"The fella who came to see you at your folks' house? The fella who deserted a little while after that?"

"He didn't desert," Mosby said. "He was following my orders when he left the rangers. He's now living in Baltimore under another name, helping to coordinate the activities of a group of Confederate agents there."

Titus was glad Mosby couldn't see the way he stared at him. "You mean Powell's a spy? We've got spies in Baltimore?"

"Both sides have spies in many places. But none are engaged in a more desperate mission than our people in Baltimore."

"They're going to kidnap Lincoln." It wasn't a question, but Titus still sounded as if he were having trouble believing it.

"Yes, and he'll be brought back to Richmond through the Northern Neck, escorted by Major Chapman's men. It's true that I sent them there so that they wouldn't be a drain on our supplies here, but the plan was already in the works at that time. Major Chapman is aware of the duty that may fall to him and his men."

"What do you want me to do?" Titus asked bluntly. "Am I supposed to go to Baltimore, too?"

"No, I want you to stick close to me. I may need you to ride fast with orders for our agents. Also, I want a man to be aware of what's going on, so that if anything happens to me the operation can continue." Mosby fumbled in the darkness for Titus's hand and pressed something into it. Paper crinkled. "Keep this document with you at all times. It's a memorandum in my own hand identifying the bearer as someone who can be trusted. Also, it authorizes you to take command of such of our men as you deem necessary to successfully complete the mission."

Titus was thunderstruck. "You . . . you're tellin' me that I'm to take charge of the rangers if something happens to you?"

"Not the day-to-day actions, but in everything relating to these secret plans . . . yes. I'm placing my trust in you, Titus. The entire Confederacy is."

"Damn," he muttered. Wouldn't old Duncan Ebersole mess his drawers if he ever heard something like that? Ebersole had always considered Titus to be nothing more than contemptible white trash.

But of course Ebersole wouldn't ever hear that, because the old bastard was dead, Titus thought. And a well-deserved death it had been.

He pulled his thoughts back to the present. "All right, Colonel," he said as he thrust the folded paper under his coat. "But nothin' is gonna happen to you."

"We don't know that, and no one can guarantee anything. I've been wounded several times already."

"Yeah, but I hope it don't come to that. I ain't no spy."

"Perhaps not, but you're a man who will do whatever it takes to win." Mosby reached out in the darkness, found Titus's shoulder, and squeezed it hard. "That's exactly the sort of man I need now."

A cold-blooded killer. A man who could murder a Yankee without blinking an eye, especially an important Yankee. Mosby hadn't said those things, Titus thought, but he might as well have. They both knew that was what Mosby meant.

And Titus didn't mind a bit that the colonel thought of him that way.

FOR SEVERAL days as the rangers continued their conscription activities, Titus thought a great deal about the things Mosby had told him. When the time came, if he needed to help with the kidnapping of President Lincoln, he would be glad to do so, even though it would mean penetrating into the very heart of the Federal capital. The audaciousness of the idea appealed to Titus. And if he could witness the destruction of the White House, the place where the plans had been hatched that had brought so much death and devastation to his homeland, well then, that would be a bonus.

On March 20 a scout galloped up, having sought out Mosby. Breathlessly, he delivered the news that a large force of Yankee cavalry and infantry had crossed over from Harpers Ferry and was on a foraging mission in Loudoun County. Mosby was in Fauquier at the time. Immediately, he sent out orders for the rest of the rangers to converge on Loudoun and started north to meet the Federal threat.

By the next day, well over a hundred rangers had rendezvoused with Mosby. Titus wasn't sure how large the Union force was, but he was confident that the rangers would be outnumbered, as usual. They wouldn't know how to fight any other way, he thought to himself with a wry grin.

Mosby called a halt in some woods about a mile east of the village of Hamilton. Scouts rode out to locate the enemy and soon came galloping back with the news that the Yankees were coming. Not only that, but the Federals numbered more than a thousand men.

Titus grimaced when he heard that. Fighting against long odds might be commonplace for the rangers, but even they weren't accustomed to going up against a force ten times larger than theirs. Still, the Yankees couldn't be allowed to rampage through the countryside unopposed. This was still Loudoun County, part of Mosby's Confederacy.

To have a chance, they had to take the Yankees by surprise. Quickly, Mosby split his force. The main body remained hidden in the trees. A few men drifted their horses out into the road and headed slowly toward Hamilton. Titus was among them.

They had gone only a few hundred yards toward the settlement when the Yankees appeared ahead of them. Titus and the other rangers reined in sharply and jerked their horses around, trying to appear surprised. They knew the enemy probably had field glasses trained on them, so they wanted to make it look good. Titus yelled and banged his heels against his horse's flanks. The other men followed suit. They galloped back to the east, toward the line of trees.

The Yankees took the bait, charging full tilt after a small band of partisan rangers who hadn't expected to encounter the enemy this morning.

Titus glanced over his shoulder at them but waited until he was facing forward again before a grin spread across his face. The Yankees were the ones who were in for a surprise.

Titus and the other rangers raced past the trees. The Federal troopers were closing in on them. But as the Yankees rode past the woods, a wave of flame burst from more than a hundred rifle muzzles. Bullets scythed through the soldiers, knocking many of them out of their saddles. The charge broke, slowing into a confused mass.

At the sound of the shots, Titus hauled back on the reins and wheeled his horse. Yelling in excitement, he charged toward the Yankees milling in the road. The rest of the small group that had served as bait did likewise, and many of the rangers who had been hidden in the trees came pouring out to attack the Yankees' flank.

The Federals tried to put up a fight, but they had been battered and bloodied in the opening instant of the clash. The rangers hit them from two directions at once with revolvers blazing. Some of the fighting was at such close quarters that the rangers yanked out their long, heavy knives and started hacking away as if they were wielding sabers.

Titus stuck to his guns, emptying the pistols, pulling back and reloading, then charging into the fray again. He didn't try to keep track of how many Yankees he blasted off their horses. All he knew was that he felt a fierce surge of satisfaction every time one of them died at his hands.

The Northern cavalrymen broke and ran, fleeing back to Hamilton. The rangers gave chase, breaking off the pursuit only when they started taking fire from the Union infantry, which had been left behind by the cavalry. Mosby waved a gauntleted hand for the rangers to pull back. Scouts stayed in the area, though, and reported later that the Yankees retreated in a steady stream toward the Blue Ridge and Vestal Gap, where they had crossed over the day before.

Maybe they would think twice before riding so boldly into Mosby's Confederacy again, Titus told himself as the rangers rode southward toward Fauquier County that evening. Maybe . . . but probably not. If there was anything besides food and supplies the Yankees weren't short of, it was arrogance.

The important thing was that Mosby had emerged from the clash unharmed. Fighting the Yankees was important, Titus thought . . .

But striking directly at their heart the way Mosby intended with the plans for Lincoln . . . that was even more important.

Chapter Fifteen

CORY HATED SWAMPS. HE had fought in them before, most notably north and east of Vicksburg while Gen. John C. Pemberton's army tried to hold back Grant's inexorable advance that eventually became the crippling siege of the city. Cory had fallen ill with a fever during that time, and he was convinced that the stagnant muck of the swamps had been responsible for his sickness. That fever had almost killed him. It had weakened him for months. He was over it now, of course, but he still remembered what it was like to fight in the swamps: the stink, the slime, the constant rotting dampness, the mud that sucked greedily at a man's feet every time he tried to move.

From time to time as he stood on top of a narrow ridge overlooking the Cape Fear River, he cast a glance back at the swamp on the other side of the ridge. He hoped that if there was a battle today, as there probably would be, the Confederates would not wind up being pushed back into that swamp.

It was early on the morning of March 16, 1865. Hardee's command, now numbering between six and seven thousand men, had been shifting from camp to camp ever since abandoning Charleston to the Yankees almost a month earlier. Virtually all of South Carolina was now under Union control, and Sherman continued to press northward into North Carolina. It appeared that he intended to attack either Raleigh, the state capital, or Goldsboro, southeast of there. Sherman still had his army split into two columns, and those columns also had right and left wings, so it was difficult to be certain exactly what the Federal commander had in mind, other than eventually linking up with Grant's army in Virginia and causing as much destruction as possible along the way.

General Johnston had arrived in North Carolina along with some reinforcements from the Army of Tennessee. He made his headquarters at Smithfield, between Raleigh and Goldsboro, so he could shift in either direction once it was determined which way Sherman was going. Braxton Bragg was supposed to rendezvous with Johnston at Smithfield, bringing eight thousand men with him, but Bragg had been delayed by an engagement a week or so earlier with a force of Yankees on their way inland from the coast. Bragg had beaten them at a place called Southwest Creek—a rare victory for him—but the battle had cost him some time, time that Johnston desperately needed to consolidate his forces. Johnston would need all the men he could gather if he was to have any chance of stopping Sherman's advance.

The town of Averasboro was on the Cape Fear River, south of both Raleigh and Goldsboro. No matter which city was Sherman's real target, he would have to pass by Averasboro to get there. So Johnston had thrown Hardee's small army in Sherman's path. They were to be a stumbling block to old Uncle Billy, Cory thought as he stood with Abner Strayhorn atop the ridge where the line had been set up the day before.

There had been some skirmishing with Federal cavalry on the previous day. Cory had been involved in enough cavalry operations to know what the Yankees were doing. The cavalry came first, to probe the defenses, but the infantry wouldn't be far behind. Cory expected the army would see Union foot soldiers today.

The Union troops would have to pass between the ridge and the river. Confederate guns covered that route, so the Yankees would have to turn and attack the line or have their flanks chewed to pieces. All along the top of the ridge, the men felled trees and dug trenches and pits. They held the high ground, the only dry ground in these parts. The Yankees were in for a hard fight if they tried to dislodge the defenders.

"Looks like we're in about as good a shape as we can get," Abner commented. He and Cory had inspected the defenses so they could report to Hardee. "Though I reckon it'd help a mite if we had three or four times as many fellas here along the line."

"You might as well wish for ten times as many while you're at it," Cory said.

Abner laughed. "Why the hell not?"

Their horses were tied up a short distance from the crest of the ridge. Cory and Abner mounted and rode over a winding path that twisted along the edge of the swamp. Hardee's headquarters were about a mile away, on another rise beyond the swamp. As the sun climbed higher in the sky, a light breeze carried a variety of fetid smells to Cory's nose. He grimaced, thankful that it wasn't summer. Nothing stank worse than a swamp in the heat of a summer day.

The general received Cory's report with a curt nod as he stood under a tree, hands clasped behind his back. "We'll see Sherman himself today," Hardee declared. "I can feel it in my bones."

"No offense, General," Abner said, "but I'd like to see ol' Sherman over the sights of my rifle." He lifted the weapon and grinned. "Just one good shot's all I ask, sir."

Hardee gave a bleak chuckle. "I wouldn't mind having that chance myself, Sergeant Strayhorn."

They waited there with the rest of the general's staff, but they didn't have to tarry for long before artillery began to pop along the ridge. Cory trained his glasses on the crest, but there wasn't much to see, only the backs of the men firing down at the Yankees on the other side of the ridge. A courier galloped up with the news that the Yankee cavalry was back this morning.

"Not the infantry?" Hardee asked sharply.

"No sir," the young soldier replied. "Just hoss soldiers, but they's fightin' dismounted. The hosses all been tooken to the rear."

Hardee frowned in thought. "Keep me posted," he ordered. Cory thought the general had something in mind, but he wasn't sure what it was.

A short time later, another messenger reported that the Federal infantry still hadn't shown up, although a force of dismounted Yankee cavalry continued to attack the ridge.

"I want the left side of our line to attack," Hardee snapped. "We'll turn the Federal right, encircle them, and smash them before the rest of Sherman's force gets here to help them."

Cory was surprised by the general's decision. For the most part, Hardee was a careful, even a cautious, commander, as befitted the man who before the war had written *Rifle and Light Infantry Tactics*, the prewar army's standard manual on the subject. Under these circumstances, a flank attack was a daring maneuver, more along the lines of something that Bedford Forrest would have ordered.

But if it worked, if they could destroy even a portion of Sherman's cavalry, they might have a chance to be more than a bump in the road to the Federal advance. They might even be able to stop the Yankees for a while.

"I'll carry the order, General," Cory volunteered, feeling the blood pumping through his veins with excitement.

Hardee nodded his agreement. Cory and Abner hurried to their horses. A few moments later, they were galloping along the road that skirted the swamp.

Cory didn't pay attention to the bad smells now. Besides, the swamp had plenty of competition from the stench of powder smoke. Clouds of the stuff drifted over the swamp and the ridges that bordered it.

Cory found the officers in command atop the ridge and gave them the general's order. Within minutes, soldiers on the left end of the Confederate line charged down the ridge and across the open ground between there and the Cape Fear River. Troops in tattered gray and butternut poured down the slope. The Yankees on the right flank tried to swing around and stop them, but their numbers were too small. The Confederates smashed into them, firing as they came then using bayonets and rifle butts as they fought at close quarters.

From the ridge Cory and Abner watched anxiously to see if Hardee's move was successful. The Confederate thrust at the Federal right flank seemed to be going well.

Suddenly, artillery roared and shells began to burst along the ridge. "What in blazes!" Abner yelled as a nearby explosion almost knocked them off their feet. "Them damnyanks didn't have no artillery up!"

"They do now," Cory said grimly as he swung his glasses to locate the big guns. He found them in the rear, three batteries placed on a small rise near the river. Not only that, but the Yankee infantry had come onto the scene as well, rank after rank of blue-clad soldiers hurrying toward the front. They surged forward like a wave, propping up the battered cavalrymen who had carried the fight so far. The Southerners attacking the Union right flank had no choice but to turn and retreat as the resistance facing them suddenly swelled.

A thunderous outburst of fire from the far Confederate right made Cory turn the glasses in that direction. To his dismay, he saw that the Yankees were carrying out a flank attack of their own on the other end of the line. From the looks of it, they were succeeding, too. Cory saw dozens of Confederates break and run, fleeing down the ridge into the swamp. The murky water flew up as they splashed into it.

"Damn it!" Abner said. "How can things turn around so fast? Looked like everything was goin' our way, and then all of a sudden they's Yankees everywhere!"

Cory lowered the field glasses. "Come on. We have to get back to the general."

They swung into their saddles and raced back to the far rise where Hardee waited. "I see, Captain," the general said before Cory could say a word. Hardee looked as old and tired as Cory had ever seen him.

They stood and watched as the line on top of the first ridge completely collapsed. Some of the men were still fighting as they retreated into the swamp, though. The mud and the standing water, the thick roots and the vines made slow going for both sides in the battle. The Yankees who had been shouting triumphantly as they came over the crest and drove the enemy back now fell silent as they realized they had to fight not only the Confederates but the swamp as well.

The Southerners used every bit of cover they could find, and the thick trunks of the trees in the swamp provided plenty. As the Confederate riflemen fired from behind the trees, the Federal assault slowed even more.

"Would you look at that!" Abner exclaimed, excitement creeping back into his voice. "We're stoppin' em! Dadgummed if we ain't!"

Abner was right, Cory thought. The Union attack came to a standstill as the retreating Southerners stiffened and formed a ragged line across the swamp itself. Some of Hardee's staff cheered, but the general looked on with concern. He knew they weren't out of the woods yet, and so did Cory.

Over the next hour, the Yankees followed the same strategy they always seemed to follow when an attack stalled: They brought up more men and threw them into the battle. *Was there no end to them?* Cory wondered. Sometimes it seemed like there were more Yankees in the world than there were grains of sand on a beach. They never stopped coming.

The defensive line in the swamp had been tenuous to start with. As fresh Federal troops smashed into it again and again, it began to crumble. Then the Yankee cavalry, which had started the battle, came into play again, swinging wide to the right in a flanking maneuver similar to the one the Southerners had tried earlier. The Confederate left was threatened, and Hardee made a decision.

He gripped Cory's arm. "We can't fight them in the swamp. Tell them to fall back to this rise. We'll make our stand here."

Cory swallowed hard and acknowledged the order. He had to go out there . . . into the swamp.

He couldn't help but think about Lucille as he and Abner rode out into the swamp, water splashing high around their horses. Every time he went into danger, he wondered if he would ever see his wife again.

He allowed himself that luxury only for a few moments, though, and then he forced his thoughts back to the job at hand. Mud splattered so high that some got on his face and in his eyes. He pawed it away so he could see and looked for the field commanders as he came up to the rear of the fighting. The Yankee artillery on the far side of the first ridge had fallen silent, since the gunners could no longer chart the course of the battle and didn't want to drop their shells among their own. But there was still plenty of rifle and pistol fire. Bullets whined through the air near Cory's head and plopped into the water beside his mount.

Cory spotted one of the commanders and shouted to him, relaying Hardee's order. The officer acknowledged it with a wave and began ordering his men to fall back. Cory wheeled his horse and rode along the line, looking for more field commanders. Abner trailed him. Both of them hunched low in their saddles, making themselves smaller targets.

Cory found several more officers and relayed Hardee's instructions to regroup on the higher ground to the rear. That idea was already spreading of its own accord as the defenders saw their comrades pulling back.

Abner came up alongside Cory. "We'd better get out of here, Cap'n! Them Yanks are gonna be right in our laps in a minute!"

Nodding his agreement, Cory instantly hauled his horse's head around and started toward the rise. At that moment, something slapped his hat off his head and sent it sailing into the muck. He caught a glimpse of the bullet hole in the crown as he rode past at a gallop.

Fingers of ice played up and down his spine. He had come within an inch or so of a head wound. Death was everywhere around him, he thought. He rode past corpses floating face-down in the shallow water. Wounded and dying men clutched tree roots and tried to keep their heads up, but the swamp sucked them down. Men in agony thrashed and splashed.

Hell might not be a fiery pit after all, no matter what the Bible said, Cory thought as he and Abner rode for their lives.

More than likely, it was a swamp.

AS HARDEE had ordered, his men regrouped and formed a new line on the high ground beyond the swamp. That proved to be a strategic improvement over the original line, because the Yankees couldn't charge as fast or as hard through the muck and mire as they had been able to cover the open ground. In this case, their superior numbers didn't give them an overwhelming advantage.

All through the long afternoon, the Federal infantry charged up the rise and were beaten back, regrouped in the swamp and tried again. Cory lost count of how many times the Yankees attacked. All he knew was that the slope was littered with torn and bloody bodies.

The Yankees inflicted some damage of their own, though. They were unable to dislodge the Confederate defenders from the top of the rise, but they made the Southerners pay a high price for holding that ground.

At last the sun dipped below the horizon and the light began to fade. The firing slackened, and when the Federals pulled back one final time, they didn't attack again. A gray twilight settled over the swamp and the two ridges that bordered it, cloaking the grisly scene.

Even though the bodies of the dead men could no longer be seen as night fell, the screams and shouted pleas of the wounded could still be heard. Cory had to clench his fists and close his eyes for a few moments as he tried unsuccessfully to shut out the hideous sounds.

He jumped a little when Abner touched his shoulder. "Ol' General says we got to move out," he told him quietly. "Says we held 'em off for a day, and there ain't no more we can do. We're goin' back to Smithfield and join up with General Johnston."

Cory nodded. He knew Hardee was right. The day's battle had been successful in a way. The Yankees had been stopped.

But only temporarily. The toll on the Confederates had been high, too. Cory had no doubt that if they stayed where they were, tomorrow the Yankees would finally push them off this hill and maybe destroy them in the process. It would be better to withdraw and join up with Johnston so the army would be stronger for the next encounter.

All through the night the defenders slipped away to the north, being quiet about it so the Yankees, who had pulled back to the far side of the swamp, wouldn't be aware of what they were doing. Hardee's men would be long gone before sunrise the next day.

That sunrise was gloomy, as the rains that had plagued the area for several months returned. All day the Confederates slogged northeast through the mud toward Smithfield. No one doubted that the Yankees were coming on behind them, but the Northerners couldn't move very fast in this weather, either.

The next day Hardee's men were still on the march. Gunfire crackled in the distance, just enough to let them know that skirmishing was going on somewhere. That night Cory sat in on a meeting between Hardee and his commanders in which the general explained what had been going on elsewhere.

"Here is General Slocum's wing, which engaged us at Averasboro two days ago," Hardee said, his finger stabbing at a map spread out on a folding table inside his tent. Rain pattered on the canvas overhead, and the light from the lanterns flickered as vagrant gusts of wind stole into the tent.

Hardee's finger traced a line on the map. "General Howard's wing is moving up on the right. It's reported by our scouts that General Sherman is with Slocum. General Johnston's feeling is that Sherman intends to bring the two wings together at Goldsboro. He plans to prevent that by falling upon Slocum first and destroying his command."

That would be a tall order, Cory thought, but not impossible. If Johnston could manage to bring all his forces together, their numbers would be roughly equal to one of the Federal wings.

Given good ground on which to fight . . . well, anything was possible, Cory told himself.

Hardee's next words came as no surprise. "We are to proceed with all due speed to Bentonville, where we will rendezvous with Generals Johnston, Bragg, and Stewart. Today, General Hampton's cavalry skirmished with the advance elements of Slocum's column in an attempt to slow them down and give us time to join forces. From all the dispatches I have received, General Hampton's efforts were successful."

"Tomorrow, then, we'll be moving up to join General Johnston?" one of the officers asked.

Hardee nodded. "That's right." He paused briefly. "Gentlemen, this may be our last chance to stop the Yankees. I know your men will fight hard. That is all I ask of them—and you."

Solemn nods came from the bearded, gaunt, weary men gathered around the table. There had been a lot of last chances in this war, Cory thought. Would this truly be the final one?

The next day would bring the answer.

THE MEN were up well before dawn on March 19. They had to get an early start to reach the place Johnston had picked to meet the enemy, an intersection about two miles south of Bentonville.

A long wooded ridge straddled the Goldsboro road. Hardee's men circled it so as to come in from the north side, swinging far around so they wouldn't be seen by the Federals already arrayed in front of the ridge. The soldiers clad in ragged gray filtered through the woods, moving quickly and quietly. Soon they began to see the other Confederate units that had settled in atop the ridge. Men greeted each other warmly even though they were strangers. They were united in their goal, which was to stop the Yankees.

Cory looked on as Hardee conferred with Joseph E. Johnston, Braxton Bragg, and Alexander P. Stewart. Cory liked and admired

Johnston, despised Bragg, and didn't know Stewart. Johnston had had both successes and failures along the way during the war, but he had done his best with the situations in which he found himself in command. Bragg, on the other hand, had refused aid to Vicksburg when Grant was closing in on that city and had squandered the smashing victory he had won at Chickamauga, ultimately rendering it worthless. Cory had been intimately involved with both of those affairs and had seen for himself how Bragg's callousness and indecision had cost the Confederacy dearly. Stewart had served at both Shiloh and Chickamauga; in fact, his command had been part of the Confederate assault on the Hornets' Nest, in which Cory had taken part. But at that time Cory had still been a civilian and had known little or nothing about the army and its commanders. At Chickamauga, Stewart's command had been on another part of the field. So Cory would have to reserve judgment on Stewart's skill as a commander . . . not that the judgment of a junior staff officer mattered much.

Johnston's plan of battle was fairly simple. Bragg commanded the left end of the line, where the roads intersected. Hardee would be next to Bragg, to the right. Stewart would hold the right end of the line, beyond Hardee's command. The formation, with Hardee's men out in front a little, formed a rough arrow shape pointing toward the Yankees.

Wade Hampton's cavalry was still at the bottom of the ridge, where they had been since the day before, skirmishing with the Yankees. Johnston explained that Hampton would make a last sally toward the enemy then retreat over the ridge. The Union forces, believing that they faced only a small group of cavalry, would follow, right into the gun sights of the massed Confederate army.

Johnston shook hands all around. "Good luck, gentlemen," he said. "I know I need not remind you that what we do here today is vital to the survival of our nation."

The meeting broke up and the generals returned to their commands. Cory strode along just behind Hardee, and he heard the general muttering, "We have a chance. I believe we really do have a chance."

As Cory surveyed the scene, he agreed with Hardee. Luck would have to be with the Confederates, but if it was, they might actually carry the day.

Musketry rattled up and down the line as Hampton's cavalry lured the Yankees up the ridge. Suddenly the rattle became a roar as Bragg's, Hardee's, and Stewart's infantry opened fire on the advancing Federals. Cory trained his glasses on the blue-clad ranks and saw the surprise on their faces as the deadly rain of lead sliced through them. The Yankees fell back briefly. Their officers must have decided they couldn't possibly be facing as large a force as what seemed to be entrenched on top of the ridge. They came again, determined to sweep the opposition before them.

Again, volley after volley smashed into the blue ranks, breaking their charge and driving them back.

"We mustn't give them time to think too much about it," Hardee said, as much to himself as to the staff gathered around him. "We should launch our counterattack soon, while they're still reeling."

Before that could happen, however, a courier dashed up with a message from Johnston. Hardee scanned the dispatch and exploded with anger. "Blast the man!"

"General Johnston, sir?" Cory asked in surprise.

"No, I'm talking about General Bragg. He says he needs help on the left, and General Johnston has ordered me to send him a division as reinforcements."

Hardee's corps was composed of three divisions. Sending one to reinforce Bragg would seriously weaken the center of the Confederate line. Cory saw that immediately. He asked, "Are you going to do it, sir?"

"I have no choice," Hardee replied grimly. "See that the orders are given, Captain."

Hardee's adjutant quickly wrote up the orders. The general signed them, then Cory and Abner delivered them. Soon a division went tramping to the left, toward Bragg's position. The firing had died away and was only sporadic now. Time was slipping through the fingers of the Confederates.

Cory's impatience grew as they sat atop the ridge. Hours dragged past. Noon came and went, and still the army waited. The counterattack on the Yankees should have been launched long before now, Cory thought. When and if it came, it would no longer be a counterattack, would no longer be able to take advantage of the confusion of a Federal retreat. The Yankees would be waiting for them.

Shortly before midafternoon, the division that had gone to help Bragg came marching back. A furious Hardee demanded to know what was going on. Bragg responded he did not need the assistance after all. Cory had never seen Hardee angrier, and he couldn't blame the general.

When a message arrived from Johnston ordering an attack at last, Hardee pulled his saber from its scabbard. "I'm going to lead the charge myself," he declared.

"General, the Yankees have been bringing up more men all day," Cory pointed out. "They're a lot stronger now than they were this morning."

"Indeed they are. But that doesn't matter, Captain. Look how they have arranged themselves."

From their vantage point on top of the ridge, Cory could see that the Federal front was two divisions wide. The Confederate line extended a considerable distance beyond the Union left. "They still don't know how many of us are up here," Cory said as he began to understand.

"That's right. We're going to hit their front while Stewart strikes them on the left and rear. We'll pinch them off."

Cory nodded. "Yes sir. It just might work."

"It will work," Hardee said confidently as he lifted his sword. "It must work."

The general strode toward the front. Cory and Abner looked at each other for a second then followed him. They were joined by the rest of the general's staff. Cory didn't mind. Standing back and observing a battle got old after a while. Today he would be in the thick of it again.

Soldiers crouching in rifle pits or kneeling behind breast-works came to their feet as Hardee strode past them, swinging his saber a little. More and more men fell in step with him as he advanced toward the slope. Farther along the ridge, artillery opened fire as a signal to begin the belated attack. The general raised his saber, pointed at the Yankees, and shouted, "Charge!" He started down the hill at a fast walk that soon became a run.

Three divisions were right behind him, thousands of men moving almost as one.

The Yankees came out to meet them, but their movements were tentative. The blue line was already wavering as Hardee's tide smashed into it.

Just before the battle began, Cory wondered what Bragg was doing. Not much, he would have been willing to wager.

Then he was too busy fighting to worry about anything except trying to stay alive.

Chapter Sixteen

CORY FIRED SLOWLY, PICKING his targets with care. When his pistol was empty, he reloaded and resumed firing. Before he could empty the gun a second time, he was on top of the Yankees. A Federal lunged at him with a bayonet. Cory twisted aside and fired. The bullet broke the man's shoulder and knocked him off his feet. A second later, two Confederate bayonets plunged into his body and ripped him open.

When the hammer of Cory's revolver clicked on an empty chamber, he jammed the gun back in its holster and snatched up a rifle from the ground. The weapon was empty, but the bayonet was still attached to it. Cory went to work with the brutal instrument, thrusting and jabbing at the Yankees who surrounded him.

He had lost track of Hardee and of Abner. He hoped they were all right but had no chance to look for them. The hand-to-hand fighting was fast and fierce. Suddenly the Yankees began to fall back. Hardee's charge had broken them.

The Confederates gave chase, but only for a short distance. Federal reinforcements came up quickly and stiffened the Yankee line, ending the retreat that had threatened to become a rout. The fighting continued as hard as ever, but now it was more of a standoff.

Cory spotted Hardee. The general's uniform was disheveled, and powder smoke grimed his face. Cory ran to him and urged, "General, you'd better fall back."

For a second Hardee looked as if he was going to argue with him, but then the general nodded. Hardee had done his job. He had led his men into battle at great personal risk. Coming through the first few minutes of combat relatively unscathed, now Hardee's responsibility was to withdraw so that he could direct the action in the rest of the battle.

"Come along, Captain," he said as he trotted toward the rear.

262 • *James Reasoner*

Cory wanted to stay where he was, but after prodding Hardee into pulling back, he couldn't refuse to go himself. He looked for Abner but didn't see him.

Hardee and his staff regrouped at the base of the ridge. This spot would serve as a temporary command post. After a fresh burst of firing from the Confederate left, Cory turned his field glasses in that direction. Through the roiling powder smoke he was able to make out Bragg's men charging forward. He also saw that they were stopped by a particularly deadly volley of musketry from the Yankees.

That halt was only temporary, though. With unusual ferocity for one of Bragg's units, the left surged forward, despite the arrival of Federal reinforcements. Excitedly, Cory pointed out the breach in the Union line to Hardee.

The general knew what to do with this opportunity. He sent his men slashing through the gap and toward the Federal rear.

Cory learned later that was not the only gap to open in the Federal line that day. Another breach occurred on the Union left, and Johnston attacked it hard as well. Men rushed forward yelling, blinded by smoke, bullets and canister whizzing around their heads. They fought stubbornly for their lives and for their country. But they were not the only ones with such goals, and although the Yankees gave ground, they did not collapse. Again and again Johnston sent Hardee's, Bragg's, and Stewart's corps crashing into the Federals, but each time the Northerners stood their ground.

Dusk finally ended the battle. Each side pulled back slightly. Weary men slumped to the ground, leaned against bullet-pocked tree trunks, and tried to rest. In the field hospitals of both sides, surgeons hacked and sawed and tossed mangled arms and legs behind them, little knowing or caring where the limbs landed. Orderlies dumped so many buckets of blood that the ground turned to red mud. Elsewhere, commanders in the field wondered what the next day would bring.

Cory searched for Abner Strayhorn.

He looked everywhere, from the pickets on the front lines to the field hospitals in the rear. Abner was nowhere to be found. Did that mean he was lying somewhere on the battlefield, mortally wounded or already dead? Cory was afraid that was the most likely answer. Even though he didn't know for sure that Abner was gone, he felt the loss of his friend keenly. Sorrow put a hard lump in his throat, a knife of regret in his chest.

But the war didn't stop for grieving, of course. Never had and never would. Cory went back to Hardee's command post and stayed near in case the general needed anything.

The next morning, as sunlight spilled over the battlefield, Cory climbed to the top of the ridge with Hardee and studied the Federal position. The Yankees' numbers had swelled during the night, and as Cory watched, even more blue-uniformed troops came marching up in the rear of the Union formation. Occasionally a shot rang out between pickets. Other than that, a vast silence gripped the field.

"There are too many of them now," Hardee muttered. "And more coming all the time. A plague of locusts has descended on our homeland, Captain . . . locusts in blue."

"Yes sir," Cory agreed. "I can't argue with that. What do you think General Johnston will do?"

Hardee frowned in thought. "We're outnumbered now. For a time yesterday, the odds were fairly even. But now . . . Still, Sherman's men have had a long march. Those people coming in may not have spent yesterday in battle, but they're quite tired, I'd wager. And we can also hope they're running low on supplies, too. Sherman will attack, make no mistake about that . . . but perhaps not today."

Cory didn't point out that he had asked what Johnston would do, not Sherman. After a moment, Hardee added, "Since Sherman still wants a fight, I believe General Johnston will give him one. Every day that the enemy is occupied with us is one more day General Lee does not have to deal with him. If Sherman attacks us again, it will cost him both men and time. I'm certain

General Johnston intends to remain here and continue the struggle as long as practicable."

Cory nodded slowly, weighing the general's prediction. The Confederates had plenty of time to spend in occupying Sherman. They had nothing but time. They would run out of men first.

That day, March 20, passed relatively peacefully, but every man on both sides felt a sense of anticipation in the air. Something was going to happen. The only question was when.

As the sun rose on March 21 the sound of rifle fire picked up. Artillery briefly barked. Even though men were dying, there was a feeling that the armies were only passing the time, waiting until the proper moment for a real battle to begin.

Somehow that moment remained in abeyance. Cory stalked back and forth beneath the trees, impatient and relieved at the same time. The general had a visitor now: his son, Willie. The sixteen-year-old reminded Cory a little of himself when he was that age, especially when Willie lobbied his father for permission to enlist and take part in the battle, if battle there was to be. He had always been anxious to get right in the middle of whatever was going on, Cory recalled. In some ways, he still was.

Finally, an exasperated Hardee hugged his son and granted his request. The youngster rushed off. Hardee shook his head as he watched him go, an expression of mixed amusement and worry on the general's face.

The day wore on. Skirmishing escalated. In the late afternoon, though, it seemed that night would fall without an outbreak of a major engagement.

That suddenly changed with a furious outbreak of firing on the left flank, almost in the rear. Cory stared in that direction, wondering if the Federals had circled around and attacked the rear. If that were the case, and if the Yankees penetrated far enough, they might cut the Southerners' line of retreat and trap them here.

Cory was so intent on the fighting that he almost didn't hear someone calling his name. He finally turned his head, and his heart leaped as he saw Abner Strayhorn hurrying toward him. He noticed the Tennessean was limping. A bloodstained bandage was tied around his left thigh and another bandage encircled his head above his eyes. But he seemed to be in fairly good shape.

"Abner!" Cory greeted him, embracing him in a bear hug. "Are you all right?"

"Yeah, I reckon. One o' them Yankee bullets smacked me on the head a couple of days ago. Reckon I must've bled like a stuck pig, 'cause the fellas around me all thought I was dead. When I finally come to and staggered into an aid station, the sawbones in charge there wouldn't let me go until just a little while ago. I sure was worried about you, Cory."

"I looked for you," Cory replied, "but I guess I never looked in the right place at the right time."

Abner grinned. "Reckon you thought I was a gone goose."

Cory returned the grin helplessly. "Yeah, I reckon I did. Lord, it's good to see you, you gangling old ridge-runner!"

"Yeah, I'm glad to be back. After all, somebody's got to watch out for you."

Cory was about to say something else when he noticed a messenger with General Hardee. The general suddenly stiffened then bent forward a little, as if he might be about to collapse. He caught himself and straightened. He wore as bleak an expression as Cory had ever seen on the face of a human being.

With Abner trailing him, he hurried to Hardee. "General, what is it? What's wrong?"

Hardee swallowed. "The Yankees . . ." he began. He struggled to control himself. "The Yankees circled around our left flank and threatened the road to Smithfield. General Johnston rushed some men over there to turn them back. The maneuver appears to have been successful. At least, the Federal advance is stopped for the time being."

"General . . . ?" Cory said, knowing that wasn't all the news.

"My son, Willie . . . enlisted a short time ago, as you know." Hardee squared his shoulders against the grief that threatened to make them sag. "He was among the men sent to stop the Yankees. He was . . . killed in action."

"Oh, my Lord," Abner breathed. "General, I'm so sorry."

He put a hand on Hardee's arm. "I'm sorry, General," he said. The words seemed hollow, insufficient, but there was nothing else anyone could say at a terrible moment such as this.

"So many of our sons," Hardee said under his breath. "All of them out there dying . . . every one of them some man's son."

And what were they dying for? Cory thought. So that one group of politicians could bray about state's rights and keep their precious slaves for a few more years, and another group of politicians could cloak themselves in self-righteousness and boast of how they had preserved the Union and freed people who soon might have been free anyway. But by God, neither side gave an inch! They had that to be proud of, anyway.

Over the next hour, the Yankee thrust around the left flank had been withdrawn. Cory was never quite sure why Sherman had not continued with that strategy. Decisions were made in combat. Sometimes they were right, and sometimes they were wrong. Regardless of why, the Southerners had been given a respite, and for General Johnston it was now an opportunity to be seized. The Union force had grown so large that it outnumbered the Confederates by more than three to one. With supplies and ammunition lower than ever, and with their escape route threatened, as the Yankees had so capably demonstrated, the only real choice remaining to Johnston was to retreat.

By the morning of March 22 the Southerners were gone from the vicinity of Bentonville.

Sherman's road to Virginia was wide open.

THEY WERE certainly a scrawny, bedraggled bunch, Mac Brannon thought as he rode at the head of the Confederate cavalry patrol, and now, to make things worse, they were soaked, to boot. Ever since the previous December, heavy rains had fallen intermittently across Virginia and throughout the South. The downpours would stop from time to time, teasing the weary men on the battlefields with a few days of warm sunshine, but then the rain would come back, drenching them once more. It was no different now. It had started raining again during the night, and on the morning of March 30, the drops sluiced down, soaking the horsemen and their horses.

Maybe the fact that they were so miserably wet would take their minds off how hungry they were, Mac told himself. That was him, always looking for the bright side no matter how bleak things got to be.

He was having trouble finding anything to be optimistic about these days, though. The only positive development in the past month was that Fitzhugh Lee had returned to action. He was in overall command of the cavalry of the Army of Northern Virginia, the same position that Jeb Stuart had held before his death at Yellow Tavern.

The negatives in recent days were almost too many to count. In the Shenandoah Valley, Gens. Philip H. Sheridan and Jubal Early had met in battle once again, this time at Waynesborough, and the outcome had been the same as before: Sheridan had emerged victorious. Hearing of this, Robert E. Lee had become convinced that Grant would recall Sheridan to the siege of Petersburg. A fresh influx of Yankee cavalry would gravely threaten the supply lines from the west, and Sheridan might even pose a danger to Richmond itself and the Confederate rear at Petersburg.

Feeling this pressure, and knowing the defense of Petersburg was ultimately doomed because of the overwhelming numbers against him, Lee had decided to go on the offensive in hopes of smashing through the Federal line, thereby forcing Grant to concentrate his troops. Lee's real goal in this maneuver was to give him some room, enough room for his men to withdraw to the southwest, toward North Carolina. General Johnston was there with what was left of his army. Johnston had not been successful in slowing down Sherman's advance through the Carolinas. He simply did not have enough men for that. But if he and Lee could join forces, the Confederacy would have one army strong enough to fight at least a respectable battle. That would mean abandoning Richmond to the Yankees, but that price might have to be paid. Peace feelers had already been put out by parties on both sides in the conflict; President Davis and the Confederate government still held out a faint hope of negotiating a peace, rather than surrendering unconditionally, even if they had to flee Richmond to do it.

Lee's thrust at the Union lines had come in the form of a predawn attack on Fort Stedman, a heavily fortified redoubt southeast of Petersburg. This had occurred almost a week earlier, on March 25. Lee and Gen. John B. Gordon had worked out a complicated plan of battle that involved a force of men with axes to chop through the barriers of sharpened logs around Fort Stedman. At first, everything seemed to work fairly well, and by the time the sun rose that morning, the Confederates were in control of the fort. But then Federal reinforcements came up and threw them back after a fierce, costly battle. Lee had lost several thousand men he could not afford to lose.

Now the scouts brought word that the Yankees were moving farther west, beyond the Confederate right. Their successes had emboldened them. If they turned the right flank, cut off Lee's supply lines and escape route, the Army of Northern Virginia was doomed. Grant would be able to utterly destroy it almost at his leisure.

Fitz Lee's cavalry had been ordered to determine the extent of the Federal flanking maneuver and block it if possible. Robert E. Lee was also sending infantry, pulling men out of the trenches at Petersburg. That weakened an already tenuous line, but it couldn't be helped.

With Fitz Lee's return, Mac was reassigned to the general's staff. It was a happy reunion, or at least as happy as such things could be when the very existence of the Confederacy seemed to be on the verge of winking out. Lee placed Mac in charge of one of the patrols sent out to explore the Yankees' intentions. He would report back to the general as soon as he had something to report besides the fact that the men were going to start growing webbed feet if it didn't stop raining soon.

"It's a real toad-strangler, ain't it, Major?" The question came from Lt. Stephen Holland, the company's regular commander now riding at Mac's back. Holland was a pleasant-enough young man who didn't seem to resent Mac's being in charge for a while. He elaborated, "Know what I'd do if I had me a strangled toad right now?"

"No, Lieutenant, I don't," Mac said.

Holland chuckled. "I'd have me some fried frog legs."

"I doubt that, Lieutenant."

Holland looked worried, as if he thought that he might have offended Mac somehow. "Why not, Major?"

"Because there's not a dry piece of firewood in the whole state of Virginia," Mac said, grinning through the drops of rain rolling off the brim of his hat.

Holland laughed out loud. "Well, Major, I'll bet you're right about that!"

They rode on. Somewhere in the area was an intersection known as Five Forks, Mac recalled from his study of Lee's maps.

His thoughts drifted, eventually coming around to food, as they often did these days. When he shaved, he hardly recognized the gaunt face peering back at him from the broken piece of mirror. As an officer and a member of Lee's staff, he got more to eat than the men in the trenches did, and his belly still growled and rumbled most of the time. The men in the line were little more than scarecrows now. The cavalry fared slightly better because they at least got to move around, rather than being stuck in a trench, and occasionally they happened across something to eat. Not often, of course, but anything was better than nothing.

The horses were in bad shape, too. Mac had never thought his sleek, muscular stallion could ever look like an old nag, but that was starting to be the case. Bones stood out against the silver gray hide. The horse still had plenty of fire and spirit, though. Hunger could never quench that.

Mac adjusted the tilt of his head as he rode. There was an art to such things. His head had to be tipped forward enough so that the rain would run off his hat, but if he leaned too far forward, the cold wet drops went down the back of his neck and under his collar. Of course, it didn't really matter all that much. Enough rain had already seeped through the slicker he wore so that his uniform was sodden.

He forced his attention back to the job at hand. He certainly wasn't the only one to be wet and hungry and miserable today. Every man in this patrol felt the same way, and more than likely, so did those Yankees who were just emerging from some woods up ahead.

Mac stiffened in the saddle as he saw the blue-clad figures through slanting curtains of rain. They were Federal cavalrymen, probably some of Sheridan's men. Mac might have faced them in the Shenandoah Valley, at Yellow Tavern, at Gettysburg. Yellow-haired George Custer might be among them. They were the enemy.

But there wasn't much Mac's troopers could do about it. Their guns probably wouldn't be very reliable in this weather. That meant if there was going to be a fight, it would probably be with sabers.

Mac made a quick gesture, signaling Holland to stop the patrol. Maybe the Yankees wouldn't see them, even though they were in the middle of the road. Maybe the Yankees wouldn't want a battle, either.

And maybe when he got back to camp there would be a big plate of fried chicken waiting for him. That was just about as likely, Mac thought. And a second later he was proved right, because the Yankees broke into a charge toward them.

All they could do was meet that charge. Mac pulled his saber and shouted the inevitable command: "Charge!"

Mud splattered as the horses thundered toward one another. Mac picked out the officer at the head of the charge. It wasn't Custer, but that didn't matter. Mac aimed the stallion right at him and swung his saber.

The Yankee parried the blow and tried a backhand of his own. Mac swerved to avoid it. Holland came up on the Yankee's other side and drove his saber under the man's arm, into his body. The Yankee slumped forward as Holland pulled his blade free. He clutched the neck of his horse and hung on somehow.

Mac turned away and clashed steel with another cavalryman. For a moment their blades flickered in a mad flurry of stroke and counterstroke. Mac was no duelist. To him a saber was an instrument for hacking and slashing, not fencing. But he was forced to fight this way and for a short time was able to fend off the attack. Sooner or later, though, the Yankee's blade was going to slip past his and drive deep into his body. It was only a matter of time.

So he threw caution to the wind and launched the sort of attack at which he excelled. He drove in hard and fast, nothing fancy about it, hammering blows at his opponent. If the clash had lasted more than a moment, Mac would have lost. As it was, one of his first strokes happened to catch the Yankee's saber just right and snapped off the blade. Left with only a broken saber to defend himself, the man had no chance as Mac battered through his guard and used a sheering blow to cut deep into his neck. Blood spurted from the severed arteries and veins.

The Yankees broke off the engagement. Mac had the same idea, calling, "Fall back! Fall back!" to his men. The two groups were soon lost to each other in the gray, swirling rain.

That encounter was not the end of it, though. Gunfire sounded in the near distance, audible even over the rain. Mac wasn't quite sure who had kept their guns dry enough for them to work, but obviously that was the case. He and the patrol rode in that direction.

During the rest of the day, the rain tapered off, and the skirmishing continued. Mac saw Federal infantry as well as cavalry moving toward Five Forks. The Yankees traded shots with the Confederate cavalry as well as some infantry units under Gen. George E. Pickett that had been shifted into the area by Robert E. Lee. Yet a full-scale engagement never developed, no doubt due to the rain and mud. No one could move quickly enough to launch a real attack.

But as Mac rode back to the crossroads late that day, he knew he was carrying bad news to Fitz Lee. From everything he had seen, the rumors about the Yankees' trying a flanking maneuver on the right flank were true. And there were sufficient numbers of them in the area so that if they weren't stopped, they would move right through Five Forks and on up to the Southside and Danville Railroads, which were vital links between Richmond and the west. If the Yankees destroyed those rail lines, no more supplies would make it into Richmond or Petersburg. The siege would be over.

And so would the war.

Chapter Seventeen

ALTHOUGH PORTENTOUS EVENTS WERE in the offing and everybody on both sides knew it, nobody could do much of anything on the morning of Saturday, March 31, 1865, except wait for the mud to dry. At long last, the rain stopped that morning—although no one believed it would stay stopped—but the roads were such quagmires that men couldn't move over them, let alone horses, wagons, and artillery. When the sun came out, though, commanders on both sides hoped that its warmth would dry the roads. There were things to be done, battles to be fought, a war to be won or lost.

By midday the roads really weren't dry enough for troops to be moved with ease, but history had waited long enough. Federal cavalry started up the road to Five Forks. They didn't expect to run into any opposition except perhaps some Confederate cavalry. Instead, they found Pickett's infantry moving south and west, around the Federal left. Pickett, who had failed at Gettysburg to take Cemetery Ridge through no fault of his own, was an able commander and had his men in good position. Shortly before midafternoon, his men hit Sheridan's cavalry and forced them back toward the settlement of Dinwiddie.

Sheridan had gone out this morning intent on inflicting destruction. Grant had let him know in no uncertain terms that it was time to deal with the Rebels and drive them from Petersburg and the surrounding area, perhaps destroying them in the process. This sounded fine to Little Phil, who knew a thing or two about shattering an enemy. But today it seemed that the enemy was intent on doing some shattering of his own.

The Confederates continued their southward surge, pressing the forward units of Gen. George A. Custer's cavalry. Pickett's infantry, with the help of the cavalry brigades led by Gens. Thomas Rosser and W. H. F. "Rooney" Lee, Robert E. Lee's son and Fitzhugh Lee's cousin, advanced until Custer's dismounted cavalry stiffened into a defensive line on top of a ridge just north of Dinwiddie. In desperation, Custer hung on there until nightfall brought an end to the combat.

Several miles to the east, Federal troops under Gen. Gouverneur Warren engaged more of the Confederate infantry sent to the Five Forks area by Robert E. Lee. For most of the afternoon Warren was in trouble, but late in the day he was able to mount a counterattack and regain the ground he had lost. This left him poised to strike at the left flank of Pickett's force, but Warren did not realize that due to conflicting orders and miscommunication. Pickett had done well to push Custer as far south toward Dinwiddie as he had, but at the same time, his success had done much to isolate his men and leave their flanks exposed.

All through the night dispatches flew between Sheridan, Warren, and Grant, who was at his headquarters at City Point, south of Petersburg. The Yankees had been presented with a prime opportunity: By splitting his forces to counter the westward movement of the enemy, Robert E. Lee had left himself vulnerable to having those men cut off from him permanently. If Sheridan hit them on the front, and Warren carried out a flank attack on the Confederate left, Pickett's infantry and Fitz Lee's cavalry would crumble. That was the plan the Federal commanders decided upon.

The only problem was that Pickett now realized how dangerous his position was. By dawn on the morning of April 1, his men were already hurrying back toward the trenches that had been dug along the northern side of White Oak Road, on both sides of the intersection known as Five Forks.

Federal cavalry chased after Pickett, but not in time to prevent him from reaching Five Forks. Once he had gained the vital intersection, Pickett stationed his men in the trenches and then turned the left, or eastern, end of his line sharply north in an angle, anticipating that Sheridan might try to strike at his left flank. The angle was in thick woods, and the soldiers manning it piled up rough breastworks.

The Confederates waited anxiously for the attack that was sure to come, but as the day went on there was no sign of Yankees except for a few skirmishers here and there. Unknown to Pickett and Fitz Lee, Warren had been exceedingly slow in deploying his men in the order of battle Sheridan wanted. Sheridan grew impatient, but nothing seemed to hurry Warren along. The sun was out, the air was warm, it was a fine day for fighting, and hours were being wasted.

A mile and a half north of Five Forks, a creek known as Hatcher's Run twisted its way through the Virginia countryside. The stream had been the site of several clashes in the past, but today it was peaceful. Not only that, but the shad were plentiful, darting through its silvery waters.

Mac was with Fitz Lee and George Pickett as the two generals conferred behind the lines that afternoon. A messenger rode up with a dispatch for Pickett from Rosser. Pickett laughed when he read it.

"A new military development, General?" Fitz Lee asked.

"Hardly," Pickett replied. "It's an invitation. Tom Rosser has caught a mess of shad in Hatcher's Run and wants us to join him for dinner."

Lee grinned. "A shad bake? That sounds mighty good, General. I say we accept General Rosser's invitation."

The dashing Pickett returned the grin. "I concur, sir, especially since it appears that the Yankees don't plan to come calling today after all."

Mac tried not to frown at the conversation. He didn't blame the two commanders for wanting to share in Rosser's feast. These days, generals were on mighty short rations, too. But he wasn't sure it was a good idea to be leaving the battlefield at a time like this.

Still, it was their decision, not his. When Fitz Lee beckoned him to join them, Mac could only nod and fetch the horses.

Gen. Thomas Munford rode up as Mac was bringing the
generals' mounts to them. He looked worried as he swung down
from the saddle.

"General Lee," Munford said, "I've just received word that
we've lost communication with General Anderson's corps. It
appears that Federal cavalry has interposed itself between our
lines and theirs."

Richard Anderson's infantry was to the east, farther along
White Oak Road. If the Yankees were between Five Forks and
Anderson's position, that was bad news. Cavalry wasn't so bad,
but if Union infantry poured into that area behind the horse soldiers, Pickett and Lee would be cut off.

Lee didn't appear overly concerned, though. He and Munford had never gotten along that well, and Mac knew Lee well
enough to see that the general didn't put much stock in Munford's report.

"There's probably some other explanation," Lee said with a
small wave of his hand. "Keep us informed, General."

Munford's mouth tightened. For a second, Mac thought he
was going to argue with Lee. But Munford only nodded and
said, "Of course, General."

Lee motioned for Mac to mount up. He and Pickett stepped
up into their saddles and rode off to the north, toward Hatcher's
Run. Mac trailed just behind them. He realized that Lee and
Pickett hadn't told Munford, or anyone else, where they were
going. Reluctantly, he didn't say anything, either. It wasn't his
place to do so.

Rosser's headquarters was a cabin on the north bank of
Hatcher's Run. Tables had been set up under some trees, and
platters of baked shad rested on them by the time Lee and Pickett got there. Rosser greeted them warmly and invited them to
sit down and enjoy the food. An orderly produced tin cups and a
bottle of whiskey.

Several of Rosser's staff were in attendance as well. Mac
joined them at another table while the three generals sat together,

eating and drinking and swapping stories. Mac had a plate of fish, although he shook his head when the orderly tried to fill his cup with whiskey. He had creek water instead. As he ate, the hosannas of joy from his stomach drowned out the worried voice in the back of his brain. He hadn't eaten so well in a long, long time.

As the afternoon passed, Mac thought he heard noises from the south, but the air was unusually heavy and seemed to muffle everything. The sounds were faint, barely more than whispers, so he thought nothing of them. With his belly full for a change, he thought later that he hadn't been as alert as he should have been. But no one else paid any attention, either.

Finally, around four in the afternoon, Pickett sent two men to Five Forks to determine if the situation had changed there. Shots rang out as soon as the men splashed across Hatcher's Run to approach the woods. Mac jerked to his feet and saw Yankee soldiers rushing out of the trees. One of Pickett's two riders was knocked off his horse and captured; the other wheeled his mount and galloped frantically back across the creek.

"Yankees!" Pickett shouted. "There aren't supposed to be any Yankees over here!" He lunged toward his horse.

Mac started toward the stallion, too, but Fitz Lee snapped, "Mac, wait!"

Pickett threw himself into the saddle and galloped across the stream, moving so fast the Yankee skirmishers had no chance to stop him. Meanwhile, Rosser's men opened fire and drove the Federals back into the woods. Mac joined in, emptying his pistol toward the blue-clad troops.

As he lowered the weapon, he turned to Fitz Lee. "Hadn't we better get back to the front, General?"

Lee shook his head. "No, and General Pickett shouldn't have rushed off so recklessly, either. He'll just get himself killed, and then his men will be without a commander."

They had been without a commander all afternoon already, Mac thought, but he didn't voice it. Lee was uncharacteristically cautious. Perhaps his Winchester wound had something to do with that. Maybe the long recuperation had changed him, had dulled his sense of daring. Whatever the cause, it was frustrating to Mac to stand there knowing that a battle had to be going on somewhere nearby.

Rosser and his staff galloped off, leaving Lee and Mac behind. Rosser promised to send back a report as soon as he knew what was going on.

That report, and others that followed hard on its heels, quickly painted a grim picture. Sheridan's attack had finally gotten under way, and it was proceeding with great success, especially on the Confederate left. Mac didn't discover until later that not only had Warren been late with his advance, but he had been in the wrong place as well. Luck, however, had been on the side of the Federals even then, because Warren's men wound up situated so that they were able to drive into a gap in the Rebel line. Continuing the string of misfortune for the Southerners, another force of Yankee troops missed the Confederate line entirely in their advance but wound up in the rear, threatening Pickett's line of retreat to the north. The commands of Pickett and Lee were very near to being encircled and destroyed.

Lee took action at last, sending orders for the cavalry to converge on his position along Hatcher's Run. Munford answered that call, but Rooney Lee's command, which had been fighting dismounted on the far right end of the line, was already being routed and had no chance to make the rendezvous. Thus it was only a small force that met the advance of Federal cavalry from the east, not long before dark.

Lee's uncharacteristic caution disappeared in the heat of battle. He fought the Yankees with Mac at his side. When their pistols were empty, they used their sabers. But despite their best efforts, Lee and his men had to give ground before the larger Union force. Lee finally turned his grim, wide-eyed face toward Mac. "Pull back! Pull back!"

Mac repeated the order to retreat. The Confederate horsemen broke off the engagement and raced toward the north; the

Yankees harried them from behind. It was a bitter defeat, and the bleak scene was repeated up and down the line as the defenders were routed. By the time darkness descended, the Yankees were in firm command of Five Forks and the White Oak Road, and what was left of the commands of Pickett and Lee were little more than a disorganized rabble making its way north toward the Appomattox River.

FIVE HUNDRED miles to the southwest and a few days earlier, things had not gone at all well for the Confederacy in Alabama. On March 22 James H. Wilson's more than twelve thousand cavalrymen had crossed the Tennessee River and headed south toward Selma. Nathan Bedford Forrest reacted to this threat by shifting men eastward from the camps in Mississippi, trying to get them in Wilson's way in order to slow down the Federal advance until Forrest himself could get there.

The weather was a considerable hindrance to Forrest's plans. Although the rain had stopped for the most part, the rivers were still out of their banks. The flooding had stopped Wilson north of the Tennessee for a while; now the rivers between Forrest and the Yankee line of advance—the Tombigbee, the Sipsey, the Black Warrior, and the Cahaba—kept Forrest from moving quickly. So Wilson was able to penetrate several hundred miles into Alabama without any real opposition, foraging and destroying anything along the way he deemed to have military significance.

It was the last day of March, although Henry Brannon wasn't sure of that at the time, when he and Ernie Murrell and the rest of Forrest's men approached a place called Six Mile Creek, a short distance south of the village of Montevallo. Henry was tired of riding over muddy roads, tired of fording swollen streams, just plain tired. But when he looked at Forrest at the head of the column, tall and straight as ever in the saddle, he felt some renewed energy go through him. Forrest was a natural leader, no doubt about that. His example caused his men to find strength within themselves that they hadn't known existed.

"How far south you reckon them Yankees have gotten?" Murrell asked idly.

Henry shook his head. "Not this far, or we would have run into them by now. We'll be between them and Selma."

"I knew a gal named Selma once."

Henry smiled, thinking that Murrell was about to launch into some sort of ribald story. "Is that so?" he prodded.

"Yep. I married her."

Looking over at his friend in surprise, Henry said, "I didn't know you were married. You never said anything about it."

"Well, I ain't married no more. She up and died."

"Lord, I'm sorry, Ernie."

Murrell shrugged. "It was awhile back. She was gonna have a baby, but something went wrong. Wasn't no sawbones within fifty mile. Her ma and my ma did all they could for her and the young'un, but it wasn't no use. Lost 'em both."

Henry shook his head. "I sure am sorry." Murrell's story eerily paralleled what had happened with Polly and her unborn child. Henry had never talked about that, so he understood why Murrell had not mentioned the tragedy in his own life. Maybe it was time, Henry thought, that he unburdened himself. If anybody ought to understand what he had gone through, it was Murrell.

But before Henry could speak, the sound of gunfire came drifting through the warm spring air. The shots came from up ahead. Instantly, Forrest waved a hand forward and shouted for his men to follow him. The general put his horse into a gallop. The group wasn't very big, but they would go wherever Forrest led them, no matter how outnumbered they might be.

The gunfire moved to the south. The battle was being pressed in that direction. Henry had no doubt the Yankee cavalry had finally encountered some of the men Forrest had sent over here to block their path. But from the sounds of it, the Confederate troopers were being pushed backward.

A few minutes later Forrest's men came within sight of a long railroad embankment: the line that ran from Montevallo down to Selma. The right-of-way made a natural path for the invading Yankees, and dozens of blue-clad riders streamed southward alongside the embankment. The Federal column stretched as far as Henry could see in both directions.

Forrest never slowed down. He led his men against the right flank of the Yankees, pistols blazing as he spurred forward. Henry raked the Northerners with his Spencer repeater. Beside him, Murrell emptied a pair of pistols into the blue host.

Like a keenly honed saber, Forrest's riders sliced right through the Yankees, splitting them. The bunch to the south continued after their quarry, probably a small Confederate cavalry detachment. Forrest swung his men to the left and hit the Yankees still coming down from the north, hit them head-on. With sabers and roaring pistols and crackling carbines, the Southerners slammed into the enemy.

The Federals had been taken by surprise, and Forrest's men fought with such ferocity that, within minutes, the portion of the column still to the north was in confusion. Some of the Yankees broke under the pressure and fled. The ones who stayed to fight were either killed or captured.

Forrest paused long enough to reload his revolvers. He called out, "We'll go after them others now and hit 'em from behind!" He whirled his horse and took off to the south.

Henry looked around for Murrell, intending to go with Forrest instead of remaining behind to guard the prisoners. For a second he couldn't find his friend, but then he spotted Murrell sitting hunched forward in the saddle. Henry's eyes widened with fear. He rode over and caught hold of his arm.

Murrell looked up, gray-faced and trembling. As his horse turned, Henry saw that the right leg of Murrell's trousers was soaked with blood.

"Caught a bullet . . . in the hip," Murrell grated. "Feels like it . . . busted a bone."

"You'll be all right," Henry said. "We'll find a surgeon—"

"No!" Murrell shook his head. "You go on . . . with Forrest . . . Get some more o' them . . . Yankees . . ."

"Damn it, Ernie, you're wounded! I have to—"

"You have to fight," Murrell gasped. "That's what all of us got to do . . . as long as we're able. I ain't able . . . no more . . . but you are."

Henry knew Ernie was right. Forrest had only a small force to begin with, and a portion was already remaining behind to look after the prisoners. Yet the general hadn't hesitated to ride off in pursuit of the much larger group of well-mounted, well-armed Yankees.

"All right," Henry said. "But I'll be back to check on you, Ernie. That's a promise."

"You just . . . go on," Murrell urged. "Get one or two of 'em for me, Henry."

Henry heeled his mount into a run. He didn't look back at Murrell, afraid that if he did, he would turn back to try to help his friend. If the situation had been reversed, Murrell would have gone after the Yankees, too. Henry knew that, but it didn't make things any easier. He still felt like he was abandoning his friend.

He rode hard, reloading his rifle on the way, and caught up with Forrest and the others in a few minutes. The fight was already under way. Forrest had come up in the rear of the Yankees and slashed into them with deadly effect.

Henry spilled a couple of Yankees from their saddles with shots from the Spencer. Several of the Federal cavalrymen charged him, their attention drawn by his dangerous accuracy. He snapped a couple of shots at them then rode into some trees, twisting around the trunks. For the next quarter of an hour he played a perilous game of cat-and-mouse with the Yankees, but when it was over he had dropped two more and was still unscathed himself.

Forrest's shouts drew him to the general. Although the attack had done some damage to the Federals, there were simply too many of them for Forrest to wage a real battle. With his men following him, the general broke off the engagement and galloped up and over the railroad embankment. They headed east, leaving the Yankees behind. For their part, the Yankees seemed glad to let Forrest go. Holding him would have been like trying to hold a bobcat by the tail.

The men left behind with the prisoners and wounded had pushed east, too. The groups rendezvoused as night fell and paused to regroup. Henry took advantage of the moment to look for Murrell.

His anxiety grew when he didn't find his friend. Finally, he located a man who had seen Murrell after he was wounded. The man shook his head in response to Henry's worried questions.

"Naw, sorry, I don't know what happened to him, only that he fell off his horse about the time the Yanks started comin' back down from the north. Reckon he must've passed out . . . or bled to death."

"You mean you just left him there?" Henry asked incredulously.

"Wasn't nothing else we could do, Brannon. The Yanks were comin' back. We had to get movin', or they'd have grabbed us."

In a bitter voice, Henry said, "Then by now Ernie's either a prisoner, or dead."

"Yeah, I reckon that's about the size of it."

Seething with anger and grief, Henry stalked away. He didn't really blame the man, but reasonable or not, he was still furious over the way Murrell had been left behind. Henry should have stayed behind, he thought. He could have looked after Murrell and made certain that he wasn't abandoned to the Yankees. But instead he had galloped off to fight.

Nothing could be done about it now. Henry thought about riding back, but that wouldn't accomplish anything except to get him captured by the Yankees, too. No matter how guilty he felt, he had to go on. More than likely, the next day would bring another battle.

Murrell had told him to fight the Yankees. That was exactly what Henry intended to do.

ON THE night of March 31 Forrest sent out messages to the leaders of other groups of cavalry in the area. One bunch had been bypassed by the Federal column, so they were now in the Yankees' rear. Another was coming in from the west. Forrest himself circled wide to the east around the advance units of Wilson's cavalry and rendezvoused with the men who had been driven south toward Selma during the day, so the general was in front of the Yankees. It seemed to him that if he hit them from three directions at once, his men would have a chance despite being outnumbered.

Henry managed to sleep a little on the muddy ground underneath a tree next to Ebenezer Church, which Forrest made his headquarters. When he woke up in the morning, he found that a small group had marched in during the night to join up. Altogether, though, the soldiers who lined up beside the church, the railroad embankment, and the narrow stream called Bogler's Creek numbered no more than fifteen hundred. The Yankees would outnumber them by at least five to one.

Forrest sent out scouts to look for the reinforcements that were supposed to be coming in from the north and west. The men reported back that there was no sign of them. Forrest cursed as he heard the bad news. "Blast it, where are they? My dispatches must've gone astray somehow." He paced back and forth for a moment then stopped to glare northward. "Well, we'll fight 'em with what we got, then!"

They didn't have much choice, Henry thought. No matter what the odds, it was fight or run, and Bedford Forrest seldom ran when he could fight.

The Yankees came at them hard. There was nothing complicated about it. Thousands of riders galloped down the railroad right-of-way, firing and shouting as they came. Forrest's defenders, who had found every speck of cover they could, returned the fire.

Henry was crouched behind the tree under which he had slept. He braced the Spencer against the trunk and opened up, blazing away at the onrushing Yankees until the repeater's magazine was empty. He had enough cartridges to reload a couple of times, but then the Spencer would be useless.

The Yankees seemed to know where they were going. Their main thrust was directed straight at Forrest himself. The general stood in the open, pistols in hand, as the action swirled and swarmed around him. Some men tried to form a protective ring around him, but it was difficult. Many of them were hacked down by sabers as the Federal charge carried the blue-clad troopers into the midst of the Confederate defenders.

At close range, Henry fired the Spencer again and again. His shoulder was numb from the repeated recoil of the rifle. From the corner of his eye he saw a dismounted Federal trooper rushing at him, swinging a saber. Henry twisted and pressed the Spencer's trigger, but nothing happened.

He gripped the barrel of the rifle with his left hand, burning it on the hot metal. Ignoring the pain, he used the Spencer to block the downward slash of the saber. The steel rang as it struck the rifle barrel. The Yankee yelled in pain as the impact shivered back up his arm. Henry slid his other hand onto the barrel and swung the Spencer like a club, smashing the stock against the Yankee's head. The wood shattered, but so did the man's skull. He went down in a heap; blood poured from his nose and ears.

Henry spun away and used the broken rifle to crush the skull of another Yankee before a saber cut across the back of his left hand forced him to drop it. He grappled with the man who wounded him, panting with desperation in the hand-to-hand struggle. Henry finally managed to trip his opponent, and as the man fell, Henry jerked the saber out of his hands. He grabbed the hilt and drove the blade downward, all the way through the

Yankee and into the ground. The man screamed and thrashed and pawed feebly at the blade where it stuck up from his chest. After a moment his hands dropped away, and his head fell to the side; bloody drool leaked from his open mouth.

Shaking a little from exertion and fear, Henry looked up in time to see one of the Yankees attacking Forrest. The man hacked at Forrest's arm with a saber. Blood flew in the air. Forrest roared in pain and anger as he sustained the wound. But the saber fell only on one arm, and with the other Forrest fired his pistol at point-blank range. The Yankee flew backward as the heavy lead ball ripped through his body.

Henry rushed to Forrest's side in case the general started to fall, but Forrest stayed on his feet. "To horse! To horse!" he bellowed. His wounded arm covered with blood, he staggered toward his own mount.

Henry snatched up a couple of pistols from the ground and looked for his horse. He didn't see the animal, but another horse was running loose nearby. He stuffed one pistol behind his belt and used that hand to grab the trailing reins. With a vault, he leaped into the saddle and rode hard after Forrest. He twisted and fired behind him at the Yankees.

More of Forrest's men joined the retreat, which soon turned into a running battle. But the Southerners were too scattered to put up any kind of real resistance, and soon their flight became a race for life itself. Only the fact that much of the surrounding terrain was thickly wooded and that darkness soon fell enabled them to slip away from the Yankees.

Henry stayed close to Forrest. The general had incredible vigor and somehow remained in the saddle most of the night trying to gather his scattered men. He was able to regroup some of them and led them to Plantersville, less than twenty miles north of Selma. That short distance was all that stood between the Yankees and the city that Forrest had sworn to defend.

He couldn't stop the Federals with his ragtag band of survivors. All he could do was fall back to Selma itself and try to keep the Yankees out of the city. Covered with gore from his own wounds and those of other men, Forrest rode into Selma early on the morning of April 2. Henry was close behind him, along with several other men who had appointed themselves as the general's bodyguard.

Forrest found remnants of several other commands in Selma and pressed them into service along with any citizens who were willing to take up arms. Trenches had been dug around the northern outskirts in preparation for this day that everyone had hoped would never come. During the morning and early afternoon of April 2, Forrest arranged the defenders in those trenches. No more than three thousand men lined up to face the attack of at least three times that many Union soldiers.

Behind the trenches, Selma was evacuated. The railroad to the west was still open, and steamers could navigate the Alabama River to the south. Supplies and Federal prisoners were loaded on railroad cars and boats. An air of mingled desperation and resignation gripped the city.

Wilson's cavalry arrived at about two o'clock, but the Yankees did not launch an attack until nearly five in the afternoon. Henry stood with Forrest and the rest of the general's escort behind the center of the Confederate lines. The numbers were too few for the trenches to be manned properly; there were gaps in the defenses. Henry felt sure the Yankees would be able to pour through those gaps. Still, the defenders would fight as long as they could and as hard as they could.

As musketry rattled and artillery roared and shouts came from hoarse throats on both sides, the line, amazingly, held. The Confederates met the attack and stopped it.

Yet only for a few moments, and then the overwhelming rush of the Federals began to shatter the defenses. Just as Henry expected, the Yankees exploited the gaps, sending men through to attack the flanks. He and Forrest and the men with them stood fast, firing into the trenches with pistols as the Yankees broke through the center. Forrest's wounded arm was bound up so that he could use it again. He shot with both hands, coolly, a savage expression on his face.

As a tremendous Federal surge came at them, Henry had to pluck at Forrest's arm to get the general to backpedal away from the onrushing Yankees. Night was falling, and with the gathering dusk and the swirling clouds of powder smoke, it was difficult to see any farther than a few feet. Some of the men around Forrest had sabers, so they used the blades to cut a path through the Union troopers who tried to surround them. Whenever one of the defenders fell, another rushed forward to take his place. Henry found himself slashing at the Yankees with a saber that had been pressed into his hand by a dying comrade. He held it with both hands and felt the hot splatters of blood on his hands and face as he hacked at the enemy.

Then, suddenly, they were through the ring of fire that had threatened to close around them, and men ran up to them with horses. Forrest swung lithely, naturally into the saddle and called out for others to follow him. This time he cleared the path with his mount's slashing hooves and the two pistols that flared and bucked in his hands.

Darkness closed in, but some of the buildings in Selma were already on fire, torched by the first Yankees to penetrate the line and enter the city. The garish orange glare of destruction illuminated the night skies as Forrest, Henry, and the others fought their way free of Selma and circled north and east of the city.

Forrest had a brooding nature at times, and on this night he had plenty of reason to brood. Behind him, Selma was in the hands of the Yankees—and in flames. Black curses flowed from the general's lips. Henry agreed with Forrest's sentiments, but he was too tired to utter them himself. At the same time, the strain of battle had left his nerves drawn tight, and he felt as if he might never sleep again, no matter how exhausted he was.

There was no chance for sleep this night. They stayed on the move, skirmishing with some scattered units of Yankee cavalry. Henry didn't know exactly what Forrest intended to do next, but he figured the general would find a way, somewhere, somehow, to fight the Yankees.

But with so few men, what could Forrest really accomplish? Maybe it was time at last, Henry thought.

Time to go home, no matter what awaited him there.

Chapter Eighteen

SUNDAY, APRIL 2 was a decisive day for the Confederacy. Perhaps the most decisive since the April day almost four years earlier when guns in Charleston had shelled Fort Sumter. Not only did Selma fall to the Yankees in Alabama, but with Sheridan's victory at Five Forks the day before fresh on his mind, Gen. Ulysses S. Grant ordered an all-out assault on the Confederate lines south of Petersburg. The attack began before dawn with a thunderous artillery barrage, so heavy that it must have seemed to the embattled defenders that the very heavens had opened up and were crashing down upon them.

Then, when the murderous barrage finally ended, the Yankee soldiers charged, thousands upon thousands upon thousands of them. Hell had come to Petersburg.

The defenders hung on valiantly, pouring their hearts and souls and blood into the battle, but the odds were too great for them to overcome. The Yankees broke through the right side of the line west of Petersburg. The fortified redoubt known as Fort Gregg fell after long hours of intense fighting. Fort Mahone, in the center of the line, followed. The defenders, those who were still alive, fell back closer to Petersburg. There was no hope. Robert E. Lee sent couriers to Richmond. Get out, he told Jefferson Davis and the rest of the Confederate government. Get out of Richmond while they still could.

Because the city was doomed.

IF ANYONE had been able to watch the retreat from high above, it would have looked like a total rout, Mac thought. While the last flickers of resistance held back the Yankees, what was left of the Army of Northern Virginia streamed out of Petersburg. Officers tried to keep the men in orderly columns, but it was a hopeless task. The exhausted soldiers found the strength to trot then run. Wagoners whipped their horses and mules. Civilians trying to escape the surging tide of Federal occupation were pushed out of the way. Every road leading to the west from Petersburg and Richmond was packed. The atmosphere of despair was overwhelming and clogged the air like thick clouds of smoke. And like smoke, it burned the throat and made the eyes sting and water.

"Dear Lord," Fitzhugh Lee muttered as he sat his horse beside Mac and the stallion where they had paused atop a ridge overlooking the landscape west of Petersburg. "What can we do now? How can we hope to stop the Yankees?"

Such pessimism had been foreign to Fitz Lee in the past. But it was hard not to be pessimistic in the face of such over-powering odds.

Lee had ridden in to see his uncle and find out what the commander of the Army of Northern Virginia planned to do. Robert E. Lee's objective was the same as it had been ever since it became obvious that the Confederates could not hold Petersburg. The army had to move southwest and rendezvous with Johnston's army in North Carolina. That was the only way they could continue the war. To do that, the multiple columns that left Petersburg would converge on the village of Amelia Court House, where supplies were supposed to be waiting for them.

Fitz Lee's job was fairly simple. His cavalry would move out in front of the army and keep the way clear for the escape to proceed. Lee and Mac were on their way to implement those orders when they stopped to take a final look back.

Now, grim-faced, Lee motioned them on.

By the end of the day the Confederate government was gone from Richmond and the city was in flames. Chaos and anarchy had taken over. Mac knew nothing of that until later. He was busy helping Lee to get the cavalry moving toward Amelia Court House.

Not surprisingly, Sheridan came up behind them and harassed them. Several running fights broke out between Confederate and Union horsemen over the next twenty-four hours. Sheridan didn't seem to be after the columns of infantry marching westward for Amelia Court House. Mac decided that Little Phil was trying to get around them and cut them off. When he and Lee studied the maps, it seemed obvious that Sheridan didn't care if the army reached Amelia Court House. Sheridan's objective was farther west, at Burkeville, where the Richmond and Danville Railroad headed south into North Carolina. That was the spot the Yankees had to prevent the fleeing Confederates from reaching.

The rains came and went, and sometimes the roads were so full of refugees that the soldiers could not make their way through. Exhaustion and lack of food took a heavy toll on the Confederates. Men fell by the side of the road, unable to continue. Some just stopped where they were, unwilling to go on. It was easier to sit and wait for the Yankees to engulf them.

By April 4 the various columns that comprised what was left of the Army of Northern Virginia had staggered and stumbled into Amelia. They expected to find rations there that had been sent out from Richmond prior to the evacuation. Although there were plenty of other supplies on hand, no food could be found. The rations had never been sent from the capital.

This was the worst blow yet, Mac thought when he heard the news. The men who had kept moving had done so in hopes of being fed when they arrived at their destination. Now there was nothing to eat.

Robert E. Lee sent out foraging details, but the farms in the area had already been picked clean. Nothing remained. The civilians were starving as surely as the soldiers were. There was nothing left for the army to do except move on.

They could not go southwest to Burkeville. By the time the troops marched out of Amelia Court House on April 5, scouts had already brought news that Sheridan's cavalry was at Jeterville, between there and Burkeville. Fearing that in their present condition his men were no match even for a force of cavalry, Robert E. Lee directed a march north and west, around the Yankees. The rain was heavy all that afternoon and night and did nothing to make it any easier on the fleeing troops.

The next morning, with the infantry leading the way and the wagons following—a reversal of the usual arrangement that Robert E. Lee had ordered in hopes of speeding the army's progress to the west—the column reached the bottomlands along Sayler's Creek. The hard rains had made the area even more of a sea of mud than usual. The wagons veered north in hopes of finding easier going, and the rear guard commanded by Gen. John B. Gordon followed them. That left two corps of infantry pressing on alone, following the creek.

Shots rang out as Federal infantry poured out of the woods on the Confederate left flank. The Southerners retreated beyond the creek and tried to form a defensive line, but the odds were overwhelming against them. After a fierce but short fight, the Rebels began to surrender. Capitulation spread, and before the day was over, more than eight thousand men of the Army of Northern Virginia had been taken prisoner by the Yankees, including half a dozen generals. When Mac Brannon heard about it that night, he understood why some of the Confederates had already started to refer to the day as Black Thursday. A full quarter of the army had been captured, and there was nothing anyone could do about it.

Out in front of the main column, skirmishing continued between Fitz Lee's cavalrymen and Sheridan's troopers as the two groups carried on their deadly race. So far they had stayed about even, but even wasn't good enough. The Confederate cavalry had to secure a path to freedom for the rest of the army; otherwise, their efforts were accomplishing nothing except to prolong the inevitable.

With the Federals in control at Jeterville, Robert E. Lee had to abandon his plan to use the Richmond and Danville Railroad in his quest to unite his army with that of Gen. Joseph E. Johnston. Lee still wanted to merge the two forces, but right now he had a more immediate problem: His men were starving to death. There were supplies to be had at Lynchburg, and in Lee's estimation the town could be defended against a Yankee assault. He decided to cross the Appomattox River to the north and then head due west toward Lynchburg. Once his men had full bellies, he could see about working out a plan to join Johnston. Accordingly, Lee and James Longstreet and the men with them began to pull out of the village of Farmville that they had reached the day before, while the fighting was going on at Sayler's Creek.

Yankee troops struck before all the Southerners could leave; on April 7 some of Longstreet's men had to fight their way out of Farmville. Once clear of the town, they crossed the river on a towering railroad bridge, then the battered, famished army again turned west. Lee received word that railroad cars of supplies had been sent from Lynchburg to Appomattox Station, a depot near the tiny village of Appomattox Court House. The supplies were there, but no soldiers to protect them. The army would have to march all night to reach Appomattox Station before Sheridan's cavalry could do so. They had to have those provisions.

On the night of April 7 from Farmville, Grant sent a courier under a white flag with a message to General Lee. The message was a simple one: In order to save lives and prevent further bloodshed, the time had come for the two men to meet and discuss the surrender of the Army of Northern Virginia.

THE COLLAPSE of the line at Petersburg and the subsequent evacuation and occupation of Richmond had far-reaching effects elsewhere in the Confederacy. In Fauquier County, Titus was with Mosby on the night of April 3 at the colonel's headquarters when a sentry came in with the news that a couple of men were there to see Mosby.

Titus remembered Lewis Powell's earlier visit to Mosby in Amherst County and halfway expected to see the burly former ranger stride into the room. Instead, the two visitors were strangers to him. One of the men withdrew quickly, leaving Mosby and Titus alone with the other man.

"Titus, this is Tom Harney," Mosby said as he shook hands with the visitor. "Tom, meet Titus Brannon."

Titus could tell from Mosby's attitude that the colonel was excited about something. He wasn't sure what it might be, since all the news that had been filtering in from elsewhere in Virginia was bad. Richmond had fallen, and Robert E. Lee's army, what there was left of it, was hightailing it to the west, trying to stay out of Grant's clutches.

"You're ready?" Mosby asked.

Harney nodded. "Yes sir. I have an adequate supply of fuses and detonators. When I get to Washington, our agents there will provide the necessary explosives."

Titus's eyes widened in surprise. Mosby nodded. "Good, good," he said. "We'll get you there, Tom." Mosby looked over at Titus and added, "Sergeant Harney is an expert on explosives and explosive devices. He's from the Torpedo Bureau."

"Son of a bitch," Titus breathed. "You're goin' to blow up Washington."

Mosby shook his head. "No, just the White House—while Lincoln and his cabinet are meeting there."

"Shouldn't be too hard to do," Harney said with self-effacing modesty.

Titus smacked his right fist into his left palm. "I'm with you, Colonel," he declared. He had known that Mosby had something like this in mind for quite a while, but now that the time had come, he was seized with an undeniable eagerness. To Titus, it seemed that Abraham Lincoln was personally responsible for everything that had happened to him over the past four years. If he could help blow up the president, he would do anything in his power to make the plan a success.

Mosby nodded. "Indeed you are with us, Titus. I'm sending you with Tom. It's your job to see that he reaches Washington safely . . . and blows the White House off the face of the earth."

THE NEWS of Richmond's fall and the army's desperate flight had not reached Alabama by April 3. Bedford Forrest was still concerned with Wilson's massive Union cavalry that had driven the Confederates out of Selma the day before. Despite the defeat, Forrest was still in the mood to fight. In fact, during the night of April 2, while circling around Selma to the north after the city's fall, Forrest's men had stumbled upon a group of Yankee cavalrymen at the house of a Union sympathizer. Forrest's wounded arm was still giving him trouble, so the men insisted he stay back and let them take care of this chore. He agreed, and the small group of Confederate cavalrymen approached the house.

Henry was with them, still carrying the saber with which he had hacked his way out of the debacle at Selma. Even hours later, his brain was still half-stunned. He had seen his share of death and destruction since joining Forrest; he had killed more men than he could count. But never had he fought with such pure savagery, such sheer bloodlust as that which had possessed him this night. Deep down, he felt ashamed. And yet he knew that, faced with the same situation, he would do the same thing again.

He was as bad as his brother Titus, he thought. And though he wanted to blame it on the war, he couldn't bring himself to do so. The war had brought out that barbarism, but it had been within him all along, he told himself.

Perhaps all men carried that inside them, a darkness in their hearts that needed only the right time, the right place, the right circumstances to bring it out in all its ugly glory.

As the riders approached the house, one of the Yankees challenged them, then without waiting for an answer he opened fire. The shot was like touching a spark to a powder keg. Howling, the cavalrymen swept down on the place and gunned down every blue uniform they saw. Henry used his pistols, leery of drawing the saber again for fear that the ravening beast inside him would awaken once more. Of course, he realized later that the men he shot were just as dead as they would have been had he cut them down with cold steel . . .

By the morning of April 3 Forrest's men rode into Plantersville, north of Selma. One of the running fights that had occurred several days earlier had ended here, and the cavalry had spent the night. Today Forrest barely paused to rest his men and horses before starting on west. He hoped to find the men who had never reached Selma and rejoin them.

They had barely left the town when a large force of Federal cavalry rode out of some trees ahead, on the far side of a stretch of open ground. Forrest reined in sharply, as did Henry and the rest. The Yankees kept coming, and it was soon obvious that there were more of them than there were men in Forrest's command. "Lordy, what'll we do now?" one of the men muttered.

Forrest heard the question. He sat straighter in the saddle and jerked his head around. "We charge them, of course," he said with a savage glare. Hatless, his long coat bloodstained and bullet-torn, he was still a magnificent figure as he pulled his pistols from their holsters and sent his mount lunging ahead with a defiant shout.

Henry didn't hesitate, and neither did any of the other men. They galloped after Forrest, yelling and shooting.

The Yankees stopped short and began spreading out as their officers shouted orders at them. Hurriedly, they swung down from their horses and formed a defensive line. Carbines came up as the wild-eyed Southerners thundered toward them.

Then, with no warning, while he was still just out of effective range, Forrest turned his horse. His men followed his lead, and as the flabbergasted Yankees looked on in confusion, Forrest rode right around them and disappeared into the woods. The rest of his men were right behind him.

Henry's pulse gradually calmed down as he realized there wasn't going to be a battle. He laughed softly, humorlessly to himself. He didn't know whether to be happy or disappointed that he wasn't going to get yet another chance to spill more Yankee blood.

Be patient, he told himself. The opportunity would surely come again.

By THE morning of Saturday, April 8, the rains had stopped again. It showed every sign of being a warm, pleasant spring day. The night before, Grant's message had been delivered to Lee. The always dependable James Longstreet had read the message and barked a curt "Not yet." Lee sent a message back to the Federal commander asking what terms Grant proposed. By that morning there had been no response from Grant, so Lee got his weary army moving again. Their destination was Appomattox Court House. Lee's plan called for the men to halt there while the supplies were brought from Appomattox Station, two miles away. Negotiations could continue with Grant while the soldiers ate and rested. If no agreement could be reached on a surrender, then it would be time to fight or march again, whichever was required to keep the dream of the Confederacy alive for another day, another hour, even another minute.

Grant's response, when it came, was more generous than his heavy-handed reputation might have indicated it would be. This was, after all, the man known as "Unconditional Surrender" Grant. On this occasion, Grant had one condition: The men who surrendered would give their parole not to take up arms against the U.S. government unless and until they were properly exchanged. Of course, there would be no exchange of prisoners, and the commanders on both sides understood that. This surrender, if it came, would mean a final end to the hostilities, at least where the Army of Northern Virginia was concerned.

Mac Brannon knew nothing of this as he accompanied a patrol bound for Appomattox Station late that afternoon. Fitz Lee's cavalry was somewhere behind him, and Lee had sent Mac to see if the way to the depot was clear. Sheridan's cavalry was close by; Mac could sense that, could almost feel it in his bones.

The next moment he had more concrete proof as a rifle cracked and a bullet hummed past his ear.

Mac reined in the stallion and drew one of his pistols as a group of Federal horsemen spurred out of a stand of trees up ahead. He looked past the trees and spotted the depot building a mile or so ahead, with the sun shining on the rails leading to it. Blue-uniformed men were everywhere. Mac's heart sank as he realized that Appomattox Station and the vital supplies cached there were in the hands of Yankees.

"Fall back!" he shouted to his men as he wheeled the big silver gray horse. "Get out of here!" He snapped a shot at the oncoming Yankees. The range was too great for the shot to be effective, but he did it anyway, an empty show of defiance. Then the stallion took off at a gallop. It could still outrun any horse in the Yankee cavalry . . .

Then, with a terrible lurch, the stallion went down.

Mac cried out involuntarily as he flew through the air, out of control. Instinctively, he had kicked his feet free of the stirrups when the stallion fell. He tried to roll when he landed, but instead he slammed heavily to the ground. His left arm took most of the impact, and the bone snapped with a sickening crack that sent a dagger of pain all through him.

Screaming silently from the agony of his broken arm, Mac tumbled over a couple of times then came to a stop. Even through the pain that consumed him, he thought about the stallion. The horse was so sure-footed that it never would have fallen if it had not stepped in a hole or something like that.

Or perhaps one of the Yankee bullets had struck the stallion. That possibility hurt Mac almost as much as the fractured bone in his arm.

But when he blinked away the tears that had sprung unbidden to his eyes, he didn't see the big silver gray horse anywhere. Clearly, the stallion had been able to get up and gallop off. Mac felt a surge of relief. He was a little surprised that the stallion had left him, but better that than for the animal to fall into the hands of the Yankees. The bastards would capture him, but the stallion would run free.

If he had been thinking more clearly, he might have felt differently. The Yankees would have seen what a fine horse the stallion was and taken good care of it. Left to run loose, the horse would be in danger as long as the war continued. But in his pain and his hatred of the Yankees, Mac couldn't see that. He lay there for a moment gathering his strength and then with gritted teeth pushed himself into a sitting position to watch the Federal cavalrymen riding toward him. He glanced around, hoping to spot the pistol he had dropped. He didn't see it, and his second pistol had fallen from its holster, too. For a moment, he had thought he might put up a fight and force the Yankees to kill him rather than capture him, but it looked like that wasn't going to happen.

Suddenly, hoof beats sounded behind him. He twisted his head, thinking that the stallion had returned for him. Instead, he saw one of the men from his patrol. The man galloped hard toward him, obviously bent on a rescue attempt. Mac tried to wave the trooper back—no point in both of them being taken prisoner, he thought—but the man ignored him. A glance toward the Yankees told him that they had seen the same thing and were coming on faster now. It would be a race.

The Confederate cavalryman won it. He swept up beside Mac and held a hand down. Mac reached up with his good arm and clasped the man's wrist. With a jerk, he came up off the ground. The trooper grunted in effort as he swung Mac onto the horse behind him. Wheeling the animal, he put it back into a run.

Pistols and carbines thundered behind them. Mac hung on as best he could with one arm as they raced for safety. He heard bullets sizzling through the air around them, but somehow, none of the hot lead found its target. They reached a stand of trees and darted into it.

"Hang on, Major!" the trooper called over his shoulder. "We're gonna make it!"

Mac might not have believed that if he had stopped to think about it. But the pain that shot through him with every lunging step of the horse had made him only half-conscious. His brain was stunned, dull. He knew he had lost his horse and broken his arm and that the Yankees were chasing him and the man who had rescued him, but those things all seemed far away and inconsequential. A gray fog shrouded his thoughts and grew thicker with each passing moment.

Gradually, he became aware that he couldn't hear shooting anymore. Had they gotten away from the Yankees . . . or had they been captured? No, the horse was still running, he thought. They were still riding hard over the Virginia countryside.

He was only vaguely aware of it when they came to a stop. After hanging on for so long, his strength failed him and he started to slip. Hands reached up and caught him before he could fall. He heard voices. One of them said, "Good Lord, what happened to him?"

Later, he remembered thinking in surprise that the voice belonged to a woman.

Then the gray cloud around him turned black, and he knew nothing else.

Chapter Nineteen

So THIS WAS WHAT it felt like to come back from the dead, Mac thought as awareness slowly penetrated his brain. That awareness brought with it a considerable amount of pain, but now it was only a dull ache, not the sharp agony he had felt before. He blinked his eyes, wincing against the light.

"You're awake."

Again, a woman's voice. The same woman? he wondered. Her voice was low and soft.

"Would you like some water?"

Mac suddenly realized then just how thirsty he was. His lips were dry and cracked, and his tongue felt swollen and enormous. He tried to lick his lips, but his tongue was clumsy and wouldn't work.

"I'll take that as a yes," the woman said with a hint of sympathetic humor in her voice. "Easy, Major. Here."

Blessedly cool water touched Mac's lips and tongue and then trickled down his arid throat. He had never tasted anything better in his life.

When she took the cup away, he tried to move his arm. He cried out as a fresh wave of pain went through him. "Don't do that!" the woman said sharply. "Your arm is broken. I've set it, splinted it, and strapped it down. You need to rest, Major, instead of moving around."

His mouth worked well enough now for him to croak, "The . . . Y-Yankees . . . ?"

"You're safe here," she assured him. "There are no Yankees. At least not yet."

The words had a sardonic fatalism to them. Mac's vision had been too blurry at first for him to see anything, but now it was beginning to clear. He turned his head enough to peer up at her, drawn by an intense curiosity.

She was beautiful, with reddish-brown hair and green eyes. Not young but not old, either, somewhere around his own age. Even under the circumstances, her eyes sparkled with intelligence and humor.

Mac knew now that he was lying in a bed, in a room with faded paper on the walls. The faintly flickering light that had seemed so strong to his eyes when he first regained consciousness came from a single candle. Shadows cloaked the corners of the room.

"Wh-where . . ."

"Where are you?" she finished the question for him. "You're in my home, Major. This is my farm, not far from Appomattox Court House. One of your men brought you here. You'd been hurt, and he wanted to know if I'd take care of you. He said he didn't want to take you to your own surgeons, because they might cut your arm off. Of course, I took you in. Does that answer your questions?"

Mac tried to force his brain to assimilate all she had said. "The man who . . . brought me here . . ."

"Yes?"

"Did he . . . tell you his name?"

"No. He was just a Confederate cavalryman."

Mac began to laugh. He didn't know his rescuer's name, either. The trooper had saved him from being captured, had maybe even saved his life, at considerable risk of his own. And Mac didn't even know his name. That was just one of the oddities of war, he supposed. Those who died seldom knew the names of their killers, and those who were spared sometimes didn't know who saved them.

He was still chuckling over it when he went to sleep again.

HER NAME was Norah Malone. Her husband, Terrence, had been a soldier of the Army of Northern Virginia and had died at Fred-

ericksburg. Mac had been there, of course. There was every possibility he had seen Terrence Malone, either alive or dead, but he
hadn't known the man. Norah had two young children, a boy and
a girl, and they stared wide-eyed at Mac as he sat up in bed the
next morning and ate the thin soup their mother fed him. He
smiled at them, but that made them duck back around the corner
shyly and brought a laugh from their mother.

"They've seen so many soldiers that you'd think they
wouldn't be scared of you," she said. "The army is camped very
near here."

"I've got to get back," Mac said. "I'm sure my commanding
officer is wondering what happened to me."

"You're not in any shape to be riding. Especially not with
that broken arm."

"If the army is as close as you said, I can probably walk over
there," Mac said.

Norah thought about it then nodded. "You probably could.
But I still think you should stay here for a few days and rest."
When he looked like he was about to argue, she went on firmly,
"The army doesn't need you anymore, Major. It's over."

Mac caught his breath. "You mean we've surrendered?"

"Well . . . I don't know about that," she admitted. "But there
are so many Yankees, and they're all around. Where can you go?
What can you do?"

"Whatever General Lee tells us to do," Mac replied. He sat
up straighter and swung his legs out of bed. He still wore his
uniform trousers, though his boots had been taken off as well as
his shirt. When he stood up, he said, "I'd appreciate it if you'd
rig a sling for this arm, ma'am." He was dizzy, and it took an
effort not to show it.

Norah sighed. "All right. You're a stubborn fool, Major. But
my Terrence was exactly the same sort of stubborn fool, may his
soul rest in peace." She had been sitting on the foot of the bed,
an intimate pose despite the fact that she and Mac were relative
strangers. Now she stood up. "I'll help you."

He had to grit his teeth against the pain as she got his shirt over his right arm and shoulder, fastened a sling around his neck to support the broken left arm, then draped the shirt over it. He sat down in a straight-backed chair while she knelt and worked his boots onto his feet.

"I'm sorry, I don't know where your hat is."

He shook his head. "Don't worry about it. I lost it when I was unhorsed yesterday. My guns, too."

"I'm not sorry about that. If you're not armed, you can't fight."

"You said the fighting is over," Mac pointed out.

"I don't know that for certain. Yesterday afternoon there was quite a bit of firing down toward Appomattox Station."

Mac nodded. That would have been Sheridan's cavalry over-running the small Confederate detachment that had reached the depot. No doubt it had been captured along with the supplies.

He heard the sound of hoof beats at the same time as the two children came running into the room, shouting that soldiers were coming. With Norah trailing him, Mac hurried out through the parlor to the farmhouse's small front porch. He didn't know whether the men riding up to the house would be wearing blue or gray.

Relief washed through him as he saw the gray Confederate uniforms. Not only that, but the bearded face of Fitz Lee himself grinned at him as the general drew rein in front of the house. A large force of cavalry was with Lee. It was a beautiful early Sunday morning.

Fitz dismounted and came up onto the porch to grab Mac's hand. He started to grab his friend but stopped when he saw the sling under Mac's shirt. "Thank God you're all right," he said fervently. "I finally got word this morning that you'd been hurt and brought here."

"It's good to see you, General," Mac said, swallowing the lump in his throat. "I'm ready to ride with you. You'll have to find me a horse, though. I'm afraid mine is gone."

Lee nodded, his expression solemn now. "I appreciate your loyalty, Mac, but you're not going anywhere. Not with that busted wing you've got."

"But, sir—"

Lee stopped the protest with an uplifted hand. "You're to remain here and rest, Major. That's an order." He looked over at Norah Malone, who had come onto the porch behind Mac. "Stay here and let this fine lady take care of you," he added. "That is, if she's willing to let an old horse soldier clutter up her house."

"Perfectly willing, General," she said. "And I appreciate your talking sense to the major here."

"You hear that, Mac?" Lee said with a grin. "I'm talking sense."

Mac knew he had no choice but to accept the general's decision. Still, he had to know what was happening today. "Where are you bound for, sir?"

Lee's expression grew more serious again. "We're to break through Sheridan's cavalry and secure an open route to the west. General Gordon's infantry is moving up to join us in the effort."

"Then . . . then there isn't going to be a surrender?"

"All I know, Mac, is that I'm on my way to a fight," Lee said softly. "For what it's worth, I wish you were going with me."

"So do I, General," Mac said, his voice trying to choke a little. "So do I."

HE SPENT most of the morning sitting in a cane-bottomed chair on Norah Malone's front porch. The children gradually lost their fear of him and came out to talk. Mac heard the rattle of gunfire in the distance, no more than two miles away, and felt himself torn inside. His friends, his comrades, were fighting and dying, perhaps even Fitz Lee himself, and Mac could do nothing except sit and listen. He tried to distract himself by forcing his attention onto what the youngsters were saying, but it was difficult.

Every instinct Mac had told him that this was a momentous day, perhaps the most momentous of the entire war. And here he was, forced to sit to the side, no longer part of the great drama unfolding around him.

Looking across the fields, he noticed a red brick house a few hundred yards away at the edge of the village. "Who lives over there?" he asked, pointing to it.

The boy, Patrick, answered, "Oh, that's Mr. McLean's house. Mama says he used to live up at Manassas, where we fought the Yankees the first time. Was you at Manassas when we fought the Yankees, Major?"

"No, I wasn't." Mac swallowed. "Not the first time. My brother was, though."

"Was he a hero?"

Mac thought about Will Brannon and nodded. "Yes, he was, Patrick. He was a hero." He blinked away tears as he stared across the fields at the McLean house.

The sounds of battle seemed to surround the area of the railroad station and the small town. Later, in talking with the men involved, Mac learned that Longstreet's infantry had fought to a near-standstill with the Yankees to the northeast, near New Hope Church. To the west, Fitz Lee's cavalry and Gordon's infantry made their push against the Federals blocking the army's escape in that direction. At first, it seemed that Lee and Gordon would break through. In fact, they forged a gap in the Union lines and did break through. But then, as they looked to the west and saw thousands upon thousands of Yankee troops marching over the rolling hills to block their path once more, both generals knew the cause was lost. There would be no escape for the Army of Northern Virginia on this day. Gordon's men stayed in their lines, halting their advance; Fitz Lee gathered his cavalry and galloped off to the southwest, circling around the massive Yankee army.

They were the only ones to escape from the trap.

Although Mac didn't know about these developments until later, word of them soon reached Robert E. Lee. Some of his subordinates still argued against surrendering, but the gallant old warrior knew that the end had come. Enough of his men had given their lives in a lost cause. It was time. He had already agreed to meet with Grant to discuss the terms of a surrender. Now, unless Grant changed the conditions radically when the two commanders met, that surrender would take place.

As the sun rose in the sky and approached noon high, skirmishes broke out around the village of Appomattox Court House itself. The Yankees were crowding the embattled Confederates on all sides. Mac heard the nearby firing and stood up. Patrick Malone and his sister, Kathleen, had gone back into the house earlier. Now, as they tried to rush out to see what was going on, disregarding their mother's order to stay inside, Mac moved to block their path. He stood in the doorway, "Go on back, children. This is no place for you."

He glanced over his shoulder and saw both Confederate and Union soldiers running through the fields. They stopped behind trees and rock fences and took potshots at each other. The shooting was sporadic, but even so, men on both sides were hit. They stood up, cried out, died. Mac's heart pounded as he watched the skirmish. Suddenly, several Yankees came running around the corner of the house. One of them saw Mac standing there in his cavalry uniform, skidded to a stop, and threw his rifle to his shoulder. Mac stood still. He heard a step behind him, and Norah Malone said, "Major . . . ?" He put out a hand, motioning for her to stop where she was, but he never took his eyes off the Yankee who was drawing a bead on him. The soldier was a grizzled old-timer with more gray in his beard than black. Probably, he had been a member of the regular army before the war, and he had fought and survived all the way through four years of combat. Mac met his gaze steadily as the Yankee peered at him over the barrel of the rifle.

Then the man lowered the weapon, shrugged, flashed a grin at Mac, and turned to trot after his companions, who were heading toward Appomattox Court House. Mac let his breath out slowly. He felt both relief and anger. There had been an arrogance in the Yankee's grin as he spared Mac's life. It was as if Mac were no longer a threat. As if a single Confederate soldier no longer mattered.

The bitter truth of the matter was that that was probably true.

In a frightened voice, Norah asked, "Are they gone?"

"That bunch is," Mac told her. "But there are more of them all around. You and the children stay inside, Mrs. Malone, and keep all the doors and windows locked." His mouth twisted. "That won't keep them out if they really want in, but maybe it'll discourage enough of them that you'll be safe."

"Then you should come inside, too."

Mac shook his head. "I want to stay out here, so I can keep an eye on what's going on." He thought about asking her if she had a gun in the house. Chances were that she did. But if he had been armed when those Yankees ran by, they would have shot him. He was certain of that. He had never wanted to take up arms in the first place. Maybe it would be better if he didn't now.

Norah Malone was still arguing as Mac firmly closed the front door. He went to the corner of the porch and looked around. Tendrils of powder smoke drifted over the countryside. Rifles cracked, pistols barked, and in the distance artillery rumbled. As Mac stood and watched and listened, however, the sounds of battle became fewer and farther between. Finally, the shooting stopped entirely.

Was it over? Had a cease-fire been called? Mac held his breath, halfway expecting the ugly symphony of combat to begin playing again at any moment. But the silence remained, broken only occasionally by a man's shout. A sort of hesitant peace reigned over the beautiful Virginia landscape.

Movement in the distance caught Mac's eye. He saw a small party of Confederate officers riding toward the McLean house. One of them looked familiar, and a moment later Mac's breath caught in his throat and his blood seemed to freeze in his veins as he recognized Robert E. Lee.

Over the years, Mac had seen Lee several times. He would never forget how the general had ridden past the cheering troops at Chancellorsville while the Chancellor house and the woods surrounding it burned. Mac had stood there on that day with his brother Will, and they had cheered themselves hoarse just like everyone else as Lee trotted past on his horse Traveller, holding his hat above his head in celebration of their triumph.

Now as Mac watched, Lee brought Traveller to a halt in front of the McLean house and dismounted. He moved like the old, tired, sick man he was as he climbed the steps to the columned porch and went inside with the two officers accompanying him.

Without thinking about what he was doing, Mac stepped down from the porch and started across the open ground that separated the Malone place from the McLean house. Behind him, Norah opened the door and called after him, "Major, where are you going?"

"To see the finish of this," Mac said. "Stay inside, Mrs. Malone. It's almost over."

He kept walking. Every step pained his broken arm, but he ignored the discomfort. Something called him on. An instinct for history, perhaps.

A few more Confederate soldiers walked up but remained outside the house. Mac did, too, not wanting to intrude on something important. Just being this close was enough. Through a curtained window to the left of the house's front door he caught a glimpse of General Lee moving around, taking off his hat and gloves and placing them on a small table.

Mac stood there waiting patiently like the other men gathering in front of the house. After about half an hour, hoof beats announced that someone else was coming. The Confederates moved aside to allow a party of Yankee officers to ride up to the house and dismount. One of them, in a rather plain uniform with mud-splattered boots and trousers, was short, compact, and bearded. He had a brusque air about him. Mac had heard the man's description often enough to know that he was looking at Ulysses S. Grant.

Everything he suspected was true, then. There was only one reason Lee and Grant would meet here at this house. Lee was going to surrender. It was over at last, truly over.

Unless, of course, Mac thought in a moment of mad whimsy, Lee intended to ask Grant for his surrender.

That would not be happening today. Mac knew it, accepted it, was even glad for it. To everything there was a season, the Good Book said, and the season for killing had come to an end.

The yard around the house was utterly hushed. Inside, the two commanders greeted each other then sat down at small tables, facing each other over a distance of five or so feet. Mac couldn't hear what they were talking about, but he knew anyway. After a time, Grant began to write something with a pencil, scrawling the words in a small book. When he was finished, one of his subordinates carried the book over to Lee, who took it and, after fidgeting for a moment, began to read what Grant had written.

Surrender terms, Mac thought.

Finally, Lee and Grant spoke again, perhaps clarifying some point or other, and then junior officers on both sides took out paper and ink. The settlement had been reached.

When the official documents were ready, Lee and Grant both signed them. With that few seconds of pen-scratching, it was done. The generals stood up and shook hands. Lee put on his hat and tucked his gauntlets behind his belt. He left the parlor and stepped onto the porch of the McLean home.

Instantly, all the soldiers gathered in the yard, mostly Federal but with a few Confederates scattered through them, came to attention and saluted. Lee returned the salute then stepped forward, but he paused at the top of the steps. Mac saw him gaze off into the distance. Perhaps he saw his army, or the past four years that had been filled with so much smoke and blood, or a future in which the Confederacy was nothing but a dim memory.

Whatever vision came to him, it caused him to sigh, and he slowly tapped his right fist into his left palm.

Lee came down the steps. A soldier had his horse ready. He stepped up into the saddle, took the reins, and looked at the men around him.

At that moment Grant stepped onto the porch, ready to depart as well. But Grant stopped on the porch and reached up to take off his hat. Without hesitation, all the Yankee officers did likewise.

Lee nodded gravely at them and raised his own hat for a moment. Then he turned his horse and rode away toward his army, moving at a deliberate pace.

Tears stung Mac's eyes as he gazed after the general. He looked past Lee and stiffened in shock as he saw a horse step out of a distant clump of trees. He knew the animal instantly, recognized the smooth, silver gray coat he had brushed and curried hundreds of times over the past years. The stallion was alive and evidently unharmed by the tumble he had taken the day before. He tossed his head, shaking the long mane. The saddle was gone. Someone had taken it off him.

Mac took a step forward. Then Lee rode past the stallion. The horse turned his head to look toward Mac once again, and Mac froze, returning the gaze, feeling the bond that had grown up between them. That bond was as strong as ever, he sensed, but something was different now. After a long moment, the stallion turned and trotted off into the woods without looking back.

Mac let him go. It was the only thing he could do. On foot, with a broken arm to boot, he couldn't hope to catch the stallion. He'd had enough trouble catching the horse in the first place, and he'd been healthy then and had had the help of Henry and Cordelia. The stallion was gone, and he had to accept it.

He walked slowly back to the Malone house, where Norah and the two children stood on the porch, waiting for him.

☆ ☆ ☆

WORD OF Lee's surrender spread quickly, and there was no question but that the cease-fire would hold. Grant gave orders that the Confederate soldiers were to be regarded not as the enemy but as fellow countrymen. They were to be fed and treated decently, also given medical care if they needed it. When rumors began to fly among the Confederates that they could get rations from the Yankees, many of them put down their weapons and walked unarmed into the Federal ranks. For the most part, the Northerners greeted them warmly and shared food and coffee. A festive atmosphere began to spread. Here on this Sunday afternoon, it was almost like dinner on the grounds following the morning church service. Generals Lee and Grant had pronounced the benediction, and the congregation in blue and gray uttered a heartfelt "Amen!" and pitched in to the food.

There were still some reminders of the grim business so recently concluded. A detail of Federal troops with wagons made its way across the fields where a major battle had almost been fought. But even without a full-scale engagement, there had been plenty of skirmishing prior to the cease-fire, little battles that had proven equally deadly to some of the men as Antietam and Gettysburg had been to the soldiers who fell in those places. The Yankees picked up their dead and loaded them carefully onto the wagons.

Two of the troops bent down to lift the body of a young officer who had been struck in the chest by a single bullet. A small line of blood had trickled from one corner of his mouth and dried there; otherwise, his handsome face bore no sign of his violent death. It was peaceful, as if he had drifted off to sleep.

One of the soldiers grunted then paused as he was about to grasp the young officer's feet. "This fella's insignia says he's from our company, Sergeant, but I don't recognize him."

"That's because he was just assigned to us a week ago," the other soldier answered. "Barely got his feet wet before some Johnny Reb killed him, the poor son of a bitch." The sergeant

leaned over and spat then grasped the corpse under the arms.
"Come on, get his feet."

"What was his name?"

The sergeant shook his head. "Kelleher, or something like
that. Hell, I don't even remember for sure. Now, damn it, quit
stalling. We got more bodies to pick up. The war may be over,
but it'll be awhile before all the graves are dug."

Chapter Twenty

T HE WAR WASN'T OVER, of course, even though the Army of
Northern Virginia had surrendered. What was left of the
Army of Tennessee was still in North Carolina with Joseph E.
Johnston. In Alabama, Nathan Bedford Forrest's cavalry and
Richard Taylor's sizable infantry had not yet given up the cause.
In Texas a force of irregulars led by Col. John S. "Rip" Ford,
nominally under the command of Edmund Kirby Smith, contin-
ued to campaign against the Federals in the Rio Grande Valley.
All these men would have to either surrender or be subdued
before the war would truly be over.

Despite the many who might wish otherwise, there were still
shots to be fired in this conflict.

TITUS BRANNON'S eyes never stopped moving, although the
night was dark as he rode along with a small group of men near
Burke's Station, Virginia, only fifteen miles from Washington,
D.C. Titus's keen vision searched the shadows along the road,
alert for any sign of danger. Tom Harney rode beside him. It was
vital that Harney make it into Washington. Once he did, Abraham Lincoln's days were numbered.

It was April 10. During the past week, Titus, Harney, and a
small escort had made their way across Virginia and then waited
in one of the safe houses until the order came to launch their
mission. Tonight a Yankee wagon train was supposed to be on its
way from Washington to Burke's Station. Federal cavalry was
stationed nearby at Fairfax. A company of rangers would attack
that wagon train and draw out the cavalry at Fairfax, leaving the
way open for Harney's party to slip into Washington and set
about the work of blowing up the White House.

"Just think, Titus," Harney said in a low voice. "A few days from now, the White House will be nothing but rubble and Abe Lincoln will be doing his meddling in the hereafter."

"In hell, as far as I'm concerned," Titus said. A part of him didn't much like the idea of murdering Lincoln with explosives. Anybody who had caused so much trouble ought to be killed head-on, in Titus's opinion, while looking over the barrel of a gun at the man who would press the trigger and deliver justice. But that wasn't likely to happen anytime soon, so he and his companions had to do what they could to put a crimp in the Federal war effort.

Holed up as they had been, they hadn't heard any news. Titus was aware that the Army of Northern Virginia had been pushed out of Petersburg and had headed west, on the run from that stubby little bastard Grant, but that was the last Titus had heard. He couldn't help but wonder what had happened. He was pretty sure the war wasn't over, though, or somebody would have told them.

As he rode, he listened for the sounds of gunfire that would signify the rangers' attack on the Yankee wagon train. So far the night had been silent, and that was getting a little worrisome. What if the rangers hadn't been able to find the wagons? Without that attack to draw the Yankees' attention, Federal cavalry patrols might be abroad tonight, and they could pose a real threat to the saboteurs heading for Washington.

He was about to voice that worry when he suddenly heard the swift rattle of hoof beats behind them. Twisting in the saddle, Titus looked back and saw a sizable group of riders come around a bend in the road and gallop toward them. Muzzle flame bloomed in the darkness as guns began to crack.

"Yankees!" Titus exclaimed. Somehow the Federal cavalry had gotten wind of what was going on. He snatched off his hat and slapped it across the rump of Harney's horse. The startled animal leaped forward into a gallop. "Get out of here!" Titus called to Harney. "You gotta get through! We'll hold 'em off!"

Without waiting to see if Harney did as he was told, Titus yanked out his pistols and wheeled his horse around so that he was facing the onrushing Yankee cavalrymen. He brought the pistols up and began firing, alternating hands and squeezing off the shots as fast as he could cock the revolvers. The shots rolled out like thunder.

Several of the other men in the party joined Titus in fighting the rear-guard action. The hail of lead they threw broke the back of the Yankee charge and had the Federal horsemen milling around in the road in momentary confusion. Titus whirled his mount and galloped after Harney. The rest of the men followed suit. As he rode, Titus jammed one gun back in its holster, took the reins in his teeth, and started reloading the other revolver.

When he looked up, he saw to his horror that Tom Harney was dropping back. "Harney!" he shouted through teeth clenched on the reins. "Go on, damn it!"

A moment later, he saw that Harney had no choice in slowing down. The man's horse had gone lame and was lurching along in a slow, uneven gait. Somebody had to change horses with him, even though that would mean whoever did would almost certainly be captured or killed by the Yankees.

Titus was willing to make that sacrifice. Some of the men were still trading shots with the Yankees and holding them back, so there would be time to swap mounts if they moved fast enough. Titus drew his dun alongside Harney's horse and was reaching for the other animal's bridle to draw it to a halt when something smashed into his left arm just below the shoulder. Titus cried out in pain as his whole left side went numb. He lurched forward but somehow stayed in the saddle.

Spooked, the dun lunged ahead, increasing its pace even more. The horse swept past Harney, easily outdistancing the lame animal. Titus had dropped the reins, so the dun was running free. Stunned, Titus struggled against the pain that threatened to overwhelm him. His instincts took over and made his own survival their first concern. He clutched the saddle with his good hand, hanging on for dear life. The numbness that had gripped him for a moment went away quickly and was replaced by a fiery pain. He felt blood running down his arm.

His thoughts tried to get back to Harney and the mission that had brought them here, but he couldn't seem to think straight. Anyway, it was too late now, a part of his brain told him. Harney had fallen far behind him, and there was a good chance the Yankees had already caught him. Or killed him. That would be better, Titus realized fuzzily. A dead man couldn't talk.

Gritting his teeth, Titus forced himself to find the trailing reins. He hauled back on them, slowing the horse. When he finally brought the animal to a stop and turned around to look back along the road, he didn't see anyone. He had completely outrun the fight. For all he knew, he was the only one who had gotten away from the Yankees.

Colonel Mosby had to know about this. Although Titus hated to go back to the colonel and report such a dismal failure, he had no choice. Maybe Mosby could come up with something to salvage the operation. Maybe there would be another chance to strike at Lincoln and the rest of the Federal leaders. All Titus could do was hope . . .

Fighting to remain conscious, hoping that he wouldn't bleed to death before he reached some place he could find help and shelter, he rode on into the night.

THE WOUND wasn't as bad as Titus had thought at first. A Yankee bullet had clipped his arm, digging out a chunk of flesh and leaving a bloody furrow. By the time he reached one of Mosby's safe houses not long before dawn the next morning, he was confident he wasn't going to bleed to death. The farm family took him in and cared for him. The mother and daughters fussed over him, cleaning the wound and binding it up with strips torn from their threadbare petticoats. There was only enough food in the house for a meager breakfast, but even that made Titus feel stronger.

"I got to be goin'," he said when he was finished with the meal.

"Are you sure you're in good enough shape to be riding, Major?" the farmer asked.

Titus didn't correct the man about his rank. "Don't have any choice in the matter," he said curtly. "I got to find Colonel Mosby." He didn't explain why he had to find Mosby. The less these people knew about the operation, the better. They couldn't give away any secrets they didn't know.

The farmer's sons had grained and watered the dun. The horse was tired, but that couldn't be helped, Titus thought. He was about played out, too, but he had to go on anyway.

He didn't like riding in broad daylight like this. There was too good a chance he would be spotted by the Yankees. He thought about hiding out somewhere until nightfall, but he couldn't afford the delay. Mosby had to know about Harney as soon as possible. Of course, he told himself, he didn't know that Harney had been captured or killed. He didn't see any other likely outcome to the encounter with Yankee cavalry, though.

By the time he reached Mosby's headquarters the next morning, some of the other men who had escaped from the running fight with the Yankees had already returned. Mosby clasped Titus's hand. "I didn't expect to see you again. I was told you'd been shot."

Titus flashed a grin. His arm was stiff and sore as hell, but he knew it was already healing. "I'll be fine, Colonel," he said. "Reckon I've got some bad news, though."

"If it's about Tom Harney being captured by the Yankees, I already know about that," Mosby said with a bleak expression on his face.

"He was captured then, not killed?"

Mosby nodded. "Some of the men saw him being led off on horseback by the Yankees."

"You reckon he'll talk?"

"Tom Harney is a good man. I'm sure he'll tell the Yankees as little as possible about our plans."

Titus nodded. "If I'd had the chance, Colonel, I'd have put a bullet through his head just to make sure of that."

Mosby regarded him with keen interest. "You would have, would you?"

"You know me, Colonel," Titus said with a humorless grin. "I'd kill just about anybody if it meant we stood a better chance of hurtin' the Yankees."

"Yes," Mosby said. "I believe you would."

TITUS WAS with the colonel two days later when a rider came in from one of the ranger patrols. The man handed Mosby a sealed message. "Got this from a Yankee who came up under a white flag, Colonel," the ranger explained. "He said it was mighty important that the message get to you."

Mosby turned the paper over in his hands. "I'm not sure I want to read anything a Yankee has to say to me." Then, with a shrug, he added, "But I suppose I had better see what it's about."

Titus noticed a change in Mosby's demeanor as he read the note. The colonel's features hardened with anger, but Titus thought he saw something like despair in Mosby's eyes as well.

Even though Titus didn't ask, Mosby said, "General Hancock calls on me to surrender my command and offers us the same terms that Grant gave to General Lee."

"What?" Titus burst out.

Mosby raised his eyes from the message. "Apparently General Lee surrendered the Army of Northern Virginia three days ago at Appomattox Court House. The men had to surrender their arms, but they were allowed to keep their horses."

"That was mighty big o' those damn Yankees," Titus said bitterly. Lee surrendered! He could barely bring himself to believe it. Did that mean the war was over? What about the other Confederate armies in the field? "What are you goin' to do, Colonel? Do you plan to surrender?"

Carefully, Mosby placed Hancock's message on a table. He looked like he wanted to crumple the paper and put it down so that he wouldn't give in to that impulse. Looking up at Titus, he shook his head. "An outright surrender? No. But I will ask Hancock for an armistice, a cease-fire."

"Why? Why don't we just keep fightin'?"

"There are plans a-foot, as you well know, Titus—"

"But the Yankees got Harney. He can't do anything from inside a prison cell."

"Tom Harney was not our only agent," Mosby said softly.

Suddenly, Titus understood. There were other agents in Washington. He didn't know the names of all of them; Mosby might not even know all of their names. The Confederate espionage network was set up so that everyone didn't know everybody else who was involved. "You're talking about Booth and that bunch?"

Mosby nodded. "It was expected that our people in Washington would assist Harney in his assignment, but contingency plans were made. Booth has wanted to kidnap the President for some time now. He was even at the inauguration, you know. With Lincoln in our hands . . . well, there's no telling what the Federal government might be willing to do to ransom him back. Peace with honor, perhaps."

Titus wasn't interested in peace, whether it had honor or not. But without Lee's army, the Confederacy couldn't even begin to hope for anything better than that.

Mosby turned toward him. "How's your arm?"

The question took Titus a little by surprise. "It's all right. Still hurts, but not too bad."

"Can you ride?"

"Damn right, beggin' the Colonel's pardon. Just tell me where you want me to go and what you want me to do. I'll light out for Washington if you want and do what I can to help our boys there."

Mosby waved a hand. "No, no. Not yet. Let's just see how things play out. But be ready to ride at a moment's notice. There's no telling when I might need you. Who knows, Titus? You might be the man who tips the balance. Think of that. One man in the right place at the right moment in history can make all the difference in the world."

"Yes sir, Colonel," Titus said. Mosby sounded like he was about to start philosophizing, and Titus had no interest in that. History was for somebody else to worry about, not him.

His thoughts were consumed by the possibility that he might just get ol' Abe in his sights after all . . .

☆ ☆ ☆

FOUR DAYS later, on the morning of April 16, shouting voices roused Titus from sleep. He was outside, his blankets rolled under a tree. He came awake with a pistol in his hand, his thumb looped over the hammer ready to cock and fire if necessary. As he rolled over he threw the blankets aside and surged up into a crouch with the gun leveled. His eyes darted from side to side as he sought the source of the disturbance.

Several men had just ridden into the ranger camp. One of them was Mosby, who had been at a safe house nearby. As Titus realized this and lowered the revolver, the colonel swung down from his saddle and walked quickly toward him.

"There's news from Washington, Titus," Mosby said in a low, urgent voice. "Lincoln was killed the night before last."

Titus's breath hissed between his teeth. "The son of a bitch is dead?"

"That's right," Mosby replied with a nod. "He actually died early yesterday morning."

"Who killed him?" What Titus really wanted to know was who had cheated him of the chance to kill Lincoln himself.

"Booth was recognized. He shot Lincoln at Ford's Theatre."

John Wilkes Booth . . . Titus knew the name of the actor by reputation only. He had never seen him perform, had never cared to. Play-acting was a waste of time as far as Titus was concerned. Clearly, though, the man did have some courage; otherwise he never would have killed Lincoln right there in the middle of Washington.

"You said he was recognized. The Yankees didn't catch him or kill him?"

Mosby smiled faintly. "No. He leaped from the president's box to the stage and escaped. Reports say that he may have injured himself, but I don't know about that."

"Well, well." The wheels of Titus's brain turned over rapidly. "So he's still on the loose somewhere?"

"As far as I know."

"I reckon Booth knows a lot about all the plannin' that's been goin' on. It wouldn't be too good for the Confederacy if he spilled everything he knows."

Despite Lee's surrender and the collapse of the Confederate government, the war wasn't yet over. Negotiations were still going on between Sherman and Johnston in North Carolina. And there were other scattered holdouts. Yet with Lincoln dead, everything might change. The rangers had heard that the Yankee president had taken a conciliatory tone in his orders to the army, that he wanted a peaceful conclusion to the war and had no interest in making things hard on the Confederates. But even if Titus had believed that—and he wasn't sure he did— there was no way of knowing what might happen now. Whoever took over as president might feel completely different. Andrew Johnson was vice president of the Yankees, but Titus didn't know much about him.

"The war won't continue because Lincoln is dead," Mosby declared. "But if word gets around in the North that we've been plotting against him and the rest of the Federal leaders in Washington for quite a while, things will go harder on all of us down here in the South, Titus. Those politicos up there already hate us. We can't give them any more of an excuse to take vengeance on our people."

Titus nodded in understanding. "You want me to see if I can get Booth out of there?" he asked.

"I'm sending details to cover several routes between here and Washington." Mosby's voice dropped until only Titus could hear what he was saying. "Their job will be to help Booth get away. Your job is to find Booth and see that he gets into the hands of one of those groups of rangers."

Titus rubbed his lean, bearded jaw for a second and then said, "And if I can't get him out?"

"I'm going to leave that up to you. Use your best judgment."

"Yes sir," Titus said. "I'll do that."

THE ACTUAL surrender of Robert E. Lee's army, not just the agreement on surrender terms, took place on the morning of Wednesday, April 12. The sky was overcast at first, but the clouds broke after a short time and the sun came out. Gen. Joshua Lawrence Chamberlain's troops lined up on both sides of the road leading to Appomattox Court House and waited for the Confederates to march in and officially lay down their arms.

Gen. John B. Gordon rode alone at the head of the column, looking neither right nor left. The Stonewall Brigade, Will Brannon's old outfit, followed him, a mere shadow of what it had been in the Shenandoah Valley and at Sharpsburg and Chancellorsville. Mac Brannon had no arms to lay down, so he watched the ceremony from the porch of the Malone house. He had to swallow hard when a lump formed in his throat as the Stonewall Brigade's battle flags went past. In a way, he was glad Will wasn't here to see it.

There were no drums or bugles, no shouts of victory, only the tramp of feet as the Confederate army marched in and laid down their rifles and flags. For these men, the war was indeed over. They would be given written passes allowing them to go home.

No one had any thoughts of going elsewhere. Not now.

On the same day in Raleigh, North Carolina, rumors of Lee's surrender began to fly through the ranks of Johnston's command. At first the Confederates refused to believe it. When Cory Brannon and Abner Strayhorn heard the news, Abner shook his head and said, "It ain't so. Ol' Marse Robert wouldn't surrender to no damnyank."

"He would if that was all that was left for him to do," Cory said. "I don't think his pride would let him sit by and allow every man in his army to be killed."

"Maybe not, but I just don't believe—"

Abner stopped short as the sound of wildly cheering men floated through the air. Sherman's army was close by; in fact, the Confederates had been getting ready to evacuate Raleigh and let Uncle Billy have the place. They would find somewhere else to make their next fight.

Now it looked as if there wouldn't be a next fight. Slowly, the numbing realization sank in on the Confederate troops. The Yankees wouldn't be carrying on like that unless it was true. General Lee had surrendered. The war was over.

The next day, Johnston and Beauregard met with Jefferson Davis at Greensboro, North Carolina, in one of the railroad cars that formed the temporary home of the Confederate government following its flight from Richmond. The president summoned his remaining commanders to see what could be done about continuing the war.

Johnston and Beauregard told Davis in no uncertain terms that the war could not continue. Desertions, already heavy even before the news of Lee's surrender arrived, were now higher. At the rate things were going, there might not be an army to surrender before much longer.

A bitter Davis argued the matter but finally agreed with his generals. He instructed Johnston to seek an arrangement with

Sherman that would establish a cease-fire. Johnston did so, exchanging messages with the Union commander, and they set up a meeting on April 17 to discuss the details. This truly would conclude the war if it came about. Johnston's army was the only Confederate force still large enough to fight a real battle, if it came to that.

But there was a hitch. When Johnston and Sherman had their face-to-face meeting, Sherman had just received a telegram from Washington. It contained the shocking news of Lincoln's murder two nights earlier in Washington.

Sherman was determined to act in good faith and negotiate a settlement with Johnston, as he had agreed to do. But no matter what these generals agreed to on this day, there was still the matter of whether a furious, vengeance-seeking Congress, along with the rest of the North, would accept it.

EVER SINCE John S. Mosby had received the message from Winfield Scott Hancock informing him of Lee's surrender and suggesting the possibility of a cease-fire, communications had been ongoing between the two men. Mosby was a realist and knew that without an actual army to support, his partisans could accomplish little or nothing against the enemy. He agreed to meet with the Yankees to discuss a settlement.

That meeting took place on April 18 at a home in Millwood. Gen. George H. Chapman represented the Federals. They arranged a cease-fire to last for a minimum of forty-eight hours, but although Chapman offered Mosby the same terms that Lee had agreed to, Mosby refused to accept them. This was not an outright refusal to surrender, he made clear; he was merely waiting for instructions from his government on how he should proceed. Also, although Mosby didn't state as much to Chapman, he was waiting to see if Johnston still had any fight left in him down in North Carolina. In the meantime, the shooting would stop, and Mosby had already told the rangers that if any of them wanted to surrender to the Yankees on their own, they were free to do so.

So far, there hadn't been any takers on that offer.

At the end of the cease-fire, set for noon on April 20, Mosby met once again with the Yankees and requested an extension of the truce. Word had come down from Grant himself that Mosby's request was not to be granted. The cease-fire had come to an end, and now Mosby had to surrender or resume hostilities.

This meeting took place in a tavern in Millwood, and it was a tense moment. Despite flags of truce, a skirmish might break out right then and there. All Mosby had to do to start the ball rolling was to nod to his men. But instead he walked out and took with him the small party of rangers that had accompanied him. The Yankees let them go, but no one knew what the next day would bring. More than likely, most thought, it would be a resumption of the guerrilla war that Mosby had been fighting for so long.

Instead, Mosby sent out orders for all the rangers to rendezvous at Salem. They did so on April 21, and there Mosby wrote an end to yet another chapter of this long, bloody war. Rather than surrender to the Federals, he chose instead to disband the rangers. It would be up to the individual men to go in and sign the paroles that the Yankees demanded. The rangers scattered out from Salem, most of them heading home, others going straight to the nearest Yankee headquarters to surrender themselves.

Mosby's Confederacy was no more.

THE SURRENDER of Johnston's army in North Carolina did not go well. The surrender terms presented by Sherman and agreed to by Johnston were rejected by Washington. Now in a rage over Lincoln's assassination, the North was in no mood for anything that even remotely smacked of leniency. The secretary of war,

Edwin M. Stanton, who had announced the president's death on the morning of April 15, now sent Grant to North Carolina to take over the negotiations with Johnston.

Grant, through Sherman, presented Johnston with the same terms that Lee had agreed to. Johnston was more than willing to accept them, but Jefferson Davis refused. Instead, he ordered Johnston to scatter the army with the intention of regrouping later and continuing the war. Now it was Johnston's turn to refuse. He told Davis that he planned to negotiate a settlement with Sherman and Grant, and an impotent Davis, stripped of any real authority by developments of the past two weeks, could do nothing to stop him.

On April 26 Johnston and Sherman met again, and Johnston signed the surrender agreement Sherman presented to him. The Army of Tennessee, like the Army of Northern Virginia, was now a thing of the past and belonged only to history.

VERY EARLY on the morning of April 26, a long way from where Johnston and Sherman were making their final pact later that day, Titus Brannon held his breath as he waited for the Yankee trooper to step past him.

Titus stood behind a tree on the Garrett farm between the villages of Bowling Green and Port Royal, Virginia. For more than a week now, he had been roaming stealthily through this area of eastern Virginia, not far from the Potomac River. Rumors were everywhere concerning the fugitive, John Wilkes Booth. The army's efforts to locate the killer of the president had resulted in one of the largest manhunts in history. The investigators had turned up a number of clues . . .

But so had Titus.

Earlier in the night, he had discovered from an overheard conversation in Bowling Green that Booth and a companion, David Herold, were thought to be hidden on the Garrett farm.

Titus had heard plenty of hints like that during the past ten days, and none of them had turned out to be true. He might not have put much stock in this rumor if he hadn't noticed soldiers surrounding the Star Hotel in Bowling Green about midnight. Earlier, he had seen young Willie Jett ride into Greensboro from the direction of the Garrett farm. It was Willie whom Titus had overheard telling a young woman whose father owned the Star Hotel about how he had helped a couple of men hide out on the farm. Willie just wanted to impress a girl; Titus wanted to cut the young blabbermouth's throat. But that wasn't going to accomplish anything now. The damage had already been done, Titus decided when the Yankee soldiers stormed into the hotel. They had to be after Willie Jett, he thought, and if the Yankees believed Willie's story, then maybe Titus ought to take it seriously, too, at least for the time being.

So he had set out immediately for the Garrett farm, beating the Yankees there. But not by much. They were in a damned big hurry, he thought. Not surprising since they were after the man who had killed their president.

Titus had been slipping around the farm buildings, looking for some sign of Booth and Herold, when he heard the horses approaching. The family's dogs started to bark. Titus ducked back hurriedly into some trees and hid in the thick shadows underneath them.

The troopers rode up to the house. Richard Garrett opened the door in response to the commotion. As Titus watched, Garrett found himself staring down the barrel of a pistol in the hands of the officer commanding the Yankees. Titus couldn't make out everything that was said, but he could tell that Garrett was being stubborn and refusing to say whether or not Booth was there.

The other Yankees began spreading out, surrounding the farmhouse and the outbuildings.

As the officer ordered Garrett dragged out and hanged if he wasn't going to talk, one of the soldiers started past the tree where Titus was hidden. Titus let the trooper pass then struck silently, bringing the butt of one of his pistols down on the man's head. The Yankee grunted and fell. Titus grabbed him to keep him from making too much noise when he landed.

Then it was only a moment's work to strip off the soldier's tunic and cap and put them on. In the dark, that would be enough to let Titus pass himself off as a Yankee.

As he tucked his long hair up under the cap, he hoped the son of a bitch didn't have lice.

Shouts from the farmhouse drew his attention as he picked up the Yankee's rifle and took his place in the line of men spreading out around the Garrett place. A youngster, probably one of the farmer's sons, had emerged from the house and was yelling and pointing toward an old tobacco barn. Titus caught the words, "In there! They're in there!"

So this was it, he thought. The Yankees had found John Wilkes Booth at last.

And so had he.

THE OFFICIAL records of that night's events showed that the army detail commanded by Lt. Edward P. Doherty—accompanied by a pair of detectives named Conger and Baker—surrounded the barn on the Richard Garrett farm. Inside the barn were John Wilkes Booth and David Herold, and unknown to them, Garrett's son Jack had locked the barn door when they went inside the previous evening, because his father was afraid they might try to steal a couple of horses. Booth had to use a pair of crutches to get around on the leg he had broken when he sprang from Lincoln's box to the stage of Ford's Theatre, and even though he gave Garrett a false name, the farmer knew perfectly well who his visitors were.

Once the barn was surrounded, Doherty shouted for the men inside to come out. When there was no response, Jack Garrett was told to unlock the door and bring out the fugitives. A nervous Jack did as he was told, or at least tried to. But he turned and ran out of the barn when Booth, now aware of what was going on, threatened him.

Booth opened a conversation with the soldiers, calling through the door that the man in the barn with him wanted to surrender. Booth pretended that David Herold was a stranger to him and knew nothing about any crime, certainly not about the murder of the president. Herold came out with his hands in the air, babbling that he was innocent. Soldiers grabbed him, dragged him to a nearby tree, and tied him to it so that he would be out of the way.

Now Booth was alone in the barn. The detective Baker demanded his surrender, but Booth refused to come out. He suggested instead that he and Baker fight it out man to man, but clearly he was stalling for time. The ploy backfired on Booth, because it gave Conger a chance to make his way around to the back of the barn and toss some burning hay through one of the gaps between the slats of the barn walls. The flames spread rapidly inside the barn. Now Booth was truly trapped and had to choose between surrendering or burning to death in what promised to be an inferno.

Some of the soldiers outside could see Both through the four-inch gaps between the slats of the old tobacco barn.He had a crutch propped under each arm and carried a carbine. If he hadn't been injured, he might have burst from the barn and fought it out. But with a broken leg, that was out of the question. As the flames crackled and spread from the rear of the barn, Booth started limping toward the door.

From somewhere—no one ever seemed quite sure where—a shot was fired. Booth dropped, shot through the neck.

The soldiers slammed open the doors and rushed in, grabbing Booth and dragging him clear of the burning building. He was mortally wounded, although he lingered until seven o'clock that morning before dying. He was awake part of the time and spoke a few sentences, but nothing of any great importance. Nothing about the assassination that had made him such an infamous figure in such a short time.

A somewhat mentally unstable sergeant named Boston Corbett claimed to have fired the fatal shot through one of the gaps because he believed that Booth was about to shoot the officers in front of the barn. Most people accepted that explanation, despite Corbett's unreliability. And perhaps it was true.

But nowhere in the official record was there any mention of a trooper who woke up with one hell of a headache and his cap and tunic lying on the ground beside him. Probably the man didn't want to admit that he had been knocked out and had missed the whole thing.

And nothing was said, either, about a lone rider who slipped away from the Garrett farm before dawn, vanishing into the shadows, vanishing from the pages of history.

Chapter Twenty-one

CAPTAIN GRIFFIN REINED SIZZLE to a halt and pointed to a plume of smoke rising into the blue Texas sky several miles away. "I don't like the looks of that," he said to the other rangers with him on the top of this long rise. "I'd say it's coming from the Lloyd place."

Pie Jones thought there was a little extra tension in the captain's voice. He knew the ranch Griffin spoke of and had visited there several times with the rangers. It belonged to a woman whose husband was off in the war. She was running it with her kids, and Pie knew that Cap'n Jim was fond of the whole family.

"We better get on over there, Cap'n," Pie suggested. "That don't look like enough smoke to be a cabin on fire, but it ain't normal, either."

"That's what I thought." Griffin put Sizzle into a long, ground-eating lope. The rest of the rangers followed.

Pie glanced over at the man beside him. Phin Carnevan wasn't officially a ranger, but the Englishman had been riding with them quite a bit lately. Pie suspected it was because Carnevan was sweet on Lucille Brannon, but nothing was ever going to come of that because Lucille was married and would never think of being unfaithful to her husband. And Carnevan, to give credit where credit was due, hadn't pressed his suit. Instead he stayed gone most of the time from the Harrigan place, where Lucille and Mildred Thompson and Allen and Fred Carter had fit right in, helping Rachel and Tad run the ranch.

To tell the truth, it was a good thing Carnevan rode with the rangers, Pie thought. Their numbers had dwindled over the past few months of the spring of 1865. Confederate conscription officers showed up every now and then, looking for men they could bully into the army, and every time they did, more of the rangers took off for the tall and uncut. It wasn't that these men were not loyal to Texas or to the Confederacy, but they saw no point in leaving home to serve a lost cause. News from back east was slow to arrive, but by now, the middle of May, it was obvious even out here on the frontier that the war was lost.

Pie sure as hell didn't intend to go back. Texas was his home now, just as much as if he'd been born and reared here. And it wouldn't be much longer until Rachel had the baby. Then the roots she and Pie had planted in the Brazos country would really be deep and unshakable.

Griffin pushed his paint horse into a gallop as they neared the Lloyd ranch. Sizzle responded tirelessly. The other horses did their best to keep up. As the rangers came in sight of the double log cabin and the outbuildings, they saw that the smoke came from the barn. Several men broke from the barn and ran toward the cabin, firing revolvers as they came. One of them spun off his feet as return fire from the cabin chopped him down.

Those weren't Indians attacking the ranch, Pie noted, but rather white renegades. Outlaws and deserters, more than likely. Puffs of smoke from the brush told Pie that more of the varmints were holed up out there. There might be as many as twenty or thirty of them, he estimated.

The patrol numbered ten men, including Phin Carnevan. Inside the cabin would be Renee Lloyd, her children, and maybe a couple of hired men who worked on the place. Those weren't good odds. Griffin never slowed down, though. Rangers didn't turn their backs on trouble, no matter what the odds.

They drew their pistols and started blazing away as they galloped down a hill toward the ranch. Two more of the renegades were knocked off their feet by ranger lead. Several men charged out of the brush and foolishly tried to block the charge. Griffin rode down one of them on his way to the cabin. The others dove back into cover as the rangers opened fire on them.

Griffin reached the cabin first; Pie and Carnevan were right behind him. The captain left the saddle in a dive that sent him rolling into the dogtrot. As he came up on his feet, blood flew from his thigh as a bullet clipped it. Griffin grunted in pain and dropped to a knee, but he held on to the revolver in his hand.

The door of one of the double cabins was thrown open, and a woman with a rifle clutched in her hands stepped out. She moved over behind Griffin as a couple of the renegades rushed them. Smoke and flame geysered from the rifle's barrel as she fired over his shoulder. The ranger captain's Colt blasted simultaneously. The two outlaws were driven backward by the slugs as if they had run into a wall.

Pie left his saddle in a dive, too, a flying tackle that sent him crashing into a pair of renegades. His weight smashed them to the ground, and they broke his fall. The men were stunned. Before they could recover, Pie had grabbed a throat in each hand. He pulled their heads up off the ground and slammed their skulls together. Bone crunched as it shattered.

Meanwhile, Carnevan was still mounted, and his accurate fire accounted for another renegade. The other rangers raked the outlaws as well. The odds were evening up in a hurry. It was all too much for the renegades. They had figured on raiding what they thought would be an isolated, defenseless ranch, and instead they had found themselves in the fight of their lives. The ones who were left alive broke and ran for their horses. The rangers pulled rifles from saddle boots and threw a few more shots after them, hurrying them on their way.

Pie stood up and saw Renee Lloyd helping Griffin to his feet. Pie moved over to take the captain's other arm and steady him. Renee Lloyd was an attractive woman in her late thirties or early forties, with dark blonde hair and green eyes. She said worriedly, "Jim, you're hit!"

The old ranger captain forced a grin past the pain on his face. "Just nominated, not elected," he said. "It doesn't amount to much, ma'am." He looked at Pie. "Any of the boys hit?"

"I don't think so, Cap'n."

"You come right on in," Renee Lloyd said to Griffin, "and I'll patch up that bullet hole." She looked over at Pie. "Maybe some of the rest of you boys can put out that fire in my barn before it burns all the way to the ground."

"Yes ma'am," Pie said with a grin of his own. "Did those renegades torch it?"

"No, when some of them holed up in there, I lit a lantern and tossed it in there before I ran in the house. Figured I was willing to burn down the barn if I could get some of those skunks at the same time."

Pie chuckled as he waved the rangers toward the barn. Texas women would sure do to ride the river with.

IT WAS almost like her other life was a dream, and she had been here in Texas all her life, Lucille thought. But thoughts of Cory were her anchor, holding her to everything that had happened in the past.

She was hanging clothes on the line to dry after washing them in the big washtub. A warm breeze flapped the arms of the shirts and made her laugh because the shirts looked like they were waving to her. When she was done she turned and looked around the place, feeling a sense of satisfaction as she saw all that had been done.

There was another double cabin on the small rise above the river. She and Mildred each had a side of it, where they would make their home once their husbands came back from the war. It was a short distance away from a second double cabin built on the site of the original homestead, which had been burned down by the Comanches. Pie and Rachel were in one side of it while Tad Harrigan lived in the other. Farther along the creek was a single cabin shared by Allen and Fred Carter. The barn had been rebuilt and expanded, and now there was a hog pen and a corral for the milk cow. The place was coming along just fine. Pie and the other rangers had done most of the work between patrols. Allen, Fred, and Tad kept everything in good repair.

Lucille and Mildred worked the vegetable garden. Rachel had helped with that at first, but she was getting too big to work comfortably anymore. She would have to wait until after the baby came to resume such chores.

Lucille was proud of the place. She didn't know if Cory would want to stay here or if he would prefer for them to strike out on their own, somewhere else along the river. Whatever he wanted was fine with her, as long as they were together.

She picked up the clothes basket and propped it on her hip, but then the sound of horses made her look around. She saw three riders approaching from the east. They weren't soldiers, and she didn't recognize them as rangers. All three men wore broad-brimmed hats, and as they came closer, Lucille saw that they wore guns and carried rifles in saddle sheaths. A bad feeling suddenly made her shiver, as if a snake had just slithered over her feet.

She walked quickly toward the closest cabin. There was a shotgun just inside the door. She put the basket aside, reached in the door, and picked up the shotgun. Mildred was inside, sniffling as she cut up some wild onions for stew. She looked at Lucille and saw the grim expression on her face as she picked up the scattergun. "Land's sakes, girl, what's wrong?"

"Riders coming," Lucille said. She had adopted the brusque speech patterns of the Texans.

Mildred came toward her, wiping her hands on her apron. "Do you know them?"

"No, but there's something familiar about a couple of them," Lucille replied. She hadn't really realized that until just now, when she spoke. But as she stepped away from the cabin and looked at the riders again, she was convinced that she had seen two of them before.

Allen, Fred, and Tad were downriver, looking for some of the rangy longhorn cattle that had wandered off. Rachel was resting in the other cabin. If there was trouble, Lucille thought, she and Mildred would have to deal with it by themselves.

Well, it wouldn't be the first time, she told herself. She thought about Cory, and she thought about her father, and as always, she drew strength from the memories.

The three riders were close now, close enough for Lucille to spot the sunlight reflecting off a badge of some sort pinned to the vest of one man. She felt a little relieved as she realized what that meant. This man wasn't a ranger—they wore no badges—but he was a lawman of some sort. Surely he didn't mean them any harm.

But a moment later she stiffened in alarm as she figured out where she had seen the other two men. It had been over in East Texas, when she first met Phin Carnevan. They had been Carnevan's partners in the smuggling operation that had brought supplies to Texas from England, past the Yankee naval blockade.

One more man had been involved in the smuggling, but he was dead now. Lucille knew that because she had killed him.

She hadn't meant to, but the man had been trying to kill Phin Carnevan, and he had run right into the heavy blade of the knife that she had thrust at him in self-defense. She knew the law blamed Carnevan for that killing, even though his partners had double-crossed him and had been trying to kill him. The plotters had also murdered one of the men working for them and framed Carnevan for that crime, too. Carnevan's status as a fugitive was one reason they had all left East Texas and headed for the Brazos country.

Now it appeared the law had caught up with them.

The three men reined in. The one with the badge smiled and tugged on the brim of his hat. "Mornin', ma'am. How are you this fine day?"

Lucille ignored the pleasantry. "What can we do for you, Sheriff?"

The man grinned. He had a bushy black mustache and a prominent nose. "Oh, I ain't a sheriff," he said. "I'm a special deputy from over East Texas way. These gents are lookin' for a fella, and I came along to help 'em out."

So the man was little better than a bounty hunter, Lucille thought, rather than a real lawman. Her hopes sank. She had thought that she might be able to explain the situation and make the man understand that Carnevan was a victim, not a criminal. But this so-called special deputy was probably in the pay of the two men with him, and he wouldn't be in the mood to listen to the truth.

"I don't think we can help you," Lucille said. "We haven't seen any strangers around here."

One of the other men snapped back, "He's not a stranger to you, Mrs. Brannon. We're looking for Phin Carnevan, and you know it."

So they remembered her name from the tavern and hotel where she and the others had lived and worked for a time. She wasn't surprised. It had been less than a year. Considering how big Texas was, it really hadn't taken them long at all to find the people they were looking for.

"He's not here," Mildred said abruptly. "He's dead."

"Dead?" the other smuggler echoed in surprise.

That was a good tack to take, Lucille thought. She followed up on Mildred's declaration by saying, "That's right. You killed him. He died on the road, and we buried him before we ever got to Dallas."

If they believed that, they might turn around and ride off. After all, Phin wasn't here, and there was no telling when he and the rangers would be back.

To her dismay, both of the smugglers shook their heads. "No offense, ma'am, but that's a damned lie. We talked to folks in Weatherford who saw Carnevan with you. He's somewhere around here." The man waved a hand at the cabins. "Hell, he may be hidin' in one of those shacks. You'd better do your duty and take a look, Deputy."

Lucille shifted the shotgun in her hands, letting the barrel come up a little. "There's no one in there except a lady in a delicate condition, and she needs her rest. You shouldn't disturb her."

The deputy looked at the other two men, reluctance on his craggy face. "I don't reckon I should be botherin' a lady like that, gents."

"Damn it, do as you're told," one of the smugglers growled. "Carnevan's a murderer, and you're bein' paid to bring him in."

"Yeah," the deputy muttered as he swung a leg over the back of his horse. "Dead or alive."

Lucille lifted the shotgun even more. "Stop right there."

The deputy froze halfway off his mount. He looked at the other men, clearly unsure what he ought to do next.

"Go ahead, damn it." The man who spoke laughed scornfully. "She's not goin' to shoot you."

"Maybe you should ask Palmer Kincaid about that," Lucille said softly.

"Who?"

She shook her head. There was no way these men could know what had happened in that cave in the bluffs below Vicksburg. She made one last attempt to deal with this peacefully.

"Phineas Carnevan isn't here," she said. "I don't know where he is. We haven't seen him for a long time. So you might as well leave us alone and go look for him somewhere else."

One of the smugglers jerked a hand toward the deputy. "Go on," he snapped. "I don't believe a word this hellcat says."

"Now, there's no call for that," the deputy said with a frown. He pulled himself back up onto his horse and settled into the saddle. "I said I'd help you boys find this Englishman, but I won't stand for talk like that about a white woman."

Lucille felt a surge of hope. Without the deputy to help them, maybe the two smugglers would give up and leave.

"Damn it, you're bein' paid—"

"I don't care," the deputy cut in. "I told you, I won't stand for talk like that, whether you're payin' me or not."

One of the smugglers wanted to argue, but the other one stopped him. "Let it go," he said. "It's not worth it." To the deputy, he went on, "We're quits. Get out of here."

The deputy fidgeted for a second. "You don't want your money back?"

"No, I just don't want to see your sorry face anymore."

"Well, if you feel that way about it . . ." The deputy looked at Lucille and Mildred and gave a little shrug. "Ladies." With that, he turned his horse around and started walking it away from the cabins. Lucille's heart sank. The man was going to just ride off and leave them at the mercy of the two smugglers.

The one who had told the deputy to ride away moved his arm, and when his hand came up, there was a gun in it. He eared back the hammer and pulled the trigger, and the whole thing happened so fast Lucille had no chance to react. The gun roared.

The deputy slumped over the neck of his horse and let out a groan as blood started to spread on the back of his coat. The animal was spooked by the gunshot and started to buck. The deputy tumbled out of the saddle and pitched to the ground, landing face down. He twitched once or twice and then lay still.

The man who had shot him turned back to Lucille, smoke curling from the barrel of the pistol. "Put down that scattergun, Mrs. Brannon, or you're next," he said. "Carnevan cached a bunch of money and didn't tell us where, so you'd better hope he's still alive and you'd better know where he is. We don't get that loot, we're gonna have to take what we can get from you and this old woman."

The other smuggler looked a little surprised at the callous murder of the deputy, but he dragged the back of a hand across his mouth then grinned. "Don't forget about the other gal," he reminded his partner. "The one they said was expectin'."

"Yeah, her, too." The smuggler holding the gun jerked the barrel of the weapon. "Now, are you goin' to put that shotgun down?"

The twin barrels of the greener had sagged a little at the thunderous sound of the shot. Lucille wasn't sure she could lift them high enough to bring them to bear on the man on horseback before he would be able to get off a shot.

But if she gave up the shotgun, she was sure the men would kill her and Mildred and Rachel before they rode off. After all, she and Mildred had seen him murder the deputy. He wouldn't want to leave witnesses behind. And if Allen and Fred and Tad had heard the shot and came hurrying back to the cabins, the men would probably kill them, too. Allen was a former soldier and a tough man, but he was no match for these killers, especially with only one leg. There was no getting around it, she realized in the split second that followed the killer's ultimatum: She held the fate of all of them right there in her hands.

But before she could move, a rifle cracked and the killer jerked in the saddle as blood flew from his chest. The gun in his hand went off as his finger involuntarily jerked the trigger, but the bullet plowed into the ground. The other man yelled a curse and slapped at the pistol holstered on his hip.

Lucille turned and raised the shotgun, touching off one barrel. One load of buckshot was enough. At this range it hadn't spread much before it slammed into the second man, shredding his flesh and blowing him backward out of his saddle. Lucille backed off and tracked the shotgun toward the first man in case she needed to fire it at him. But he had already dropped his gun and was swaying sideways. His horse bucked and threw him off. The limp way he landed told her that he was dead.

Her mouth was dry and her pulse hammered loudly in her head. She thought she was going to be sick. She forced down the reaction and looked around, saw Rachel standing in the dogtrot of the other cabin, a rifle in her hands. Her belly was enormous, but that hadn't affected her shooting eye.

Slowly, she lowered the rifle. "Are they dead?"

Lucille nodded. "They're dead."

Rachel let the rifle slip out of her fingers and put a hand against the cabin wall to support herself. "Good," she said in a weak voice, "because my water broke a few minutes ago. I think I'm about to have this baby."

☆ ☆ ☆

THE RANGERS rode in that evening. Pie heard the baby crying before he even dismounted. He let out a howl, flung himself from the saddle, and raced into the cabin to find his wife and daughter waiting for him. Rachel smiled up at him from the bed and handed him the beautiful redheaded baby. The rest of the rangers crowded into the dogtrot, trying to catch a glimpse of the squalling youngster, then Mildred shooed them away.

"That young'un's got a powerful set o' lungs on him. You can bet a hat on that," Curt said.

"It's not a him, it's a her," Lucille told him. "I mean, she's a girl. Now you boys go on, like Mildred told you. Give the family a little peace and quiet."

"You heard the lady," Captain Jim said. When the rangers had backed off, he and Carnevan came over to Lucille. The captain said quietly, "Uh, Mrs. Brannon, I noticed some odd-looking shapes with some old canvas thrown over them, out by the barn . . ."

"Allen and Fred and Tad are downriver digging some graves," Lucille said. "We had some unwelcome visitors today."

"Comanch'?"

She shook her head. "No." She looked at Carnevan. "They were trying to find someone, and they didn't believe us when we told them we didn't know where he was."

His breath hissed between gritted teeth. "I hoped they'd never find us."

Griffin looked back and forth between Carnevan and Lucille, frowning in thought as he did so. After a moment, he said, "Phin, you ever committed any offenses against the laws of the state of Texas?"

"No, Captain, I can honestly say I haven't."

"Then whatever you and Miz Brannon are talking about isn't any business of mine, and I'll leave you to it." He touched the brim of his hat. "Evenin', ma'am."

"Good evening, Captain."

When Griffin had moved off to join the other rangers, Carnevan said in a low voice to Lucille, "It was those former partners of mine?"

She nodded. "And a special deputy they hired to come with them and do their bidding."

He let out a groan. "You had to kill a lawman on my account?"

"No, one of your friends did that. Shot him in the back when he tried to leave."

Carnevan shook his head. "Those two were no friends of mine. They tried to kill me, remember?"

"I remember. According to them, it was because you held out on them and stole their shares of the money you all made." That was a bit of a guess on Lucille's part; the smuggler hadn't actually said that. But it made sense.

Carnevan stiffened. "That's a bloody lie. They got their shares. It was my share that they were after when they betrayed me, and they couldn't find it."

"Oh." Lucille blinked. Now that Carnevan had explained it, his version of the story made sense, too, and certainly cast him in a better light. She realized she had jumped to a conclusion, and an unfair one at that. "So you hid your money so they couldn't get at it."

"That's right. But it wasn't really my money, at least not all of it." Before she could ask him what he meant by that, he went on. "I planned to give part of it to the Confederate government." A grin spread across his face. "After all, I wouldn't have been making money off the blockade in the first place if there hadn't been a Confederacy."

"You mean if there wasn't a Confederacy."

"Well . . ." Carnevan grew solemn again. "We heard some news over at the Lloyd ranch a couple of days ago. They say the war is over."

Lucille's heart thudded heavily. She whispered, "Oh, my. We . . . we lost, didn't we?"

Carnevan nodded. "I'm afraid so. One of the tinkers who travels up and down the river had been over in Weatherford, and he heard about it there. General Lee surrendered last month in Virginia, at some place called Appomattox. I didn't catch many details. I'm afraid that's all I know."

"Then there's not a Confederacy anymore."

"It appears not."

Lucille felt a surge of excitement to go along with a sense of bittersweet loss. The South was her homeland, or at least it had been, and she hated to think of it as defeated and ravaged by the enemy. But now she called Texas home, and if the war was truly over, that meant Cory would be coming for her. She didn't know where the war had taken him, but she was sure he would head for Texas as soon as he could. They had talked about it often enough, back in those dim, dire days in Vicksburg.

"Well," she said, "I suppose I'm glad. The war had to end sometime." A thought occurred to her. "But what about the rangers? Will they disband?"

"No reason for them to do that," Carnevan said. "They ride for Texas, not the Confederacy. I'm sure they'll keep right on with what they're doing."

"I hope so. The frontier wouldn't be safe without them." She laughed softly. "Not that it's all that safe now . . .." After a moment, she asked, "What about you? What are you going to do now that it's all over?"

Carnevan shook his head. "I don't understand."

"Those two men are dead. They were the only ones who could tie you to any crime, even though it was a lie. I suspect that with the war's being over, the authorities are going to be too busy to worry about you anymore. You can go back to sea or do whatever you want." She smiled. "After all, if you go back and get that money, you'll be a rich man, I imagine."

At that moment, Pie emerged from the cabin, gently cradling his tiny daughter in his massive arms. "Boys," he called to the rangers, "there's a jug of whiskey down in the root cellar. If somebody'll fetch it, we'll all have a drink to Miss Amelia Arabella Jones!"

An enthusiastic cheer went up from the rangers. Lucille expected the baby to start crying, but she just cuddled against her father's broad chest.

Carnevan looked at the celebrating Texans. "I am a rich man, Lucille. Richer than I ever expected to be. Cap'n Jim asked me to join the rangers. I told him it would be my honor to do so."

"But that was before—"

"No. It was after we already knew about the war being over." He reached out, touched her shoulder quickly, lightly. "Besides, I can't leave Texas now. I want to meet that husband of yours."

"Of course. I'm sure you and Cory will be friends."

Carnevan nodded. He stood there beside her as the rangers passed around the jug and drank to Pie and Rachel and the baby . . . and to the future of the Lone Star State.

Chapter Twenty-two

I T HAD BEEN A long, hard winter in Dakota Territory. For the men of the First U.S. Volunteers, all of whom were Southerners, the temperatures of forty below zero were unbelievable and almost intolerable. On top of that, although Two Bears' band of Yanktonai Sioux was friendly, the other tribes in the area became more aggressive. Several times troopers away from the fort were attacked, and some were killed. British fur trappers from Canada came across the border and stirred up sentiment among the Indians against the American forts and even provided rifles so the Indians could attack the bluecoats. It was an explosive situation.

Not all the dangers came from outside the fort, however. Short rations and malnutrition meant that scurvy ran rampant through the regiment before spring came. Disease killed more men than the Indians did. It was truly a miserable existence. Some of the men even wondered aloud if they had made a mistake by volunteering to become Galvanized Yankees. They thought they might have been better off back in the Union prison camps.

Nathan Hatcher knew that wasn't true. Dakota Territory might be pretty much the godforsaken end of the earth, but it was still better than Camp Douglas.

During the spring the weather grew warmer, and the thick blanket of snow on the ground began to melt. While there were still white patches of snow showing, shoots of green grass began to poke up from the earth. Men who had thought they would never see warm weather again began to have hope.

But along with the improvement in the weather, the Indians grew even more hostile. A large war party attacked the fort itself and killed a couple of troopers before being driven off. The Indians fled, but they took a good number of horses and cattle with them.

On a more positive note, Elizabeth Cardwell was pregnant, although it was a wild, untamed land into which she would be birthing her baby. At least there were a few women around now to help her, the wives of fur traders who had come upriver when the worst of the winter was over.

Finally, the ice on the Missouri itself cracked and melted, and steamboats could make it upstream again. It was May when the boats began to arrive, and they brought news as well as supplies.

The war was over. The South was defeated, the Confederacy was no more. That was exciting news to the Yankee officers, but the enlisted men, all of whom had fought for the Confederacy, received the information somberly. True, they were Yankees now themselves—although galvanized ones, to be sure—but their hearts still beat with loyalty to their homes.

Nathan heard the news with mixed emotions. He had never supported the Confederacy, never believed in it or what it had fought for. He felt sympathy, though, for people like the Brannons, who had fought because they felt they had no other choice. To them, a person's home had to be defended above all else.

Nathan was sitting on one of the benches next to the parade ground when Patrick Cardwell sat down beside him. He and Patrick had been friends since before the First U.S. Volunteers had ever left for Fort Rice. Now Patrick slapped him on the knee. "What do you think of it?"

"What do I think of what?"

"The war being over, of course!"

"I'm glad," Nathan said honestly. "It never should have been fought in the first place."

"Aye, that's true enough. The Yankees should have left well enough alone." Patrick held up a hand. "No, I didn't come over here to argue with you. I know how you feel about such things, Nathan. I was just wondering what you're going to do now."

Nathan frowned. "What do you mean?"

"Well, the Confederacy is dead and gone. The Yankees don't have to worry about us fighting them anymore. So they don't have to keep us out here in the middle of nowhere. They can send us home."

Nathan shook his head. "The war ending doesn't have anything to do with that. We still signed on to be soldiers and to protect the frontier."

"Yes, but the army doesn't leave its men in a place like this forever!" Patrick said. "They send replacements, even for troops that didn't used to be Rebels. From what I hear, they'll be replacing us sometime this summer." The jubilant young man shook Nathan's shoulder. "We'll be going home before you know it!"

"You're sure?"

"That's what I hear."

Nathan looked down at the ground. It was muddy from melting snow. By the middle of summer, it would be cracked and dried out and hard as stone. "That's good," he said. "Maybe your child will be born in civilized surroundings."

"We can only hope." After a moment, Patrick asked, "What about you? What will you do when you get home?"

"I don't know," Nathan said honestly. Considering the circumstances under which he had left Culpeper County, he wasn't sure if he had a home to go to. If he went back, no one would want anything to do with him. Especially not Cordelia . . .

"Maybe I'll just stay in the army," he said. "They can't make me leave."

Patrick stared at him. "Man, have you gone daft?" He waved a hand at their surroundings. "Can you honestly say you'd rather stay here than go back to Virginia?"

Nathan looked at the rolling hills with their interspersed patches of green and white and at the huge blue sky that arched over everything, dotted here and there with puffs of white cloud, and he smiled.

He knew the answer to Patrick's question.

☆ ☆ ☆

MAC BRANNON came home first, and his mother and sister and Louisa hugged him and cried, then they all laughed, then they cried some more. A week later Cory rode up to the farmhouse for the first time in more than five years, and at first no one knew him as he stepped hesitantly onto the porch and called a tentative hello. Then Cordelia shouted and flung her arms around his neck, and the crying started all over again.

Henry didn't make it home until late May. Forrest hadn't disbanded his cavalry and sent them home until May 9. That sounded like Forrest, Cory commented when he heard about it. The general always had been one to hang on until the last. Even with the war ended, Henry didn't know if it was safe for him to come home, but he had nowhere else to go. When the women told him that the army had never been after him, that the man he had killed had been a deserter and a criminal, he wryly smiled at the news. "Well, what do you know about that." There was nothing else he could say.

Cordelia was thrilled to see her brothers, of course. All of them were gaunt and bearded and dirty when they got home. Mac's arm, although he could use it now, was stiff and hurt when it rained. He said it probably always would. Cordelia didn't care. She was just glad they were all home. All but Titus. Nobody knew where he was or if he was still alive. Abigail prayed for him, but she didn't expect to see him ever again.

Cordelia was waiting for one more person to arrive. She sometimes stood on the porch for hours at a time, watching the road. But Lt. Joseph Keller never came. With each day that passed, the certainty grew within Cordelia that he never would. He had finally gotten what he wanted, a transfer to a different regiment, and he had left Culpeper County ten days before the surrender at Appomattox. She told herself that he had forgotten all about her, that he had gone back to his home and family and had no more time to spare for a foolish Southern girl.

That was easier than considering any other explanation for his absence.

Cory didn't plan to stay on the farm. He couldn't, he said, because he had a wife waiting for him somewhere in Texas. But he had been close enough to home that he wanted to visit his family before searching for Lucille.

"It's a good thing you did," Abigail said. "You would have starved to death on the road to Texas."

Cory grinned at her. "I've almost starved to death a bunch of times, Ma. I'm sort of used to it by now."

Several evenings, the brothers sat up late on the porch and talked about the war, about where they had been and what they had done, things that they could never really share with the women or with anyone who hadn't been there. They spoke of their friends—Ernie Murrell, who had survived his wound and been sent home to recover; Abner Strayhorn, another survivor now back in the bosom of his family; Bedford Forrest and Fitz Lee, generals, great men, but not above being steadfast friends to some common soldiers—and after a while they were even able to talk about Will. Mac had been the closest to him, in both life and death, and though his voice cracked with emotion, he was able to share his memories, good and bad.

"Could you find where he's buried?" Henry asked in the quiet night as some of the first mosquitoes of the summer buzzed around them.

Mac nodded. "I'm pretty sure I could."

"We ought to go down there sometime. I reckon Ma would like to see the place. I know I would."

"Me, too," Cory said. He could hardly believe that Will was gone. While they were growing up, Will had been as much a father to him and Henry as John Brannon had been. Cory wished he hadn't been quite so stubborn about leaving home.

But if he hadn't, he reminded himself, he never would have met Lucille or her father, never would have seen and done all the things he had done. Some of those experiences, he could have done without . . .

But some of them he wouldn't trade for all the world.

That was life for you, he thought, swallowing a lump in his throat. Even when there wasn't a war going on, it was a hellacious thing, full of uproar and upheaval. But then just when you thought it was all too much trouble and not worth all the pain that came with it, you saw a sunset or a bird flew by or a fish jumped in the creek or the woman you loved with all your heart touched your hand—then none of the trouble really mattered and you were happy you had gone along for the ride.

Cory was damned glad it was dark on the porch so his brothers couldn't see his tears.

☆ ☆ ☆

A FEW days later a buggy came down the road and pulled up in front of the house. Judge Darden was at the reins, Mac saw as he stepped out onto the porch, but a stranger sat beside him. The man was middle-aged, well-dressed, and had a ginger-colored mustache that drooped over his wide mouth.

The judge called out to his horse as he brought the buggy to a stop. From the top of the steps, Mac nodded and greeted the two men. Mac wore civilian clothes now, and they felt good after years of wearing a uniform.

Darden grunted and nodded, but Mac could tell from the expression on the lawyer's beefy face that something was wrong. "Mornin', Mac," the judge said. He jerked a thumb at his companion. "Like to have you meet Mr. Malachi Carlson."

The stranger bounded down from the buggy, came to the bottom of the steps, and thrust a hand up at Mac. "Pleased to meet you, Mr. Brannon," he said with a grin. His brisk accent marked him as a Northerner.

Mac felt an instinctive dislike for Carlson, but he shook his hand anyway. "What can we do for you?"

"Why, nothing, Mr. Brannon. I've come to do something for you. I'm working with the Federal authorities, trying to straighten out everything that's got messed up the past few years. All the records and paperwork, things like that." Carlson took off his hat and waved it in front of his face, fanning himself. "Reckon we could sit on the porch for a spell, out of the sun?"

"Sure," Mac invited. "Come on up and have a seat. You too, Judge Darden."

Darden looked very uncomfortable now, but he joined Mac and Carlson on the porch. As he sat down, Mac said, "If this is about business, I'd better fetch my mother. She's really the one who owns this farm."

"No sir, it's in your name," Carlson said. "You are the oldest surviving son, I believe?"

Mac nodded. "That's right."

"Then legally, this is your place."

Mac looked at Darden. "Judge, is that right? You handled Pa's will—"

"Technically, Mr. Carlson is correct. Under the law, Abigail is not allowed to own property. Therefore, when John passed, title to the land devolved to Will as the oldest son. Now it's yours," Darden said.

"Nobody ever said anything about that," Mac protested.

Darden shrugged his beefy shoulders. "We all knew what John's wishes were, and we knew this place belonged to Abigail Brannon regardless of what some piece of paper said."

"The truth is, the farm belongs to all of us," Mac declared. "Cory and Henry are out in the fields now, trying to get in a crop, and Ma and Cordelia have kept it going while the rest of us were gone." He looked at Carlson. "Like the judge says, no matter what's on some piece of paper, we all own this place."

Carlson chuckled. "Well, now, not exactly. No taxes have been paid on it in the past four years."

Suddenly, Mac felt cold inside. "That's not true," he said, struggling to keep his voice level and calm. "Ma always paid the taxes. She's got receipts—"

"From an illegal, treasonous government, a government that, in point of fact, never existed." The grin had disappeared from

Carlson's face. "Of course, you'll be given the opportunity to repay those back taxes, along with a penalty for failing to pay them in the first place. But if you're unable to do that, I'm afraid this farm will be forfeit, and the Federal government will take it over for proper disposal."

For a moment, all Mac could do was stare, unable to accept or even comprehend what he had just heard. Then he said in a choked voice, "The Yankees are taking the farm?"

"It's all quite legal. And as I said, you'll be given a chance to pay—"

"How much?" Mac cut in. "How much do we have to pay to keep our own land?"

"Let me see . . ." Carlson reached into his coat and took out some papers, but as he flipped through them, Mac got the impression that the man already knew the amount in question right down to the penny. He was just putting on a show. Finally, Carlson announced, "The total including the penalty is $847.35."

"Good Lord!" Mac couldn't stop the exclamation from coming out. "We don't have that kind of money. There's probably not twenty dollars on the whole place!"

"Well, you don't have to pay it right away." Carlson turned more pages in the sheaf of papers. "It says here you have ten days from the date of notification. How's that?"

Mac looked over at Darden and said in a low, dangerous tone, "Judge . . ."

"Now, Mac, there's no use in gettin' upset," Darden said quickly. "I don't like this any more'n you do. And I got to go all over the county with this fella breakin' the bad news to folks. You just got to come up with the money somehow, that's all."

Mac looked down at his hands. They had clenched into fists. Slowly, he forced them to relax. After a moment, he looked at them and confessed, "I can't." With a hollow laugh, he added, "I couldn't even scrape up that much Confederate money."

"No Confederate money or scrip," Carlson said promptly. "United States currency only."

Mac couldn't seem to get his breath. His voice trembled slightly as he said, "Judge, get this fella out of here."

"Do I understand that you intend to relinquish title to this property?" Carlson asked.

Mac stood up. "You can understand that I intend to thrash you if you don't get out of my sight!" he said as he took a step toward Carlson.

Judge Darden got between them with surprising agility for such a big man. "Now hold on, Mac," he pleaded. "You can't do that. Carlson's just doin' his job—"

"It's a damned dirty job!" Mac burst out. "It's thievery, pure and simple."

The Northerner's veneer of affability had vanished completely. "It's all a damned dirty Rebel like you deserves," he snarled as he came to his feet. His hand slipped under his coat, and Mac knew he was reaching for a gun. With an effort, Mac brought his temper under control. He had been shot at plenty of times by the Yankees. He didn't intend to be gunned down by one of them on the front porch of his own home.

"Get out," he said hoarsely. "You gave me ten days. This is still my land until then, so get the hell off of it!"

"I'm going," Carlson said, "but I'll be back. And I'll have the army with me, just to make sure you comply with the law. You'd best remember that, Brannon." He turned and started down the steps to the buggy, but he added over his shoulder, "The war may be over, but I'm sure the soldiers won't mind killing a few more of you Rebs."

Mac didn't say anything. He waited until Carlson had climbed into the buggy, then he asked Darden in a low voice, "Can he do this, Judge? Can he really take away the farm?"

"They won the war, Mac," Darden said miserably. "They can do any damned thing they please."

Mac stood there, his hands gripping the porch rail, and watched the buggy roll away. He didn't know what he was going to do.

He didn't even know how he was going to tell the others that the last vestiges of the world they had known were about to be ripped away from them.

☆ ☆ ☆

"**I** SAY we fight!" Henry smacked his fist down on the dining room table to emphasize his declaration. "They can't get away with this!"

"The Yankees make the rules now," Mac said wearily, echoing what Judge Darden had told him earlier. "They say they can take the farm, and they've got the guns to back it up."

He had waited until after their meager supper to tell them. The dining room was lit only by a couple of candles, but they gave off enough light for him to see the devastated expressions on the faces of his family. He looked around the table at his mother, at Cory and Henry and Cordelia, and at Louisa Abernathy, who was pretty much a member of the family now, since she didn't have anywhere else to go.

Cory, always the hothead, surprised his older brother by saying, "Mac's right. We can't fight them. Is there any way we can get the money?"

"Turn outlaw, maybe," Mac said with a grim shake of his head. "But who would we rob? Nobody around here has any money. Everybody's in the same fix we're in."

"No one in this family is going to turn outlaw," Abigail snapped. "Brannons are not thieves."

Mac was standing at the head of the table. He leaned his hands on it and asked, "What do you think we should do, Ma? You've been here the longest."

"Yes, I have," Abigail said quietly. "I gave birth to all of you here." She smiled at Louisa. "Well, not you, dear, but you know what I mean." She took a deep breath. "I watched you children grow up, and I buried a husband here. This place has been my life for so long, I . . . I can't imagine being anywhere else."

"That brings us back to fighting," Henry said.

Abigail shook her head as tears ran down her cheeks. "No. There's been enough fighting. We . . . we've all lost enough to the Yankees. We won't give them anything else."

Mac frowned. "I don't understand, Ma. You say we shouldn't fight, but then you say we won't give them anything else . . ."

"We won't give them any more blood," Abigail whispered. "Let them have the land. It doesn't mean anything anymore. Not after what they've done."

"But . . . where will we go?" Cordelia asked brokenly.

Cory spoke up again. "I never planned to stay here. You all know that. Another week and I'd have been gone anyway. The Yankees don't care about us. They won't stop us from leaving. Why don't you all go with me?"

Henry looked sharply at him. "You mean to Texas?"

"Lucille's waiting there for me," Cory said with a nod. "I know she is. I feel it stronger than I've ever felt anything in my life." He smiled. "I can't think of anything I'd like better than to have all of you meet her."

"What would we do in Texas?" Henry asked.

Abigail said, "There's farmland there, isn't there?"

Cory nodded again. "Yes ma'am. From what I've heard, some of the best farmland you'll find anywhere. And lots of it, too. Plenty of room to grow. Plenty of room to spread out."

"You'd like that, Cory," Cordelia said with a smile. "You never liked to stay in one place for very long."

"That's the way I used to be," he said. "I reckon I've gotten over a lot of that now."

Mac wasn't so sure. He didn't think Cory would ever get all the wanderlust out of his system. But maybe he was wrong.

There was only one way to find out.

Ever since Carlson had threatened him with the army, Mac had known in the back of his mind that there was only one real answer to this problem. They had to leave. Maybe they could find some other place in Virginia or somewhere else in the South.

But they would be likely to run into the same sort of problems there, the Yankees coming in and taking over everything, pushing out the people who had settled the places and made something out of them in the first place. A clean break might be best, a fresh start a long way from all the bitter memories . . .

"I think we should do it," he said. "I say we go to Texas with Cory."

"So do I," Cordelia said.

They looked at Henry. He hesitated then shrugged. "Might as well. It could work out all right."

Mac looked at Louisa. "What do you say?" he asked.

She said, "You want me to go with you?"

"Of course we do," Cordelia said as she reached over to take Louisa's hand. "You're one of us now. Isn't she, Ma?"

Abigail nodded. "You'll always be welcome, no matter where we are, Louisa. If you want to come with us, that is."

"I do," Louisa said, tears shining in her eyes. "I do."

Mac turned his gaze to his mother, who was seated at the other end of the table. "That puts it up to you, Ma. What do you say?"

Abigail looked at Cory. "You said there was good farmland there. What about churches? Are there Baptist churches?"

"I don't know for sure, Ma, but I reckon there probably are," Cory said, trying not to laugh. "You can find a Baptist just about anywhere you look."

"Well, then, I suppose it's not a totally heathen place." Abigail took a deep breath. "We'll go. We'll go to Texas. And may God be with us."

"Amen," Mac said.

THE WAGON rolled along the edge of a large field bordered with trees. The vehicle was piled high with all the possessions the family had been able to take with them. Henry was at the reins, handling the team of scrawny mules. Abigail sat beside him; Cordelia and Louisa perched on the pile of goods in the back. Mac and Cory rode alongside, Cory on the horse he had brought with him from General Hardee's command, Mac on the mount Henry had used as one of General Forrest's cavalry. It wasn't like being on the stallion, Mac thought, but this was a good horse and Mac liked him.

His eyes swept over the field. The first time he'd seen this place, not far from the village of Cold Harbor, it had been covered with thick, waving grass, but then that grass had been pounded down by bodies and drenched with rivers of blood. Once it had been a pasture; now it was a graveyard.

Most of the thousands of men who'd died here had been buried here as well, interred where they lay or in mass graves not far away. When Mac closed his eyes he could still see it as it had been after the battle, broken and bleeding bodies lying everywhere, piled on top of each other. What should have been a sunny, pleasant field had been turned into a charnel house.

But now the bodies were gone. Almost a year had passed. The mounds of freshly turned earth had receded. Grass had grown over them. Some of the graves were marked with crosses or stones, but many were not. Another year, and it would be impossible to tell even where they had been.

During the week it had taken to get down here after they left the farm, Mac had worried that he wouldn't be able to find the right place. But as soon as he saw the open spot between two trees at the edge of the woods, he recognized it. He and Roman had dug the grave themselves, had wrapped Will in a blanket and laid him to rest in it.

Roman had never gone back to the Brannon farm as Mac had told him to do. Mac wondered what had happened to him. He hoped that wherever Roman was and whatever he was doing, he was happy. The young man had been a good friend to Will, and he deserved a chance for happiness. Mac prayed that misfortune hadn't befallen him. Somehow, he didn't think that was the case.

"This is it," he called to Henry, waving a hand toward the spot between the trees. "Right here."

Henry hauled back on the reins and brought the wagon to a stop. He hopped down from the seat and turned back to help Abigail climb to the ground while Cordelia and Louisa slipped down from the back. Mac and Cory dismounted. Cory held the reins of Mac's horse so Mac could take their mother's arm.

Abigail clutched a flower in her hand as Mac led her to Will's gravesite. "Are . . . are you sure this is right?" she asked. "I can't see anything."

"This is it, Ma," Mac told her softly. "This is the right place. I'm sure of it."

Abigail's chin lifted as she struggled with her emotions. "I'm glad we came down here," she managed to say. "I couldn't leave Virginia without . . . without saying good-bye."

It had been hard enough on her leaving her husband's grave on the farm. This was probably even worse, Mac thought. She had never had a chance to say good-bye to Will, to her firstborn, at least not until now. It was difficult for Mac, too. His chest felt tight, as if a giant band had closed around it, and his eyes burned with tears. Behind them, Cordelia was crying. Louisa put an arm around her shoulders to comfort her. Cory and Henry cleared their throats and wiped away tears.

Abigail stepped forward and leaned down to place the flower on the ground. "He should have had a marker," she said as she straightened.

"Yes ma'am," Mac agreed. "But there wasn't time then, and we can't do it now. Maybe someday . . ."

Abigail shook her head. "We'll keep his memory in our hearts. That'll have to be marker enough."

Mac thought it would be.

That was it, then. Henry and the women climbed back into the wagon. Mac and Cory got onto their horses. Henry took up the reins, turned the mules.

Pointed the wagon west.

"It's going to be fine," Cory said. "Mighty fine."

The Brannon family moved on, toward whatever destiny a new land held for them.

And behind them, unseen in the shadows under the trees on a rise overlooking Will's grave, a lone figure—tall, lean, and cold-eyed—swung up onto his horse and rode away, heading west as well.